THE WHITE LIAR

Arctic Fire Press
PO Box 1445
Jacksonville, OR 97530

Edited by: Sue Kenney

Illustrations by: Mad Scientist

Cover Design by: Books Covered

Cover Photographs © Shutterstock

Interior Formatting: Streetlight Graphics

ISBN 0-692-88101-8

10 9 8 7 6 5 4 3 2 1   17 18 19 20 21 22

First Edition

Also by Dannal

The Rum Runner

For Mom and Dad.

CHAPTER 1

MAXWELL SUTHERLAND STEPPED INTO PSYCHEDELIC streaks of neon light reflected across rain-slick Pearl Avenue to reach the indecorous bar across the street. A Miami-Dade Metrobus nearly wiped him out halfway across. Max stopped just in time to let the colorful graphic-wrapped people mover whoosh by, allowing almost a foot between the vehicle's sweeping left side and the end of Max's nose. But he made it across in one piece.

He always tried to gauge the quality of a watering hole based on the particulars of its exterior. Max had patronized so many different dives in the Little Haiti area, and the other surrounding boroughs of Miami, that he now considered himself to be a real connoisseur of these places.

A casual glance at Amador's Oasis betrayed several merits this particular lounge had on offer: oxidized steel bars over dirty windows and its glass front door told Max the proprietor valued security; weather-beaten stucco siding and faded green paint suggested the place was well-seasoned and long-established; the skinny Cuban man in the soiled pink tank top who loitered outside, panhandling change to buy a bus ticket back to Vermont, suggested Amador's to be a diverse and multi-cultural business; and the flickering neon double X's in the window, along with the electric glow promising a virtual deluge of Miller High Life, Pacifico, and Pabst Blue Ribbon, had drawn Max across the steamy gray street like a doomed mosquito seduced by the allure of a bug zapper's deadly whitish-blue brilliance.

Max struggled with the door for about a minute and a half. No matter how hard he pulled, he could not budge it, despite the neon red and blue Open sign that flashed intermittently in front of him, promising the establishment was in fact open for business.

After another few seconds of struggle, Max watched two young ladies in cowboy boots and questionably short dresses push open, then step out of the door, about six feet from where he stood. And yet it still took Max a moment to realize he'd been struggling his mightiest to pull open the bars over one of the tavern's windows.

At last, Max found the door, and he stumbled inside, scanning the place deliberately from left to right. The bar was dank, and smelled of stale, spilled beer and sweat, while a stereo blasted songs through distorted speakers that must have played from an album titled *Lame Songs of the Nineties*.

"My kind of place," Max muttered to himself. He glanced around at Amador's clientele, finding it to be a colorful mishmash of what appeared to be a wide assortment of troglodytes, vampires, and serial killers.

Max wobbled toward the bar and leaned onto it, using both hands to right himself, as he glared longingly at the kaleidoscopic congregation of bottles behind the surly-looking, bald-headed bartender. The barkeep wore a strange, white, ruffled shirt— Amador's must have had a pirate theme—and glared back at Max as if expecting some kind of trouble or scene to be made.

"Hmphh," Max said, unable to suppress a snigger at the sight of the man's attire. "Sorry, sir. That's a lovely blouse."

He looks like a Curly, Max thought to himself. Maybe he said it out loud, Max wasn't sure. *He's surly and he reminds me a bit of a cue ball. So, maybe that makes his name Curly.* The guy looked like he could have been a cousin twice removed from that Three

Stooges guy, although Max wasn't sure which one of the three he meant.

Max's eyes gravitated toward the rums behind the bartender. There were so many different kinds of liquor available to defile one's self, Max sometimes wondered what it was about the rum that tempted him. Whatever it was, the sweet distillation of sugarcane was his poison of choice, of that he was certain.

"What can I do for you?" Curly said, placing his palms on the bar. He glared at Max in an angry, condescending way. Max wondered what he had done to have given the drink server such a foul first impression of him. "And don't say you want a drink, because we don't serve guys as gutter-pissing wasted as you obviously are."

Max looked around at the axe-murderers and the hookers, each one likely to possess a heart of gold. "Color me surprised you have such high standards…let alone any standards at all."

"Would you like to turn around and walk out?" Curly said. He reached down behind the bar and found a four or five iron, its handle broken off. Close inspection of the instrument revealed it had grip tape wrapped around the broken shaft to make it work as a perfect close-quarters striking weapon. "Or would you like to be escorted out? Either way works for me."

Max noticed that Curly's face swirled around in his field of vision in slow disorienting circles. He suddenly wondered if Curly was actually Amador. Max concentrated on the bartender's nose and brought the man's face into distinct focus.

"A wager," Max said, slapping his hand on the bar top.

"A wager?" Curly said, lowering the weapon in his hand. "For what?"

Max turned to his left and noticed a young woman—or was she actually in her mid-sixties?...he was having a hard time telling the difference—sitting on a barstool about three seats down. *She* seemed intrigued by his offer of a wager.

"I realize you must have a policy of withholding the precious elixirs so solemnly interred in their glass tombs behind you," Max said, feeling as if the words flowed from his lips with an unusually articulate eloquence; though he conceded to himself that he probably slurred every other word, "from anyone who stumbles in with a countenance of obvious intoxication. But my wager is this: I'll bet you I can perform a handstand on your establishment's bar top—"

Curly burst into wheezing laughter. The sexagenarian a few stools down—Max laughed when he thought of that last—seemed intrigued. But Max wasn't finished.

"And I will perform ten pushups from the handstand position," Max continued. "If I'm successful, you'll give me that bottle of Bacardi eight-year-old. For free."

"And if you can't?" the smooth-pated bartender asked. His smug smirk suggested doubt in Max's acrobatic prowess.

"If I can't do ten pushups while standing on my hands on your very bar top," Max said, in his best impression of the crowd-pleasing showmanship of the late P.T. Barnum, "then I will give you a hundred dollars for that same thirty-dollar bottle of rum."

"A hundred. For Bacardi Eight? All right," Curly said, showing an unflattering grin; so many teeth were absent from the bartender's mouth that Max thought the man was better off keeping it closed. "Deal. Let's see you do it."

Max doubled over with laughter. His laugh was a drunken snorting guffaw that would have embarrassed Max if he had not already had so many drinks. He laughed so hard that he teetered and almost toppled forward onto the ground. Fortunately the knee-worn pine bar front caught his forehead and stopped him. Max uprighted himself and looked Curly square in the face.

"What's so funny?" the barkeep asked, staring with narrow squinted eyes.

"Of course I can't do that," Max said, slapping a fresh green hundred on the bar top in a loud gesture that snapped to attention most of the night crawlers in the bar. "But I *will* be havin' that bottle of Bacardi Eight."

CHAPTER 2

After practicing *Tire Machèt*, the dance-like martial art performed with fine-edged eighteen- or twenty-inch machetes, Josue Remy used the front of his white t-shirt to wipe the perspiration from his forehead. With a delicate swish of the young Haitian's wrist, he slung his machete onto the weathered stump whose gnarled roots grew up out of the ground and threatened to grab hold of the old wooden tool shed nearby. The sharp carbon steel of Josue's blade sunk deep into the wood with a bright zing, and Uncle Guillot patted Josue on the back.

"*Oke fè*," Uncle Guillot said, *well done*.

Josue had practiced with his uncle since his first memories. The old man now looked grizzled and slightly hunched at the shoulders, but Josue, despite standing at 190 centimeters, knew that his uncle could defeat him with ease, even at only 167 centimeters himself. The practiced hand of the master at work with the razor-sharp jungle machete always opened Josue's eyes wider, made him stare at the old man with even greater awe. And Josue cherished every moment he spent getting whipped by his septuagenarian uncle.

"*Mèsi, mèsi*," Josue said with a huge grin.

"You are getting to be very good, young man," Uncle Guillot said, adjusting the bright green Heineken hat he always wore with some measure of pride. No one remembered how long Guillot had had the blue Izod Lacoste polo shirt, but Josue's mother always insisted he take it off at least once a week so she could wash the tattered and faded garment. "I'm afraid that soon you will have surpassed me in skill."

"That is not possible," Josue said, speaking in earnest protest to his uncle's words, in his native tongue of Haitian Creole. "I will never achieve *your* level of skill."

"But you can still become the world's finest chicken farmer," Joliette said. Josue's sister was twelve years old, and she flashed an impish smile as she handed Josue the basket used to collect eggs from the chicken coop behind the old house. "I beat you squarely, and you're doing my chores for three days. Remember?"

It was true, Josue and Joliette had made a series of wagers as they gambled with the worn-down dice they took turns rolling from a cup. Josue was pleased, though; at one point during the game he had owed his sister nearly three weeks' worth of chores, but he had managed to win his way back down to only three days.

"You will owe *me* next time we play," Josue promised.

"*Pa janm*," Joliette said, shoving Josue good-naturedly, *never*. The girl's floral sundress was new; Josue's mother had sewn the dress and bought Joliette the elastic ponytail holders with the chestnut-colored beads that matched the girl's eyes.

Josue dropped the basket and tickled his sister's ribcage, just above her hips. Joliette's body jerked as she wriggled to get away from the unbearable electric shock feeling made by Josue's powerful fingers. She slapped his arm and ran into the house.

"Josue, Joliette!" Josue's mother, Emitilada, shouted from the kitchen window. "Supper is almost ready!"

Josue rushed up the hill to where the noisy chickens flapped inside their coop. They struggled to flee from the tall, dark-skinned predator trying to steal their eggs. But Josue made short work of the task, reaching into each wooden nesting box, feeling around, and snatching out the warm brown eggs in the blink of an eye. Before long he had looted the fruit of each one of the coop's two dozen black and white speckled birds.

Josue stepped outside and enjoyed a cool breeze that blew up off of Port au Prince Bay. As he gazed down the hillside toward the glistening water, Josue reflected on what a good farm Uncle Guillot had built. The farm's several acres of land produced abundant crops of sugarcane, sorghum, and corn, and a small garden yielded all the tomatoes, cucumbers, and eggplants the family could eat, with an overage to trade with their neighbors. The house had been built by Guillot's own hands, of cinderblocks, found wood, and other materials.

But Josue thought the house was remarkable. His uncle, the craftsman, had taken his time. He had built the two-story structure with aesthetics in mind, not just function. Wide windows gave a view toward the bay, and a wooden balcony spanned the full width of the structure, affording one a peaceful place to sit and watch the boats on the bay, to enjoy a sip of rum, and maybe a cheap cigar. A big cooking stove in the kitchen, built of smooth stones Guillot had gathered over a period of years, gave the family a convenient place to cook their meals. Guillot had even chipped away the flat bottoms of dozens of glass bottles, grouting them in place to create a few windows of "stained glass".

Josue considered how much more fortunate they were than so many others in their community. Neighbors called their place the Palace. Most of them lived in squalor by comparison and struggled with hunger, despite whatever help Josue and his family could offer them.

Over-deforestation of the hillsides had left the soil eroded and depleted, and growing anything was always a greater chore than it should have been. It was a landscape of largely dry and barren dust, inhospitable and unforgiving.

By contrast, Uncle Guillot had taken the time to plant a grove of palms and conifer trees, along with about a dozen mango trees. He had started developing the farm nearly thirty years ago—at least that's what Josue was always told—and many of the trees were quite mature and tall.

The farm's lush gardens had renewed their soil, quenching it with nutrients and breathing life back into it. Uncle Guillot's farm was like an oasis in a desolate place. Josue was happy to have been able to live there, but he could not help but feel deeply for others around them.

Josue also worried about his uncle. The old man still sparred with Josue, having taught him both the martial arts of jujitsu and Tire Machèt. But the elderly farmer grew more tired each time they practiced. Josue saw the pain in the man's eyes as he would place his hands on his lower back. The shortness of breath, and the swollen hands and feet were the symptoms of the painful diagnosis Guillot had received from the doctor: chronic kidney disease.

Josue wondered how long the old man would last. Josue didn't know if he was ready to take over, to become the man of the farm. But he feared that that fate would be decided for him, sooner than later.

Josue looked through the kitchen window. He saw his mother's face. Beads of sweat dotted her forehead as she toiled with a rolling pin, making delicious flatbreads out of stone-ground corn. Despite her strict nature, Josue loved his mother. He loved to hear her singing from the kitchen while preparing food. He longed to hear more of the stories she sometimes told about Josue's father, before he had passed, when Josue was only a baby.

The next instant, the earth began to rumble beneath Josue's feet. Fear gripped his heart as he saw the house transform into a moving bright white blur in front of him. He struggled to remain on his feet.

One by one the brown eggs inside the basket tumbled over the side. They shattered into gooey blobs on the ground near his feet.

What is happening? Josue thought. *What is happening?*

Josue fought hard to keep his feet. At last he lost his balance and stumbled backward, reaching out his hand to arrest his fall. Josue felt the ground move under him like a wild, kicking mule.

He wanted to cry out. He wanted to shout for help. Josue's lips formed the words to scream to his family, all of them inside the white house.

And then, in a lightning-quick blur of motion, Josue watched the house crumble into thousands of broken pieces. The crumbled shards tumbled down to the ground.

Unable to understand what had happened, Josue could only stare at the massive rubble pile that had, seconds earlier, been his good home.

The Palace stood no more.

CHAPTER 3

MAX SHUFFLED THROUGH THE FRONT door of Max's Hardware and Paint, dodging a guy with a snow-white comb-over who was on his way out with a couple of ten-foot PVC pipes over his shoulder. Somehow, the dexterous older man managed to hold open the door while Max stepped past him, before slipping out with his pipes.

I should've had a drink before I came in here, Max thought. He felt a bit queasy from drinking the night before, and his mind filled with an unsettling degree of clarity. He didn't like the feeling. And lately, the only thing that seemed to make Max feel better was more rum.

The Yellow Pages in his room at the Deep Blue Sea Motel had told Max how to find the hardware store. It pleased him to learn the store was only a two-block walk from the bright turquoise motel that Max had called home for the past several weeks.

"Help you, son?" said a silver-haired man with a white shirt, sleeves rolled up, and a red vest adorned with the embroidered name Roy. The elderly shopkeeper had the palest skin Max had ever seen in Florida, and the man's neck reminded him of skin he had seen sliding off a chicken his wife had once boiled. But the shopkeeper had a pleasant smile, and he seemed eager to be of help.

"I need a hammer, a file, a punch, and something to hold something down with," Max said, doing his best to remain as vague as he could about his little DIY project. The well-aged store clerk seemed like a decent fellow, and Max knew that telling him about his plans would likely upset him.

"Well, I can show you where the hammers, punches, and files are," Roy said, adjusting his Max's Hardware and Paint baseball cap over his thin silver hair, "but I don't know what you mean when you say you need something to hold something down with."

Max stood silent as Roy stood by, waiting for him to answer. The old man must have gotten the message that Max would not be elaborating on the details of his project, because he wandered off toward an aisle, mumbling something about a vise.

Max trailed behind, wondering if Max's Hardware and Paint sold booze.

"Are you looking for something like this?" Roy asked, slapping his hand down on the thick cast iron body of a six-inch bench vise. He twisted a little handle to open and close the gaping metal jaws of the substantial vise.

"That looks like it's gotta be a little heavy," Max said. "I just need to clamp something down to a table top."

"Maybe you need a clamp," Roy said.

For a second, Max thought a light bulb might actually appear over the ancient hardware man's head.

"Yeah," Max said. "That sounds about right."

Roy showed Max all of the wood clamps, C-clamps, and bar clamps the store had in stock. Max ultimately chose a pair of quick-release bar clamps, then he grabbed a ball-pein hammer, a small set of punches, and an eight-inch file. He dropped them all into a bright blue handbasket.

When he was ready, Roy rang up Max's purchases, and Max pulled his fist-sized cash roll out of the pocket of his cargo shorts and peeled off a hundred. "And here's something for you, Roy," Max said. "I didn't know there were still helpful guys in stores like this anymore."

Roy looked down at the extra hundred Max held in front of him. "I couldn't take this from you, fella."

He tried to hand it back, but Max shook his head and showed Roy the palm of his hand. Truth was, something about the man's features reminded Max of himself; at least what he thought he might look like, if he lived to be as old.

Life could present a man with so much pain. Max stood in awe of another who had lived to such an advanced age, having likely endured so much trouble, so much sorrow, so much loss. Yet the elder man still possessed the will to get himself out of bed each day. To function. "Please take the money, my friend. I really want you to have it. You...deserve it."

"Very well, son," Roy said. He extended his hand for a shake, and Max shook the man's hand. "Max would have been proud to have you for a customer," the seasoned old man said, as he closed the cash register. "Nobody seems to have much respect for anyone anymore."

Max nodded and made a solemn grin at the shopkeeper, and he headed out the door.

In his motel room, Max used the clamps to secure his Smith & Wesson 6906 pistol to the top of the cheap, laminated, fake wood table that occupied half the living space in the room. His hands shook as he held the hardened steel punch over the side of the pistol's front sight. Max took the hammer in hand and tapped away gently at the punch.

Max had picked up the gun a few days earlier at a seedy pawn shop not far off of Biscayne Boulevard in Little Haiti. The store had specialized in firearms, and Max figured that half their inventory must have been Army surplus or survival-related gear. Max had been browsing the gun selection when the dicey-looking salesman had pulled the pistol out of a box that had contained several handguns and magazines, likely just acquired by the shop.

The 6906 had caught Max's eye because of its shiny stainless steel slide and frame; it reminded Max of one of the guns carried by Charleston Corbin on an old TV show from the eighties, called *Miami Crime Squad*, which Max had watched a lot when he'd been a kid. He'd liked the 9mm pistol, even though he was fairly certain Corbin's piece had been a .45 caliber.

Max had asked the clerk if he could see the pistol, and he'd noticed that the pale-faced pawnbroker was missing several fingers on his right hand. Max didn't know the first thing about guns. But he had taken the weapon in his hand and articulated the slide. He had pointed the pistol toward the ceiling and pulled the trigger, hearing a crisp, dry click.

Max had liked how smooth the muzzle of the pistol felt between his fingers. When he had told the man at the counter he'd wanted it, the clerk had taken a last look into the cardboard box he'd removed it from and said, "Wait, there's a few spare mags in here that go with it."

At the shop, Max had done his best to steady his shaky hand while filling out the Form 4473 the salesman had used to run his background check through the NICS system, to confirm that he could legally buy the weapon. But something had told Max that even if he'd failed the background check, he could have still walked around to the back door of the shop to buy the pistol; it just might have required a bit more cash.

"You all right?" the pawn shop clerk had asked. Max had watched him scratch his cheek with his sparsely fingered hand, causing Max to fight off a shudder. Max remembered wondering whether one of the shop's shady guns had maimed the man, or perhaps it had been something from the military surplus aisle. Did they sell grenades?

"You don't by any chance sell rum, do you?" Max had asked the clerk.

In his motel room, Max tapped the Smith & Wesson's front sight as delicately as he could out of its dovetailed groove on the semi-automatic pistol's slide. Then he employed the more aggressive side of the brand-new file to begin grinding down the sharp edges of the dovetail.

Max worked hard at the task. Beads of perspiration dripped onto the vinyl tabletop as he toiled. He had to stop a couple of times to redo the clamps which had loosened during the aggressive abrading process. Max rubbed the file against the stainless steel pistol slide until what remained was a smooth, burr-free surface.

Max ran his fingers back and forth over the muzzle of the pistol, admiring his own handiwork. It looked good. He had done a good job.

With the front sight now completely absent, Max knew the 6909 wouldn't be winning any target shooting competitions. But when the time came, Max didn't know if he would put the gun to his temple, or if he might want to stick it in his mouth and "eat" it. If he chose the latter—maybe it was silly—he wanted the last few seconds of his life to be as comfortable as possible.

CHAPTER 4

J OSUE DUG THROUGH THE RUBBLE like a demon. Each
cinderblock must have weighed thirteen kilos. Josue grabbed
them and threw them aside as if they were made of Styrofoam.
He dug gingerly, but diligently, knowing he had to be as careful
as he was swift.

Josue had started where he had last seen his mother: in the
kitchen. But the kitchen was now nothing more than a pile of
toppled, broken blocks and splintered planks of dry wood.

Josue grew more frantic and agitated with each passing
moment. He threw the blocks aside faster until a stark sight gave
him a second of pause; he spotted the fabric of his mother's faded
red and white quadrille dress.

"Aaahhh!" Josue screamed as he snatched the broken cast-
concrete blocks away from his mother until her entire body was
uncovered. It was at that moment that Josue realized the severity
of her injuries. The way the woman's neck twisted to the side
suggested her neck was almost certainly broken. Both of his
mother's legs had snapped into gruesome compound fractures.

Josue knew her body must have been broken inside from head
to toe, riddled with unseen internal injuries. He prayed that she
had died quickly, that she had not suffered for even a moment.

Josue paused as he thought of his uncle and his sweet, young
sister. Seeing his mother like this broke his heart. He didn't want
to see the others the same way.

As he stood, dripping with perspiration, panting to regain his breath, Josue heard wails from a cluster of his neighbors' houses nearby. Women shrieked like banshees and a general moan of pain and loss resounded in his ears.

Some of the voices screamed, "*Jezi, gen pitye. Jezi, gen pitye pou nou.*" *Jesus, have mercy. Jesus, have mercy on us.*

Josue clung to the last vestige of hope inside himself. He tore into the task, digging through the rubble like a ferocious animal.

Some of Josue's fingernails cracked, and he ached with pain that radiated outward from his back and his shoulders. But he would not give up.

He unearthed the ruined shelf that had once contained all of his books. Volumes by American authors Hemingway, Steinbeck, Mark Twain, and Edgar Allen Poe, among others, had once occupied the simple plywood shelf attached to the wall. Now the books lay buried, looking ancient under the dust and crumpled debris.

The sun had already fallen when Josue uncovered the bodies of his uncle and his sister. They were gone. Their devastating injuries were a testament to a cold truth that burned in Josue's brain: there was nothing he could have done to have saved them. They would have perished almost instantly in the devastating ruin of the now crumbled farmhouse.

All of the care and the toil Uncle Guillot had poured into the building of the stout cinderblock house had only ensured there would be no surviving its destruction. The warm building that had always inspired a feeling of home and family in Josue was the very thing that had destroyed his family, and had taken them away from him.

Josue made a fire out of some of the broken wood from the house to give himself some light. He spent another hour unearthing the clean white linens his mother kept folded inside a cupboard. Josue used them to wrap the mangled and broken bodies of his mother, his uncle, and sister, enshrouding his dead loved ones into white, tightly wrapped mummies. He labored to move them to the tall grass in front of the farmhouse's rubble, by the dirt road.

Josue sat beside the bodies of his dead family members, and he echoed the sentiments of his wailing neighbors. "Jezi, gen pitye. Jezi, gen pitye."

And then Josue doubled over and wept. Sharp, wracking sobs overtook the young Haitian's body until he thought he might vomit from the effort.

Josue wept until he could weep no more. He wept until sleep overtook him, and he fell back asleep in the tall grass by the dirt road.

The next morning Josue awoke late, for the sun was already high up in the sky. For a fleeting moment he believed he might have imagined the deaths of his family members as a vivid and visceral nightmare. But Josue sat up to see the shrouded bodies of his dear mother, beloved uncle, and gentle young sister.

Blood had seeped through the white fabric around his uncle's face and his sister's stomach. The sight made Josue sick. The pain of their loss was difficult enough to bear. The continuous reminder of their afflictions was like coarse salt rubbed into the wound he felt inside his heart.

Josue knew he had to bury them. There would be no better place to inter their mortal remains than the small grassy yard overlooking Port au Prince Bay. Josue set about finding a shovel. He was dismayed to find the shed behind the house completely intact. It was a cruel joke that the shovels, hoes, machetes, and other farm tools would survive the wrath of the violent earthquake, while his precious family would not.

Josue grabbed a shovel and began to dig the first hole beside his mother's body. He plunged the freshly-sharpened blade of his shovel into the dry earth. As he dug, Josue realized he was angry. No, he was incensed to have his family taken away so quickly, so cruelly, without having even had a single moment to bid them goodbye; to remind them of how much he loved them.

As Josue stabbed the shovel into the earth, he spotted a dusty cloud sent up from the tires of an approaching vehicle. It appeared to be from an off-road truck with no roof. *What is that called, a Jeep?* Josue thought, as he spat into the dirt.

The driver, a child of maybe fourteen years, wore a black headband and mirrored sunglasses. He stopped the vehicle on the road in front of the farm. Josue spotted a familiar face in the passenger seat.

"Hello, Janjak," Josue said, his tone as tart as the flesh from the bitter melon that grew out back behind the farm's shed.

"*Bonjou*, Josue," said the young man of maybe twenty. He stepped out of the Jeep, and took off his own sunglasses. Josue spotted the long scar, thin and white against the man's deep russet-colored skin, from the corner of his mouth to the bridge of his nose. "Who have you lost?" Janjak said, speaking in Creole.

Josue stared at the dirt. Something inside him suggested that if he didn't speak the words, the truth would not become real. But after a long moment, in which the Port au Prince gang member stood, staring, and waiting for a response, Josue at last spoke. "My mother. Uncle Guillot. Joliette."

"*Kondoleyans mwen*," Janjak said. *My condolences.*

Josue nodded.

"It is time for you to take your place in Scorpio," the dangerous inner-city criminal said, sounding like a strict father speaking to his son. "Benoit wishes it. It is time now, Josue. There is nothing left for you here."

"Uncle Guillot said he would kill Benoit if he ever set foot on this farm," Josue said, speaking back to the other man, still in Haitian Creole.

"That is why I am here now," Janjak said. "Benoit received

19

word of the farmhouse's destruction, and that Guillot was dead. You must come to the city. Take your place in the gang."

"No," Josue said. "I will not."

Janjak put his sunglasses back over his eyes and sat back down in the Jeep. "One day, Josue. To mourn. I will return for you tomorrow. There will be no say for you in this matter. You *will* join Scorpio."

Then Janjak nodded at the young driver, who stomped on the gas pedal, spinning the vehicle's large tires, kicking up a cloud of dust as the Jeep sped away.

Josue spat a glob of thick saliva into the road after them.

The thought of joining the violent Port au Prince gang terrified Josue. He knew Uncle Guillot had done everything in his power to keep Josue away from the nefarious organization known as Scorpio—Haitian Creole for scorpion. Josue didn't know what he would do. But he *could not* join the gang well known throughout the region for its violent robberies, hijackings, and murders.

Josue heard the rumbling of another vehicle, a heavy dump truck lumbering up the long dirt road, well before he saw it. The deep murmur of the vehicle's engine had, at first, suggested another aftershock. Josue had already experienced so many of those since the devastating first quake that he was far from afraid of them. But he saw the cloud of dust kicked up into the air by the huge truck's wheels, and a moment later he smelled the stench that the vehicle had brought with it: that of death.

The truck stopped on the dirt road in front of Josue. Two men with pale blue helmets stepped down from the cab, along with another man, who had blond hair, blue jeans, and a dirty, gray t-shirt. The two soldiers lowered the tailgate of the dump truck's bed. The sight made Josue sick inside his stomach.

Dozens of bodies, piled one on top of the next, occupied the big box of the truck like so much refuse to be dumped. Some of the faces seemed to stare at Josue, watching him with blank, glassy eyes. He felt anxious and nauseated by the sight. And he was confused. Why were these men stopping here?

Then the two soldiers stooped over Josue's sister. They began to lift her shrouded body.

"No!" Josue shouted, picking up his shovel and raising it to strike the men. They let go of Joliette's shoulders and ankles, letting her body fall back to the grass. They looked at Josue, both terror and confusion apparent in their eyes.

"We must take these bodies with the others," one of the soldiers said in Creole. "They will be dumped in the ground and covered with earth near Titanyen. They cannot stay here. It is not sanitary."

"No!" Josue shouted again. "You will not take them!"

"They must be buried," the second soldier said. "It is not sanitary to allow them to sit like this. Think of the disease they will bring."

"I will bury them myself!" Josue shouted.

The two men seemed to ignore Josue and they turned back to the task of picking up Joliette's corpse. Josue lunged forward to assault one of the men with his shovel. The blond-haired man from the truck stepped between the men, and he put up his hands.

"Wait," the man said. He spoke English. He was an American, maybe fifty years old, very tan skin. "Don't hurt anybody, son." The American's face showed kindness; his voice suggested empathy.

Josue lowered the shovel.

The American turned toward the UN soldiers. "I'll stay here and help the kid bury his family. You guys pick me up on the way back, and I'll help you as long as I can. Okay? Just pick me up on the way back."

The UN soldiers looked irritated, but they closed the dump truck's tailgate and drove off, kicking up another wide cloud of dust as the heavy truck's wheels rumbled away over the parched dirt of the road.

"I'm Austin," the American said. He held out his hand for a handshake.

Josue looked at the man's hand for a few seconds before embracing it, realizing that the skin of his own hands was raw with ripped-open blisters. But the men shook hands. "Josue."

"I'm sorry for your loss, Josue," Austin said. "This is your family?"

Josue nodded. "My mother, my uncle, my sister."

"What were their names?" the American asked. He picked up Josue's shovel and began digging, expanding the grave that Josue had started. "My mother called Emitilada. She was most good woman I ever know," Josue said, knowing his English wasn't very good—he could understand spoken English and read it quite well, but speaking the language was harder. Josue figured the fair-haired American almost certainly didn't know Haitian Creole. "I grab another shovel, dig with you."

Josue found another shovel, one with a square blade, which he used to move away some of the dirt that Austin had loosened with his digging shovel. He continued to tell the American about his family as the two men worked together. Josue told him about Uncle Guillot, and how they had trained together in jujitsu and Tire Machèt since Josue had been only a small boy. He told him about the jokes Josue and Joliette would play on each other as they tended to the daily tasks of the farm.

Austin seemed interested in hearing Josue's stories, and he smiled as he dug. Josue saw the blisters that quickly formed on the other man's soft hands. He knew the American was not likely used to such manual labor, yet Austin did not complain once as he worked.

Before the big dump truck made its way back down the dirt road, Josue and Austin had finished burying his family. They marked the graves with round rocks placed into the shape of crosses.

From his mother's body, Josue had removed the silver pendant of Our Mother of Perpetual Help, which had still hung around the woman's crooked neck when he had found her body in the rubble. Josue had wanted the token to remember his mother. It was now all he had left of her.

Austin bowed his head as Josue prayed over the graves of his precious family.

"Hey, Josue," Austin said, when the impromptu funeral had concluded, "what do you think you are going to do now that you are alone?"

Josue saw the tenderness in the American's eyes. He did not know who the man was, but it seemed fortuitous that they had met. "I don't know," Josue said. "Perhaps I will stay and rebuild the farm." The thought felt hollow and empty to Josue. What good would life on the farm be without his family? And what would happen when Janjak came to take Josue into the city, to join Scorpio. What would Benoit do when he refused to join?

"If you're interested in getting to the US, I know of a boat leaving tonight at around midnight," Austin said. "I arranged it myself. I can't get you a visa or a passport or anything. But when you get to Florida, you claim you're a refugee, okay? Just say, 'refugee,' and they should give you protected status—in consideration of the earthquake and all."

"You arrange a boat to take people to US?" Josue asked. "Why? You want money?" Josue had found the shattered jar in the destroyed kitchen where his mother and uncle had kept all of their savings. Josue now had all of the money in his pocket, almost seven thousand Haitian gourdes, which amounted to around a hundred dollars, US. But Josue wasn't sure he wanted to give it to someone to take him to America.

"No, no, no," Austin said, sounding as if he had been misunderstood. "I don't want your money, Josue. I was in Miami when I heard about the quake. I came here as soon as I could; I came over on my own boat. I am only here to help out in whatever way I can. The boat will not be a dangerously-overloaded refugee boat. It is a fast motorboat, and I am handpicking people to go back over on it. When all the seats are filled, it's going to leave. I'm counting on the US government to show mercy on refugees from Haiti—they have to. After all of the devastation, there's no way they'll turn you all away."

The big dump truck stopped in front of Josue and Austin. Josue shook Austin's hand again, grateful for the kindness the stranger had shown him. Austin let go of Josue's hand and stepped in to give him a full hug. Josue was shocked by the gesture. At first he didn't know what to do. But then he put his arms around Austin.

"Take care, Josue," Austin said, as he turned to climb up into the UN dump truck.

"Austin," Josue shouted after him. He waved Austin back over toward him.

The blond-haired American trotted back over, a hopeful look on his face.

"Where is boat?"

CHAPTER 5

J OSUE WALKED FIVE MILES TO the village of Aubry, following the directions Austin had scrawled on a scrap of paper. Josue knew of the village, and suspected that the private boat dock the directions led to were not far from the cement plant, with its huge machinery, mountains of sand and crushed stones, and seemingly endless conveyors tumbling the materials from here to there. Josue had asked for directions along the way to the specific address written on the paper. He was surprised to find that they led to a magnificent villa built right beside the bay.

Josue was reluctant to approach the black wrought iron gate set into an imposing stone wall around the villa. Two men, Josue suspected they were members of a gang or militia, stood guard outside the gate holding AK-47 rifles.

One of the men spotted Josue, and shouted, "*Vin sou isit la.*" *Come over here.*

Josue approached cautiously, his hand clutching the bundle of gourde notes in his pocket; it was all he had in the world, and he would not let anyone take it without a fight.

"What are you doing here, farm boy?" said the man who had called Josue over to the gate, speaking in Creole. He wore white shorts and a red football jersey. The man let the rifle swing down on its sling to his side.

"Someone tell you to come here?" the other man asked. He could have been the first man's twin brother.

Josue nodded. He handed the first man the scrap of paper.

The dodgy-looking man scrutinized the note and looked up at Josue. "Austin give you this?"

"*Absoliman*," Josue said, *absolutely*. He stabbed his finger at Austin's signature on the note. "He told me there would be a boat waiting here. He said I could have passage to the US and it would not cost me any money," Josue said, speaking Haitian Creole back to the men.

The second man unlocked the gate. "There are others waiting in the villa. We have room for three more, and then the boat will leave. Please go and join the others."

"*Beni ou*," Josue said. "*Beni ou*." *Bless you*.

Josue walked the flagstone steps to the villa's front door, and he came to a sudden realization: every house he had passed along the way had been leveled by the mighty earthquake, or by one of its devastating aftershocks. Yet this elegant Spanish-style villa seemed to be almost perfectly intact, with only a cracked window or two, and a few missing roof tiles. *The rich can build much safer homes*, Josue decided.

He was surprised to find the villa's front door unlocked. He twisted the knob and entered, finding himself in a mirror-lined hallway. Elegant marble flooring led the way toward a huge living room with a wide window that offered a magnificent view of the late afternoon sun flickering off of Port au Prince Bay.

Josue stepped into the room and felt the stares of dozens of eyes, all peering at him. Some seemed distant and uninterested; some looked at him with intense stares; others looked at him hopefully, as if he were the one they had been waiting for.

"I am here for the boat," Josue said to the group. He noticed the group seemed quiet and subdued for its size. There were maybe twenty people present, all Haitian, men, women, and children.

"Take a seat," said one man, maybe a couple years older than Josue's nineteen years. The man wore black-rimmed eyeglasses, and Josue noticed one of the lenses had a large crack through the middle. A gash on the man's face appeared to follow the direction of the crack in the lens. The man scooted over on his bench seat to make room. "*Non mwen se Foret*," the bespectacled man said. *My name is Foret.*

Josue thanked the man and sat down beside him. "I don't suppose you have any fresh water," Josue said, knowing that most everyone present was likely as deprived as he was. Some folks were injured, some with seeping bandages, one or two moaning in constant pain; some were just quiet, clinging to a handful of belongings that represented all they had left; others just stared out the window as if in a trance. Everyone present had experienced great loss in the last twenty-four hours, maybe the greatest loss of their lives. Josue figured no one in the room had anything keeping them in Haiti any longer. It was now time to move on.

"There is a kitchen through there," Foret said, pointing a bony finger toward a doorway opening. "Water runs right out of the pipe. You may go and help yourself to a glass."

Josue walked tentatively toward the kitchen. He approached the big sink that appeared to be made of shiny polished steel. A couple of empty glasses sat inside the bottom of the deep sink. Josue held one of the glasses under the water pipe and tried to figure out how to make the water come out. There were two knobs on either side of the water pipe, and Josue turned one of them. *This is much different than the hand-crank-operated pump Uncle Guillot had installed beside the shed, to draw water out of our well,* Josue thought.

Water gushed out of the pipe, quickly filling his glass and overflowing it with clean, cool water. Josue nearly dropped the glass trying to stop the flow of water. He didn't want to waste a drop. As he brought the glass to his lips, Josue felt as if his tongue was a warm, dry sponge soaking in the sweet, cool water. He swallowed the water quickly and sighed with relief. *Do all the wealthy people have sinks and faucets like this?*

Josue glanced around furtively and then filled his glass again. He gulped down the refreshing water. Then he sat down next to Foret. And he waited.

About an hour later a young mother came in the door, clutching a baby who must have been asleep, for as quiet as it kept. It was dark when an old man with a long gray beard stumbled into the front door, his cane bouncing noisily off of the marble flooring. A few minutes later a white man with deeply-tanned skin, short gray hair, and a face punctuated by a network of thin wrinkles, entered the room and spoke to the group. His white button-up shirt with black epaulettes, and white short pants suggested he must have been the boat's captain.

"The boat will be leaving in about fifteen minutes," the man said. "Women, children will board the boat first. Then the men. The trip will be fast, about eight to ten hours until we arrive in Miami or Fort Lauderdale. Godspeed to all of you."

Josue had looked at maps before. He knew that Florida was around seven hundred miles from Haiti at its nearest point. *Was it even possible for a boat to travel that far that quickly?*

Outside the villa, Josue heard the rumbling of a loud engine starting up. And then he heard another, doubling the sound of the deep mechanical growl. The women and children were led by the tanned, gray-haired man, and another white man—short with bright red hair and a white and black uniform, who must have been a crew member of the boat—down to the end of a long pier. A few minutes later, some of the older, frailer men were taken down the pier as well. Josue and Foret were among the last men led out of the villa and down the long pier to the awaiting boat.

As Josue got his first glimpse of the boat, he could not believe the sight his eyes took in. The boat looked like a racing boat he had seen on TV once while at Darcourt's Market in the city. The vessel must have been seventeen or eighteen meters long and looked like a rocket ship, with its loud, grumbling engines and its long, narrow, pointed tip. Black lettering stood off from the boat's shiny silver paint, spelling the words *Silver Bullet*.

One of the crewmen grasped Josue's hand to steady him as he stepped from the wooden dock, over the boat's railing. "Here, here," the younger white man with red hair said, pointing to a row of four seats at the rear of the boat. "Sit here."

Josue caught a glimpse of the narrow door leading through to a long, narrow cabin in the front part of the boat. The women, children, and most of the men sat on cushioned seats, and a few of the worst injured lay out on a big double-sized bed. Josue spotted a sink and a toilet through another door far up in the bow, and he wondered if fresh, cool water flowed from that sink as well.

Josue and Foret took seats at the very rear of the open cockpit. Their seats fronted the compartment where the two thunderous engines rumbled. Josue and Foret sat on either side of two other men who occupied the row of four comfortable, cushioned seats. Red plastic gasoline containers covered almost every centimeter of spare space on the cockpit's floor, each one lashed to the other with ropes and elastic cords.

Two other seats occupied the cockpit area, directly in front of Josue; they would be for the captain and the first mate. A complicated panel of controls sprawled out before the captain, who stared intently into what looked like a big TV screen built into the dash board in front of him. Josue squinted to make out some sort of map on the screen.

Then the first mate threw off the ropes tying the boat to the dock. He shoved off from the pier with his foot.

"You," the first mate shouted, pointing his finger toward Josue's chest.

Josue's heart leaped. "Yes?"

"Can you help me and the captain add fuel when the tanks get low?" the first mate asked.

"Yes!" Josue shouted, nodding his head vigorously. "Yes!" He was eager to prove himself useful on their journey.

"Good man," the first mate said, slapping Josue on the shoulder. Josue knew the man meant the gesture good-naturedly, but his shoulders throbbed from first digging his family out of the ground, and then burying them back in it, and he could not help but wince.

The first mate pulled two straps from behind Josue's back and tugged them down across his chest. At first, Josue thought he was being restrained against his will. Then he noticed Foret and the others beside him had all pulled the same restraints over their heads, securing the straps in front of them. Each man adjusted his own safety belt for comfort. Josue wondered how fast a boat must move that a person should be tied down to his seat.

"We're off!" the captain shouted to his first mate, as the mate snuggled himself into his own seat and put on a headset with silver cups that covered his ears, and a communication device that extended in front of his mouth. The captain wore the exact same device. The two men touched fists, and then the captain pushed a pair of long silver levers forward and the engines roared as the boat began to speed away from the dock.

Josue turned around and watched the dock grow smaller and smaller behind him. A short time later he saw what must have been the entirety of Aubry diminishing into nothing behind him.

Heading further out toward the open sea, the captain gave the boat even more throttle, and the boat sped up faster. Wind whipped over Josue's face and body. He felt exhilarated.

A long time ago, Josue had ridden into the city on Janjak's motorcycle, back when they had been close friends; he had never traveled so quickly before in his life than when the speedy motorcycle had zipped through the city, winding in and out of busy traffic. Now, skimming across the waves faster than he could have imagined possible, Josue wondered if this was what flying in an airplane felt like.

He looked across the row of seats at Foret. The bespectacled man looked back at Josue, a massive grin spread across his face. As horrible as the last two days had been, it was nearly impossible to suppress the feeling of elation that had exploded inside of him.

Josue turned back to look toward Port au Prince. He was dismayed to see the city, normally bright with city lights, now looming dark, with the odd fire burning here, and only a few bright lights—probably temporary lights set up by emergency services—glowing here and there. The electricity in the city must have been cut off by the destruction of the earthquake.

Josue had not witnessed the destruction in the city. It must have been horrible there, likely even more so than in his village. So many people lived in the city, their houses built practically one on top of the other.

As he watched Haiti growing smaller behind him, Josue considered the words of a Kipling poem his uncle used to be fond of reciting. The words felt deeper to him than they ever had, now more meaningful:

If you can meet with Triumph and Disaster

And treat those two impostors just the same;

If you can bear to hear the truth you've spoken

Twisted by knaves to make a trap for fools,

Or watch the things you gave your life to, broken,

And stoop and build 'em up with worn-out tools:

If neither foes nor loving friends can hurt you,

If all men count with you, but none too much;

If you can fill the unforgiving minute

With sixty seconds' worth of distance run,

Yours is the Earth and everything that's in it,

And—which is more—you'll be a Man, my son!

"*Bondye ka ede ou,*" Josue said aloud, though no one could hear him over the din of the speedboat's engines and the wind that whipped across his face like a cyclone. He took one last glance at the ruined city before setting his eyes forward.

God be with you, he whispered.

CHAPTER 6

SERGEANT LORENZO FERRIGNO CLUTCHED THE wheel of the unmarked Dodge Charger as it cruised slowly through a sleepy street rimmed by gumbo-limbo trees and shabby houses fortified by rusted and broken chain link fences.

"What does that mean?" his partner, Detective Arthur Parks asked. The tall Trinidadian and Tobagonian American detective sat in the passenger seat, his arm propped up between the top of the door and the bottom of the unmarked black police car's window frame. "He just called it a mass?"

"Yeah," Lorenzo said, slapping the wheel with his hands like a drum. "He just said he found a mass."

Arthur stared out the passenger window. The quiet detective seemed even more subdued than usual.

"Until I hear otherwise, I'm not making any assumptions about it," Lorenzo added. "It's just a mass. Could be anything."

Arthur just nodded, wearing a grim smile on his lips. "Hmm."

Lorenzo stopped the car abruptly in the middle of the street. His eye had caught something odd in front of a dilapidated yellow house with only black bars for a front door.

"What is it, Zo?" Arthur looked sharp, peering all around the vehicle, trying to ascertain what had caught his partner's attention.

"Aw, man. Why did I have to see that?" Lorenzo asked. He stabbed his finger toward a pile of trash bags nestled between a set of green and blue city trash containers awaiting pickup. "Why did I have to turn my head and see *that*?" The detective's irritated tone resounded through the thick accent he had brought south with him from Queens.

"Is that a *guy*?" Arthur said, adjusting his old-school prescription Ray Bans, the kind with pale yellow lenses and tan leather trim pieces.

"Do you think we can give this one a miss?" Lorenzo asked. "Someone'll wake up, go out to walk their dog, and spot him soon. We call this in, we're gonna miss breakfast service."

"What if he's alive?" Arthur asked. "Wouldn't be right, we didn't stop and administer aid."

"We could make an anonymous call?" Lorenzo said.

"Got an anonymous phone?" Arthur asked.

"Not with me."

"We pass this up and someone sees us, calls it in..." Arthur said. "Don't wanna spend the rest of the day gettin' my ass grilled by Chato, or worse, I.A., over somethin' stupid like this."

"Biscuits and gravy at Trina's, though?" Detective Ferrigno said. "Might be worth it. She puts sausage *and* bacon in the gravy. And you know how big the biscuits are." The ex-New Yorker made a wide ring out of his hands over his lap to show the impressive size of Trina's biscuits.

"I ain't throwin' out my whole career for a plate of biscuits and gravy, Zo," Arthur said, opening his door and stepping out of the car. "As good as they are."

"You know I was just messin'?" Detective Ferrigno said, chuckling with the wheezing laugh of a career smoker.

"Uh, yeah," Arthur said, stepping toward the body that now lay in a contorted heap beside some unlucky person's driveway. "Looks like he's been dead for—Whoa! He moved!"

"Ha ha ha ha!" Detective Ferrigno burst, in a gasping bout of laughter. He stabbed an accusatory finger in his partner's direction. "You jumped about a foot. You thought he was *dead*."

"You didn't?" Arthur asked, obviously annoyed. He reached

into his back pocket, beside his leather-holstered Beretta pistol, and removed a pair of black nitrile gloves, which he snapped on before he began digging through the pockets of the unconscious man who lay on the pile of trash.

"Oh, man, Art," Lorenzo said, his voice now assuming a rather serious tone, "I just wish I had a quarter for every morning I woke up like *that*." Then he bellowed with laughter until he had worked himself into a wild coughing attack.

Arthur looked at his partner and smirked. "I got his wallet. Says his name is—"

<hr />

Max woke up, face down, his arm draped around a black plastic trash bag. His legs extended into the gutter, and his body lay sprawled across the curb, onto a patch of brown grass in front of a small house worn out by both time and neglect. Max's mind slowly cranked to life as he labored to remember how he had gotten here, wherever *here* was. And then he felt the headache.

"I'll ask you again, Sport," a booming man's voice sounded from somewhere behind Max's head. The tone and accent sounded to Max like a guy who might have been a prison guard at Riker's Island. "Can you stand, or do you need assistance?"

Max craned his neck and looked over his shoulder. The rising sun's rays sprayed his eyes, temporarily blinding him. "Uggh," he said, as he began to wiggle like a bug, testing the waters to see if he could stand up.

When he'd made it to his feet, Max realized two men were standing over him, one shorter and red-faced, like a man who spent most of his time outdoors; he wore a black leather jacket over a blue button-down shirt and tie. A thick rope chain of yellow gold dangled over the tie, matching the bracelet that jangled against the gold tone watch on his wrist. A gold sergeant's badge hung from his neck on a stainless chain.

The other guy was a lanky, lighter-skinned black man. He wore a blue polo shirt, a two-inch afro, and a pair of glasses he must have had since the late eighties. A gold badge glinted in the sunlight from his black alligator skin belt.

Max guessed the overly-tanned guy was the one who had addressed him. A black unmarked Dodge Charger sat idle in the street behind them, both doors ajar. Max spotted the vertically-secured twelve-gauge shotgun, the console-mounted data terminal, and the cage that separated the front seats from the back. Max wasn't used to being in trouble with the law, but he knew these features, along with the peculiar antennae protruding from the vehicle, told him it was definitely a cop car.

Max felt his pants for his wallet. *Had he brought his gun?* These guys pat him down, find the Smith & Wesson tucked into his pants, and him without a concealed permit—Max's going to jail. He might be going to jail anyway.

Then he noticed the black cop holding his tan eel skin billfold, the one his wife had bought him for last Father's Day, telling him it was actually from the kids. The tall cop flipped through its contents, scrutinizing every bill, every credit card, Max's driver's license.

"No, I'm good," Max said to the other cop. "I think I must have blacked out or something."

"Ouch, brother. What the hell happened to your ear?" the black cop asked.

Max's hand reached up to his left ear. Pain seared throughout his earlobe as his fingers touched it, and he looked down to see blood on his fingers. He felt again and found a thick gauze pad dangling from the back of his ear by medical tape, and he yanked it free, finding it saturated with blood and pus.

His mind wandered back to the scuffle he had had the night before in that tavern he'd stumbled into by the sewage treatment plant. Had that guy actually cut him with that broken Pabst bottle? Must have. It felt to Max like his ear had gotten caught on a barbed wire fence and he had yanked his head to free it.

"You have a lot to drink last night?" Riker's Island asked. "You get pretty pissed and pass out here?"

"I...I think I only had a couple of beers," Max said, nervously wringing his hands together. "But I recently started taking Xanax and Lexapro. They must have reacted adversely with the alcohol." Max rubbed his cheeks. He felt like he had been run over by a steam roller. For all he knew, he had been.

"Your address is up north," the tall cop said, holding up Max's driver's license in front of his face. "Windermere. Orlando area. What kind of work you do up there, Maxwell?"

"I'm...I'm in accounting," Max said, running his fingers through his short dirty blond hair. "I work for a...TV ministry up there."

"So why you down here in Little Haiti, face down in the gutter, hugging someone's bag of banana peels and chicken bones?" the brusque, ruddy-faced officer said, sounding skeptical.

"Honestly," Max said, rubbing his eyes and straining to focus them at the two police officers, likely detectives by the badges and their hip holsters, "I don't remember. All I know is I went into a sports bar over on Biscayne and had some hot wings, drank a couple of beers. That's the last memory I can recall."

"Down here soliciting?" Red-face continued. "Cruising for chicks? Maybe dudes? An' what happened to your car? You get rolled by her pimp an' he take off with your ride?"

"It wasn't anything like that," Max said, unable to suppress a smirk at the suggestion. "Is that what goes on down here?"

"What do you think we gotta assume?" the detective with the New York accent asked. "We drivin' down the street, see you layin' in the gutter. I say we keep going. I got an appointment with some biscuits and gravy at Trina's. Art says, 'No, Lorenzo, we gotta stop, check this guy out. Make sure he's not freakin' dead.'"

"Listen, Zo, I think the dude might be legit," the black officer said, slapping his hand with Max's wallet. "This fella's got blue cards, gold cards, platinum cards, and there's like six hundred in cash right here. Guy's got a cozy zip code, lives not far from that huge mansion Shaq's got up there. Sounds like our friend here's just havin' the worst day of his life."

Not the worst, Max thought. *Not by a long shot.*

Then something clicked in Max's mind. "Art?" he asked, looking at the tall black cop with a newfound sense of familiarity. "Arthur Ashe?"

The shorter cop burst out into raucous laughter. "Every time, Art. Every time!"

"No," the black officer said, obviously irritated. "I'm Detective Arthur Parks, with the Miami Police Department, not Arthur Ashe. The late Arthur Ashe was a tennis player who died in the early nineties. If I was Arthur Ashe, I'd be almost seventy by now. Wouldn't I?" The detective's speech sounded rehearsed, as if he'd given it a hundred times before.

"I'm sorry," Max said. "I didn't mean to offend. I just thought… well…you know. There's a…resemblance."

"Yeah," Detective Parks said. "I do get that from time to time."

"Maybe if you didn't wear the same glasses and keep your hair cut the same way," Max suggested. He frowned and shrugged his shoulders.

The cop named Lorenzo burst out laughing again. It was an intense asthmatic laugh that almost made Max wonder if the guy was going to keel over right in front of him. When he had finally stopped wheezing and had collected himself, he said, "You know, Art, the man may have just woken up in a gutter, literally lying facedown on a pile of garbage, unable to remember anything from the night before, but you gotta admit he's got a point."

"Yeah, whatever, man," Arthur said.

"You gonna be able to get yourself home or back to your hotel safely, Maxwell?" Detective Parks asked. The look in the lawman's eyes told Max the cop was about a twitch away from arresting him and stuffing him in the back of his Charger—and Max knew these guys wouldn't be happy about missing breakfast.

"Yeah," Max said, nodding. "I'm good."

"Be safe out there, Maxwell," Arthur Parks said, tossing Max his wallet.

Max waved as the two cops piled into their car and sped away down the quiet street on their way to Trina's. Then he turned and took a shaky step toward the sidewalk. Max's hand reached for his waist and he felt the weight of his heavy steel pistol through his light green cotton shirt. *That was too close*, Max thought.

And then Max wondered aloud, "Where the hell can I get a drink around here?"

CHAPTER 7

JOSUE SPOTTED LIGHTS FLICKERING OFF of the water. It was nearly impossible to gauge the distance as dark as it was, and as swiftly as the long speedboat whisked across the surface of the water. Once, the boat had stopped, and Josue had worked hard to help the first mate load fuel from gas cans into the fuel tanks below deck. Another time the boat had stopped in the middle of nowhere to meet another boat. The old fishing boat—Josue guessed it might have been a shrimp trawler or a crab boat—had tied up to the speedboat and transferred even more fuel from a big rusty tank on the trawler's deck.

The ride had been the most exhilarating of Josue's life. He had squinted through the wind to see the bright screens on the control panel. He was certain he had once seen the gauge read over one hundred miles per hour. Josue made calculations in his head to figure out exactly how that translated into kilometers per hour.

At times, Josue had even managed to forget about Joliette, his mother, and Uncle Guillot. But memories of the devastating collapse of their home, and the pitiful cries of wounded and sorrowful neighbors while Josue had desperately dug for his family, came rushing into his mind like a torrent. The rushing wind whipped away Josue's tears as the boat cut through the night like a hurtling bullet.

"Just another hour or so!" the first mate shouted back toward Josue and the three other men seated beside him. The first mate looked pleased. He seemed happy to be helping Josue and the others, even if it was a bit of a clandestine operation. "We're seeing the Keys now. See those lights on the islands in the distance?"

A piercing searchlight shone onto the deck of the *Silver Bullet*. Josue didn't know what was happening. The captain slowed the boat and turned it hard to the port side. It was then that Josue spotted the huge white vessel with red and blue stripes bearing down upon them. Men with combat helmets stood on the deck, some manning spotlights, others clutching shotguns.

The captain of the *Silver Bullet* added throttle and tried to turn back and speed away in the direction they had just come. Another spotlight shone ahead of them. A second vessel, this one small, inflatable, but fast, bore down on them like a streak of lightning.

Josue's heart raced.

"Can all of you guys swim?" the captain shouted back at Josue and the others.

"What?" Josue asked. *Why would the captain ask me such a question?*

"You four look able-bodied," the captain shouted back. "Can you swim?"

Josue and two of the others nodded. The fourth man shook his head. He looked terrified.

"I'm going to get as close as I can to the shore. Then I want you three to jump overboard," the captain shouted. "The Coast Guard is going to board us. They'll process the rest of the refugees, detain them, and make a decision about their statuses. But you guys can make a run for it, get free. I'll get you as close as I can to shore, but you've gotta jump. Then swim to shore, as fast as you can!"

The captain steered the boat back toward the Coast Guard ship, and then accelerated the boat. They shot past the big white vessel, pursued by the smaller craft that zipped along in the white foam behind the *Silver Bullet*.

Then the boat suddenly slowed down.

"Jump!" the captain shouted. "Jump!"

Josue fumbled with his restraint. Foret and the other man who could swim climbed over Josue and dove into the dark water as the small Coast Guard boat neared. At last Josue unbuckled the latch. He threw off the black fabric belts from his shoulders.

Josue mounted the *Silver Bullet*'s railing and turned to look at the captain and first mate. "Thank you," he said, just before he dove headfirst into the cool winter water near the Florida Keys.

Josue swam harder than he had ever swum in his life. As his head bobbed above the surface so he could gulp in a breath of air, he spotted moonlight glinting off a sandy beach. They only had about a hundred yards to go.

"*Ede!*" a voice nearby shouted. *Help.* It was Foret, and he was foundering in the water. Josue wondered if he had lied when he said he could swim.

"*Pa pè. Pa pè,*" Josue shouted back. *Do not be afraid.* "I will help you."

Josue slipped his arm around Foret's neck and pulled hard with his other arm, struggling toward the moonlit beach. The other man who had jumped with them struggled beside them. He could keep afloat, but he was not a strong swimmer.

"Stop!" a booming robotic-sounding voice shouted. Josue realized it came from the small inflatable Coast Guard boat. One of the men shouted at them through a loudspeaker. "Do not flee. Do not try to run."

Josue did not know if he should keep swimming for the shore, or if he should surrender to the Coast Guard. Would they hurt him? Would they imprison him? Josue knew they very likely would send him right back to the devastated land he had just fled.

Josue kicked his legs. He pumped his free arm with all of the strength he had left. Even more strength than he had realized he had. He swam until he and Foret were close to the shore, where the sand rose up to meet their feet, less than a meter below the surface of the lapping waves.

"*Kanpe*," Josue shouted to Foret. *Stand.*

Josue saw that the Coast Guardsmen in the small boat had grabbed the third man, the struggling swimmer, and were now helping him aboard their craft. But Josue just turned back toward the shore.

He and Foret waded out of the water, onto the beach, both gasping for air. The search lights from the Coast Guard boats gleamed across them, and Josue heard sirens in the distance.

"Run, Foret," Josue urged. "Run, hide."

The two men ran pell-mell away from the beach. They hadn't made a hundred yards, running under a bridge with cars and trucks loudly racing by overhead, before they encountered another beach on the opposite shore. "How small is Florida?" Josue asked Foret, who shrugged his shoulders.

The men ran in the opposite direction from which they heard the sirens. It wasn't long before they reached a thick cluster of dense mangroves. Josue rushed into them, followed by Foret. It wasn't long before the sand fell away and they were once again wading through waist-deep water, pushing their way through the thick tufts of bright green leaves.

"Which way?" Foret asked. His head shook from side to side. He looked frantic.

"This way," Josue said, pushing on through the mangroves. He had no idea where he was going, but he thought it might settle Foret down if he sounded as if he had a plan.

Then the two refugees came face to face with an old white man, probably an American.

The man sat in the bow of a white boat, and he looked

surprised, his eyes wide, as he glared down on the two frightened men. The white-haired man wore a blue baseball cap and clutched a fishing pole in his hands.

Josue eyes darted around; he wondered which way to run next.

"Wait, wait," the old man said. He set the fishing pole down. He held up his hands in front of him. "You refugees? From Haiti? You two just flee the quake?"

Josue and Foret nodded vigorously.

"I'll help you," the old man said. He reached his hand down toward Josue.

Josue didn't know why an American would help him escape his own Coast Guard. He was skeptical. But there was something about the way the man looked down at Josue that suggested something kind. Was it compassion?

Josue took the man's hand and climbed up onto the boat. Josue helped Foret behind him. The old man wasted no time. He fired up the boat's engines and sped through a twisted maze of green foliage that appeared shockingly vivid in the boat's brilliant headlights.

Sometimes the green foliage would slap them in the face as the boat flew past. When they had reached a clearing the old man turned to Josue and said, "Here, take the wheel."

The old man pulled what looked like a tiny glowing TV screen out of his pocket. He tapped on it a few times. And then he shouted into it. "Danny? Yeah, it's Edgar. Want to do your good deed for today?"

The old man, Josue guessed his name was Edgar, took the wheel again. He drove the boat close to the shore for awhile until they reached a dock with a long pier that led to a cluster of buildings, most of which appeared dark and unoccupied.

"Get to the end of the dock. My friend'll be waiting. Danny

will help you. He's a good man." The old man smiled at Josue and Foret. "You'll be free. You'll be okay."

Josue could not help himself. He threw his arms around the old man and hugged him tightly. "Thank you. Thank you."

Foret hugged the man as well.

Josue reached the end of the dock and crept low between two dark buildings, wondering where he was supposed to go next. He stopped short as he spotted a huge truck, the largest he had ever seen. Orange and white lights adorned the full length of the truck, which must have been as long as the *Silver Bullet*, maybe longer.

Then Josue spotted a white-haired man with a thick, bushy beard in the window of the truck's driving compartment. The man was looking right at Josue, and he was waving his hand toward himself.

Josue didn't know what to do. He stared at the man.

"Come here," the man shouted out the window. "It's okay. I'm Danny, Edgar's brother-in-law. I'll drive you where you want to go."

Josue and Foret approached the truck with caution. "Yes?" Josue said to the driver.

"Get in the truck," the man said. "I'm heading up north far as Titusville today. Where do you fellas want to go?"

"Miami?" Josue asked. "Can you take us Miami?"

The driver nodded enthusiastically. "Sure. I can take you there. It'll be right on the way." He handed Josue a big bag of some kind of food.

"What this?" Josue asked.

"Pork rinds," the driver said. "They're delicious. Try one. You'll love 'em."

In no time, Josue and Foret were on the highway driving toward the city that seemed almost mythical in his mind. He had read descriptions of the sparkling city by the sea from his aunt, who had lived there for six or seven years after leaving Haiti. Josue couldn't wait to see it. But as much as he wanted to take in all the new sights along the way, Josue struggled against the urge to sleep. As the sun peeked over the surface of the ocean, Josue finally succumbed. He nodded off to sleep in the comfortable seat of the kind stranger's massive truck.

CHAPTER 8

J OSUE HANDED THE TRUCK DRIVER the wrinkled folded envelope from his pocket. It contained a card with a picture of a dog wearing a party hat that Josue's aunt had sent him for his birthday. Josue had plucked the envelope from the rubble of his shattered house, remembering his aunt's address had been printed in clean blue handwriting on the outside of the envelope. Josue hoped the driver, Danny, could use it to help him find his aunt.

"Lemon Street?" the bearded man said between gruff hacking coughs and the noisy clearing of his throat. "I know where it is. Little Haiti. Probably the best place you could go. A lot of folks there from your home country."

Josue sat back in silence for a long time watching the scenery that flew past as the truck chewed away the kilometers toward Miami. He couldn't believe how lush the whole state was. Rich, green trees of all kinds lined the road, almost like decorations. Most of the trees in Haiti had been chopped down and burned to make charcoal for fuel, leaving the earth parched, dry, and barren. Bright cars of all colors and sizes surrounded them as they drove, yet everyone seemed to drive in an orderly and controlled manner.

The long truck rumbled as it crested a hill, and Josue caught his first glimpse of the city. The towering buildings of Miami, taller even than trees, loomed ahead of them in the distance. Josue gasped. He had never seen structures so tall. Sunlight glinted off countless glass windows like sparkling diamonds. It nearly took his breath away.

"Not long now," the kind truck driver said, his meaty hands wrapped around the large steering wheel.

The truck rolled on for about another fifteen minutes before the driver stopped on the side of the road while keeping the chugging diesel engine running. He pulled a piece of paper from a leather bag which he had grabbed from the sleeping area behind his seat. The wild-looking man scrawled lines all over the paper and wrote a few numbers.

"We here?" Josue asked. He wrung his hands together. "Lemon Street?"

"Truck's too big to drive all the way there," the truck driver said, speaking loudly. Maybe he thought it would make Josue understand him easier. "So I drew a little map to help you find your way."

"Thank you," Josue said. He took the piece of paper from the driver.

"Go that way," the driver said. He pointed out his window toward a gray street lined with palm trees. "Follow this map."

Josue hugged the truck driver. He felt so much warmth inside to have been shown so much kindness in such a foreign land. "Thank you. Thank you."

The truck driver nodded. "Take care. It's been my pleasure, young man. Be safe."

Josue turned toward Foret. He grasped the other man's hand and spoke to him in Creole. "Do you have somewhere to go, my friend?"

"My destination is further north," Foret said. The refugee's dark brown eyes looked bright and eager as he spoke. Josue guessed the man's heart was filled with as much hope as he himself felt. "The city is called Hollywood. The truck driver said he would take me all the way there. I have a brother there, and I believe he will allow me live with him."

"I am counting on my aunt's mercy and kindness," Josue said to his new friend. The truck driver looked as if he were trying to understand what the two conversed about, but he mostly just appeared confused by their language. "I am hoping she can give me a place to sleep, provide me with some food."

"Bondye ka ede ou," Foret said, shaking Josue's hand firmly. He grasped his other hand on top of Josue's. "You *will* find your way, my friend. Thank you for helping me to the shore. You are now my brother."

Josue embraced Foret around the neck. Then he cautiously crossed the street, peering down at the map the truck driver had drawn for him. He turned and waved as Danny the driver rolled slowly away with Foret in the massive building-sized truck.

It took a few minutes to find his way. Once, Josue turned left instead of right, and he misread one of the signs. But he finally found a green sign that read Lemon Street. It was one of the most beautiful sights Josue had ever seen. His heart fluttered with excitement. The journey had been long and trying, but he had, at last, arrived.

After everything he had experienced over the past couple days, Josue was ready for a meal and a comfortable place to rest his head. He followed the map, walking down Lemon Street, checking the numbers on each of the houses. It didn't take him long to figure out the odd-numbered houses were on one side of the street, while the even-numbered addresses were on the other. And it was soon clear the numbers beside the doors ascended in sequential order.

Josue found himself faced with number two hundred twenty-one: his aunt's address. The pale green house was small, but had a neat little yard with lush, freshly cut grass. A large terra cotta pot beside the front steps swelled with tiny tomatoes growing among tall stalks of gangly green foliage. Josue hadn't seen his aunt since he was about twelve years old. Would she even recognize him?

Josue approached the door and knocked. And then he waited, wringing his hands together once again, unable to shake the nerves that squirmed in his gut. It took a minute, but at last he heard a fumbling sound inside the house, as if someone was working a lock or a latch. And then the door opened and Josue saw the face of his Aunt Corantine.

"Yes?" the woman said. She wore a bright blue dress and matching head wrap. Her eyes were a light greenish brown color, and Josue instantly thought of his mother's eyes, nearly the same color.

Josue laughed inside himself. She didn't recognize him. The boy she had once known had grown to become a man.

"Josue," he said, his lips splitting into a massive joy-filled smile. "Josue Remy. *Sonje mwen?*" *Remember me?*

"No," Aunt Corantine said, her mouth gaping open. "Josue?" She threw her arms around Josue and gave him the tightest, warmest hug he had ever felt in his life. Tears welled up in his eyes. The journey had wearied him. His recent losses had been so great. But at last, he had found a new kind of home. And hopefully, some peace.

"How did you get here?" Aunt Corantine asked, speaking in Haitian Creole, her face beaming in a bright smile. "Did your mother and sister come? Are they with you? I have been so worried about you all. I've been watching all of the destruction on TV. Port au Prince is ruined. It is *ruined.*"

Josue told his aunt everything that had transpired with his home and family. How they had perished suddenly in the devastating collapse of their house. How he had resisted the government workers who wanted to dump their bodies in a pit, a communal mass grave. How he had dug their graves at the farm and marked them with crosses made of stones.

"They're dead?" Aunt Corantine asked, her chin and her cheeks quivering as the ground had during the quake. She held her hands to her face and she began to sob. "My sister is dead? My brother is dead? My niece? Dead?" And then she shrieked with a horrible wail that made Josue shiver. She reached out her arms and clung to Josue for support.

"How did you get here?" Aunt Corantine asked, looking at Josue with huge eyes.

Josue quickly recounted his adventures, telling his aunt about the speedy boat, swimming away from the Coast Guard, the kind fisherman, and his friend the burly truck driver.

"You cannot be here, Josue," his aunt said, pushing him away from the door. "You cannot stay with me. You will get me in trouble. I am a legal citizen. If they find out that I helped you, they will take my citizenship away. They will send me back to Titanyen. They'll send me back to that hellish place!"

"Where should I go?" Josue asked in a panicked voice. He felt a flutter of fear inside him. He was in a foreign land, and Aunt Corantine was the only person he knew in the entire country. He didn't know what he would do without her.

"I don't know," she said, continuing to push against his chest. "You must go, and you must go now. Do not return here. I do not know you."

Aunt Corantine slammed her door, and Josue heard the metallic sound of the latches on the other side. He stumbled down the little path in front of her house to the street.

Josue's own aunt had turned him away. He did not know what to do.

Josue turned and made faltering steps toward the end of the street. He felt like a fugitive from justice. Maybe he *was* a fugitive from justice. He felt as if someone might take one look at him, see that he did not belong, and start screaming.

"Fugitive! Fugitive!" they would say. And they would call

for the police, who would lock him up in their jail. Maybe they would beat him. Then they would send him back to his village near Titanyen.

Josue found a cluster of sea grape shrubs growing wild in a big vacant lot down the street from Aunt Corantine's house, the plant's big, round, leathery leaves billowing in the light, warm, morning breeze.

Josue crawled into the tangle of shrubs, nestling himself deep inside, concealing himself from the sight of passersby. In the shady crevice of the tropical plant, Josue sat, hands on his face, elbows on his knees. He looked at the envelope, still in his hand. He tore off the part with his aunt's name and her address. He wadded up the ripped piece and threw it on the ground in disgust. It felt to him as if he had never known his aunt.

He began to cry, softly at first. And then Josue wept as hard as he could weep until he thought there weren't any more tears left in the world. And then he fell asleep.

CHAPTER 9

MAX GRABBED HOLD OF THE handle on the tinted glass door of the South Beach Savings and Loan in the Upper East Side of the city. Max had chosen the bank branch because it was the same institution where he and his wife had kept their accounts since the first year they were married. It was also the first bank Max had spotted when he had stumbled out of Tippy's Hideaway after a quick round of morning cocktails.

Max entered the bank—which he thought looked like a big box made almost entirely of smoked glass panels—and he stumbled to the podium where they kept the deposit slips, withdrawal slips, and those annoying pens attached to the counter with those too-short beaded chains. Max's foot kicked a potted bamboo palm beside the podium, knocking it over, and spilling some of its soil on the white tiled floor.

A man in a white short-sleeved shirt and blue and silver spotted tie rushed over from a desk to pick up the plant. He smiled at Max. Probably the bank manager. *And he probably doesn't care if I burn the place down as long as I keep my money in his bank,* Max thought.

"Sorry, sir," Max said, looking down at the back of the man's balding scalp. "My fault. Entirely my fault."

Max fumbled with the withdrawal slips, grabbing a thick bundle of them instead of just one. As he tried to peel one off the top of the stack, the remainder slipped out of his hand. The fifty or so withdrawal slips fanned out, cascading over his shoes and all over the floor.

Max detected the stare of a thick-throated, bespectacled woman with a big tuft of brown, curly hair who sat behind one of the new accounts desks, as well as those of several people standing between purple velvet ropes waiting for the next available teller. Max bent down to pick up the slips and banged his head hard on the surface of the podium. A bright flash of white light shocked his vision, and his hand instinctively rose to his smashed forehead.

An elderly woman let go of her tennis ball-footed walker to bend over and take a knee. She gathered up the white papers from the floor and looked at Max eye to eye, as he had dropped to one knee as well.

"Everything okay, son?" she asked. Kindness shone in the woman's eyes. It would have normally melted Max's heart. But he had seen so many eyes looking at him with similar expressions in recent days. So many stares of polite pity. Seeing it now made him feel sick. He didn't want to feel this way anymore.

"I'm good," Max said, standing quickly, almost too quickly—he had to grab hold of the podium to right himself—and he broke away from the kind woman's gaze. "I just need to make a transaction."

The elderly woman nodded and scooped up the papers, and placed them on the podium. Max isolated one of the withdrawal slips and began to fill it out. He didn't realize his hand was shaking so badly until he saw the face of the elderly walker woman, as well as those of two kids, whose heads barely crested the podium's top.

Max used two hands to slowly fill out all the fields. He amazed himself that as unsteady as he felt, as cloudy as his mind swirled, he had had no trouble remembering his account number. He supposed that you do something enough times and it becomes automatic.

Max looked at the withdrawal slip. *That's a lot of zeroes*, he thought. *I wonder if I did it right. I suppose the girl at the counter will tell me if it's wrong.*

Max entered the queue. Standing in the roped-off area he felt like an ill-fated cow being herded to his doom. Maybe he was. Perhaps the money he pulled out today would buy the incendiary liquid that would ultimately finish him off. He had a feeling it wouldn't be that easy, though. He would probably be back again and again for more before it was all done.

Max leaned on one of the brass or bronze pillars that allowed the velvet ropes to be clipped and unclipped. The support nearly toppled over once, but Max managed to regain its balance. He felt like a magnet for people's peering, prying, judging eyes. He couldn't possibly care less.

Max looked down at his shirt. Was he wearing a shirt? He saw the wrinkled green button-down and creased navy blue blazer. *Fancy*, Max thought. *When did I put this on?* But the bank clientele looked upon him as if he were a homeless vagabond who had entered the bank solely to ruin their day.

"Next," a sweet voice called. Max waited, wondering how long it would be until his turn. He hoped it wouldn't be too long. He thought he'd had enough drinks at that shabby dive—what was it called, Tippy's or something?—to steady himself and stave off the shakes, but that was clearly not the case. He needed more drinks, and he needed them soon, or things would really start to get ugly.

"Next," the sweet female voice said again. Max turned his head and noticed no one between him and the young blonde teller. "Sir, you're next," she said, and it was the least judgmental face Max had seen in a while.

He shuffled his feet over to the young teller's window, grateful for the opportunity to place both of his arms down to support himself. He looked the teller in the eyes and almost got lost in them. They were the biggest and bluest eyes he had ever seen, a pale crystal blue like shallow tropical water over white sand.

"Can I help you, sir?" the young teller asked.

Max must have been staring, because the petite blonde looked down at the counter, cutting off the lock he had with her eyes. Max looked down as well. He noticed the slip of paper in his hand and he slid it out away from himself until the teller picked it up with two hands and looked at it. Her big blue eyes grew in size even more.

"Are you sure this is how much you would like to withdraw?" she asked. "Are you sure you have an account with us, Mr...Sutherland?" And there it was, the judgment Max had been anticipating.

"Um...I think so," Max said, reaching his hand down to the withdrawal slip for another look. "Why? How much does it say?"

"It says you want to withdraw a hundred thousand dollars, sir," the young teller said. Max noticed that the name tag on her pink sweater said Chloe. "Is that right?"

Max laughed. It was an exaggerated laugh. He wasn't sure if he did it on purpose, or if it had just come out that way. "No... Chloe," Max said, using the counter to steady himself. "You're right, that is wrong."

"Well, how much do you want to withdraw?" she said. Chloe seemed so innocent to Max, like a doe or something. For some reason Max thought about Bambi's mother being shot in the forest.

"I thought it sounded like a lot of zeroes," Max said, looking again into Chloe's crystal eyes. "I meant to write *ten* thousand."

Chloe's mouth hung open slightly. She looked as if she didn't know what to do. Then she started punching numbers onto a computer keyboard as she stared at a small computer monitor. Her eyes bulged as she peered at the LED screen's face.

"If you don't mind, sir, I'd just like to call my manager over here to verify this transaction. I'm pretty new here, and just want to make sure I don't make any mistakes." Max halfway wanted to ask Chloe out for a round of cocktails. He knew how well that would go over, though.

The balding plant picker came over and stood beside Chloe, looking like the beast to her beauty. "Yes, Chloe?"

"Mr. Sutherland wants to withdraw ten thousand from his account. It looks like he has...two hundred and ninety thousand in his account, so that's not a problem. I just wanted to make sure...everything was...okay." She looked at the bank manager intensely, as if her face was a giant question mark.

The bank manager looked over Max for a moment. "Is everything all right with you today, sir?"

"Sure," Max said, looking around behind him. "Why?"

"You just seem a bit unsteady today," Mr. Short Sleeve said, running his hand over what hair he had left. Max noticed his name tag said Brett Mordecai.

"I am a little," Max admitted. "Is that going to keep you from letting me withdraw money from my account today?" Max intentionally allowed his tone to become a bit confrontational.

"Honestly, sir," the bank manager said, "I just want to confirm that you are not extracting money from your account during a state of duress. Would you humor me and tell me that you are not under duress?"

Max nodded. "It's good of you to be so careful. I am not in a state of duress. I am very likely going to go into a series of bars, taverns, and possibly even saloons this evening, and I will probably burn through most of the ten thousand on various and sundry. But it *is* my money, and I know what I am doing."

"Very well, sir," Brett said. "Chloe will proceed with your transaction, and I hope you have a wonderful day, Mr. Sutherland."

"Just make sure you confirm his identity," the bank manager said to the young teller. "And then give him his cash."

Chloe glanced up at Max furtively. She looked like she

was participating in a drug deal. "I just need to see your ID, Mr. Sutherland."

Standing in the parking lot, Max flipped his thumb over the end of the paper wrapped ten thousand dollar bundle in his blazer pocket, feeling the hundreds slipping by under his skin. He thought about how much his wife would disapprove.

Who cares? Max thought. *It's not like she's around to do anything about it. Besides, I'm a big boy. I can make my own choices.*

A dirty guy with a bike trailer full of dilapidated belongings, towed by his rust-crusted ten-speed, leaned over and tipped his whole torso into the deep trash can outside the big glass bank. With great effort the wild-haired man righted himself, clutching a dented silver beer can in each hand.

"Hey, man," Max said, peeling off a percentage of the thick cash bundle in his pocket. He slipped his hand out and flipped through the loose bills. "Here's…twelve hundred. Should be able to get a good meal for that."

The destitute man's eyes bulged wide. He must have thought it was some kind of trap the way he held his hands by his sides, still clutching the cans.

"No, really," Max urged. "Take it. I want you to."

The guy took the bills and hugged Max. But Max still felt greedy. As if this offering had been a mere tithe before he utilized the rest to completely degrade himself.

Max spotted a sign in a building across the street that advertised ice-cold Jager shots. He didn't know what that was, but he was always willing to expand his repertoire and try new things. Max waited by the stoplight until the red hand had changed into a green walking man, and he scraped his feet across the asphalt, being careful to stay within the white painted lines of the crosswalk.

CHAPTER 10

BY THE TIME JOSUE AWOKE, darkness had fallen over him. An eerie and disorienting feeling gripped him. Waking up inside a thick cluster of sea grape leaves gave him a sickening, claustrophobic sensation. But the worst experience for him, and Josue had already experienced it twice in as many days, was the cold reality of waking up believing he would see his family, and then learning once again that they had perished.

Josue scampered out of the shrubs. He gasped for a fresh breath of air. He found himself facedown on his hands and knees like an animal in the middle of the vacant lot. What would he do next? What could he do?

In a matter of seconds, Josue's life had become a cruel joke. One minute his heart had swelled with a great deal of hope; the next minute the hope had vanished. He felt like a boat adrift at sea, its sails swollen from a great gust of wind, but only for a moment, before the doldrums set in, and the wind blew no more.

Josue fought back tears. His brain grappled with so much pain, fear, and doubt; somehow letting himself weep managed to drain some of these feelings from his body, at least for a short time. But there was only so much that crying could do. He steeled himself and stood to his feet.

Streetlights illuminated Lemon Street intermittently; foliage from palm trees, massive weeping willows, and the odd gumbo-limbo tree dappled and diffused their artificial light. The lush green of the foliage juxtaposed itself against the stark reality of the impoverished neighborhood. The seedy street was opulent by Haitian standards, but the general run-down nature of the vicinity did not pass by Josue unnoticed. The faded, peeling paint, the trash-strewn lawns, and the general state of disrepair shared by most of the homes suggested residents either didn't have much, did not care, or perhaps suffered from a combination of both factors.

Josue saw the warm glow of lamplight in a nearby window. He thought about knocking on the front door and asking for a merciful handout of food. His stomach felt hollow and made groaning sounds from time to time. The last thing he had eaten was the strange fried snacks Danny the truck driver had offered him from a big plastic bag. Though they had been food, they had also left Josue feeling rather sick to his stomach.

He stood at the edge of the grass in front of the house, wondering what to do. A noisy vehicle pulled up behind him and stopped. Loud booming speakers announced the vehicle's arrival, and Josue turned to get a look at the driver. The man behind the steering wheel was the smallest full-grown man Josue had ever seen. The petite driver wore a sleeveless sports jersey. His head was bald and about the size of a coconut with its fibrous green husk removed. The small man looked quizzically at Josue.

"Yo, you lost?" the driver said. His diminutive arm hung over the side of the vehicle's door, which had been painted with the shiniest, most dazzling orange paint Josue had ever seen. Except for the huge, shiny silver wheels, the car's bright color reminded Josue of a hard sour candy he had sucked on as a child.

Josue did not know what to say. He was not lost exactly. But he also did not have any place that he could go. "I come to Miami today. But I have...no place. No place I can go."

"You came here *today*?" the little man said, his voice sounding high-pitched, sort of small, like he was. "Where from?"

"My village, near Titanyen," Josue said. "Close by Port au Prince."

The miniature driver looked surprised. "My mannnnn," he said in an exaggerated way. He held out his hand as if he wanted Josue to grasp it in some sort of handshake or other gesture. Josue obliged, and the little fellow clasped hands with him. They shook hands in a strange way where they wrapped their hands around each other's thumb. "Port au Prince, brother. You flee the quake?"

"Earthquake, yes," Josue said.

"Speak Creole?" the man said. "*Ou pale kreyòl?*" *Do you speak Creole?*

Josue nodded and spoke to the man quickly in Haitian Creole, hastily telling him everything that had transpired over the past few days. He left out the part about his aunt turning him away. She lived right down the street, and he was wary about causing her any trouble.

"Sorry about your family, man. You among friends now," the little fellow said. "My name's Derrick, but everybody calls me Tiny Deege."

"Tiny Deege?" Josue said, thinking the name sounded funny, like a clown name or some other kind of performer. "I am Josue. Josue Remy.

"Are you..." Josue tried to think of the word in English, but it escaped him, "*Miniatures?*"

"Naw, man," the little man said, scrunching up his child-size face. "I ain't no midget. Just born smaller'n everyone else. Ya know? Normal-sized dad, normal-sized mom. I just turned out the way I turned out. Dig?"

Josue stared back with a blank expression. He nodded softly.

"Good to meet you, brother," Tiny Deege said, drumming his fingers on his car's steering wheel as if playing a djembe. "Tell you what, I'm gonna take you over ta my house, get y'all some grub, introduce you to the boys. Then we gonna set you up with a place to sleep. You gonna be okay fro' here on out, Josue. All right?"

Josue could not help but smile. His prayers had suddenly been answered in an unexpected way. The bone-weary traveler stepped around to the passenger side of the vehicle, and Tiny Deege popped open the door for Josue, who took a seat. Josue had only ridden in cars a couple of times before. This one was strange, with carpeting below the front window and hand-painted skulls here and there.

Josue spotted a colorful fabric object on the back of the boosted tan leather driver's seat that raised up Tiny Deege's stature behind the steering wheel.

Tiny Deege noticed his stare. "Oh that? It's a quilt that my Grandma made. Nice, huh? My seat be custom-made to jack me up high. An' look at them pedals," the small driver said, nodding his head and looking down at the floor in front of him. "They got extra long arms to reach 'em up where my feet at. Had 'em made just for this ride."

The miniscule man drove the car two driveways down and stopped on the grass in front of a weathered turquoise house.

The two men stepped out of the car, and Josue followed Tiny Deege to the front door, which was accessible only by first opening another door made of black metal bars. The smaller man pushed the door open, and Josue stepped into a dimly lit room fogged with billows of strange-smelling smoke, and the din of many people sitting, conversing inside.

Tiny Deege led Josue into the middle of a room, which was crowded by about a dozen people who sat upon ripped couches, or faded reclining chairs, some smoking hand-rolled cigarettes, others smoking odd-smelling cigars. Most of the folks present— mostly men, except for three young, immodestly dressed women—drank from bottles of beer or hard alcohol, and stared at what looked to Josue a lot like a football game on a huge flat television. But instead of the players kicking around a round white ball, these footballers wore body armor and crashed into each other as they groped for the oblong brown ball.

"This here is my man, Josue Remy," Tiny Deege said to the group. "He goin' stay with me for awhile. He just come over from Port au Prince today."

A roar bellowed from the group as they clapped hands and cheered for Josue. A couple of the men stood up from the couch and clasped hands with Josue in that strange way Tiny Deege had shaken his hand before.

Josue's pint-sized friend started making quick introductions between Josue and the other men. "This is Hazy Junior," Tiny Deege said, pointing to a tall, thin youth with medium dark skin, about the color of a coconut's husk. "He an' Wily Beeve be twins, brothers." The small man pointed toward another man, slightly shorter than Hazy Junior, who had the identical skin tone, and a similar short nose.

"Other fellas be Rocket Mike and his lady, Treena; Momo; Jessie Bae; that orange-haired fool off in the corner smokin' a bowl be Zann." Tiny Deege rattled off a few more names, but Josue quickly lost track of everyone who was mentioned. It was too much to take in all at once.

"Josue lost his family in the quake," Tiny Deege added. "Young 'un lost it all, my brothers, so show him some love. Feel me? Let's all show 'im some love."

Most of the men in the room reached into their pockets and pulled out thick rolls of American currency. They peeled off a lot of bills from their bundles and handed them to Josue. He felt awkward about receiving such great amounts of money, but the men seemed adamant about him taking it.

"Thank you," Josue said, nodding with humility as he gazed down at the heaping mound of green paper money between his hands. "Mèsi, mèsi."

Tiny Deege explained to Josue that everyone in the room was either a Haitian refugee, a legal immigrant from Haiti, or had been born in the United States to Haitian parents. "Imma refugee like you, Josue," Tiny Deege said. "So I feel what you feelin'. But you all right now. You among friends."

One of the men, a huge man, nearly two hundred centimeters tall, stood up and passed a flat box over to Josue. "Have some pizza, guy," the man said, placing a hand on Josue's shoulder. The big man's hand nearly covered it.

"I'm Momo," the man said. He wore a similar sports jersey to that of Tiny Deege. But the two men were like opposites of each other, Momo with a white jersey and Tiny Deege's black. Tiny Deege was the size of a child and Momo stood nearly the size of a mountain.

Josue nodded at Momo as he accepted the food, and then he ate ravenously. Momo laughed as he watched Josue eat. "Slow down, slow down," he said. "There's a lot mo' where that came from."

The front door opened and a woman of about thirty years stepped into the crowded living room. The dark-skinned woman was colorfully dressed in a bright red and yellow dress and matching head scarf. Josue noticed her hand clenched tightly around the neck of a bespectacled black kid, maybe twelve years old. The brightly dressed woman practically dragged the kid inside the house after her.

"I must speak with you, Momo," the woman said, as she glared at the largest man in the room.

"What is it, Mama Dorah?" Momo said. Josue thought he looked irritated.

"It is time that you consider taking Reginald into the gang," the woman said. "Time to start teaching him the ways of Ti Flow, to make him one of your own."

"Imma tell you one last time, Mama," Momo said. "We can't

take no kids into the Flow. We ain't that kinda gang. Kid's gotta grow up a few afore he can join. Besides, we got enough guys."

The one called Mama Dorah glared at Josue. "Who is this?"

Josue extended his hand for a shake. "I am Josue Remy."

Mama Dorah looked at Josue's hand as if he had just wiped himself with it.

"You will take in young Reginald, Momo," Mama Dorah said, raising her voice as she turned her attention back toward the hulking gang member. "You will take him in, or you will regret the consequences that may befall you."

Josue noticed that as she spoke the woman fiddled with the beads of her necklace. Closer inspection suggested, at least to Josue, that the beads were actually finger or toe bones, possibly human.

"We gonna talk about this later, Mama," Momo said, sounding perturbed. "Like maybe in fo' years."

Mama Dorah turned on her heels and grabbed the neck of the kid. She shoved him out the door in front of her, before storming out after him.

"Hey, Momo," Tiny Deege said, looking up at the larger man. "S'okay if'n Josue stay here fo' awhile? He can bed down on my flo'."

"Sho thing," Momo said. "Your room's your room, brother. You can do what you like. Dig?"

"Thanks, Momo," the little man beamed.

After Josue had eaten four slices of pizzas, and drank two cold Prestige beers, Tiny Deege led him the length of a short hallway to a darkened room. The little man clicked a switch on the wall to turn on the electric overhead light. Josue saw a bed with messy bedclothes; a brown wood cabinet with drawers and a strange clock on top with bright red numbers; and an orange-carpeted floor strewn with empty wine bottles and other debris.

"This is *my* room," Tiny Deege said. He slid a door on the wall to reveal a smaller compartment behind it. Tiny Deege fumbled with a pile of things behind the sliding door until he produced a cloth bundle. He untied a couple of knots and unrolled the fabric, kicking aside some of the trash so he could lay it out on the carpeted floor. A long zipper ran down the side of what looked to Josue like a thick folded blanket. "My old sleeping bag," the diminutive man said. "You can sleep here as long as you like, my brother. You in a safe place now."

"Thank you," Josue said, hugging the other man. "Mèsi, Tiny Deege."

"I know, man," Tiny Deege said. "I know. It seems like it was only a few days ago when I'd just got off the boat too. Get some sleep. We'll talk more when you're rested." Tiny Deege clicked off the light switch and left the room.

Josue nestled himself into the cozy sleeping bag—though it smelled a bit musty and old—and he tucked his hands under his head. He felt something dig against his side painfully. Josue reached into his pocket and felt the thick silver pendant he had taken from his mother's neck before burial. Josue slipped out the small icon and chain, placing them on the small bedside table of Tiny Deege's room. *It will be safe there until I wake,* Josue thought.

He wondered how it was possible that in a matter of minutes he had gone from being completely destitute to having food, shelter, and friends. But as he drifted off to sleep, he thanked God for being merciful and not forgetting him. He did not know what he had done to deserve such kindness and generosity.

"Josue!" a voice called from the doorway. The overhead light was still turned off, and Josue saw Tiny Deege's silhouette in the doorway. "You awake, man?"

"I am," Josue said groggily. He looked at the clock with bright red letters. Nearly five hours had passed. "I am awake."

"Someone here I want you to meet," Tiny Deege said, and Josue detected a hint of excitement in the little man's voice.

Josue got up and rubbed his eyes. He followed Tiny Deege down the hall. Fewer men occupied the living room now, and one man with very dark skin sat on the arm of one of the couches, gazing in Josue's direction with a sense of anticipation in his eyes. The man's head was covered in a wild thicket of long, tangled dreadlocks, and the man's eyes were wide and vibrant. He reminded Josue of a lion.

"Is this *him*?" the man asked in Creole. "Is this Josue?"

Tiny Deege nodded. "Big Flow, meet my new brother, Josue Remy."

Big Flow stood up from the couch and approached Josue with arms outstretched. Josue noticed his partially-buttoned shirt was half blue, half red, and emblazoned with the crest of Haiti's flag, adorned with its familiar cache of weapons and its lone palm. The charismatic man embraced Josue in a warm, gentle embrace.

"I feel so deeply for you, my friend," Big Flow said, speaking to the sleepy man in Haitian Creole. "But I dare not call you friend, for you are now my brother, Josue Remy. It is no accident that you have arrived here. The tide has brought you to me. It is destiny that you should arrive here, to find Ti Flow."

"Ti Flow?" Josue asked.

"Ti Flow is the name of our organization, Josue," Big Flow said, releasing Josue from his embrace and holding out his hand and slowly waving it about the room, as if showcasing all of the men present. "Each man here is a vital part of Ti Flow. One cannot exist without the others. We work as one, we believe as one, we hurt as one, we weep as one. The thing that has brought us all together is that we are all refugees, wayward sons, orphans from the same mother, Josue."

"Haiti?" Josue asked.

Big Flow laughed. "Yes, Josue. Our shared mother is our homeland. We take great pride in it. We live for her. We will die for her if need be.

"Would you like to belong, Josue? Do you wish to be a part of something greater than yourself? To do whatever work we call upon you to do? To share in our great joy, weep with us in our brief sorrows, to enjoy the great spoils of our most triumphant moments? To be one with the other parts of Ti Flow?"

Josue's heart began to pound. He was scared. He knew about the gangs in Port au Prince. Their violence, their disregard for the sanctity of human life, their willingness to take anything they pleased, claiming it for their own. Janjak had intended to recruit him into the Scorpio gang, in Port au Prince. It was part of the reason he had chosen to step onto Austin's boat, to try to find a better life.

Josue knew his mother would not approve of his membership into such an organization. She would have died first. But Josue now saw no other way for himself.

"I do," Josue said. "If you allow me."

Chapter 11

MAX WASN'T SURE WHY HE had chosen the Deep Blue Sea Motel. The ambiance of the place certainly hadn't factored into the decision. Or maybe it had without him realizing it. As Max considered his surroundings, the gloomy room's stark amenities—its lumpy bed, cheap laminated table and chairs, and the paper-thin walls that allowed all manner of hair-curling noises and sounds to seep through—were likely the very reason for Max's choice in the first place.

He had plenty of money for one of the colorful 1930s era hotels on Ocean Drive in Miami Beach. But lodging himself in one of the luxuriously renovated Art Deco or Nautical Moderne places seemed at odds with his mission. The ambiance of that locale, with the mellifluous sounds of its Latin and Caribbean music; the appetite-whetting aromas wafting from its restaurants; and its vibrant people, all determined to enjoy their lives as much as possible, would surely make Max's purpose in coming down to Miami nearly impossible.

He preferred the grittier streets of Little Haiti. The occasional crack of a resounding gunshot, the frequent sing-song of semi-distant or imminently close police sirens, and the intermittent voices shouting at each other from windowsills with such great disdain, were more like music to Max's ears. They were a constant reminder to him that this world was no longer a place he wished to occupy.

No, more consideration of the matter proved to Max that he

had chosen this particular seafoam green motel for its ambiance. But for exactly the opposite reasons most people chose their overnight accommodations. Most folks searched for the most comfortable bed, the greatest tourist-friendly location, the highest reviews. Max had chosen the Deep Blue Sea, with its peeling paint and creepy clientele, because the ramshackle inn looked exactly the same way as he felt.

Max sat at the foot of his bed, its filthy quilted bedspread pulled off and spread across the floor in front of him. He decided the only omission to the room's mossy covering of thick orange carpeting was the white outline of a man's twisted body. *Maybe it'll have one soon*, Max thought.

He leaned forward and gazed across the room into the smudged mirror above the shabby room's tacky dresser.

Max's own face looked ugly to him. He didn't remember growing so old. When had that happened? His cheeks wore at least twelve days of gritty stubble, and his short, dirty blond hair looked greasy, and as messed-up as it could be. But it was the dark circles around his eyes that made him almost unrecognizable to himself. The eyes were mostly the same as he remembered them, but even they had changed in the short time since he had lost everything he'd ever had that was worth a damn.

Max picked up a rum bottle from the floor by his feet. The rum was Papa's Pilar dark rum, and it was named after Ernest Hemingway's beloved fishing boat. The rum was nice: dark, rich flavors of caramel and vanilla, strong aromas of brown sugar and spices. He brought the short, bulbous bottle's neck to his lips and cursed the glass container's limited flow of liquid as the last trickle of sweet spirit drained into his mouth. He checked the magazine of the recently purchased gun. He made sure it was loaded with the three 9mm Federal hollow point bullets he had brought with him.

Max slapped the magazine into the pistol and pulled back

the slide. He watched one of the bullets through the ejector port sliding off the top of the magazine, being pushed into the chamber.

The gun was now cocked. Loaded. Ready to fire.

He placed the muzzle of the pistol to his right temple. Again, he looked at himself in the mirror across from him. The sight embarrassed him. It pissed him off. People he once cared about would be ashamed of him if they could see him like this. The saliva in Max's mouth felt thick, bitter. He stood up and placed the pistol down on the crappy table. He approached the mirror.

Max appraised his appearance once again. Then he pounded his fist into his reflected visage, smashing himself in the jaw. The mirror shattered into a thousand prickly shards that scattered onto the top of the dresser.

Max looked down. A few of the jagged pieces protruded from his knuckles as warm crimson blood began to drip, drip, drip onto the pile of mutilated silver glass that had settled in front of him.

Disregarding the flow of blood, Max picked up the gun and once again took his place at the foot of the bed. Again, he placed the muzzle of the gun to his head.

Knock, knock, knock.

The rapping on the door startled him. At first he had thought the gun had gone off, but he hadn't pulled the trigger.

Max rested the shiny silver pistol back down on the table and rushed into the bathroom to grab a hand towel to wrap around his hand. He walked over to the door and opened it. The flimsy door jerked to a stop as the security chain caught. Through the gap Max saw the face of a young Latin American woman wearing a faded blue housekeeping uniform. Her shoulder-length hair was a striking dark chocolate brown color adorned with several streaks of bright, almost metallic blue. She forced a smile.

"Yes?" Max said, not bothering with the chain. Opening the

door further would only increase the chance of the room cleaner seeing the broken mirror.

"Housekeeping," the young woman said. Max thought her voice sounded both sweet and salty at the same time. She was in her early twenties, and Max guessed by her short nails and rough hands that she worked very hard to make her living. "Do you need your room cleaned? Fresh towels?"

"Um, no," Max said. "I didn't know this motel had maid service... Not yet. Maybe a little bit later."

"What happened?" the housekeeper asked.

"What do you mean?" Max asked. He looked over his shoulder, wondering what the housekeeper might be able to see through the gap in the door.

"Your hand," she said. "Blood is seeping through the towel you've got wrapped around it. Are you okay?"

"Oh, this?" Max said. "Yeah, it's nothing."

"I can bring you some Band-Aids," the young housekeeper said. Max noticed that her name tag read Tori. "We have a big first aid kit in the break room downstairs."

"No," Max said, tightening the bloody towel around his hand. "It's okay. You don't need to do that."

"It's no trouble," Tori said. She looked Max squarely in the face with a probing expression. "Sir, are you sure you're okay?"

Max wondered if she had seen that look before. The look people had in their eyes before they ended it. It was the same expression that had made him smash the mirror in the first place.

"I'll bring by some bandages and some fresh towels," she said. "If you want me to, I can just leave them by the door."

"That would be nice. Thank you."

"Take care of yourself, okay?" Tori said, looking Max in the eyes as he closed the door.

Max grabbed the gun and stumbled back over to his place at the foot of the bed. He leaned forward over the bedspread on the floor and for a third time placed the muzzle of the Smith & Wesson pistol to his temple. His hand began to shake.

He thought about Tori coming back to clean the room and finding his body. She seemed like a nice girl. It was a terrible thing to do to her. For his part, Max had not unlatched the chain, so at least she wouldn't be able to enter the room. She would probably see his legs sprawled across the floor through the gap and call the cops.

Max's hand still shook. The muzzle of the pistol scraped back and forth against the side of his face. He reached up his left hand to steady his right arm, but it was no use. He hadn't had enough to drink today to steady himself. Withdrawal symptoms were settling in. If he proceeded, the chances were good he would do it wrong. He would injure himself, maybe be paralyzed for life, sitting in a chair, spending the next decades thinking about everything that had gone wrong in his life.

No, Max thought. *This isn't something you want to get wrong. You only get one chance to do it right.*

A few minutes later, Max heard another knock at the door. He waited a minute or so before he took a peek out the room's curtained window. No one stood by the door. But he saw the folded white towels that Tori the housekeeper had left for him.

Max took off the chain and opened the door. He picked up the pile of clean towels on top of which sat an unopened box of adhesive bandages and a note. Max stepped back into the room and set down the towels. He unfolded the note and read its three short lines of curly handwriting along with a local phone number.

If you need help, please call.

Don't give up hope.

You are not alone.

Max read the words and almost became overwhelmed. But he strode into the bathroom and washed his hands with soap and warm water, finding he had to pick out a couple more broken glass shards from his skin. Then he bandaged his wounds as best he could with his shaky hands.

Max removed the magazine from the pistol and ejected the chambered bullet, returning it to the magazine before placing the weapon down on the table. These bullets were special, and he was reserving them. He reached into his suitcase and grabbed one of the empty magazines that had come with the gun, slapping it in place inside the grip of the Smith & Wesson pistol.

The streets were rough, and Max carried the pistol as a deterrent. He didn't want to shoot anyone, but he also didn't want to get killed for his wallet outside of some dive bar. His death was a privilege that Max was reserving for himself.

Max tucked the pistol into his waistband and made sure he had a bundle of cash in his pocket. Then he left his room, determined to drink his fill until he could hold the pistol with a steady hand. Then he would come back to the room and finish the job that had brought him down to Miami.

Chapter 12

J OSUE GRABBED THE BOAT'S PORT side railing and held on
for his life. "Where we going?" he asked Tiny Deege, who sat
on the seat beside him. It was the second time in as many
days that Josue had sat in the rear seat of a powerful speedboat as
it skimmed like a rocket across the surface of the ocean.

"Got a job to do tonight," Tiny Deege said, shouting to be
heard above the roar of both the speedboat's engines and the
wind that whipped over them. "But right now, we heading out to
do some target practice."

Josue had no idea what the job would be, but he was unsettled
by the fact that the others had brought guns, lots of guns. Each
man, except Josue, had a pistol tucked into his short pants, covered
over by his shirt. Momo had brought a short military-style rifle,
and Zann, the orange-haired member of Ti Flow who wore thick-
rimmed black glasses, had a small machine gun suspended by a
leather sling and covered over by a lightweight yellow jacket that
flapped as the boat raced over the choppy waves.

Zann drove the boat, and Momo sat beside him, shouting
orders to him. Josue figured the massive man was in charge of the
job they were going to perform. Big Flow, the dreadlocked leader
of the gang, lay on his back on a cushioned seat at the bow of the
ten-meter boat, his fingers locked together behind his head, as
he stared back toward the others. Dark sunglasses covered the
magnetic leader's eyes, and a long-barreled black rifle with an
elongated scope lay slung across his chest.

"Yo, yo, Josue," Tiny Deege said, reaching into a black bag and pulling out a long black gun and passing it over to Josue. "You gonna wield the gauge."

Josue took the weapon. He did not know much about firearms, but he figured it was a shotgun.

The agile speed boat hurtled out toward open sea, bobbing now and then as the waves grew choppier. Josue looked over his shoulder at the potent twin outboard motors and the thick white wake that churned behind them. He looked further behind still, and watched the immense buildings of the big city disappearing into the distance behind him.

The view reminded Josue of his last look at Port au Prince, and how it had broken his heart to see the ruined city for the last time, and to have left behind the graves of his family, and the shattered remains of their once-good home. Josue did not know what peril or fortune the evening's job would bring, but a nagging feeling of trepidation percolated inside him. He wondered if his recent choices had plummeted him out of a sizzling skillet, only to toss him onto a smoldering bed of searing hot flames.

When the boat had traveled so far and so fast that all other boats, and any sign of land, had vanished, and all Josue could see was rolling blue water all around him, Zann powered down the boat until it slowed to a crawl and the outboard motors rumbled softly behind Josue's back.

"We gonna get in some target practice," Momo said. He stepped toward the back of the boat. "Gotta find out if this new kid can shoot worth a damn." The mountain-sized man opened a long black bag at Tiny Deege's feet and removed dozens of flat, colorful, plastic objects. The bright colors made Josue think they were children's toys, and Momo started tossing them onto the lap of each man on the boat. Josue noted he did not throw one to Big Flow.

Each man opened a little plastic valve on the object and began blowing into it. In no time, Tiny Deege had puffed and puffed into one until it had expanded into a vibrant red, yellow, blue, and white plastic ball. Momo tossed it out onto the ocean. "All right," he shouted. "Just about a hundred mo' to go."

The gang members blew up the balls until the ocean around them was littered with the colorful floating objects. Momo grabbed the shotgun from Josue's lap. He produced a box of ammunition from the black bag on the deck and began stuffing shells into the weapon. He pulled back on the pump action, jerked it forward, and handed it to Josue. Then the gargantuan gang member pointed at the floating balls. "Let's see what you got."

Josue had never fired a gun before. He had read about a hundred books in which characters fired guns: books about war; Western books with cowboys and gunfighters; books about killers, whose guns were the tools of their trade. Josue raised the gun and looked down the barrel, lining up the little bead on the end with one of the air-filled balls. He squeezed the trigger. Nothing happened.

"Safety's on, fool," Momo said, grabbing the gun and flipping a little switch on top. A little red marker appeared next to the switch and the big man handed the gun back to Josue. "Weapon's hot now."

Josue aimed the shotgun again and squeezed the trigger once more. The shotgun kicked into his shoulder like an energetic punch; it reminded him of his uncle's fist when they used to spar, practicing jujitsu and boxing.

The floating ball exploded. It disappeared into shredded bits of colorful flotsam on the surface of the sea. Josue could not keep the grin off his face. He pulled the weapon's foregrip as he had seen Momo do, and the spent shell flew out the side of the shotgun, dropping into the ocean. He aimed and fired again, destroying another ball.

Then everyone on the boat began firing at the colorful

balls that floated all around them. Josue watched Big Flow peer through the scope on his long rife. The steel-eyed leader slowly squeezed the trigger. His bullet ripped through a ball that floated at what must have been two hundred yards away from the boat. Tiny Deege fired shot after shot into the water from a small shiny pistol that looked to be way too big for his hand.

Momo removed a bulky pistol from the waistband of his long black short pants and stabbed it toward the floating targets. The pistol sounded like a cannon going off each time he fired, seven shots in all, until the pistol's fast-moving slide locked open.

Tiny Deege took pictures of the gang members on a small device, his phone maybe. He showed the pictures on the device's tiny screen after he took each photograph. Then he had some of the members of the gang pose together and he took more.

"What you doin' that fo', you little homunculus?" Momo asked, sounding irritated.

"I ain't no homo nothin'," Tiny Deege protested.

"Don' want you takin' any more o' my picture," Momo protested.

"It's an important thing to do," Big Flow said, sitting up from where he sunned himself in the bow of the boat. "It is good to document our activities. Someday, people will want to know about us; the back story of the greatest gang in Miami history."

"Whatever, man," Momo hissed.

After hours of shooting their guns into the water the sun began to sink low on the horizon. "Getting close to time," Big Flow said to Momo. "Yacht's comin' in around midnight."

Big Flow walked back to the stern of the boat. He settled comfortably into a seat across from Josue. "Tonight you are going to be our lookout," Big Flow said, speaking in Haitian Creole. Josue appreciated that he spoke in their native tongue; the gang leader obviously understood it was easier for Josue. "I would not give you this important job if I did not believe in you, Josue," the charismatic gang leader said.

The bitter face Momo made while he watched Big Flow speak did not go unnoticed by Josue. He wondered if Momo didn't like him, didn't trust him, or both.

As Josue understood the plan as explained, a yacht would travel to a place near the big city, called Fisher Island, from somewhere in the Bahamas. On the yacht was a large amount of something that belonged to Big Flow. Josue was unsure why the people on the yacht possessed what Zann called "units" that belonged to the gang's leader. But the plan involved boarding the yacht, taking back Big Flow's units, and then driving the speedboat up the Miami River until the gang reached a private dock, where their car would be waiting.

It sounded easy to Josue. His job would be to wait at the dock upriver and stand guard with the shotgun. And if anyone got close he was supposed to scare them away. At least that was how he understood the plan.

"Ain't nobody gonna get hurt," Tiny Deege said, speaking in Creole to Josue. "We get our units, we take off, we good."

Zann drove the boat back to Miami. As the city's imposing buildings grew taller as they drew closer, Josue watched the orange-haired gang member pilot the boat toward an enormous dock where huge, towering cranes unloaded house-sized steel containers from a black cargo ship streaked with stripes of rust. Another ship, a vast tanker likely used to transport gasoline or fuel oil, occupied the dock nearer the city. Zann approached the dock between the ships and powered down the boat.

A white pickup truck sat waiting on the dock, and when Zann cut the engine, one of Ti Flow's other members exited the truck, and he tossed down the end of a hose. Momo unscrewed a gas cap and plunged the hose into the gaping mouth of the boat's fuel tank. The man with the truck opened a valve on a big barrel in the back of the truck.

"We need to make sure we fueled up good," Tiny Deege explained. "Used up a lot of gas going out for target practice."

With the boat fueled, and everyone's gun reloaded with ammunition, Zann drove the boat toward the skyline of towering skyscrapers built of glass, concrete, and steel. Josue felt as small as a speck of dust next to the colossal structures. He craned his neck and watched in amazement as the silver-toothed man piloted the boat directly under a bridge. Cars and trucks passed overhead as the boat rumbled into shadow beneath the bridge. Josue cowered as they passed underneath the speeding vehicles.

"All right?" Tiny Deege asked. He must have seen the anxiety in Josue's wide eyes as the boat emerged from under the bridge into sunlight again.

Josue nodded. "Amazed."

"You ain't in Haiti no mo'," the minute gang member said.

People strode peacefully along a palm tree-lined path beside the river, enjoying themselves as Josue and the others rumbled past in the boat. The pedestrians walked in and out of fancy shops and upscale restaurants. *What a magical place*, Josue thought. He had read books and poems about so many remarkable places in the world, but now that he was here, he could scarcely believe a place like this was real.

Another bridge, this one made of concrete and stretching high overhead, supported a train that rumbled across as the boat neared. Josue wondered if he was dreaming.

Eventually the boat made its way further up the river. They passed substantial, luxurious boats big enough for many people to live on. The river seemed to be littered by massive yachts, expensive sport fishing boats, large cruise boats with dozens of people standing on the top deck.

Josue wondered if everyone in Miami was wealthy. But in answer to his own question, he noted that the further they traveled upriver, the more the assortment of opulent yachts and other seagoing craft changed into more aged, ramshackle vessels, and some timeworn hulking cargo ships that looked as if they might have arrived from Port au Prince or some other impoverished locale, as derelict as they appeared. The lateral view of breathtaking skyscrapers was replaced by fancy homes; then smaller and more industrial buildings; and then some shabbier homes and run-down shacks.

Josue detected a pattern; the closer you were to the bay, the more rich you were. The further inland you drew, the less opulent your home or business.

Eventually Zann drove the boat to a dock beside a compact twelve- or fifteen-slip marina. Josue had spotted many boat docks and small marinas during their journey. This one, he noted to himself, contained none of the affluence of the others. The boats secured here looked worn out, broken down, or possibly abandoned. Josue observed that in the shade of the overpass nearby, where more vehicles crossed the river via a drawbridge, sat Tiny Deege's brightly-colored car with the shiny wheels.

"We get out here," Tiny Deege said to Josue, tucking his shiny pistol under his shirt. "Grab your shotgun. We gonna stand watch here until the job done."

Josue and Tiny Deege disembarked. On his first step, Josue's foot passed almost clean through the dock beside the boat, as a rotten board gave out under his weight. He righted himself and followed the tiny little man to his car, turning his head to watch the others shove off and head back downriver, the way they had come.

Josue watched Big Flow raise his hand in a sort of wave as Zann kicked the boat away from the dock with his foot. Momo glared at Josue with a piercing look that gave him a chill.

Josue didn't know much of the details about their job, but he knew he did not want to let down the leaders of the gang: Big

Flow, the dynamic head of the organization; and Momo, who was apparently Big Flow's right hand man.

"Hide your twelve under the dash," Tiny Deege said. He plunked down into the driver's seat and turned the key in the car's ignition so he could roll down the vehicle's windows. Josue sat down in the seat on the passenger side. "No need to draw too much attention to ourselves."

The sun hung low on the horizon. It was disorienting to Josue, sitting in the stuffy car under the overpass, listening to the sounds of car tires passing by on the bridge overhead. Josue found the sound somehow strangely familiar; then it occurred to him the rolling tires sounded to him like a long zipper being slowly ripped open as they passed.

It was only about a half hour before twilight had reached them. And not long after that, night flooded in, a nearly all-encompassing darkness with only a few distant lights visible from passing cars, distant buildings, or random boats along the river.

"Miss home?" Tiny Deege asked, handing Josue an open bag of some kind of salty snack chips.

Josue nodded as he crunched his teeth down onto one of the stale chips. All the new sights, sounds, and smells were a wonder to behold. And they all made an excellent distraction from Josue's grief. But as he sat quietly in the darkened vehicle, the crushing weight of Josue's painful loss seeped in again like floodwater. It was not long before tears began to trickle down again.

Tiny Deege reached up and rubbed Josue's shoulder. "It's all right, man. It's all right. Eything gonna get better now, you'll see."

Josue wiped his eyes and his nose on his shirt and forced himself to smile at Tiny Deege, who had become his best friend in the world in a matter of hours. All that was visible of the diminutive man in the dim light was his white teeth as he grinned back at Josue.

"Gonna be much better now," he said again.

CHAPTER 13

MOMO PLACED HIS FISHING POLE in one of the stainless steel rod holders at the rail of the stolen boat and grabbed his binoculars, placing them up to his eyes. He gazed through the lenses, straining his eyes intensely, doing his best to focus the binoculars in the nearly moonless evening.

The purloined Trophy center console boat rested at anchor in Norris Cut, a shallow inlet next to Virginia Key, which was a sandy barrier island with recreation areas frequented by locals for the bike trails, picnic tables, and carousel, as well as the miniature train you could actually ride on. Most of the park patrons and mountain bikers had already left with the setting sun, leaving Momo and the others virtually unnoticed by anyone. Their fishing rods offered their excuse for being so close to Fisher Island after dark, although Momo still half-expected to be questioned by the authorities, who tended to watch the upscale island like protective mother hens.

Fisher Island resided on the other side of Norris Cut, and the small island contained the marina the gang now watched. An inlet, protected by two staggered rocky breakwaters, guarded the entrance into the big square marina, at the heart of the affluent island.

Courtesy lights illuminated each of the marina's hundred or so slips, most occupied by long sport fishing boats, cabin cruisers of varying lengths, and a handful of sweet-looking super yachts.

"Looks like one security guard makin' the rounds in the marina," Momo said to Big Flow, who leaned forward on the cushioned bow seats of the purloined pleasure boat. The dreadlocked leader of Ti Flow cradled his scoped rifle in his arms like a baby. "Guarantee there's a lot more where he came from. Be best not draw any mo' attention than we need."

"The marina's quiet tonight," Big Flow said. He twisted a nine-inch-long titanium suppressor onto the threads machined on the end of his rifle's barrel. Momo recalled the rifle was a 300 Winchester Magnum: heavy bullets, long range. "Such a nice night," the charismatic gang leader cooed, as he pulled on the bolt handle. He slid the bolt forward, stripping a long cartridge off the three-round magazine, chambering it.

"Don't do anythin' you don' have to," Momo said, putting down his binoculars and looking at Zann, who looked scared. The bespectacled man clutched his own Glock 17, its thirty-three-round magazine protruding well out from the bottom of the 9mm pistol's grip. "We need to get in an' out quick, dig? Best if we leave an' nobody knows we was ever here."

Momo knew Fisher Island had possibly the highest per capita income of any other piece of real estate in the country. These folks were as rich as rich came, and they were well-protected. There would be a lot more security on the island. Miami-Dade, Miami Beach, Miami PD, the Coast Guard, all had fast patrol boats, and they were only a couple of minutes away. Momo knew they would have to act lightning quick before they were detected.

"Gonna be a sporty one tonight," Momo said to the others. He thought about the risk involved in the mission of stealing the ten or so kilos of cocaine from the Stein couple who lived on the island. Luther Stein was a retired orthodontist who had bought a five-million-dollar condo in one of the island high-rise buildings. His wife, Gwendolyn or Guinevere or something, taught tennis lessons to kids. Retirement must have bored them, since they had taken up running units of coke between Fisher Island and Nassau. It made sense to Momo, though; who would suspect them? But tonight, as the couple offered easy prey for Momo and the others, their illicit lifestyle would prove to be far more ill-chosen than they might have ever imagined.

The more Momo thought about the inherent risk of their mission, the more it incensed him that Big Flow would allow an untried man to participate. That new guy, fresh off the boat from Haiti. Kid might even have ICE come knocking on Momo's door looking for him. The more he ruminated on the situation, the more it pissed Momo off.

"Yo, Big," Momo said to the gang's leader, realizing he was unable to let it go, "why you let that new fool in on this? What's his name, José or somethin'? Don't you think we can't afford a goof on this job? Stakes are high on this one, my brother."

"Is it the ability of our newest member you question, Momo?" Big Flow said, gently laying down his rifle on the seat cushions. "Or is it the loyalty of the man you doubt?" The dangerous gang leader stepped over to where Momo stood, behind the helm of the stolen boat, next to Zann. Big Flow's nose reached the middle of Momo's neck. But the gang's charismatic leader peered into the larger man's eyes with an almost psychotic resolve. "Or perhaps you question *my* leadership."

"Naw, man," Momo said, trying his best to keep his tone nonchalant despite his racing pulse. "Nonna that. Just wanna make sure *you* sure about 'im. You down, I down. Dig?"

"Yes, Montgomery," Big Flow said, placing his hand on Momo's arm like a father comforting a child. He reached his other hand into the pocket of his lightweight linen pants, where everyone knew he kept his weapon of choice, the razor-pointed screwdriver he used to dispatch many of his victims. "Yes, I dig. I know I can count on you as well tonight. Remember, there was once a day when you were an untried member of our number as well. And I put my faith in *you*. I gave you the chance to prove yourself. I believed you would show me that you were my brother, Momo. Remember? And now I know I can count on you. I know this, because you know what I will do if you fail me. You don't want to disappoint me, do you?"

Momo had heard Big Flow talk to people in this tone of voice before. It usually occurred right before he stabbed them with the sharpened hand tool, or drew his nickel-plated Colt 45 pistol with lightning speed, usually placing it to someone's temple before pulling the trigger. That was Big Flow's trademark: close-quarters kills, executed with snake-like precision and fury. It was the reason why Momo's heart now threatened to pound right out of his chest.

"No, my brother," Momo said, doing his best to keep his voice even and steady. "I don't ever wanna let you down, man."

"Good," Big Flow said, turning back toward the bow. He gathered up his Savage rifle and rested its barrel on the bow rail, lying prone on one of the cushioned seats and lining up his eye with the rifle's powerful scope.

Momo thought about shucking the tiny Kahr PM9—a miniature semi-automatic pistol he carried as a backup to his powerful Israeli-made hand cannon—from his pocket and smoking Big Flow before he could even blink. Zann wouldn't do anything—Momo knew the orange-haired gangbanger's loyalty would shift from Big Flow to Momo in less than a second. The things that gave Momo pause were the what-ifs: What if he missed? What if he shot Big Flow and the .355 caliber bullets weren't enough to kill the larger-than-life leader? What if he did kill him? Was Momo actually ready to lead the gang?

"Check the GPS," Big Flow ordered. "How long?"

Momo gazed down at his smartphone. Its bright display showed a map slightly wider than Biscayne Bay. He spotted a blue circle on the map. "Only two miles out now," Momo said. "Should be seein' 'em comin' in directly."

"Soon as they pass us, we shadow them into the marina," Big Flow said. "We move as one."

Momo nodded.

As much as he liked killing in close quarters, Momo knew that Big Flow was equally deadly from well downrange. But he wondered why the gang leader had chosen the powerful rifle for this job. It seemed like close-quarter weapons were a better call. But Momo would not question Big Flow's choices.

In no time, Momo spotted a sixty-five-footer, probably a Sea Ray or something similar, well-lit with bright LED running lights, moving in their direction. He made out the red port light and the starboard green. He gazed again through the binoculars.

"That's them," Momo said.

"Wait until they turn toward the marina," Big Flow said, "then catch up, follow."

"I got it," Momo said, flipping a switch to raise the boat's anchor. "Gimme a minute and we'll get movin'."

Momo started the outboard motors and Zann reeled in all three fishing poles whose lines dangled into the water, devoid of bait. "Wish we was fishin' for real," Zann said, adjusting his glasses that threatened to slip off his face and fall into the ocean. "An' I wish I could smoke a bowl or somethin'. I'm on edge, man."

"Gotta keep our wits, brother," Momo said to Zann as he eased the throttles forward, steering the bow of the boat north toward the Fisher Island marina, with the Stein's boat looming directly ahead. Momo read the words *Catch Me If You Can* lettered in gold on the back of the wealthy couple's Sea Ray. He trimmed the twin outboards, and the bow began to settle as the boat glided forward across the waves. "Gonna burn it up later, though, dig? Gonna party at Momo's, know what I'm sayin'?"

"S'what I'm talkin' bout," Zann said, slapping Momo five.

"Steady the boat!" Big Flow ordered, as he peered through the lens of his riflescope.

Momo fine-tuned the motors' trim switches to steady the boat's ride as they followed the sixty-five-foot sport yacht into the marina. He raised his binoculars once more to try to spot the security guard making his rounds, checking each slip in the marina. Their goal was to slide in next to the Stein's yacht, transfer quickly to their boat, grab the kilos, and take off on the stolen Trophy. By the time anyone knew what had happened, they'd be long gone up the river.

Momo nearly jumped out of his skin as he heard the muffled report of Big Flow's suppressed rifle, which stabbed a bright burst of exhaust gasses out the end of the muzzle, lighting up the night. Momo peered through the binoculars in time to see the dead security guard slump, face-forward, into the stern of a docked Boston Whaler he'd been checking, disappearing from sight into the back of the otherwise empty sport fishing boat.

Momo gasped. He hadn't expected Big Flow to kill anyone unless they had to. "Big Flow…" Momo started to say, but stopped himself short.

"Close the distance," Big Flow said, "catch up to the Stein's boat!"

Momo pulled the stolen fishing boat alongside the Stein couple's brand-new Sea Ray, just as they both reached the dock inside the protected waters of the marina.

Big Flow was out of the Trophy before it had even touched the *Catch Me If You Can*'s port side. The dreadlocked leader pulled his Colt pistol from his waistband and dropped onto the sundeck at the stern of the Stein's boat. He pounced up the stairs into the rear of the opulent yacht's salon.

"Stay with the boat, Zann," Momo ordered the terrified-looking gang member. "I'm goin' to back up Big."

The second Momo stepped onto the *Catch Me If You Can* he

heard the next gunshot. He yanked his .50 caliber Desert Eagle and ran into the salon where he found a few spatters of blood on the walnut flooring. With some degree of reluctance, Momo descended a few steps to the forward part of the yacht, where the staterooms were located.

The first body he found was at the bottom of the companionway steps. It belonged to Mr. Stein. The gray-haired septuagenarian's body lay in a twisted heap wrapped in a bright pink shirt adorned with dozens of tiny manatees. A compound fracture showed the bones sticking through his right forearm. Momo guessed he'd been shot in the back at the top of the steps and fallen down, breaking his arm in the process. And Momo figured the wealthy drug runner had been dead before he'd even hit the floor.

"Big Flow?" Momo said cautiously, but he cringed, instantly realizing he shouldn't use the real name of anyone in the gang. Momo pushed open a port side door, then one on the starboard side, finding both small but well-appointed staterooms empty.

Momo pushed open the door to the forward stateroom. The scene inside made him sick to his stomach. An elderly woman lay sprawled on her back across an elevated queen-sized bed. An expanding circle of blood soaked through her white tennis shirt over her abdomen. The unfortunate woman's face stared blankly at the ceiling, eyes open, mouth agape. Blood streaked down her cheek from a hole just off center from the middle of her forehead. Big Flow stood a few feet away, rifling through the handsome stateroom's maple wood cabinets, his hands wrapped in latex gloves.

"What you do, Big?" Momo asked, upon the realization that a small pool of the woman's sticky scarlet blood crept across the hardwood floor, close to his feet. The metallic mineral smell of the blood made his stomach cramp. He felt like he might throw up from the whole of the experience.

"Help me find the coke," Big Flow ordered, glaring at Momo

with a stern look. He gestured with his Colt pistol. "We don't have a lotta time."

In the interest of self-preservation, Momo set his mind to the task of finding the bundles of cocaine the gang's informant in the Bahamas had promised over the phone would be on the Stein's yacht when they arrived back at the island. Momo opened drawers, flipped over seat cushions, dug deep into all of the vessel's cabinetry, searching anywhere one might think to stash no small amount of bundled contraband.

Momo wanted to scream at Big Flow. He wanted to ask him, "Why didn't you ask them where them kilos were before you smoked 'em?" But he knew Ti Flow's leader would not hesitate any longer than he had with the Steins before placing a bullet into Momo's brain.

"You check the engine compartment?" Momo asked.

Big Flow ran past Momo, toward the stern of the vessel. The dreadlocked man was like a flurry of dangerous energy, streaking through the sport yacht like a bolt of lightning.

Momo rushed up the steps behind him, finding a hatch open in the teak wood flooring of the aft cockpit. He slipped down a short ladder and crouched his six-foot-six frame to fit into the engine compartment, with a height of only about four feet. Maybe ten feet away, crouching between the Sea Ray's twin engines, Big Flow stood, blocking Momo's view of what lay beyond.

"Anythin'?" Momo asked.

Big Flow turned around and tossed two silver-duct-tape-wrapped kilos of cocaine at Momo's feet. Then he tossed another. Then another, until there were twelve bundles in all.

Momo stood up to his full height through the hatch opening. "Zann," he hissed toward the stolen center console boat, "bring the bag."

Zann trotted over with a huge black duffel bag. Momo grabbed it and hastily stuffed the bundles inside. "We good. Let's get outta here, man," Momo said to Big Flow, as the blood-splattered gang leader scampered up the ladder and made for the dock, at the *Catch Me If You Can*'s starboard side.

"No," Big Flow said, looking Momo in the eyes intently. "Change of plans. We take the Stein's yacht. Grab anythin' we left on the other boat."

"Big, man," Momo said, beginning a carefully-worded protest. "We all spent all day on the Trophy, got our prints all over it. We should grab our booty and take off in it. Leave this crime scene behind."

"Zann, drive the Trophy upriver. Wipe it down good. Dump it. Maybe try to sink it. We'll pick you up on the way to Deege's car." Big Flow was improvising, thinking on his feet. Every new decision he made put them one step further away from the objective of their meticulously planned mission. It gave Momo an uneasy feeling in the pit of his stomach. Or perhaps it was the sight and smell of so much blood that still lingered in his mind.

"Momo, stick with me," Big Flow urged. "We take the *Catch Me* upriver to the meeting place. Dig?"

Momo nodded, feeling reluctant.

"You drive," Big Flow said to Momo.

It took a bit of time to figure out the controls. But soon Momo navigated the elegant vessel out of the small marina, leaving one dead security guard behind and keeping two dead elderly people as passengers.

As Momo steered the boat toward the city, one thought nagged inside him, making him anxious and afraid—he hoped they would reach the Miami River before the police or Coast Guard made contact. They'd slip away easier once they reached the river.

Momo felt a shiver against the chilly late night air as he considered what would happen if someone tried to stop the boat, to impede Big Flow from his mission. As impulsive as Ti Flow's leader was, Momo didn't think any of them would survive such a confrontation.

CHAPTER 14

"YO MAN, I THINK IT'S them," Tiny Deege said, pressing out his stubby cigar into the small ashtray that folded out of the dashboard of his flashy orange car. The little man waved his hand in front of his face, apparently trying to dissipate the odd-smelling smoke more quickly.

Josue knew it was marijuana that the small man smoked. He had known of several farmers living near his family farm who grew crops of the peculiar five-leafed cannabis plant for some of the gangs in the city. Janjak had been coming around the farm, bothering Josue for years, urging him to grow the plants for the gang called Scorpio. Only Janjak and Benoit's fear of Uncle Guillot had kept Josue and his family from being forced into the production of the illicit substance.

Josue spotted the bright white, green, and red running lights of a large boat that cruised through the darkness toward the shabby marina near where Tiny Deege's car was parked under the bridge overpass. As the boat drew closer, it became clear to Josue that it was not the same boat he had spent the day on. This one was much larger, far fancier.

"Not them," Josue said, pointing his long index finger toward the sporty yacht. "See?"

"Naw, you're right, man," Tiny Deege said, gazing suspiciously at the incoming yacht. He lifted a small pair of pocket-sized binoculars to his eyes.

"Why he dockin' here fo'?" Tiny Deege asked.

Josue wondered as well. Why would such an expensive vessel dock here among such a dilapidated and derelict smattering of other boats? Then Josue spotted Momo's monolithic silhouette at the rear deck of the yacht. The hulking man hastily tied off the opulent craft to a piling that supported the rotting wooden dock over the black water of the river.

"Deege," Momo shouted, "come and grab this bag." His tone suggested to Josue that the big gang member was on edge; he wondered if their job had gone badly.

"Why you drivin' *that*?" Tiny Deege shouted to Momo after stepping out of his shiny car. "What happened ta the other boat?"

"Complications," Momo said, reaching into his shorts pocket and slipping out his Lilliputian 9mm pistol, and pulling the slide partway back to check for ammo. He stepped back into the yacht's salon, and it sounded as though he shut off the vessel's engines.

Zann appeared on the rear deck of the yacht beside Big Flow. He waved over Tiny Deege frantically with his hand, his orange hair barely visible from the light of one of the marina's murky sodium lights.

Tiny Deege glanced at Josue, who sat still in the passenger seat of the car. "Grab your shotgun. Keep a sharp lookout, man."

Josue climbed out of the car, which was so low to the ground, he felt as if he had been sitting on the ground. He grabbed the shotgun off the vehicle's floor, clutching it with a grave sense of unease. He didn't know who he was on the lookout for: a rival gang, nosy pedestrians, or worse—the police. Josue had been told to scare away anyone who interfered with their mission, but he now wondered: what if someone shot back?

Bright blue lights burned Josue's eyes. Another boat approached the shabby marina on the river, a police boat. A piercing siren jolted the frightened refugee. It startled him, and he almost felt as if his heart has stopped, just for a second. Josue didn't know what to do.

Before he could think, Josue spotted the twisting dreadlocks of Ti Flow's leader on the rear deck of the long yacht, just beside Zann. Big Flow raised a short black rifle and fired. The bright flashes from the muzzle of Big Flow's rifle, burning hot and fast with rapid gunfire, competed with the colorful, blinding lights of the police boat.

With remarkable speed, Big Flow dropped a magazine and swiftly reloaded his fully automatic carbine. Momo appeared beside Zann on the sundeck of the yacht. He lifted his big pistol and stabbed it toward the police boat. He fired shot after shot, each one ringing like a gong in Josue's head.

Josue dropped the shotgun at his feet. He turned and bolted, running in the opposite direction from the terrifying melee unfolding before him on the Miami River.

Josue barely knew these gang members. But he knew he wanted no part of this violent altercation with the police.

"Hey, where you goin'?" were the last words Josue heard Tiny Deege say before he ran out of earshot of the gang members.

Josue's breath came in short gasps as he ran under the graffiti-painted concrete foundation of the overpass, emerging alongside a long concrete ramp beside an apartment building with barred windows and doors. He paused when he reached a stairway leading up from the single lane road where he stood, to the avenue that passed by across the bridge.

Josue glanced back once more toward the scene he had just fled. Beyond tall sailboat masts illuminated by the flashing blue police lights and a few murky street lights, and past the fronds of a palm tree that blocked his view of the skirmish, a volley of gunfire continued unceasingly from the direction of the yacht and the police boat.

Terrified, Josue mounted the steps. At the top, Josue spotted a green sign that read Ponce de Leon Avenue. A few cars and trucks raced past him in both directions. Josue flailed his arms, frantic to flag down anyone who might help him. Cars honked ear-splitting horns as they swerved and revved their engines to speed away from him.

Once more, Josue felt lost, alone. He had only been in Miami for two days, and he was no closer to having any idea what he should do.

One car, this one a bright pinkish-orange color, with white and black lettering, along with a glowing wedge-shaped sign on its roof, stopped beside Josue. The driver had deeply dark skin, like Josue's, and he rolled down the passenger window. "Where you wanna go, man?" the driver asked.

Josue noticed the man's short afro was mostly gray, as was his stubbly beard. The driver bent low to look up through the passenger side window at Josue, and he twisted a knob on the dashboard to turn down the brassy jazz music he had been listening to.

"Please," Josue begged. "Lemon Street."

"Got money?" the older man asked, a skeptical look pinned to his face.

Josue dug his hand in his pocket and felt the roll of cash Tiny Deege and the others had given him at Momo's house, interspersed with the Haitian currency he had brought with him. He pulled out the roll and held the bundle toward the driver of the coral-colored car.

"Okay, okay," the driver said, waving his hand back at Josue. "Put it away, my brother. Don't be flashin' a wad like that around here." The gray-haired man looked from left to right, a look of concern on his face. "Get in the back, son."

Josue tugged open the rear passenger-side door. He almost dove into the back of the car. "Hurry," Josue urged. "Please."

The pink car raced forward, away from the scene of the shooting. "You in trouble, son?" the driver asked, looking back at

Josue, his suspicious gaze apparent in the little mirror attached to the vehicle's front windshield.

"I just want to get free," Josue said. "To get home."

"I ain't gonna ask you no mo' questions, man," the apprehensive driver said. "Don't wanna know too much about you, someone comes askin'. You just better not be up to nothin' untoward. Name's Grover."

"I'm Josue."

Josue sat in the back of the car, silent for the rest of the ride. His beating heart pulsated in his ears for most of the way. He continuously turned to gaze back through the rear windshield. He feared Big Flow or the others might catch up to him at any time.

Grover turned the music back up, and saxophone music soared inside the cabin of the taxi as it trundled through the dark city, punctuated by red, yellow, green traffic lights, and the piercing white glow from the headlights of about a million cars.

Josue wanted nothing more than to drive away from the city. He wanted to keep going and not stop until he had no more money left to pay the driver. But he would not leave his mother's pendant behind, not at the home of one of Ti Flow's bloodthirsty leaders. Josue cursed himself for having left the silver chain on Tiny Deege's bedside table.

The small token was all Josue had left of his mother besides his memories. His heart felt empty as the pink-orange car sped through the city as lighting crackled through an ominous canopy of clouds in the distance.

The driver navigated the post-midnight traffic for about fifteen minutes before he turned onto the narrow street Josue recognized as Lemon Street. The car idled past the vacant lot where Josue had slept in the shrubs, trundling onward between the weathered palms that lined both sides of the sultry street.

"Which one?" the driver asked, turning his head from left to right quickly, scanning the whole street with a vigilant gaze. He must have been wary of trouble, possibly recognizing some of the more crime-riddled streets of the city.

"Light blue-green house," Josue said, rubbing his hands together in his lap. He spotted Momo's house. From the noise and flicker of lights inside, Josue surmised that several of Ti Flow's members still occupied the small turquoise structure. "The one with many cars in front."

"Okay, okay," the driver said, peering out his window as he pulled up in front of the house.

Josue threw open the door and then slammed it shut behind him. He pulled the roll of cash out of his pocket and handed it to Grover, who leaned out of his window. Josue looked over his shoulder, wondering what to expect from the gang members in the house. Maybe Momo or Big Flow had contacted them, and warned them Josue had fled the gunfight between the police and gang members.

"No, no, no," the aged driver said, taking the bundle from Josue and slipping off two of the bills with the number twenty on them. "You can't jes' go handin' out your whole package like this, young man. I'm takin' forty—includes my tip, since I know you was runnin' from somethin' outta sorts. Now be careful, son. Don't let nobody take advantage of yeh. All right?"

Josue nodded and turned to face the front door of Big Flow's house as the coral-colored taxi sped away. He was about to grab the handle on the barred door that covered the door opening, when a tall, slender form stepped in the way and swung it open. Josue recognized the skinny, shirtless man as one of the other gang members he had met the previous night. He remembered the others calling him Junior or something.

"Josue, right?" the man said, standing aside so that Josue could enter the house. "Where Momo? Big Flow?"

Josue did not say a word. He strode toward Tiny Deege's room, giving the chipped door at the end of the hall a good shove. His mother's pendant was not on the bedside table. Panicked, Josue dropped to his knees and began rubbing his hands over the thick pile of the carpeting, in search of his mother's missing Our Lady of Perpetual Help necklace.

He wanted to scream as his quick search turned up nothing. Frantic, he rifled through the strange zippered blanket the small gang member had given Josue to sleep in.

Almost desperate, Josue lifted it and shook it out on the ground. The envelope and letter from his aunt fluttered to the tall, dirty carpet, and Josue snatched it up greedily.

His eye spotted something shiny on the ground, and he looked closer, seeing the slight tarnish of his mother's silver necklace. He breathed a heavy sigh of relief. He slipped the necklace around his neck.

Now to get away from here and not ever look back, Josue thought. This place and this time spent with these violent men need only be a sore memory for him, a dark time in his life he hoped he would look back upon as one of the worst of his days.

Now, Josue needed to place as much distance as he possible between Big Flow, Momo, and himself. It saddened Josue that he would never see Tiny Deege again. The diminutive man had become the only friend Josue knew in the United States. The little man had shown him so much kindness that Josue wished he could repay. But it would be better this way, for him to make a clean break from these dangerous men.

Josue rushed through the living room where three gang members sat on the dirty sofas, watching some kind of boxing match on their expansive television. One of the men smoked marijuana from a long green tube, as two others cheered on one of the boxers, who kicked his opponent repeatedly in the chest.

"Hey, man," said one of the gang members, a burly man wearing a bright red plaid shirt with the sleeves cut, or ripped, away. "Where you goin'?"

Josue ignored him and pushed on the barred door, holding his breath as he rushed outside. His feet moved so fast that he stumbled on the cracked concrete paving stones, which led down to the weathered gray street which grew darker as rain drops began to pelt its surface.

Josue righted himself and prepared to start running. He looked up just in time to see Tiny Deege's vivid orange car screeching to a halt in front of him.

Momo and Big Flow sprang out of the passenger side door and rushed toward Josue. Before he could take another step, the dreadlocked man grabbed the .50 caliber pistol from under Momo's shirt and pointed the heavy weapon toward Josue's face.

The frightened refugee stopped moving. He gasped.

"Hello, Josue," Big Flow said, his brilliant teeth showing through a broad, charming grin.

CHAPTER 15

MAX LOOKED DOWN AT THE handwritten note in his hand. He read it for about the hundredth time. The chambermaid's large looping letters suggested something innocent to him, almost childlike in the way they formed the words in bright purple ink. *You are not alone.*

Reading the note from Tori, the kind-hearted chambermaid, Max knew he could not take his life—not in the hotel room at least, lest she find his body, and have to live the rest of her days reliving that trauma.

Max would go somewhere else, drink as much as his body would hold, enough to make him forget all of the pain, sorrow, and loss in his heart, even if only for a few precious seconds. And then he would end it all.

Max tucked the pistol magazine, the one with the three hollow-point bullets, into the pocket of his khaki cargo pants. He was still new to handling guns, and was worried about it going off in his pants pocket. So he carried the pistol with one of the empty magazines in the box from the pawnshop. He would find just the right spot, maybe next to a dumpster behind one of the dive bars along the boulevard, and he would do it.

Max left the hotel and walked a few blocks, until the bright red, blue, and yellow neon signs called to him, drawing him in. He yanked open the barred door to a windowless establishment with rockabilly music reverberating inside.

Forgot my chaps and ten-gallon hat, but it'll do, for now. Max

100

entered and strode to the bar. He set his palms down on the lacquered pine of the bar top. He watched his fingers twitch.

"What can I get for you?" the bartender asked. Max noticed he wore a checkered shirt, a tan leather vest, and a bolo tie. *Strange attire for Little Haiti*, Max thought.

Max looked past the bartender, and his eyes voraciously soaked in the sight of the glass bottles beyond, flickering with sweet liquid contents, as the sound of a steel guitar seared the insides of Max's ears.

Max reached his hand into his pocket to pull out his wallet, but instead felt the steel of his pistol magazine. "What kind of rum do you have?"

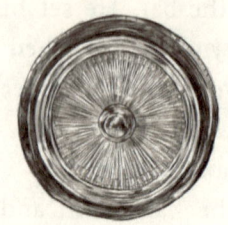

CHAPTER 16

MOMO GRABBED JOSUE BY THE neck and marched him into the middle of Lemon Street as the sprinkles of rain changed to heavy drops that saturated the street. "I knew you was not one of us the second I seen you," Momo shouted, as his sinewy arms forced Josue to his knees.

"Big Flow gave you a chance, chump!" the colossal gang member shouted into Josue's face as he squeezed his hand like a powerful vice onto the back of Josue's neck. Momo brought his fist down hard on Josue's cheek in a sharp strike, disorienting him. Josue fell down face-forward onto the wet pavement.

"Ughh," Josue gasped, as his cheek smacked the street. He planted his palms to push himself up to his feet, but a heavy foot pressed into his back, forcing him down, stealing his breath.

"We gave you a chance!" Momo snarled. Josue wondered if the gargantuan second-in-command had been waiting for this moment all along. He had seemed to distrust Josue almost since the moment they had met, and now he seemed to relish his role as Josue's punisher.

Big Flow just stood by, arms crossed, still clutching Momo's huge pistol as the large man continued to abuse Josue.

Momo reached both of his hands around Josue's neck and pulled the frightened refugee to his feet. "Why you run?" Momo shook Josue violently, his hands clinging to his throat like cast iron claws. "Why you run? Why you not do your job, chump?"

Josue gasped for breath. He glanced over at Tiny Deege who

looked as scared as he was. The little man clearly wanted no part of the abuse, but also seemed too afraid of the others to speak out against it.

Josue's eyes grew blurry as Momo clutched his neck, choking him. But he saw Big Flow's shiny teeth as the gang leader watched, with apparent pleasure.

Josue's airway was cut off. Momo held his throat in such a way it was impossible to draw breath. Josue wondered if this would be how his life would end. He had survived an earthquake that had leveled his home, killed his family. He had managed, through some miracle, to make it safely to Miami before his own aunt had turned him away. And now he would die here, in the middle of Lemon Street, strangled publicly by a violent criminal for refusing himself to participate in a violent criminal act.

Josue felt his mind slipping away as his oxygen supply quickly ran out. His blurred vision grew even more fuzzy. He was about to pass out and lose consciousness. At least then he would feel no more pain.

"Wait!" Big Flow ordered.

Josue collapsed to the ground as Momo released his hands from his throat. Josue gasped, sucking in a great gulp of air, coughing forcefully, and then drawing in another deep draft of breath.

Josue wondered what prompted the gang's leader to show such a sudden display of mercy. He looked up at Big Flow from where he sat, crumpled in a heap in the wet street. The gang leader passed the pistol back to Momo, who tucked it away in his waistband. Josue felt great relief as he watched the pistol disappear under the big man's shirt.

Perhaps Big Flow was going to give Josue another chance to join the gang, another chance to prove his worth. Or better still, maybe the dreadlocked man was going to set Josue free. Instead the gang's charismatic leader turned toward Tiny Deege.

"Step forward, my brother," Big Flow said, speaking Haitian Creole in a calm, yet frightening, tone.

Tiny Deege did as he was ordered.

"What are you packin', little man?" the gang leader asked. He lifted the front of Tiny Deege's bright red, sleeveless sports jersey.

"Beretta Cheetah," Tiny Deege said. "9mm."

"May I see it?" Big Flow asked.

The short man's face crumpled into a despondent look that suggested he might be sick. "Sure, sure, Big," Tiny Deege said, pulling the pistol out of the front waistband of his long short pants. He handed the pistol to Big Flow.

"Niiiice," Big Flow said, as he appraised the small nickel-plated weapon. He turned it over in his hands, eying it carefully, and Josue noticed it appeared much smaller in the hands of the larger-than-life gang leader. He pointed the pistol toward a street light, closing one eye and sighting in the pistol. He pulled back the slide to check that it was loaded. "Accurate?"

Tiny Deege nodded slowly. "Yeah, man. Shoots straight."

"Very nice piece, my friend," Big Flow said, handing the pistol back to the smallest member of Ti Flow.

"Thanks, Big," Tiny Deege said, and the relief was obvious in his voice.

"Shoot him," Big Flow said. He rubbed the thick gold chain that wrapped his dark throat, as he glared down at Josue.

Tiny Deege just stared blankly at Big Flow.

Momo reached into his pocket and pulled his own 9mm pistol, the tiny Kahr, and he racked its slide.

"No!" Big Flow ordered, with a wave of his hand in Momo's direction. "No. I want Deege to do it."

"What?" the small, child-sized man said.

"I made Josue your responsibility," Big Flow said, placing a fatherly hand on Tiny Deege's shoulder. "You were to look after him, to make sure he did his job. But he abandoned us. All of us. So you need to hold him accountable."

The gang leader still spoke in Creole. Josue guessed that Big Flow wanted him to understand every word clearly. Josue now knelt in the street, considering bolting to his feet and running for it. He knew he would just be shot in the back. But at least he would be resisting these savage, homicidal men, not staying put to be shot in the street like a dog.

Josue lurched to his feet. But the unyielding grip of Momo's hand clutched his neck. Josue was forced back down to his knees. At least it would be over quickly, Josue thought. It was a shame that his new friend was being made to kill him. He knew it would not be the little man's fault, and it would be a bitter memory the other man would carry with him forever.

Tiny Deege stepped forward, clutching the Cheetah pistol in his left hand. He raised it up to point it toward the back of Josue's head.

Josue lowered his head. He thought of his mother, his sister, his uncle. He closed his eyes and prayed for mercy.

CHAPTER 17

MAX STEPPED INTO THE BLOTCHY half-light behind the shabby tropical-themed dive bar where he had just been drinking. It was Max's fourth bar of the evening in what promised to be the final pub crawl of his life. The flip-flop- and Hawaiian-shirt-wearing bartender had handed him a half bottle of Montanya Oro rum, saying it was the finest rum the low-rent establishment had on offer. Max had been skeptical. Could you really make good rum in the high altitudes of Colorado? But he had taken a sip and was surprised by the spirit's spicy notes, which included coffee, vanilla, and chocolate.

When the delicious bottle of Rocky Mountain rum had been drained, Max found himself looking for a dry spot beside the dumpster outside to drain himself. Then it would be on to more pressing matters.

He relieved himself on a waist-high shrub out back, and then reached under his shirt. His hand touched the Smith & Wesson's back strap, and his fingers curled around the pistol's grip. The weapon felt warm in his hand as it had been tucked in against his stomach, even as the night felt cool and the sinister clouds above began to pelt his face with heavy drops of rain.

Max slipped the pistol out of his waistband, even as the twangy guitar of Alan Jackson's and Jimmy Buffet's *It's Five O'clock Somewhere* filtered its way through the dive bar's faded back wall to reach Max's ears. His senses felt prickly as he took one last look at the gun. It wouldn't have been his first choice of places to end his life, but he wondered now how that mattered.

Max reached into his left pocket to retrieve the loaded magazine. He was about to depress the pistol's magazine release button and drop out the empty magazine when he heard a loud grunt through a cluster of what looked like cotton plants beside the dumpster. The plants cut off Max's view of a dingy street that ran down past the shabby tiki bar.

Max pushed aside some of the shrubs' branches, hoping to get a clear look at what he had just heard. Though his vision was blurred, and seemed to swirl around in a strange square motion in front of him, Max witnessed a cluster of rough-looking guys standing around what looked like another guy, pressed facedown in the street.

Several cars, customized with huge hula-hoop-sized rims and bright candy paint littered the front yards of a pair of houses, one with faded salmon-colored paint, and the other covered in peeling turquoise latex, both situated about halfway down the street.

Max absent-mindedly looked up and spotted a green street sign that read Lemon Street. The abrasive rap music pulsating from one of the small houses, and the sight of the dangerous-looking characters congregated in the middle of the street, standing over a helpless man, suggested to Max these guys were possibly members of a street gang. Catching sight of a nickel-plated semi-automatic pistol in one of the men's hands only added fuel to Max's suspicions.

Max didn't know what the young man had done to be forced to his face in the middle of Lemon Street. But as the tiny man with the cannonball-sized head pointed his pistol at the defenseless man, even as his hand shook with apparent fear, Max knew that he could not just stand by and watch some kid's execution.

"Hey!" Max shrieked, stepping through the cotton shrubs and pulling back the slide on his Smith & Wesson pistol, brandishing the weapon in what he hoped was a menacing fashion. "Let him go!"

"Who the hell *you*, chump?" the largest member of the gang shouted, sounding incredulous.

"Let him—" Max didn't finish his sentence. His gun went off in his hand, stabbing bright orange flame toward the assembly of men. Max's bullet ricocheted off the hood of a bright orange car. Dazzling sparks flickered across the hood, and the window of another car shattered. Max's pistol fired several more times before his brain told him he was actually pulling the trigger.

Gangbangers scattered like frightened rodents as the hail of gunfire from Max's "unloaded" pistol rained down around them. In seconds, the man on the ground lay alone as the others had scampered to find cover behind their parked cars.

Max watched the tall black man lying in the street stand up, take a quick look around, then sprint headlong toward Max. At first Max wondered why the kid would run toward the gunfire. But as the terrified man approached, Max figured he assumed that Max had fired his pistol in an attempt to rescue him from the others.

The young man reached Max and stopped. "Thank you," he said.

Max noticed the kid's teeth were very white in the shadowy light of the alley behind the tiki bar. The spindly youth was tall, standing a good couple of inches over Max's six feet. Max fully expected the man to take off running, to get free from the violent thugs who had been a step away from executing him like a dog in the middle of the palm-tree-lined street.

But the younger man, whom Max guessed to be between the age of eighteen and twenty, stood still, facing Max with an expectant look on his face.

He thinks I'm gonna get him out of here, Max thought.

Max wondered what he should do. A bullet whipped past his shoulder.

He knew it was close—the bullet had a distinct sizzling hiss about it. All of the old war movies he had seen told Max that sound was the indication of a near miss.

"Come on!" Max shouted, grabbing the younger man by the wrist and running around the side of the tiki bar. He and the other man found themselves facing a busy avenue. A fair amount of traffic ran both ways for as late at night as it was—or as early; Max had completely lost track of time.

Max spotted the bright coral-pink paint of a Coral Cab Company taxi approaching from the north. He ran into the street, stopping directly in front of it, holding out his hand as if to commandeer it.

The driver hit the brakes and the cab's tires squawked against the wet pavement as the vehicle pitched forward, sliding to a stop. The front bumper struck Max's knee, which buckled under him. He fell, crumpling to the ground.

"You all right, man?" said the driver, an Indian man in a blue turban. He threw open his door and stepped forward, approaching Max with obvious trepidation. "Why you stand in front of my cab? How can I miss you if you are standing right in front of this cab?"

"It's okay," Max said, picking himself up off the street and limping over to the rear passenger side door, tugging it open, and waving over the young man he had rescued from certain death. He practically shoved the lean, wide-eyed man into the back of the cab before diving in behind him.

"I'm fine. Now get us out of here!" Max shrieked. He reached for his wallet and pulled out a few hundreds, tossing them on the seat beside the driver, who was just buckling himself in. "Go! Go! Go!"

"Are you in some kind of trouble?" the cab driver asked. He

looked back over his shoulder with a skeptical, judgmental look on his face. "Perhaps I should leave you here. It might be best for you to walk to wherever—"

The cab driver's rant was cut short by a bullet that ripped through the front windshield, shattering it. "No! Not again! Not on my birthday!"

The driver planted his foot on the gas pedal. The rear tires of the bright coral Crown Victoria spun, leaving behind about fifty percent of whatever tread they'd had before.

In no time, the cab had sped up to well over the posted limit. It hurtled down the avenue like a stone shot from a sling, soon making great distance between them and the gang members from Lemon Street, a couple of whom stood on the avenue in front of the tiki bar, taking random pot shots in their direction.

"Turn here!" Max shrieked.

The cab driver yanked the wheel and fishtailed the cab around the corner, steering the cab like a demolition derby car onto a darkened side street, as a high-pitched wailing sound erupted inside the cab, apparently emanating from deep in the driver's throat.

Max wondered if he'd have been safer back on Lemon Street.

"My brother gets a scholarship to go to M.I.T," the terrified cab driver said as he drove, head down, hands on the wheel at ten and two. The uptight cabbie's voice was tense and treble. "My other brother is a gastroenterologist living in London. I am now here driving a cab, and fighting for my life in Miami.

"Mother was right, I should have stayed in Mumbai instead of coming to America; I would already have my own proctology practice by now."

The cab driver's nervous rant continued until he turned the corner again. The Sikh cabbie raced the heavy car past rundown houses, gaining speed, and then hitting a dip as the cab barreled into a busy cross street.

The cab's front end dipped down hard, then bounced high up as the vehicle launched over the zenith of the four-lane avenue. The hurtling vehicle narrowly avoided t-boning a minivan and a newspaper truck, before blazing down the dark residential street on the other side.

Max and the young black man were tossed around in the back of the cab like dice rolling inside a Yahtzee cup.

The driver slammed on his brakes again. Max rolled onto the floor of the cab. He found himself on his back with the young man lying face up on top of him.

"Out!" the cab driver ordered.

"What?" Max asked, incredulous.

"Get out of my cab," the driver shouted. "You have caused me a great deal of trouble. Look at my windshield."

"Then give me back my cash," Max protested.

"I keep it for the broken window! Now you get out!"

Max reached for the door handle and twisted it, swinging the door open. The rescued man crawled out onto the dark residential street. Max slithered out after him.

The instant Max and the other man were clear, the cab driver peeled out again, racing away from the two men as if fleeing Satan himself.

"I'm Max," Max said, extending his hand toward the other man, who now stood to his full height, watching the Coral Cab speed away, a perplexed look spread over his face.

"Josue," said the man with the pearly white teeth and mysterious, inquisitive eyes. He shook Max's hand.

"Oogh!" Max grunted. He threw up forcefully on the ground between himself and Josue. All of the booze he had consumed, as well as the four carne asada tacos he'd eaten for dinner, splattered all over both men's shoes.

Max glared down at the sickening mess. He thought he saw part of a cocktail umbrella.

"Sorry," Max said, wiping his mouth with the long sleeve of his filthy blazer. He reached up to scratch his earlobe and winced when he touched the irritated scab where his ear had recently been sliced by a jagged beer bottle.

"Where we go?" the younger man asked. Max noticed the fear in the other man's eyes.

"Let's find another cab," Max said, hoping to sound as if he wasn't terrified as well. "Do you have a home? Someplace you can go?"

The scared young man shook his head. His lips curled down into a solemn frown.

Max considered his options for a long moment. He knew he had to do something to help the other man, whatever his situation may be.

"Tell you what," Max said. "We'll go uptown and I'll check us into a motel. We can lie low there until we figure everything out. Okay?"

The lithe black man just nodded. He seemed to trust Max implicitly.

The two men walked briskly in the shadows on one side of the sleepy residential street the high-strung cab driver had dumped them on. Max hoped that if they came to an avenue or a boulevard they would be able to flag down another cab. But that would also expose them; it greatly increased the chances the gang members who tried to kill Josue might drive past and spot them.

Max remembered the iPhone 3GS in his coat pocket. He used it to look up the number for Coral Cab. Then he dialed. He and Josue reached the end of the street just as the dispatcher picked up.

"I need a cab as soon as possible," Max said, doing his best to sound calm. He told the dispatcher where to pick them up based on the nearby street signs. "Two adults. Thanks."

A tense ten minutes passed while Max and Josue waited for

the cab. They both stood in silence, each man keeping a vigilant eye out for any sign of a bright candy-painted car slammed to the ground with hydraulic suspension. Once, they heard the booming bass of a passing vehicle's subwoofers, only to learn it had emanated from a Ford Escort with an illuminated pizza delivery sign on top.

Max wasn't sure where they should go, but when the sight of the pink-orange taxi appeared at the opposite end of the street, he decided just to put some distance between themselves and Little Haiti.

"Stay calm," Max said to the rescued man. He didn't want to raise any suspicions with their new cab driver, lest they get dropped off in the middle of nowhere again. Then Max had a fleeting pang of fear. *What if the dispatcher sent him the same turbaned driver they had before?* But Max decided that guy had probably already retired by now.

A grizzled Cuban, or maybe Puerto Rican, driver stopped the cab in front of Max and Josue. "Order a cab?" he asked.

Max nodded and opened the rear passenger door, allowing Josue to enter first. Max pulled the door behind him and looked at the driver who was peering over his shoulder appraising his two passengers.

"Got cash?" the driver asked.

Max nodded. The driver must have been put off by Max's obviously inebriated state, and Josue's semi-traumatized visage, not to mention the smell of the man's clothes, and both of their shoes.

The driver didn't move. He just sat, staring over his shoulder at Max, occasionally glancing at Josue.

Max pulled a twenty out of his wallet. "Here," he said. "A down payment." Max thought his voice sounded clear enough. But he knew he might have been slurring his words, sounding like a garden variety wino.

The driver squinted and nodded, and continued to stare over his shoulder. At last he said, "Well? Where to?"

"How about Little Havana?" Max said.

"Excellent choice," the driver said, putting the cab in gear and motoring away from the curb.

Max took one last look through the rear windshield of the cab. He wasn't sure what all had just happened. On one hand, he'd expected to be dead by now. On the other, he had just picked up a scared young man, who had latched onto him like a parasite. Max didn't remember the exact moment he had jumped in, but he now felt like he was swimming in deep and uncharted waters.

CHAPTER 18

MOMO CROUCHED BEHIND ZANN'S FULLY-PIMPED '83 Monte Carlo, slumping low against one of the vehicle's chromed eighteen inch rims as a hail of bullets rained down around him.

Rage swelled inside him. Momo checked his pistol, finding it fully loaded with seven massive .50 AE cartridges ready to fire from the huge pistol's six-inch barrel. Momo raised his head above the hood of his car, pissed off to see a deep scratch across the House of Kolor lime green paint. He raised the pistol to fire back at the waste of skin who had dared fire in his direction.

Momo stared in the direction the shooter had been standing, directly behind that lame tiki bar on the corner that Ti Flow used to launder cash. He turned to look at Big Flow, who was crouched nearby. The gang's leader stared back from over by the trunk of the Monte Carlo, his Colt AR-15 in his hands.

"You see him?" Momo asked, when the whizzing bullets suddenly stopped coming.

Big Flow's dreads flopped side to side as he shook his head. He looked livid.

Tiny Deege and Zann both crouched low behind Deege's candy orange Oldsmobile Cutlass Supreme. Tiny Deege shook his small head vigorously at Momo's question, while Zann, flashing his platinum grill through grimacing lips, shook his head as well.

"Go!" Big Flow shouted to Momo. "You must catch them. Don't let that traitor get away."

Momo ran toward the end of Lemon Street, his Desert Eagle clutched in his right fist like a handheld cannon. He reached the corner just in time to see a Coral Cab stopped in the middle of the avenue, its driver waving his hands and shouting at the occupants in the backseat.

Momo squinted. In the diluted light from nearby streetlights and passing headlights, he spotted the shooter. He was a white guy in a blue blazer, Momo saw his face through the open rear window of the cab. The chump wasn't alone. Whoever that guy was, he shared the cab with that punk traitor, Josue.

Momo fired his .50 caliber bullets haphazardly toward the backseat area of the cab. A couple of bullets ripped through the doors. The vehicle's windshield shattered.

The turban-headed taxi driver peeled out, and Momo fired the heavy pistol until his magazine was empty and the slide on his pistol locked open.

Standing on the corner, empty pistol in hand, the massive gangbanger watched Josue and the other guy flee the scene. Momo knew by the time they'd piled into Zann's car and he fired it up, it would be too late for pursuit; the cab would already be long gone.

Josue Remy had gotten away.

In Momo's eyes the newcomer had double-crossed Ti Flow; he'd run away from his post when he should have been standing guard. He had abandoned the gang instead of joining Momo and Big Flow's heat when they'd been locked in a gun battle with the cops on the Miami River. Thinking back over every minute Momo had spent with the young Haitian refugee made him more angry. *Shoulda just smoked him when I had the chance.*

Big Flow lowered his AR-15 when he reached Momo's side. A few intoxicated patrons stumbled out of the tiki bar, only to wheel around and rush back inside the tropical-themed dive upon seeing the gang leader with the carbine.

Momo knew most of the colorfully-dressed patrons of the bar had no idea the place only existed as a legitimate front for the gang. He didn't much care for the flip-flop-wearing bar hoppers who frequented the place more and more. Momo supposed the tiki bar was better than a country western joint or a biker bar, though.

As the Coral Cab sped away, Big Flow took a few shots at the fleeing vehicle from his rifle before lowering it again.

Momo and Big Flow walked back toward their houses half a block down Lemon Street. Momo knew none of the neighborhood's residents would call the police about the shooting—none of them would dare. They each knew the reckoning that would befall them should they cross the gang.

Momo stepped into Big Flow's house, finding several of the gang's other members standing by, AK-47s or shotguns in hand, quizzical looks spread on their faces. "Whyn't you come out an' help us, chumps?" Momo griped. "Bunch o' sissy-assed little punks."

"Wanted to stay back and defend Big's house," said one of the gang members, a stubby, obese guy with a huge afro, whom the gang called Chumbag. He lowered his MAC-10 machine pistol, looking timid. "Didn't know who might be comin' at us."

"Scared, wussy little—" Momo's sentence was cut short. Big Flow had taken a step toward him, and Momo watched the gang leader's hand slip into his right side pants pocket.

Where he kept the screwdriver.

Its handle wrapped with strands of duct tape, the tip of the forged steel hand tool had been filed to a sharp, needlelike point—it was the same deadly weapon Big Flow had carried since the day he'd killed his first man. That would have been around ten years ago—the first time the eager young banger had done time.

The dreadlocked whirlwind had only been nineteen then. And very well scared out of his mind. But he *had* found the courage to plunge the tip of the then unmodified Phillips head into the white supremacist's throat, at least seventeen times.

The tattooed neck of the muscled Aryan had ripped open, tearing blood vessels; the pathetic skinhead would have bled out in seconds. It had been the first moment other men inside had noticed the young Haitian immigrant. It had been the moment that forged the beginning of Big Flow's reputation forever—the spark that had created the gang's origin story.

"Whoa, now," Momo protested, feeling a bout of hyperventilation coming on. He knew Big Flow could kill him with the tool before Momo could even see it in his hand.

"I don't blame just you for the betrayal of Josue Remy," Big Flow said in a cold menacing tone. "I share a bit of responsibility. I trusted you to oversee our young refugee, to look after him, train him, and ensure his loyalty."

"I'm sorry, Big," Momo said, feeling his pulse beating in his temple. "Sorry I let you down, man. I shoulda—"

"It is all right, Momo," Big Flow said. He locked eyes with the bigger man. Momo could swear he was looking into the eyes of a crazy person. He knew it would only take one false breath and the gang's leader would snap. "I forgive you."

Big Flow slowly removed his empty hand from his pocket and took a half-step backward.

Momo sighed. His hand touched his throat and rubbed it, imagining what it might have felt like to be stabbed with Big Flow's barbaric weapon. Momo took a deep breath. He felt a little bit lightheaded.

"Don't let me down again, Momo," Big Flow said, casually scratching his leg uncomfortably close to the opening of his right pocket.

Sensing the end of the conflict, the other members of Ti Flow returned to their business of playing *Halo* on the Xbox 360, and blazing up a bong.

"Yo, Big, how'd the thing go tonight?" another gang member sitting on the sofa asked, probably trying to lighten the mood inside the cramped living room. "You guys get the units?"

"Yes, Tyrone," Big Flow said, taking a bottle of Barbancourt fifteen-year-old rum from Zann's hand and having a long swig. "We got the units. But all did not go quite as well as we hoped. Momo and I killed two police officers."

A grunting sound filled the room as Chumbag sucked a pork rind into his windpipe. The obese man gasped for air, clutching his throat. One of the other members of Ti Flow, a burly muscled man in a black tank top, reached his arms around Chumbag's generous midsection, and began forcibly administering the Heimlich maneuver. Another man slapped the chunky gangbanger hard on his back until the choking man spat a soggy chunk of fried pork skin halfway across the room. Chumbag wheezed so powerfully it seemed he might take in all of the air inside the room.

"But business is business," Big Flow continued. "And we shall never let anyone stand in the way of us achieving our goals. You all feel me?"

Every man in the room grunted affirmation. No one dared speak out against the dreadlocked ruler of the violent organization, even though most of the men in the room shared nervous gazes and unspoken words of fearful concern.

Momo hated Big Flow. It pissed him off that he lived in fear, wondering if each day would be the day the dreadlocked maniac would finally snap and cut Momo down with his handmade shiv or put a bullet in his head.

Momo resolved that the first moment he got the chance he would stage a coup d'état—he would rise against Big Flow, whether it meant killing the leader before he himself was killed, or by gaining the trust of enough of the other gang's members. But Momo *would* take over before long, of that he was certain.

Momo didn't know how long it would take, but he would find

Josue. He would find that skinny, self-preserving, cowardly creep. Momo pledged that if he ever met that treacherous refugee again, it would be more than pain he would inflict on the other man.

CHAPTER 19

"STOP HERE!" MAX SHOUTED AT the taxi driver. He leaned forward in the back of the cab, his hand resting on the top of the front seat. In a split-second Max chose the Paradiso Inn as the place for him and Josue to lie low. The cab driver had just crossed the Coconut Street bridge into Little Havana, and Max had spotted the squalid orange motel on a side street, a few blocks south of the Miami River. The scruffy motel's proximity to Shakey Redbone's Southern Fried Chicken—the fast food restaurant chain that specialized in hot and spicy Nashville-style chicken—was reason enough for him to want to check in there.

Max paid the driver, and he and Josue entered the hotel office, finding the small room to be faded and dated, as if it might have fit the postcard version of 1930s Miami, if it hadn't now been so shabby and timeworn.

The smell of sizzling onions, possibly bell peppers, and some kind of hot chili pepper assaulted Max's eyes as he stepped into the tiny motel office. He had to ding the bell to summon the short, balding woman who must have weighed four hundred pounds, who came waddling out from a small room off of the office, where she had been cooking, likely with an electric skillet or hot plate.

"Mmm, smells good," Max said, offering a forced grin as the woman approached the counter.

"Ten an hour or forty for the night," the woman said in a

monotonous drone that made Max question if she was actually human. He took in the sight of her food-stained floral frock, and the dour grimace on her face, and he wondered: had the woman just given up on life, or was it life that had given up on her?

"Uh, no," Max said. "I'd like your *weekly* rate. My business partner and I will be staying in the area for awhile."

"Two-fifty," the stubby woman said, glaring at Josue up and down before looking back up at Max.

"And we each need a bed," Max insisted.

"Three hundred."

"Done," Max said. He groped the roll of bills in his pants, peeling off three hundreds without pulling his whole wad of cash from his pocket. He slapped the bills down on the splintering dark wood counter.

The desk clerk gave Max and Josue each a worn-down key on a big, diamond-shaped, pink plastic keychain. Max led Josue up a mangled steel staircase with cracked concrete steps to the second floor balcony, which spanned the full length of the building. All of the rooms on the second floor had a door and a window overlooking the parking lot, and out across the street toward Shakey Redbone's.

Max opened the door to their room and was instantly hit with an old musty smell laced with the headache-inducing scent of cheap pine-scented cleaning solution. The room featured two slightly concave queen-sized beds, a small round table and two chairs, a long dresser with a missing drawer, and a twenty-seven inch standard definition television.

"I'll give you the honors," Max said, throwing open the curtains to look down over the street.

"What?" Josue asked.

Max thought the kid looked scared. Probably shell-shocked from everything that had transpired over the course of the evening. He didn't blame him. "I mean pick whatever bed you want. You get first pick."

Josue walked over to the bed further from the window and sat down. Max plunked down on the other bed, and then let himself flop down onto his back. In the instant he allowed his mind to rest, he watched the ceiling swirl in his field of vision overhead. "So where you from? Why don't you have anyplace to go?"

The kid was quiet for a long moment. Max didn't know if he was afraid to answer, if he didn't trust Max, or maybe he didn't really speak English. "It's okay, man. I just want to help."

"I come here...from my village, near Port au Prince," Josue said, wringing his hands together on his lap.

"You're a refugee? From the quake?"

Josue nodded.

"It must have been terrifying to live through all of that," Max said, trying to imagine such a thing. He'd seen footage of the aftermath from the devastating earthquake in Haiti a few days earlier, and it looked like a living nightmare. "And then, somehow, you found your way to Miami, which must have been an ordeal."

Josue gave a solemn nod.

Max felt terrible for the kid. He must have had a rough time in the past few days. "Well, you're safe now." He hoped he sounded comforting.

Max sat up and gazed out the window at the bright red-orange glow of a neon chicken in the window of the restaurant across the street. It occurred to him that his new roommate may not have eaten in some time. "You hungry?"

Josue nodded again, this time a hopeful, expectant look on his face.

"That chicken place across the street is open all night. Let's go over and get some food. We can bring it back here. It's probably best to keep a low profile—those gangbangers could be out on the street, looking for us."

They walked to Shakey Redbone's and found the place empty of customers, except for a long-haired homeless man curled up in a booth; he looked as if he might have lived there. Josue's face lit up as they reached the counter to face a stainless steel bin loaded with crunchy deep-fried chicken parts, and troughs of piping hot side dishes such as buttery corn niblets and mashed potatoes and gravy, along with cool, crispy coleslaw.

"What's good here?" Max asked. The guy behind the counter looked like he was about twelve, with a nice fuzzy starter 'stache. The kid's matted cluster of wild brown hair seemed mostly contained by the hairnet under his red baseball cap that was adorned with the bright yellow embroidered letters S.R. Max half-wondered if the youth should have also had a hairnet over his face to cover his sparse mustache.

"It's all good, sir," the young man said, and Max noticed his name tag said Eustace. "But if you pinned me down, I suppose I would have to say the Bonfire Chicken Strips are the best. But only if you like spicy stuff."

"You like spicy food?" Max asked Josue. "Like hot, fiery in your mouth."

Josue nodded.

"Let's get two of the Bonfire Chicken Strip baskets," Max said, wondering if Josue had even been inside a restaurant before. He didn't know much about Haitian culture, but he knew it wasn't much like it was here.

"Six...no, ten-piece baskets. We'll each have corn, coleslaw, mashed potatoes and gravy, baked beans, and give us each one of those little peach pies."

"Um, sir," Eustace said, absent-mindedly stroking the fuzz over his mouth, "if you order four six-piece baskets, it'll cost less than two ten-piece, since you ordered the extra sides."

"Whatever," Max said. "We just want the food. And two extra large Cokes."

Max paid for the meals, and he and Josue watched Eustace pack up all their food in four little cardboard boxes. He placed it all in a handled plastic bag and threw in napkins, sauces, forks, and wet naps. Then he handed them two empty plastic cups.

Max showed Josue how to use the soda fountain, and chuckled when Josue stood watching as his soda bubbled over the top and ran down into the overflow drain.

"Woah, woah," Max said, showing his new friend how to release the lever to stop the flow.

Max filled his drink, and he and Josue walked back to their motel room, food in hand. A strange feeling chewed away inside Max's gut as he walked. He wasn't sure yet whether it was a good one or not. It felt good to have rescued Josue from the gang about to murder him. But Max wasn't certain it was good he'd taken the younger man in, for him to now be responsible for the displaced Haitian.

Max didn't care about whatever trouble Josue was in. He just wondered how looking after him would interfere with his plans—with what he had ultimately come down to Miami to accomplish.

Max sat across from Josue at the wobbly table in their room. He watched the wide-eyed Haitian take his first bite of the spicy chicken strip. The expression on Josue's face was nothing short of bliss. "How long since you've had a meal?" Max asked, before shoveling in a mouthful of coleslaw.

"I ate some fried chips in car with Tiny Deege earlier in day," Josue said. "I had a sandwich with egg and bread today morning."

"I bet your meals have been hit or miss since the quake," Max said, eyeing the other man, trying to read what he might be feeling. "That's been a few days now."

"Yes," Josue said. "Hit or miss."

"You said you lived in a village outside of Port au Prince. Tell me about where you lived. By the way, you should try dipping your chicken in some of these sauces." Max ripped open a few of the little plastic cartons so that Josue could dip his chicken into the ranch, honey mustard, and spicy BBQ sauces.

"Mmm," Josue said, trying the ranch. "I live on farm. We grow mangoes, sugarcane, sorghum, corn, and tomatoes. We raise chickens for eggs, goats for meat. I live there with my Uncle Guillot, my sister Joliette, and my mother. We all lived in home my uncle built with own hands. It is all gone now."

"And your family," Max said, feeling a sick knot in his stomach. "Did they make it to America too, or are they still in Haiti?"

Tears swelled in Josue's large dark brown eyes and rolled down each cheek. "They did not survive."

As much of his own pain as he carried with him, Max still felt his heart break for this young man. One moment he must have been surrounded by family, happy, and with a comfortable home—the next moment it was all gone.

"Josue, I am sorry for your loss," Max said.

Josue rubbed his eyes and took a drink from his cup. "Thank you for helping. You rescue me."

Max laughed.

"Why is this funny?" Josue said. He almost looked offended.

"I thought the gun was empty," Max said. He took the Smith & Wesson pistol out of his blazer pocket and rested it on the bedside table. "There should not have been any bullets in the gun. I wasn't even thinking when I pulled the trigger. And then I just sort of kept pulling it out of reflex. It was all an accident. I was drunk. Pretty much still am."

"But you saw me," Josue protested. "You stood up to face enemies. You stood up and protect me. You a good man."

"Like I said, Josue. I was drunk. I'm not exactly a hero." Max rubbed his weary, bloodshot eyes with his fingers.

"Thank you," Josue said insistently.

"Well, you're welcome. But I don't know if you could count on me to do it again." Max wriggled out of his blazer and tossed it on the floor beside his queen-sized bed. By the look of the room's carpeting, Max halfway expected the floor to eat it.

"Thank you for helping me, and giving me good place to sleep, giving me food."

Max noticed that Josue had tucked most of his food back in the box, as if saving it for later. This was probably way more than he was used to having in one meal. Max didn't know if it was good for the refugee to eat his fill or to take it easy, but Max wanted to make sure he had as much as he wanted.

"Josue, you can eat all you want. In the morning we'll go and get more food. You don't have to save it. Okay?"

Josue nodded. He took another piece of chicken out of his box and then closed it back up.

Max smiled.

After they had eaten, Max flopped onto his bed and kicked off his shoes. Without much thought, he grabbed the TV remote and clicked on the television. He glanced at Josue, who looked curious.

"You watch TV before?" Max asked.

"See it a few times in the city," Josue said.

Max toggled through channels, switching from a cooking channel, to a fishing channel, to a religious channel hosted by a red-faced man with a thick bouffant of blond hair; he urged audience donations, pleading with enthusiastic gusto. Max stopped when he reached Channel Six news.

"...believed to be gang-related, and narcotics may have been involved." the female news anchor said in voiceover as the television showed B-roll of what appeared to be a crime scene at a marina with bright flashing blue and white lights. Josue sat bolt upright in his bed.

"The two officers killed were Reginald Van Kamp and Josephine Fuentes, both with the Miami Police Marine Patrol unit," the voice on the TV continued. "The officers engaged subjects believed to have hijacked a yacht belonging to a Fisher

Island couple, whose bodies were both found on the yacht, though their identities have not yet been released.

"The Marine Patrol officers returned fire after suspects on the stolen yacht opened fire with automatic weapons. Witnesses near the scene have suggested the suspects may have been members of an unknown street gang, and police are asking for your help in providing any information about an orange vehicle that may have fled the area after the shootings. Police are also searching for a black male who fled the scene on foot, last seen running north towards Ponce de Leon Avenue, near the Miami River." The news anchor provided a phone number for a tip line.

"Was that you?" Max asked Josue, who sat on his bed, knees now clutched to his chest. His eyes stared ahead with a blank expression. "That she described on the news? You were running to get away from the gang?"

Josue nodded.

"They made me go with them," Josue said, his voice sounding weary and distant. It must have hurt to know that the gang members had killed people. "I go with them. When I hear them shooting, I run. I run away."

"I believe you, Josue," Max said. He had no reason to doubt the other man. In truth, his heart hurt even more for his new roommate. After all of the devastation the kid had witnessed in Haiti, after the loss of his family, he made it to Miami only to fall in with a violent street gang who would put him to work on a drug deal.

Looking out for Josue would mean an end to Max's plans, and he wasn't ready to change them, not for anyone. He knew he had to separate from the kid as quickly as possible. But it wouldn't be tonight.

Max clicked off the TV and took one more peek out the faded orange curtains. He looked at the gritty street and parking lot outside, before smashing a scampering cockroach and switching off the bedside lamp. He flopped back down onto his bed. He could solve his problems later. What Max needed now more than anything, was sleep.

He'd worry about abandoning the kid tomorrow.

CHAPTER 20

LORENZO PARKED THE BLACK CHARGER among all of the chaos, near the rundown marina close to the Ponce de Leon Avenue bridge. An ambulance pulled away, slowly, as the detective put the unmarked car in park, and then he and Arthur stepped out into the chilly predawn air.

They approached the crime scene, maybe a bit more slowly than usual. It always stung when the vic was one of your own. In this case, two of your own. Lorenzo looked at his gold-tone Seiko. Just after two a.m.

There were two boats on the scene, one a sixty-five, seventy-foot yacht—a nice one, very expensive—the other boat was a Miami Police Marine Patrol boat with twin outboard motors.

The luxurious yacht was obviously out of place, docked amongst some of the shabby boats in this semi-neglected marina. It was way bigger than the other boats, much nicer and obviously brand-new, and this one was riddled with bullet holes.

The pursuing vessel, a quick center console with twin Mercury outboards, had been docked nearby, likely after the shootout, and it sat still, disquietingly so, its bright blue LED lights still flashing with retina-piercing intensity as the boat sat idle. Lorenzo noticed the Lexan windscreen, cracked apart by numerous gunshots, and splattered with someone's blood.

At the edge of the river, the veteran detective caught sight of a ghostly form, dressed in a crisp black suit with oiled black hair combed straight back, staring down into the dark water of the

Miami River. The two detectives approached the other man, and Lorenzo spoke first, "What do we got, Lieutenant?"

The grimly-dressed man turned and tossed his cigarillo into the water. His cheeks were somewhat sunken, and his eyes looked as black as the river. His white shirt looked bleach-white against the thin, simple black tie cinched tight around his throat. The man seemed devoid of any kind of facial expression at all.

"We got two dead officers," Lieutenant Chato said. "MPD Marine Patrol."

"Yeah, we heard that," Arthur said, his forehead furrowed into a mass of wrinkled lines. "Anyone we know?"

"M.E.'s already been here, just left," Chato said. "They just took away Josephine Fuentes," the somber lieutenant said, tucking his thumb inside his waistband just behind his holstered Sig Sauer semi-auto on his left hip. "Van Camp's coming off the boat now."

"Reggie Van Camp?" Lorenzo asked. "Damn. Used to be pretty close, kind of went our own ways after he joined Marine Patrol, I took the Homicide route. Our paths just stopped crossing, you know? Sucks, 'cause he had kids, too. Probably grown by now, though. Not sure if he and Kathy were still together. Maybe not."

Two EMTs rolled a gurney past the three detectives, and Lorenzo put his hand up to stop them. "May I?" he asked.

One of the EMTs carefully unzipped the black body bag down to the fallen officer's waist. Lorenzo looked into the bag and cringed. Seeing a friend in the bag sure as hell wasn't the same as seeing a random victim—he knew this guy.

The Marine Unit officer's body had been perforated by so many bullets, only the medical examiner would be able to tell which one had killed him. It might have been the one to his head, one of many in his chest near his heart, his spinal column. But he likely checked out quick, and that was good. Lorenzo nodded.

The EMTs made quick work of zipping the body back up and loading it into the ambulance, before switching off their lights and driving the dead officer to the morgue. Lorenzo shuddered against the chill in the air.

He and Arthur walked with Chato over to the bullet-riddled yacht. Lorenzo stepped onto the rear swim platform of the vessel, which bore the surprising lettering *Catch Me If You Can* against the transom. The seasoned detective found the rear deck strewn with so many spent bullet casings, it looked as if someone had taken a shower in a stream of brass.

"Damn," Arthur said, looking down at the casings. "That's a lot of rounds. Ain't seen so much brass since Heather and I seen the Boston Pops last year. Who do you like for this, Lieutenant?"

"This has Ti Flow's prints on it, Detective Parks," Chato said. He took another cigarillo out of his shirt pocket and blazed it to life with a torch lighter. "These guys like to hit boats in the harbor, drive their booty up the river, get picked up anywhere between the bay and the Glades. This time they hit an incoming coke shipment at the Fisher Island marina, killed a security guard there—looks like a sniper shot. Pretty brazen act. Lieutenant Guerrero from the Gang Unit is coming down to look at the scene, offer his two cents."

"Good," Arthur said. "'Bout time somebody wakes up those guys for once."

"What about the boat?" Lorenzo asked. "Fisher Island? Who the hell was running coke to Fisher Island?"

"A wealthy couple, one…Luther Stein, and his wife Gwendolyn, were residents of the island." The lieutenant looked at his palm-sized spiral notepad as he spoke. "They owned an upmarket two-level condo in one of the high-rises—place probably cost about five, six million. From what we've got so far, it looks like he was a periodontist before retirement; looks like he and his wife found a second career in narco trafficking.

"Seems the Steins were making lots of trips, running a good amount of coke between Nassau and Miami, while giving off the appearance of a carefree couple enjoying a well-deserved retirement. We'll be investigating who they dealt with between Fisher Island and downtown."

"How did Ti Flow know who to hit, where to hit, and when?" Arthur asked, taking off his Ray Bans and cleaning them on his shirtfront.

"You know these gang guys work a lot with informants," Chato said, before taking a drag on his cigarillo and blowing away the smoke. "Someone in Nassau probably worked with the cartel that delivered the product to the Steins. Probably betrayed their bosses and tipped off the gang, in exchange for a cut."

The three men walked over to the police boat, and boarded the stern. They found shell casings scattered about the deck of this boat as well. Personal articles belonging to the dead officers lay strewn about: a lunch cooler, a Miami Dolphin's backpack, a pair of broken Oakley sunglasses. Stepping forward past the control console, Lorenzo found the bow deck awash in his fellow officers' blood.

"Damn," Arthur said, gazing down at the crimson pool, just in front of his Sperry Topsiders.

"Witnesses spotted a bright orange low-rider, maybe a Monte Carlo or Olds Cutlass, fleeing the scene," Chato said, looking at Lorenzo and Arthur with a characteristic blank expression. "I have a feeling our investigation will lead us back to Lemon Street. We just need solid probable cause before we move in to the neighborhood. Can't take a step there a moment too soon. Do you read me?"

Lorenzo looked Chato in the eyes, and could tell he was serious. No cowboy moves or going off the reservation, whether Reggie Van Camp was a friend or not. He nodded.

"Shouldn't be too hard to track down a flamboyant whip like that," Arthur said, scratching his head. "Bright orange, flashy paint, hydraulics maybe. Probably just a few like it in the city. You want us on the car?"

"No," Lieutenant Chato said, glaring. The man was so sparing with his emotions, it was almost impossible to detect whether he was speaking with urgency, or if it was just another day at the office to him. "I've got Dice and Richardson pursuing the vehicle. We'll also issue a BOLO for the car—it'll turn up."

"So what for us, then?" Lorenzo asked, reaching into his pocket for a piece of Nicorette. The lieutenant's cigarillo had given him an annoying pang of craving for some nicotine.

"Other witness accounts have a tall black male—teenager, maybe early twenties—fleeing the scene on foot. Ran from the marina, mounted the steps up the overpass, tried to flag down a car on Ponce de Leon. Don't know if it was an attempted carjacking or what, but it sounds like he might have gotten into a Coral Cab.

"Sergeant Ferrigno, I want you and Parks to interview everyone at the apartment building next to the overpass—someone's seen something. Talk to the dispatcher at the cab company, see if one of his drivers picked up the kid. I want you two to use every resource available to locate this…'running man.'"

"Done deal, Lieutenant," Lorenzo said, stuffing a second piece of gum into his mouth and chomping down. "We won't let these bastards get away. They're gonna pay for what they done. For Fuentes and Van Camp. Mark my words, Lieutenant—we're gonna get 'em."

CHAPTER 21

MAX WOKE UP SHIVERING. HIS head throbbed, and a pronounced ringing tone resounded deep inside his ears. He touched his chest, feeling his shirt completely soaked through with chilly sweat.

Max sat up in the bumpy motel bed, finding the room nearly pitch dark except for a sliver of weak early morning light that trickled through a thin gap in the heavy curtains, casting a dull blue-gray streak across the floor. Max looked at the clock beside the bed. The bright red digital letters told him it was six eleven a.m.

Max remembered the liquor store he'd spotted two doors down from Shakey Redbone's the night before. The plain white building, its windows littered with all manner of beer, rum, vodka, and tequila-branded neon and vinyl signs, was the actual reason Max had decided to stop and check in at the Paradiso Inn. The wide windows of the well-lit store had given Max a glimpse of its myriad shelves heavy with colorful bottles, and the place had virtually called to him like a siren's song.

Max picked up his crumpled blazer from the motel carpet, recoiling his hand in a reflex action as a fat cockroach scurried across it. Max sniffed the blazer and grimaced. As he put it on, he wondered why he had bothered smelling the garment if he was just going to wear it anyway.

Max glanced at the room's second bed, finding Josue asleep, facedown, a gentle grating sound emanating from his nostrils.

It was probably the best sleep the kid had gotten since the night before the devastating quake that had destroyed his home and changed his world forever.

Max took great care in opening the motel room door, cringing as the door squeaked, and then closing it gently, ensuring it was secured behind him. As Max let go of the doorknob, he saw the trembling in his fingers. He would need a drink, and he would need it soon.

He looked both ways before crossing the street, though there was virtually no traffic here at this early hour. A gray primered Honda Civic zipped by on a nearby side street, its subwoofers announcing the vehicle's presence long before the annoying rumble from the car's motorcycle-type muffler.

Max spotted a couple of red and black-uniformed employees through the window of Shakey Redbone's. He noticed the bright blue and red Always Open sign glowing in the window of the twenty-four-hour restaurant, and it suddenly occurred to Max that the chicken restaurant also had a breakfast menu.

"Well, that's handy," Max muttered to himself as he reached the door to Captain Sergeant's Spirit Shoppe. He gave the door handle a tug.

It didn't open. Max frowned.

He pulled harder, squinting through the glass door, and noticing the place looked suspiciously empty. And then Max allowed his eyes to focus on the white lettering decals stuck to the glass door in front of his face.

Store Hours:

7am to 11pm Mon – Fri

7am to 10pm – Sun

"Damn," Max muttered, letting go of the door. *Leave it to me to pick one of the few Miami liquor stores not open twenty-four hours a day.* Max turned around and leaned his back against the door. He let himself slump down until he was in a sitting position.

The shivering started again. Though the chill of dawn did nothing to help, Max knew his body was reacting to a deprivation of alcohol. He'd been drinking so much over the past few weeks. He seemed to imbibe a bit more each day, if that was even possible. Presently, he knew he had to get a drink, and soon, or he wasn't sure what might happen. And he wasn't keen on finding out.

Max grabbed his lapels and pulled his blazer tighter around him. He could just go back to the warm motel room and return when the place was open. But Max didn't want to be even a second late in getting rum into his bloodstream. So he stayed there, slumped against the door, doing his best to stay awake, as his body twitched and shivered.

Max jerked awake. At first, he wasn't sure why. Then he spotted the goateed man stooped over him.

"You can't sleep here, man," said the guy, probably only a few years older than Max, judging by the few gray hairs that streaked the man's carefully groomed black facial hair, along with the hairline, which seemed to be making a run for it away from the man's generous forehead. "I got a shop to run here. Okay?"

"Sorry," Max said, struggling to his feet and smoothing out his blazer. "I got here about an hour ago, didn't realize you'd be closed, and decided to wait. You must be Captain Sergeant," Max said, standing aside so the other man could open the shop.

"Yeah," the shop owner said with a half-grin that revealed a gold crown on one of his front teeth, "I guess I am. You got money?"

Max nodded.

"All right," the goateed man said, opening the door, and holding it wide for Max to enter. "After you."

Max made a beeline for the rum section, his eyes immediately gravitating toward the top shelf. "Do you have any Zaya Gran Reserva?" Even though Max's body was desperate for an immediate drink, he couldn't get away from his deep-seated pickiness about what he drank. And whenever a particular spirit struck his fancy, there were no substitutions.

"Hmm," the shopkeeper said, opening a binder he pulled from a cabinet under the register. He flipped through a couple of pages. "Yeah, looks like I've got some in the back, haven't put 'em out yet."

"I'll take a case of six," Max said.

The liquor store owner laughed. "You want me to get you a bottle?"

"No, I'm serious. I'll take a case of six." Max moved to replace a bottle of twelve-year-old Flor de Cana rum from Nicaragua he'd been scrutinizing, and he missed the shelf. The bottle hit the floor and shattered. Max looked down at the glass shards and the wasted amber fluid splattered all over the floor. "And that."

Max paid for the rum and stepped outside. He set the box on the concrete curb in front of Captain Sergeant's and snatched out a bottle of the unique blended rum from Trindad and Tobago, peeling off the plastic, and uncorking the bottle. Max took a long, satisfying sip. He replaced the cork. *Should take the edge off for now*, he thought, as he tucked the bottle back into its case.

Max decided to step into Shakey Redbone's and grab breakfast for himself and his refugee friend. He purchased two southern fried chicken biscuit sandwiches for each of them, and some deep-fried hash brown potatoes. A couple of large hot coffees tucked into a recycled cardboard carrier rounded out the meal. Max arranged it all on top of his case of premium rum so that he could carry it all across the street.

Inside the motel room, Max found Josue still sleeping soundly. But the weary younger man stirred as streaks of the first rays of sunlight streamed through the door opening, striating across his face. The smell of hot food probably helped too.

Josue sat upright in bed, still dressed in his shorts and rank-smelling, dirt-smudged t-shirt. He seemed embarrassed, as if he had been caught oversleeping.

"Look, Josue," Max said, setting the food and liquor on the wobbly table, "I got some food and coffee for us. But you don't have to get up now, if you'd like to sleep longer. Just know there's food here for when you wake up."

"I am awake now," Josue said, rubbing his eyes with his knuckles. "Now is good time to eat."

The two men dug into the fast food meal in silence. Max alternated between taking sips from his coffee cup and from a glass of rum he had poured for himself. "Sorry," Max said, as he tipped the bottle to refill his glass. "Would you like some rum?"

Josue shook his head.

"Sorry, I forgot to grab cream for the coffee, but I did get some sugar packets," Max said. "How do you take your coffee?"

Josue seemed confused. He shrugged his shoulders. "I don't know. I never have coffee before."

Max ripped the tops off a couple of packets of sugar and poured them into the younger man's cup. "I think you'll like it better this way." Max stirred the coffee with a straw.

Josue swallowed a bite of his biscuit sandwich and sipped from the cup. "Mmmm. Very good drink."

Max smiled and took a long sip of rum. The alcoholic spirit warmed him through the middle, as the hot food satisfied his gnawing pangs of hunger. He felt better.

After breakfast, the two men propped themselves up in their respective beds as Max switched on the analog television set. Max flipped through the channels, hoping to find out more information about the violent robbery Josue had gotten caught up in. As he toggled through the channels, Max noticed Josue's face, beaming with amazement at almost everything he saw appearing in the square box of plastic, metal, and glass.

There wouldn't likely be too much TV watching on a farm outside of Port au Prince. Max thought the culture shock might not have been much different than if Josue had come to Miami from Lancaster County.

Max found that they had missed the local morning news programs. He thought about going online with his laptop, but remembered it was still at his other motel room. His mind rolled back over the events of the previous night. After his chance encounter with Josue and the other gang members, he had wanted to put some distance between them and the gang. That was why they had driven down south, to get out of Little Haiti. But now Max knew he needed to go back there to retrieve his stuff: the laptop; all of his rumpled, mostly dirty laundry; and he vaguely recalled a half-drunk bottle of Zacapa XO rum. That would be the time when he would leave Josue Remy behind.

Max went inside the musty bathroom to take a shower. Despite the stale smell of the dank room, and the hint of mildew that clung to the walls, he was pleased to find the courtesy bottles of shampoo and conditioner, as well as a tiny bar of soap. Some of these shadier motels didn't always feature such amenities. It felt good to get cleaned up, even though he would just be putting the same dirty clothes back on.

When he was dressed, standing in the steam of the poorly-ventilated bathroom, Max counted the bills in his pants pocket. Four thousand, two hundred and seventy-two dollars. He also turned out the twelve bucks or so he had collected in change at recently patronized bars and a couple restaurants that had ultimately kicked him out, spilling the coins onto the bathroom counter.

It would be enough to give the kid a second chance at life. He could get pretty much anywhere he wanted to go with that much cash. He could live off it for a few months if he was careful, get a job, find a cheap place. *Josue would be all right,* Max told himself. *And I can feel good that I did everything I could to help him.*

Max peeled off a few hundred bucks. It would get him a cab to his other motel, and tide him over until he could get back to the bank for more cash. The rest of the money he placed on the bathroom counter. Max took the small pad of paper with the Paradiso Inn letterhead and matching pen—again, the motel's amenities exceeded Max's expectations—and wrote out a short note to the young Haitian.

Dear Josue,

I am happy to have run into you in Little Haiti. I wish it had been under happier circumstances. But I'm glad you are safe now.

I'm leaving this money to help you start a new life. It's yours. I'm sorry I can't stay with you longer, but there are things I need to do. I'm afraid my life's on a much different path than yours.

Take care, my friend. I hope someday we meet again.

Maxwell

Max laid the note on top of the cash. He covered it with a dry washcloth, so that Josue wouldn't find it right away. Then he stepped out into the room, finding Josue watching a documentary about beekeeping with great intensity.

"Josue, I've got to run back to my other motel, grab some of my stuff, and check out," Max said, doing his best to sound nonchalant. "Stay here, and if you get hungry, you can walk over to Shakey Redbone's and grab some lunch." Max dropped a twenty on the wobbly table. "I'll see you later, okay."

Josue nodded, and Max opened the door. He thought about taking his case of rum, but he knew Josue would find that suspicious. As much as it made him feel like an ass, he didn't want the scared young man to know he wasn't coming back.

Max turned and took one last look at Josue. The Haitian smiled broadly and waved as Max stepped through the door. It was the first moment Max had seen the frightened refugee smile since he had met him. It would also be the last.

"I see you later, Maxwell," Josue said, grinning with those perfectly straight, pearl-white teeth.

Max nodded. He closed the door.

CHAPTER 22

"CAREFUL, MAN!" ARTHUR SAID, PULLING the beef kabob from deep inside his mouth, where the sharp tip of his bamboo skewer touched the back of his throat. "You almost made me stab myself in the brain stem. We ain't in a hurry anyhow. What the hell, man!"

Lorenzo cackled and glared at his partner with wild eyes. He slipped another stick of Juicy Fruit into his mouth, his foot pressed firmly on the gas pedal. The unmarked police car sped west through Allapattah, near the Miami River. "I doubt you'd die from the stabbing. Probably get tetanus or hepatitis or something from the skewer. You know that food truck got a D on its last visit from the state health inspector."

"I don't care, man," Arthur said, sliding a piece of folded-up beef off the end of the sharpened stick. "I'll take my chances."

Lorenzo pulled into the parking lot of the Coral Cab Company, directly across the street from Miami Casino, where blue-haired locals wagered their social security checks in video poker and slot machines. Daring athletes hurtled a ball from long wicker baskets in the casino's jai alai fronton, while gamblers placed pari-mutuel bets on the fast-paced action.

The Coral Cab dispatch office was situated almost directly beneath the concrete track of the Metrorail viaduct suspended high above traffic, where it curved south to cross the Miami River a short distance away, terminating at a train station near the airport. Cabs in various state of repair littered the lot: a few minivans, but mostly Crown Victorias, all painted with that same coral hue, ranging from shiny new, almost bright orange-red, to the oldest cars, whose paint had simply faded into a dull pink.

Lorenzo parked the Charger and stepped out, pausing to watch a Metro train rattle toward them from downtown, and then twist by overhead.

Arthur opened the office door and Lorenzo trailed behind. As the two men stepped into the dispatch office, their eyes needed a moment to adjust to the dim lighting inside the dank warehouse atmosphere.

They approached a desk where a dispatcher talked into a headset to one of his cab drivers. "Ten sixty-three, there're two waiting outside the Shorecrest Club apartments, Northeast Bayshore Court. Expecting you in five."

"Can I help you guys?" said the dispatcher, a bald man, with a glistening pate and thick brown hair wrapping his bulbous head.

Lorenzo flashed his gold shield. "Sergeant Ferrigno, Miami Police. This is Detective Parks."

"Ferrigno," the dispatcher said, bemused. "Like the Hulk, Ferrigno?"

"Yeah," Lorenzo said, tucking his badge and chain into the left front pocket of his 501 jeans. "Like the Hulk."

"Are you guys here to talk to Ronnie?" the dispatcher said, running his hand across his glistening scalp. Lorenzo wasn't sure if he meant to rub his skin, or if the man absent-mindedly forgot about his lack of hair up top, but the fidgety detective found the gesture a little cringe-worthy.

"Who?" Arthur asked.

"Ronnie Vikram," the dispatcher said.

"I don't know," Lorenzo said, "did he pick up a young male black, maybe eighteen, twenty, near the Ponce de Leon bridge this morning? Wee hours, like around 1:30 a.m.?"

"I'll have to check the logs," the dispatcher said, both his index fingers moving with blinding speed as he punched keys on his computer keyboard. "No, looks like you wanna talk to Grover, Grover Barberton. He's out on shift now. I can have him meet you pretty much anywhere you wanna talk."

"Thanks, man," Arthur said. "We appreciate your cooperation."

The dispatcher arranged for the cab driver to meet the detectives at the marina where officers Fuentes and Van Camp had been gunned down only hours earlier. The three men walked past the deteriorating boats of the small marina next to the drawbridge over the murky Miami River, raised to allow a decrepit cargo ship to pass downriver. The Stein couple's yacht still loomed like a ghost ship. The shot-up Marine Patrol Unit's center console boat rested nearby, tied off to the dock. Shiny yellow police tape cordoned off civilian access to the boats.

The cab driver pulled a pack of Winston Reds from his shirt pocket and offered one to Lorenzo. The detective shook his head, a pained expression of conflict spread over it. Arthur declined as well, with thanks. Lorenzo wrapped a piece of nicotine gum in two sticks of Juicy Fruit and stuffed it all into his mouth.

"Man, I didn't know all 'o this was goin' on when I drove by last night," the cab driver said. He looked at the bullet-perforated police boat with a forlorn expression.

"Tell me about the guy you picked up last night," Lorenzo said, pausing in his efforts to chew his mouthful of gum into submission. "What exactly went down last night?"

"I was heading northbound over the bridge," Grover said. "I was actually on my break. I'd been working Little Havana, but was heading up to Hialeah to pick up some Indian food. I spotted this guy running up the steps, just off the right side of the bridge. He ran right out into traffic, almost got hit a couple times. I stopped 'cause he really looked distressed. Not crazy or like a threat, but really in trouble. You know?"

"Tell me about this guy," Arthur said. "Did he look like a gang member to you?"

"No," Grover said, taking a drag from his cigarette and making eye contact with the officers as he spoke, "he looked scared. I talked to him a bit. If I had to guess, I'd say the kid was right off the boat from somewhere. Probably did fall in with one 'o these gangs, probably made the wise move of trying to get away from them real quick."

"You gave him a ride," Lorenzo said. "Even though you were on break?"

"Look, detective, I came to this country once too. I ain't tryin' to be aidin' and abettin' anyone or nothin'. But I know how hard it can be. And this guy was in full culture shock mode. Looked like he'd been dropped off on the moon without a compass. I felt for the guy. I switched on the meter and gave him a ride. He paid me. It's a documented transaction."

"I believe you," Arthur said.

"So where you take him?" Lorenzo asked.

"Said he wanted to go to Lemon Street," Grover said. "I dropped him off on Lemon Street."

Lorenzo looked dumbfounded. "I thought he was trying to get away from the gang. And he asked you to take him right back to Ti Flow ground zero? What the hell was he thinking?"

"Don't know," Grover said, breathing cigarette smoke out of both nostrils. "But he was petrified, that's for damn sure."

"Thanks for your help, Grover," Arthur said, shaking the cab driver's hand. He handed the cabbie one of his cards. "If anything comes to mind…"

Lorenzo and Arthur sat down in their car and shut the doors.

"What's your gut telling you, Art?" Lorenzo ripped the cap off a bottle of spring water and took a long drink.

"Kid's scared, but he goes back into the dragon's den," Arthur said, staring out the window at the nearby row of neglected sailboats, their barren masts teetering slightly from the gentle motion of the river. "Maybe he forgot something. Something important. Something he can't live without."

"He's fresh off the boat, gets mixed up with Ti Flow, must have come from Port au Prince, quake refugee. Probably going back for something he left behind." Lorenzo took another swig of water, staring blankly at a pair of seagulls begging by the driver's side window.

"A prize possession?" Arthur asked.

"Could be something as simple as a few dollars in cash, maybe all he has in the world," Lorenzo said, his brow furrowed. "Maybe a picture of a loved one or something like that."

"Wanna go to Lemon Street, start knocking on doors?" Arthur said, looking at Lorenzo with a sober expression.

"No, I think I'll go piss off that drawbridge while it's goin' up," Lorenzo said, smirking at his partner. "It'd probably be a lot safer."

Arthur laughed. He knew as well as Lorenzo that showing up alone on Lemon Street might cause them to suddenly disappear from the face of the earth. "Let's tell Chato what we've got, see if he's got any new information for us to work with."

"First, I think we should grab some biscuits and gravy," Lorenzo said.

Arthur nodded.

"What would mean so much to you that you'd run back to Lemon Street?" Lorenzo asked.

"I don't think I own *anything* I'd go back there to retrieve."

Lorenzo started up the Charger and put it in gear. He drove slowly down NW River Road, alongside the Ponce de Leon Avenue bridge. He looked at the steps leading up to the avenue, where the street ramped up before it crossed the River.

Lorenzo imagined the kid running up the steps. He didn't care much about how scared the young refugee was; he'd been involved in gang activity that had got his friend killed. If he and

Art were to catch up with him, Lorenzo would do everything he could to see that the kid did time—or at the very least, was sent back to that third world hellhole, Port au Prince, if that was actually where he'd come from.

But secretly, Lorenzo hoped that Ti Flow would find him first.

CHAPTER 23

MAX CAUGHT A CAB ON a busy boulevard two blocks from the Paradiso Inn. Guilt wracked his conscience; the more he thought about abandoning the young Haitian at the cheap Little Havana motel, the worse he felt.

But Max knew the more he drank, the less he'd care about leaving the younger man behind. So he directed the cab driver to the nearest liquor store, one that wasn't directly across the street from the Paradiso Inn.

The driver dropped Max off at a high-rise building in Midtown, where he found himself staring up between the green and silver fronds of two tall palms that seemed to grow right up out of the sidewalk. The building must have been thirty stories tall, housing upscale apartments and classy office spaces high up into the sky, along with a hodgepodge of ritzy shops on the ground floor.

Inside the liquor store, which specialized in rare wines and spirits from all around the world, Max bought another case of Zaya Gran Reserva. He knew it was stupid; when he had earlier arrived at Captain Sergeant's that morning, he hadn't yet thought through the rest of his day. He hadn't known he'd be abandoning the young Haitian refugee. He had only known that he had needed the rum desperately.

The cab driver waited for Max, who returned to the cab with the fresh case of Trinidadian and Tobagonian rum in hand. Then they headed north, back to Little Haiti. As the car jostled along through traffic, Max stared out at the vibrant display of humanity along the way as he considered what would come next.

Max didn't much like to think about it. It still embarrassed him. But Max forced himself to realize that he *had* stepped out behind the tiki bar the previous evening to kill himself.

Fate had intervened, and he had saved Josue from imminent execution. But now Max would experience a do-over of the failed attempt: heading out to a different bar, drinking his fill, and then going out back once more to end his life, once and for all.

Max had been certain the magazine he had slapped into the shiny stainless steel pistol had been empty, probably because all of the others in the box he'd gotten from the pawn shop had been empty. In his inebriated state, Max had taken for granted the magazine was empty, and he'd almost killed someone. He felt lucky he hadn't. There was only one person his pistol was meant to kill, and that was himself.

The cab arrived at the Deep Blue Sea Motel, and Max paid the driver, finding that, after buying the rum, he had very little cash left. He'd have to go back to the bank before going out that evening.

Max opened the door to the room and found it impeccably clean; the chambermaid had restored order to the utter disarray Max had left the room in. It relieved him to see his laptop on the room's table, beside a couple of bottles of half-drunk rum, and some of the tools he had purchased to file down the slide of his pistol, all arranged neatly as if put there with great care, right next to his Tampa Bay Buccaneers duffle bag.

His mother had ordered him a Miami Dolphins duffel bag from the JC Penney catalog for his birthday when he was a kid. But they'd sent the wrong one. Max hadn't cared too much, though, and he had just started using the Buccaneers bag. He'd carried it with him as long as he could remember.

Max spotted a neat pile of folded laundry on a chair beside

the table. He picked up a folded black t-shirt and held it up to his nose. It smelled like the same flowery fabric softener his wife had used when she'd washed his clothes. The skin on his arms prickled with goose bumps.

Why would a maid in a seedy motel go through all this trouble? Max wondered. He was about to plunk himself down onto the bed and close his eyes for a late morning nap, when he heard the sound of squeaky wheels rolling by outside his room.

Max opened the door and saw Tori pushing her housekeeping cart, loaded with spare rolls of toilet paper, tiny bars of soap, boxes of tissues, individually wrapped plastic cups. He stepped in front of the cart, and she stopped.

"Tori, is it?" Max said, feeling awkward about his entire relationship with the conscientious maid, despite his gratitude. "Did you organize my stuff in my room? Did you actually launder my clothes?"

Tori nodded, and Max noticed the blue tips of her hair bouncing as she did. "Sorry if it was inappropriate," she said, her voice leaning more toward the salty side this morning. "I just wanted to...help."

"I'm guessing you don't do that for too many people here," Max said.

Tori laughed and shook her head. "No, you're the first."

Max stuffed his hand into his pants pocket and grabbed out a couple of twenties. He handed them toward the young room cleaner. "Thanks."

Tori looked down into the trough of room trash heaped inside the trash can in the middle of the rolling cart. "I don't want your money. That's not why I did it."

"I'd feel better if you took it." Max felt the situation growing even more awkward each second that passed. "Why did you?"

"When I saw you in your room, bleeding yesterday, I thought about the day I came to Miami," Tori said, looking up at Max with wide, sober brown eyes. "I was lost. Just got to town. Seemed like right off the bus I fell in with some really messed-up people. It was only a matter of days before I found myself on meth, no job, no home, no hope, just wanting to OD and end it all."

"Wow," Max said, wondering how the maid's trying times somehow related to him. "Sorry you had to go through all of that. Things got better, though, right? What happened?"

"A kind stranger came up to me on the street one day," Tori said. "It was this kinda creepy old man, I think he was Cuban-American, and he wore this bright white three-piece suit. Anyway, he came up to me when I was sitting outside this club, leaning against the wall. I think he saw that I had track marks on my arms. He looked at me, and I'll never forget what he said: 'Young lady, your life is a great, precious gift to the world. And the sun wouldn't shine quite as bright without you in it.' Then he said that God wasn't finished with me yet."

"Hmm," Max said, not knowing what to say.

"For some reason, and I still don't know why, I believed him," Tori added. "Almost immediately I decided to get clean, got a job, went to meetings." The young maid smiled in a way that Max knew was real. The hard-working young woman breathed a powerful half-laugh, half-sob, and said, "Now I have a daughter. I have a beautiful two year-old girl, Rosie." Tears glistened in Tori's eyes. "I didn't think I'd ever have something so beautiful in my whole life. You know, something worth living for?"

Max's eyes blurred through his own tears as he thought about his own daughter, Lucy. He supposed he felt the same about her. It took him a long moment to collect himself before he could even speak. It broke his heart to realize his life had become so pathetic that a chambermaid at the Deep Blue Sea Motel in Little Haiti would feel compelled to reach out to him, seeing how fragile he was, trying to save him. But Tori's words struck Max deep in his core.

As he considered the maid's story about coming to Miami, feeling lost, falling in with the wrong people, Max thought about Josue. The poor guy had lost everyone close to him in that awful quake. He had found himself here with a tiny kernel of hope, finding it quashed when he was taken in by the Haitian gang, being forced into criminal activity.

Max wiped his eyes. "That's nice to hear. About your little girl. Do you have a picture?"

Tori dug her hand into a pocket in her faded blue dress, and removed a thin wallet. She unfolded it and slipped out a wallet-sized photo, handing it to Max. He took the photo and chortled as he saw the image of a toddler leaning against the side of a sofa wearing a blue knitted hat with a monster face on it, and nothing else but a diaper.

"Adorable," Max said with a grin. He grabbed his iPhone out of his pocket and unlocked it, flipping through his photos until he found one of him with his own daughter at the zoo. He showed it to Tori. "This was my daughter. She...died."

Tears glistened in Tori's eyes. "I'm so, so sorry," she said, clutching the phone delicately. "She was beautiful. Look, she had your nose."

Max put away the phone. "Thank you, Tori." It wasn't something he would have normally done, and he was certain he had not yet plied himself with enough alcohol to provoke such an act, but Max stepped forward and hugged the young maid. She wrapped her arms around him tightly, and the two sobbed together for a moment, before Max let go.

"Don't worry about me, Tori," Max said. "I am going to be okay."

Tori nodded.

Max didn't know if she believed it or not. He didn't know if he believed it himself. But he did feel as if something had changed. He knew meeting Tori wasn't an accident. He didn't believe in accidents. Everything happened for a reason. And sometimes those reasons weren't something you wanted.

"Are you sure you won't take my money?" Max said, holding out the two twenties. "For your daughter. A gift for Rosie."

Obviously a woman of great pride, Max knew it was with reluctance that Tori accepted his cash. But he knew it would help. And it was all he had left in his pocket.

"I hope to see you again someday, Tori," Max said.

"I hope so too," she said, dabbing her eyes with a tissue. "Wait, what's your name?"

"It's Maxwell," Max said. "Maxwell Sutherland."

"You're a good guy, Max."

Max stepped back inside his room a changed man. He had come to Miami with only one purpose: to take his own life. He hadn't been certain whether or not he would kill himself with the pawn shop pistol, or if he would have simply drunk himself into a coma he'd never wake from.

When he had entered his motel room ten minutes earlier, his life's mission had remained the same. But now he knew he couldn't do it. If only because Josue would be the one who would suffer. A stranger had showed kindness to Tori, and it had changed her whole life. She was happy now, whole.

Even though he hadn't chosen to be, Max had become the stranger to show kindness to the forlorn Haitian. Destiny had brought them together for that one fateful moment in the middle of Lemon Street. Max knew he had the power to change everything for Josue. It felt like his new reason for living. He would do anything he could for Josue, to help the younger man find a better life.

CHAPTER 24

MOMO PARTED THE CURTAINS THAT covered the front window in the dank living room of Big Flow's salmon-colored concrete house. The gang leader's shabby home was right next door to Momo's, his with the peeling seafoam green stucco walls, and the black bars over the doors and windows. The two houses were the epicenter of Lemon Street and, as far as he was concerned, Little Haiti itself. As Momo gazed suspiciously out the window, seeing nothing out of the ordinary to catch his eye, Big Flow approached him, stopping uncomfortably close to his face.

"Expecting someone?" Big Flow asked.

As Momo looked away from the window, the gang leader locked eyes with him in an intense gaze that was hard to look away from.

"Naw, man," Momo said, letting go of the curtain and stepping away from the window to break Big Flow's stare. He faced the middle of the room, where a glass coffee table sat in front of two couches, one of which was occupied by Tiny Deege and Zann, and another with two other members of the gang who were new enough that Momo kept forgetting their names. "Jus' bein' vigilant, my brother. Never let down your guard. Right?"

"You've been somewhat...distracted today, Momo," Big Flow said, tipping his head back to brush his long dreads off his shoulder as he moved forward to stand directly in front of the other man again. He reconnected his gaze into Momo's eyes.

"Seems like somethin' might be on your mind."

Momo didn't know if he should tell the gang's violent leader exactly what he was thinking, about the questions he had about the man's decision-making abilities, and by extension, his authority to be the head of the gang.

"Naw," Momo said, bringing his hand to his face to rub his eyes. He was relieved to again separate the face-lock he had with the other man. "Jus' a little tired."

"You should get some rest, my friend," Big Flow said, reaching his hand into his right pocket. "I don't want you to become... unhealthy, from a lack of rest."

Momo felt the grip of the Kahr PM9 in his own pocket. Tiny Deege always called the little 9mm pistol a "mouse gun." The truth was, the little semi-automatic pistol probably fit better into the small, high-strung man's hand. But Momo liked the petite weapon's concealment, and the idea that he could pack so much punch into such a small size. So he carried the tiny pistol with the three-inch barrel as a backup to his powerful .50 caliber Desert Eagle. Presently, he tucked his thick right index finger inside the small trigger guard of the polymer-framed weapon, and tilted the barrel upward, aiming toward the middle of Big Flow's chest.

"You can always open up to me, Momo," Big Flow said. "I would hate it if you had something important to say to me, but you held it back for some reason." Though he was virtually uneducated, the gang's leader had spent his time in prison, and the years following his release, filling his mind with knowledge, studying Plato, Nietzsche, Karl Marx. In the years that had followed prison, the volatile young Haitian had become a frightening and articulate leader of men. But Momo had had just about enough of it.

"Yo, man, I ain't scared of that icepick you carry around with you," Momo said, his eyes wide with defiance. "An' I don't think yo' tactics were on point when you shot that security guard, and when you led with the gun, took out that couple o' geezers on they yacht. An' I know we could'a got away from them cops on the River. Now we gotta watch our backs, every Miami cop this side'a retirement gonna come gunnin' for us. Dig?"

In a flash, Big Flow brought the sharp point of the screwdriver close to Momo's face. Momo had sensed him stop short of his throat in just enough time to keep himself from pulling the trigger and shooting Big Flow in the chest.

"It's not only the instrument of death that matters, Momo," Big Flow said, waving the deadly weapon back and forth in front of Momo's face. "It is also paramount one knows how best to put it to use. I've spent a great deal of time learning the anatomy of the human body. And what a wonder it is, my friend. Some guys just go for the jugular, on the right side of the neck. Here," Big Flow said, touching his left index finger against the side of Momo's neck.

Momo couldn't brush off the shudder in his body, as the menacing gang leader touched his throat.

"But I prefer to lay open the carotid artery on the *left* side, to allow one's own heart to expel the blood from his body like gas from a pump. I know you know, Momo, I always strike with purpose; I show my victim that his life was *always* in my hands. That there was never anything he could have done to have saved himself."

A zit-faced member of the gang, probably only sixteen or seventeen, walked in the front door, stopping short as he took in the sight of Momo and Big Flow locked in a hyper tense moment. The youth's Nike t-shirt must have been three or four sizes too large, and his Florida Marlin's cap was cocked sideways.

"Yo, sorry, Big," the young gangster said, closing the door behind him. He was relatively new, Momo had only seen him around a couple of times before. His name was Wily Beeve. "But I was shady dealin' weed over by the yellow house, bein' real careful an' whatnot. Sold a kid a twenty-dollar dimebag out behind the vacant lot, an' went back inside the house. Looked out the windows an' I seen two crackers in a creeper van takin' pictures o' the house. Sneaked away soon as I could, came right here to warn you, Big. Did I do the right thing?"

Big Flow lowered his unnerving weapon and looked at the kid with a relieved expression on his face. The charismatic leader placed his hand on the back of the younger man's neck. "So you spotted these men surveiling the yellow house—the same house we've been selling ganj from for years—and you came here directly, to warn me?" the menacing gang leader asked, his lips forming a charming smile.

"It's all good, right?" the kid said expectantly.

"Thank you, young Beeve," Big Flow said. "For wanting to warn me."

The kid smiled and nodded.

"Far better would it have been had you run from here, and never looked back," Big Flow said, malice obvious now in his voice.

With lightning-quick efficiency, the gang leader stabbed Wily Beeve with his well-seasoned screwdriver. He thrust the sharp point through the kid's baggy black jeans, likely stabbing right through his femoral artery. Then, in a blur of motion, Big Flow stabbed the tool through the kid's third and fourth ribs to puncture his heart. And then, a second later, he stabbed downward with the screwdriver, pounding it deep into the top of the kid's skull with a sickening thunk.

The unfortunate youth's body twitched violently, as if he was about to jump off a diving board into a swimming pool. And then Wily's body crumpled into a contorted heap on the floor.

Tiny Deege grabbed a bucket of Shakey Redbone's chicken from the coffee table and barfed into it. The other gang members offered varying groans of uneasiness at Big Flow's shocking and violent action.

"Aw, man," Zann said, sounding perturbed. He punched his fist into the little man's arm. "I's gonna eat that last breast."

"See, Momo," Big Flow said. "The idea you're unafraid gives you a stout heart, my friend. But I am afraid it does not show the greatest soundness of mind. Even a fool would look at Wily Beeve's wretched remains and see that I killed him three times, in three different ways, before he even hit the floor. To defy me shows bravery, Momo. But you gotta ask yourself, does it show wisdom?"

Momo glared at the menacing leader. His finger ached to pull the trigger.

"Get rid of this carcass," the gang's psychotic leader said. He kicked his foot hard into the stomach of the unfortunate dead teenager. Then the murderous man pulled a domino—blank on both sides with only a line in the center—out of his pocket. He wiped it down with a cloth and placed it into the kid's shorts pocket.

"Double zero?" Tiny Deege said. "Gonna make 'em think the kid's part o' that half-assed Cuban gang, Code 31?"

"You're a quick study, little brother," Big Flow said.

Momo knew that the gang called Code 31, so named for the Miami Police Department's radio code for murder, was Ti Flow's most bitter band of rivals. It was a shameful thing to do; to make one of ours look like one of theirs. He wanted no part of it.

"Take the body down to the river," Big Flow said. "Take him to where we killed the cops the other night, and dump him in the water."

Momo just glared at the dreadlocked man.

"Do this, and I just might forget you defied me, Momo."

CHAPTER 25

MAX RAPPED HIS KNUCKLE ON the door to his room at the Paradiso Inn. As he waited, Max began to wonder if the young refugee had gone out of the room to get something. "Josue," Max yelled. "It's just me, Max. I'm back. Could you let me in?"

The door finally squeaked open a few inches, and Josue's face appeared. Through the narrow gap between the splintering, faded orange door and its jamb, Max observed the hurt in the Haitian's eyes, the deep sting from Max's betrayal.

Pity, Max thought. *I'd hoped there was still a chance the kid hadn't yet seen the note.* It had been a terrible thing for Max to do, to abandon the younger man at such a critical time. But he *had* changed his mind. And now, Max wanted to make things right.

"Sorry, Josue," Max said, forcing a smile, "but I must have dropped my key somewhere uptown. Can you let me in?"

"You leave me note saying you not coming back," Josue said. He appeared to be crestfallen. "Why you even come back? You forget rum?"

"I'm sorry," Max said, throwing up his hands. He felt exasperated. The weak little chain on the door prevented Max from entering the motel room. "I was wrong. Okay? I was wrong."

Josue handed the thick bundle of cash Max had left for him through the thin door opening. He dropped it, and the hundred-dollar bills spilled all over the cracking concrete balcony around

Max's feet. "You take money. You leave me," Josue said. "I take care of myself."

Max turned around and leaned against the railing, looking over the few cars in the Paradiso Inn's parking lot, and beyond, at Shakey Redbone's. He didn't know what to do. He stared out, as if into blank space. Now *he* was starting to feel lost.

As he gazed over the bleak, sun-bleached street in front of him, images of his wife, his son, his daughter flooded his brain. The barrage of images came at him so quickly and suddenly, and there were so many of them, that he couldn't seem to control them: Max's daughter immediately after she was born, looking sunburned and bloody, cord still attached; his son falling off a Big Wheel, landing face-first on the sidewalk; he saw his wife decorating a cake for his birthday when the frosting bag exploded all over the cake and her face—first the expression of horror, then the cacophony of laughter that overtook them both; he saw his whole family at Walt Disney World, the joyful looks of wonderment on his kids' faces as they made their first steps inside the park; he saw his daughter's body riddled with bullets; he saw his wife doubled over, blood-soaked, and crying in pain; his son's body floating face down in the Atlantic Ocean, his blood staining the clear turquoise blue of the water.

Max fell down to his knees, still clinging to the second floor balcony's railing. He tried to let go, to allow himself to cry, but tears didn't come. Max struggled, his throat gurgling, and his body lurching in wracking convulsions; it sounded like some kind of piteous dry-heaving.

He didn't know what was happening to him, but it was painful. He felt as if the sorrow borne by his heart was so profound that tears were simply an insufficient expression of his grief. Max wondered if he might die, right there on the second floor balcony, his heart broken.

And then Max felt a warm hand settle gently on his left shoulder.

Max turned and looked up at Josue. The younger man's eyes looked down, filled with compassion.

Max began to sob. It was as if a plug had been tugged out of a bathtub. His shoulders shook powerfully as he wept. His hands covered his face. But the stinging tears brought an almost immediate sense of relief.

"Come inside, boss," Josue said, his voice quiet and kind. "Come inside."

Max pulled himself up on the railing and stood to his feet. He followed Josue inside the shabby room. He took off his blazer and dropped it on the floor next to his bed. He dragged in his Buccaneers bag with his clean laundry, bottles of rum, and his laptop. Max sat on the edge of the bed and propped his elbows against his thighs, resting his face on his hands.

"You want me to get you something to eat, drink?" Josue asked, standing in the center of the room, looking at Max uncomfortably.

Max shook his head.

"Max, you bleeding," Josue said, great urgency in his voice. He stabbed a long dark index finger toward Max's left hip.

Max looked down and saw the patch of blood spreading through his light blue Tommy Bahama twill shirt.

"You all right, boss?"

"Why are you calling me boss?" Max asked, as he lifted the shirt to get a better look at his wound.

"You in charge. You make decisions."

"I'm not in charge," Max said, letting go of his shirt. He rubbed his eyes. "I don't even know which end is up anymore."

"What happened to you?" Josue asked. "Why you bleed?"

Max didn't want to tell his new roommate what had actually happened to him. It seemed wrong. The young Haitian had already endured enough of his own pain. What good would come from Max sharing his?

Josue sat down at the foot of his own bed. He looked at Max with an eager, expectant look on his face.

Max looked down at the dirty carpet. "A couple months ago I was fishing with my wife, and my kids, down in the Keys." Max looked up at Josue's large, kind, almost childlike eyes. "Someone shot at us. I was shot." He couldn't bring himself to tell the other man the rest of the story.

Josue looked horrified. His mouth gaped open.

"I was shot here," Max said, poking his finger into his left shoulder, "here," he said, pointing to his left forearm, "here," he touched his finger to his thigh, "and here," he said, lifting his shirt to reveal the seeping wound on his hip.

"You shot with gun?" he asked.

Max nodded soberly.

"I am sorry, boss," Josue said. "I am so sorry."

"I thought this wound had finally healed all the way," Max said with an overwrought laugh. "Suppose I haven't been taking very good care of it, probably exerted myself and pulled it open again."

"Let me look," Josue said. He lifted Max's shirt and inspected the wound. "Needs clean bandage, disinfect. Where can we get?"

Max decided they needed a lot of things. Josue's possessions seemed to consist of the clothes on his back, and whatever was in his pockets; the displaced Haitian fiddled nervously with a silver pendant and chain, possibly belonging to a loved one who had perished in the quake.

Max decided it would be good to buy Josue some changes of clothing, some toiletries. Max could get a first aid kit with some antiseptic and some butterfly bandages to close his wound.

Max and Josue took a cab to the nearest Kmart store, which was about a fifteen-minute drive from the motel. Once inside, Josue looked around as if he had taken his first steps inside Walt

Disney World. His eyes wandered from the bright overhead signage to the racks of clothing, sunglasses, Blu Ray movies, candy, chewing gum, whatever anybody could want.

Max took Josue straight back to the men's department and had the Haitian try on some shirts for size. Once Max ascertained that Josue's long, lithe torso fit best into an extra-large, he grabbed a few button-ups, a few packages of Fruit-of-the-Loom t-shirts and underwear, and some socks. Max had Josue try on some cargo shorts and long pants. He also picked out a couple of hoodies, a light jacket, a couple of pairs of shoes, tossing it all into the shopping cart.

"You'll need a big duffel bag or something to keep all of your stuff," Max said, handing Josue a belt so that he could check its size around his waist. "And maybe a backpack, for when you don't want to carry everything with you."

"Is this how every American shops?" Josue asked, his eyes bulging as he looked at the heap of brand-new clothing in the shopping cart.

"Pretty much." Max wondered if Josue had ever been given anything new before in his life. He had to continually remind himself of the cultural differences between Josue growing up outside Port au Prince, and himself inside Orlando, the vacation capital of the world. His mind recalled the shopping trips he had made with his wife to buy clothes for his kids. That all seemed like a lifetime ago now.

Max bought toothbrushes, toothpaste, razor blades, shaving cream, deodorant—which he had to explain to Josue how to use—soap, shampoo, conditioner. Max couldn't believe how much stuff was piling up in the cart, but he simply wanted to share everything with Josue that he felt the younger man had been missing out on all his life.

Max pushed the cart past the section of the store where little girls' dresses draped across headless mannequins, and bright signage of happy little girls splashing at a water park hung over racks of tiny little bathing suits.

Max suddenly became overwhelmed.

He broke down. Max started to sob in a way that surprised him. Crying used to be something he could control, no matter what. But this was new. It was involuntary. He felt the warmth of the tears on his cheeks, causing them to itch as the salty drops rolled down.

"You okay, boss," Josue said, and it wasn't a question. He placed his hand on Max's shoulder. "You okay."

Now it felt like Josue was taking care of *him*. What a weird duo they had become. Max wondered about the nature of their relationship. Was Max the father figure? Were they more like brothers? It didn't matter. The two men clearly needed each other to get to the next rung in the ladder of their respective lives, whatever that would bring.

Max paid for all of the stuff and called a cab to take them back to the motel in Little Havana. When they got back, Max showed Josue how to rip off all the tags, peel off the sizing stickers, and fold everything to put away in the room's dresser drawers. And then they went over to Shakey Redbone's and grabbed a Fiery Feast, which was a bucket of the spicy Nashville-style chicken with large containers of spicy baked beans, and jalapeño cornbread.

They returned to the motel room with the food and sat down at the rickety table to eat. As they sat munching on the chicken, Max stopped, and looked at the other man with an expression of deep gravity.

Max hesitated for a long moment, and then said, "Josue?"

"Yes, boss?"

"I think I am going to stop drinking," Max said. "The rum, I mean."

"Okay," Josue said. He didn't seem to care a great deal either way about the matter.

But Max knew he wasn't much good to his friend wasted on booze, constantly needing another drink just to keep his body from attacking itself, and just waiting for the next moment when he'd mustered up enough courage, or enough sadness, to finally take his own life.

"What can I do?" Josue said.

Max smiled. He explained to Josue that he would use the rum he had bought to help him wean himself of dependence on alcohol. Max figured he'd been drinking way more than a fifth of rum every day. And it seemed as if he had drunk a bit more each day he had been in Miami.

He explained to Josue that they would take the first bottle of Zaya rum and pour out two shots, replacing them with water. Max would then drink the entire bottle over the course of one day. The next bottle, they would pour out four shots, which would be replaced with water, and Max would polish off that the following day. Then, they would pour out six shots from the next bottle and so forth. This would go on until Max could get through the day with no alcohol at all.

"I'll experience withdrawals," Max said. "My pulse will race, I'll get headaches, anxiety, maybe some hallucinations…"

"I will help you, boss," Josue said. He flashed that bright white grin that Max had been so surprised to see before. His smile would never betray his upbringing in a third world country.

Max took a big bite from a crispy breaded chicken breast and clicked on the TV. An old episode of *Miami Crime Squad* appeared. "Awww, man!" he beamed, turning up the volume on the old set. "I used to beg my parents to let me stay up and watch this show every Friday night. I must have been about nine then."

Max explained to Josue that each week the show's heroes, two undercover Miami detectives named Charleston Corbin and Palomar Teete, thrilled viewers with hair-raising shootouts, car and boat chases, and shocking endings that usually resulted in someone being shot, blown up, or a villain getting away.

"Palomar Teete is a street-smart detective used to taking on the violent gangs on the treacherous streets of Kingston, Jamaica. He moved to Miami as part of an international police exchange specialty task force, in order to pursue the man who killed his mother, Iris. He usually wears that black undershirt tank top, the white jeans, red suspenders, and the black Greek fisherman's hat. His .44 magnum pistol has a barrel so long that when he tucks it into his pants, it makes him walk with a limp."

"And the other guy?" Josue asked.

"Charleston Corbin is a hot-tempered redhead who cut his teeth policing on the mean streets of Belfast before emigrating to the US and becoming a Boston cop...before transferring to Miami. He carries three guns: a Smith & Wesson 645, a Walther P38 strapped to his ankle, and an Uzi submachine gun, which he wears on a sling under his turquoise linen sports coat. He was always leaving behind smoldering rubber from the tires of his 5.0L Mustang convertible. See? There it is."

Josue laughed as he watched the irritable redhead drive his ragtop, top down, through a carwash in pursuit of a fleeing vehicle. Charleston Corbin skidded out of the carwash soaked, his cherry red convertible filled with sudsy water.

Max chuckled as he watched, memories of the show flooding back to him. He nudged the bucket of chicken closer to the Haitian.

Max laughed to himself; it was the kind of laughing you might see a person doing on the sidewalk, immediately before you crossed the street and continued on your way on the other side.

"What is it?" Josue asked, his curiosity piqued.

"I always thought my life would have turned out a lot different," Max said, gazing past the TV set and staring wistfully at the chipped yellow paint of the wall across the room. "When I was a kid, I thought for sure I'd grow up and be somebody like

Charleston Corbin or Palomar Teete; I'd live a dangerous lifestyle of adventure and crazy times. I'd drive a fast exotic car, maybe fly a jet. Live in a luxurious penthouse in a downtown high-rise. I don't know how I charted a course from that thrill-seeking, wide-eyed kid, all the way to a grown-up life as an accountant. But somehow, I did."

Max felt Josue's stare. He knew the younger man couldn't fully understand the complexity of what he was trying to say. Growing up outside of Port au Prince, the lithe refugee's grown-up dreams must have been far more modest than Max's. Maybe he wasn't as concerned with growing up to be something, as he was with just growing up.

Max looked down at the cardboard case of Trinidadian and Tobagonian rum against the wall under the window. He knew a difficult couple of weeks lay ahead of him as he detoxified himself. He knew the side effects alone would be horrific. But the thing that frightened him the most was the clarity his mind would encounter. He wasn't sure he was ready to see the world as it really was.

CHAPTER 26

MOMO CLICKED OFF THE SIXTY-FIVE inch flat screen that covered most of one of the walls in his tiny living room. The mammoth gang member stood up from his couch and walked the short hallway to Tiny Deege's room. He found the petite man sitting on his bed, holding a torch lighter underneath the bulb of a glass pipe, which he held to his lips. The diminutive man looked up at Momo. He removed the pipe from his mouth, exhaling a cloud of thick white smoke.

"Yo, Tiny," Momo said, leaning against the side of the doorjamb, while the top of his short afro brushed against the top part of the jamb. "Time to get rid of your Cutlass. Just seen on the news the cops be lookin' for a bright, candy orange tuner. You gotta dump it 'fore you bring the wrong kinda heat back here. Dig?"

"Man, my ride ain't no tuner car," Deege protested. He set the glass pipe down onto a heavy ashtray on the bedside table and stood up. The Lilliputian gangbanger's head reached the middle of Momo's chest, and he probably weighed about half as much as an average-sized man. "Tuners be for chumps tryin' to get away from stuff. I ain't tryin' to get away from nothin'. Tuner guys always tryin' to go fast, go fast, beat the other guy. Man, I drive through the 'hood, I'm takin' my time, you know what I'm sayin'? Ain't zippin' to and fro, trying to outrun nobody."

"You gotta get rid of it," Momo reiterated. His stern tone made him feel as if he sounded bossy, and he didn't like it. He wasn't trying to be Deege's dad, he just knew what Big Flow might do if the conspicuous car led the police back to Lemon Street. "The car is marked. 5-0 is on the lookout for it. Gotta dump your whip."

"Can't part with my donk, Momo," Tiny Deege said, gazing up at the larger man with a desperate look in his eyes. His tone sounded like pleading. "Yo, that car belonged to my grandma. Thing's an heirloom. You can't make me dump it, Momo."

Momo knew the customized Oldsmobile looked a lot different now than it had when Tiny Deege's ancient grandmother had scooted around Miami in it in the eighties and nineties, getting prune juice and cabbage or whatever at the grocery store, and cruising to the pharmacy for Bengay, or old lady cream, or whatnot.

Tiny Deege had taken the car to a custom shop, where they had tricked it out with twenty-two inch Dayton rims, hydraulic suspension, leather interior, and fabricated special elongated gas and brake pedals to accommodate the short man's legs, and had installed a boosted seat so he could see over the dash. The bright orange House of Kolor paint was the main reason the car had to go, why it stood out like a road flare at midnight.

Momo reached into his pocket and pulled out a bundle. "Here's two grand. Wait 'til dark and take your car down to Holmes Wrecking Yard down by the river and tell Charles Roach that Momo sent you. Don't speak to nobody but Charles Roach. Give him the money and tell him you gotta make it like this car never was.

"Dig? Like it *never was*. An' you gotta watch him crush it, make sure he do it. 'Cause if he don't, if he send it out to be chopped or somethin', it could bring a lotta unwanted heat back to the Flow. An' you don't want that, Tiny. Do you?"

Tiny Deege appeared to be close to tears. "What if I put it in a storage locker or somethin', Momo? Don't take it out for a year or somethin'? The car's got a lotta sentimental meaning to me, brother. My cousin, Teezy Bertram, was almost born in the backseat. Had to replace the backseat cover and everything. Got a lotta memories fo' me."

"No, man," Momo said, doing his best to sound brotherly. "Sorry. Gotta be destroyed. Tonight."

"But—" Tiny Deege started another round of protest, but was cut off.

"You don't like it, you go talk to Big," Momo said, now glaring at Tiny Deege with a smolder in his eyes. "You go and tell him why you ain't gonna listen to Momo. Why you don't care if the 5-0 comes lookin' for yo' whip on Lemon Street."

Tiny Deege looked at the floor. "Awright, Momo. I do it."

Momo slapped the cash into the little man's child-sized palm. "Tonight."

Deege nodded.

"Gonna find somethin' new to drive in no time, my brother," Momo said, trying to sound reassuring.

"Meantime, you gonna go out with Zann this afternoon, drive around Little Haiti, keep an eye out for that chump, Josue," Momo said. "Big Flow want us all canvassing the neighborhood 'til that punk turns up. Feel me?"

Tiny Deege nodded again.

"You spot him, you tell me," Momo said. "I wanna be the one." He looked down at the smaller man, almost as if he were looking through him, as his mind drifted. "I wanna be the one to smoke that chump, Josue."

CHAPTER 27

NEARLY A WEEK OF MAX'S self-imposed detox program had run its course. Day by day, Josue had dutifully poured rum from the bottles, shot by shot, replacing the void with fresh water, handing shots of diluted liquor to Max at the appointed times.

Max knew it was working. As the violent trembling in his hands and chest had subsided, and the powerful headaches, lucid nightmares, and skin-shivering night sweats had lessened, he now found his head clearer, his heart rate slower, and himself much less anxious than before.

The downside to his newfound sobriety was becoming painfully evident; Max remembered things more clearly and coherently than when he'd been drunk. Thoughts of his wife and two young children flooded his mind like a torrent of dread.

"I can no longer tell the difference between tap water and a glass of water that's thirty percent barrel-aged Nicaraguan rum," Max said, looking down at his motel room glass with a sour expression.

Josue smirked. He looked dapper in his new khaki cargo shorts, fitted black workout undershirt, and a short-sleeved turquoise button-up. A long way from the faded black shorts and filthy white t-shirt that Max was convinced still bore the stench of death from the deceased loved ones Josue had buried with his own hands. "You drink all, or no dessert," the Haitian joked.

Max had had to explain to him that it was all right for him to take a shower every day, to change his clothes every day. But the displaced refugee caught on quickly to American culture. In no time, he was taking half-hour long showers, and smelling like the sporty deodorant Max had bought him.

Each time the young Haitian had opened the bathroom door after a shower, stepping out after a big cloud of steam that burst into the room, Max had seen him perform the same ritual: Josue would place his mother's silver chain with the pendant of Our Lady of Perpetual Help around his neck; he would dig through the pocket of the shorts he had been wearing the previous day, snatching out the torn envelope and card from the aunt who had turned him away; and then he would fold the dirty clothes, placing them in a neat pile beside his new duffel bag.

Every few days they had walked across the street, to a nearby launderette to wash their dirty clothes. Max even dropped off his rank blazer to be Martinized.

The two men had enjoyed Shakey Redbone's Southern Fried Chicken for every meal since they had moved into the Paradiso Inn: breakfast, lunch, dinner, and dessert. Having sampled virtually everything on the menu, both men had found that Shakey Redbone's menu offered such variety that the unlikely roommates had scarcely gotten tired of the tasty southern fried food.

Max and Josue had noshed on a smorgasbord of unique items: Heirloom Recipe Crispy Chicken Hands, which were chicken breasts sliced apart and fried to look like a strange, twisted hand; Chewy Cheese-Stuffed Chicken Breast Burritos; Crunchy Chicken Thigh Torpedoes; Half-Sized Herbert's Mini Chicken Sliders; Catfish-Style Chicken Breast Filets that prompted Max to wonder how they had managed to give the chicken a fishy taste—he had only ordered it once; Boneless Breadless Nuggets that were slimy bites of pale boiled chicken—Max found them annoying because the dipping sauce would just slide right off; Superlative Strips, that were excessively crispy, even painfully crispy—they tore up the roof of Max's mouth even worse than Captain Crunch cereal ever had; and, finally, the Stupidly Crispy, Triple-Breaded Thickie Chickie Sandwich.

The two men had also enjoyed more side dishes than they could keep track of, ranging from traditional coleslaw and mashed potatoes to more exotic offerings, like Gruyere and Pear Squash Casserole. But the favorite thing on the menu, for both Max and Josue, was the Perfect Petite Parfaits, which were little cups of graham cracker crust topped with sweet whipped cream, and layered with strawberry, chocolate, or coconut filling.

Max knew he'd already gained about ten pounds since they had checked into the Paradiso Inn, and it heartened him to see the extra weight packing onto the frame of the still-slender Haitian as well.

"Don't burn the bacon, Pal," Charleston Corbin said to Palomar Teete, the fiery Irish cop's tinny voice uttering the salty character's personal catchphrase from the room's outdated TV set. The afro-clad detective from Kingston flashed a pearly smile and gave two thumbs up. Max remembered that was sort of Palomar Teete's trademark, the thumbs.

"What that mean?" Josue asked. "About the burning of bacon?"

"I didn't know when I was a kid," Max said, looking at Josue with an expression of befuddlement, "and I still don't."

Miami Crime Squad had played in the background of Max and Josue's lives for the entire week; one of the local networks was running a continuous marathon, playing all one hundred and thirteen episodes, back to back, nonstop. The two men had left it on the whole time, going about their business, sometimes listening to the eighties cop show in the background as they conversed, sometimes tuning in, engaged, and watching as they ate, with rapt attention.

"That's him!" Josue shouted, stabbing his finger toward the television.

At first Max wondered what he was talking about, his curiosity only slightly piqued. But when Josue jumped up on his bed and started shouting, Max sat up, startled, wondering what was going on.

"That's him! That's him, Maxwell! That's Austin!" Josue bellowed.

"That's *who*?" Max asked, before draining his glass of diluted rum.

"It's Austin, the man who let me ride on boat," Josue said. "He told me where to go to get on boat. He made it so I can come to America. That's *him*!"

Max gazed at the TV, feeling flabbergasted. He looked back at Josue. He could tell the young Haitian wasn't messing with him.

"Austin Steelhouse is the guy who set you up on the boat?" Max asked, thinking his own voice sounded as astonished as he felt.

Josue nodded vigorously.

Max turned back to the TV, where a much younger version of Austin Steelhouse lay on the deck of a yacht next to an aluminum briefcase that had burst open, spilling its contents of hundreds of thousands of dollars in loose cash. The character Austin played clutched his hand to his blood-stained chest, covering the spot where Charleston Corbin had just shot him.

"You met Austin Steelhouse? In Port au Prince?"

"In my village outside of Port au Prince," Josue corrected.

"Austin Steelhouse?"

"Him same guy," Josue said. "Told me where to go to get on his boat."

"Austin Steelhouse is one of the most famous movie actors in the world, Josue," Max said. "His most recent movie, *The Apocalypse Paradox*, just became the highest grossing movie of all time. Everybody knows Austin Steelhouse. He's a household name."

Max thought back over his week. Many times they had checked the news to find out if the police were closer to finding the men who had killed those two cops on the Miami River. He was sure now he recalled watching a story where one of the major news networks had interviewed Austin Steelhouse because he had hopped on a jet to go straight to Port au Prince in order to help out, to do whatever he could, as soon as he had received word of the devastating magnitude 7.0 earthquake.

Max looked at Josue and laughed. *What a small and crazy world*, he thought.

"He a nice man," Josue said, sounding quite serious. "Help me bury my mother, my uncle, and my sister."

The two men watched a couple more episodes of *MCS* before Max stood up to address Josue, who was doing pushups on the floor of the room. The younger man stopped, sat on the floor. He wiped his brow with his sleeve, and looked up at Max.

"I've been thinking, Josue," Max said, "about going back home, up north to central Florida."

Josue looked wide-eyed, uncertain what Max might be saying. His sense of relaxed contentment had suddenly collapsed into blank-eyed reality. "Yes?" he said.

"That's where I am from, near Orlando," Max continued, "close to Walt Disney World."

"Walt Disney?" Josue asked.

Max half-grinned. Of course Josue wouldn't know anything about that. The hell of post-quake Port au Prince was a long way from the happiest place on earth. "I used to work at a big TV organization up there. A ministry on TV. The guy I worked for, Terry, knows a lot of people. What do you think about coming up there with me? We can find a place to live, we'll each have a room of our own. And I bet Terry knows some people who might be able to help you immigrate to the US legally—especially considering your situation. I think the idea that you were being forced into a gang in Port au Prince, that you fled from that, makes you a bona fide refugee. You could seek asylum."

"You want me to live…with you?" Josue asked, and the life flickered back inside his eyes.

"Well, yeah," Max said; he couldn't escape the feeling that he needed to protect the young Haitian like a surrogate son, as painful as it was. Max's sense of responsibility for Josue was like an irritating abrasive that continually rubbed his conscience, constantly reminding him of his own son. Deep in his core, Max knew it was the right thing to do, even if it would be difficult.

"After everything we've been through, I can't just let you go find your way on your own. I'm certain we can get you a job doing something you like. After the way I left *my* job, I'm sure I'll have to find something else as well. But we can work things out, we can find our way together."

Josue's eyes glistened. Max guessed he wasn't used to receiving such kindness, not from strangers. Somehow too, Max wasn't so used to doling out such magnanimous gestures. Rarely did he let others into his small and private world.

Josue stepped toward Max, and Max, at first, wasn't sure why. When the other man spread out his arms, it was clear he intended to hug Max. As awkward as it was for Max, hugging a man he barely knew inside a crummy motel in the Little Havana neighborhood of Miami, he realized he hadn't felt quite so alive in a very long time. He slapped Josue on the back.

"Thank you, Maxwell," Josue said. "You my best friend."

Now it was Max's turn to tear up. It seemed a long time since he had thought about anyone as a friend. He felt like if he spoke, he might break down, so Max just nodded.

The two men plunked down onto their respective beds for another episode of *Miami Crime Squad*, during which an alarm went off on the Timex watch Max had bought the Haitian at Kmart.

Josue carefully poured out another glass of diluted rum. "Now, you drink your medicine," he said, looking quite serious.

The episode of *Miami Crime Squad* that was playing on TV revealed that Palomar Teete had a son. Max couldn't keep thoughts about his own son out of his head. He and Lovelle would have been celebrating his birthday soon.

Max felt queasy.

The scene continued, showing Charity, a woman Detective Teete had once been in love with, traveling by seaplane with her infant son on her lap. Palomar hadn't even known he had a son; he'd only found out when Charity had sent a telegram saying she was fleeing the country and taking the baby with her, and that she hoped Palomar would join them in Jamaica.

Palomar's old flame laughed and played patty cake with the baby, while she peered out the window of the airplane as it circled a protected harbor near Kingston, where the seaplane was about to land.

Palomar Teete stood on a pier, waving up at the plane. He had quit the Miami-Dade police force to move back to Kingston. He, Charity, and his baby son, Simeon, were about to be united, to become a family once and for all.

In a shocking season finale, Detective Teete watched helplessly as the seaplane exploded into a massive fireball right before his eyes. He gasped, falling to his knees on the pier. The following season would reveal that the explosion had been no accident; a bomb had been planted in the plane by Teete's mortal enemy, Chico Cabrera. The devastating event would send Palomar back to Miami, partnering once again with Charleston Corbin.

Max breathed deeply, as he watched one of his childhood TV heroes losing his family. He didn't want to let Josue know he was upset.

A long camera shot, dollying past row after row of ornate pews, their hand-carved sides passing by slowly as the viewer was led down the aisle of a dark church, its features lit only by candles, and the light diffused through its sumptuous stained-glass windows. At last, the camera stopped, framing a tight shot of two caskets. One was crafted of rich dark wood, with shimmering polished hand rails. The other casket was small, white, child-sized.

Max bolted from the bed and pushed open the bathroom door. He knelt beside the toilet for a moment. His body lurched as his stomach heaved. Nothing came up, but the nausea did not pass. Max grabbed the toilet seat with both hands and hung on, as if for dear life. He dry-heaved a couple more times.

Max remembered the time he had stood by his four-year-old daughter and held her long blonde hair as she threw up copious amounts of spaghetti she'd gorged herself on that night at dinner, less than one year earlier. It had been one of the most disgusting moments of Max's life, and he now found himself kneeling before the toilet, wishing he could have that moment back.

Max sobbed until his tears gave way to wailing; pitiful, uncontrollable wailing. The sound was like the sickening high-pitched moan of a sick animal or some kind of terrifying fictional creature. Max knew he would have pitied any person or thing that could create such a deplorable sound.

Then he heard the light knock at the door.

He tried to stop himself, but Max was overcome with the clarity of his grief, now that he was mostly sober.

"You okay, boss?" Josue asked softly.

"I'll be out in a minute," Max said, when he had collected himself enough to speak. He stood up and leaned over the sink. His face in the mirror looked so much older than he had only recently seen himself. His old visage seemed like a distant shadow of what it now was—the image of a man with distant, soulless eyes, encircled by dark rings, with prickly stubble flecked with the odd strand of white or gray. Max splashed cold water on his face until it felt numb. Then he dabbed it dry with a towel.

He stepped out into the room, finding Josue standing in the middle of the room, facing him, a concerned expression on his face. Max walked past him and sat down at the foot of his bed.

Josue turned to face him.

Max looked up at the younger man. He knew Josue cared about Max, and why he might be hurting so badly. "I'm sorry, Josue. I wish you hadn't had to see me like this."

"It is okay," Josue said, sitting down on his own bed, and waiting for Max to speak. He seemed patient, as though he could wait all day to listen.

"When I came to Miami, I hadn't expected to have company," Max said.

Josue just looked at the floor.

"It's okay. I'm glad I have company...now. You see, when I told you I was shot on my vacation in Islamorada, I didn't tell you everything, Josue." Max's throat was dry. It hurt to swallow. "I didn't tell you what happened...to my family."

Josue looked at Max with wide, moonlike eyes. Max knew the young Haitian had tragedy of his own still stinging his psyche. Yet Max felt the other man's deep empathy in something as simple as a heartfelt look of concern.

"I'll tell you what, Josue," Max said, reaching down into his short's pocket and pulling out a hodgepodge of folding money. He peeled off a couple of bills and handed them across to Josue. "Why don't you go and grab us some chicken, and I'll tell you the whole story when you get back. It'll give me a little time to collect myself before we talk."

Josue stood up and smiled. "Yes, boss. I go and get food. Then we talk."

"Get all of the good stuff," Max added. "Let's have a feast

for lunch. And get a bunch of those little parfaits; man, I love those parfaits."

Josue grinned.

Max watched the lithe Haitian step out into the warm light of the late morning sun and close the door behind him. It would be good to tell someone his story. He had been carrying it around like a great, hundred-pound weight on the middle of his chest for the past few months. It would be good to let it out. As soon as Josue came back, Max would tell the young refugee everything.

CHAPTER 28

"WHEN THE HELL WERE YOU going to share this information, Lassen?" Lorenzo shouted, a pronounced purple vein pulsating on the right side of his neck as he screamed at the other man. "*There was a shooting on Lemon Street? Hours after the shooting at the River on the morning of the 16*th*? And no one bothered to tell the task force investigating the deaths of two Miami PD officers?"*

"Bring it down, Zo," Arthur said, positioning himself between the detective and the uniformed patrol officer.

"I'm sorry, Sergeant," said Officer Lassen, a young patrol officer, only slightly more seasoned than a rookie, "me and Lister filed our report last week, before he went on leave. I didn't make the connection until I heard someone talking about the 'running man' dropped off by cab on Lemon Street. And I just received that information for the first time this morning."

"What's all this?" Lieutenant Chato said in his typical soft-spoken yet no-nonsense way. The grim, black-clad lawman had stepped out of his office, and he now stood at the edge of Lorenzo's desk; placing one fist on the desktop, he tucked the thumb of his other hand into his belt. The lieutenant's face appeared expressionless, as usual.

"Supercop here withheld important information that could be critical to our murder investigation, Lieutenant," Lorenzo said, still fuming. "We could have closed this case by now."

"Share your side, Officer Lassen," Chato said, his voice even and calm, as he turned to face the young uniformed cop.

"Sorry, Lieutenant," Lassen said, his face growing redder by the second, "but my partner and I responded, along with a couple other units, to a possible 3-0 near Lemon Street in Little Haiti last Friday night...well, it would've been Saturday a.m. by the time. We received orders to take witness statements at the bar, but not to arrest anyone without approval."

"Lemon Street is volatile, Officer Lassen," Chato said, his voice barely above a whisper. "It's a little bit like the wild west. Nobody is above the law, but we try not to make any arrests there unless our evidence or probable cause is airtight, and then we go in force. The risk of harm—or worse—to one of our professionals is just too high if we're not going to make an impact."

Officer Lassen flipped through pages in his notebook. "Witness accounts said two guys—one black, one white—got into a cab in front of a bar on the corner of Lemon Street and Stonecrab Avenue. Two or three other guys gave chase and opened fire, hitting the cab. There were no injuries reported, and no one was killed. So we took the statements, filed our reports, and moved on."

"Without telling us about this," Lorenzo protested.

"Keep your conduct in check, Sergeant Ferrigno," Chato said, a serious, fatherly cadence to his tone. "Officer Lassen didn't thwart your investigation, nor was he derelict. It's unfortunate the connections weren't made sooner. Sergeant Brummagem and Officer Lister were both on leave last week—might have contributed to this falling through the cracks. It's an oversight, but it was not intentional. We have the information now. I expect you and Detective Parks to pursue this to its conclusion. Starting now."

"Yes, Lieutenant," Arthur said, grabbing his partner by the collar and pulling him toward the elevator. He collected Officer

Lassen's report, questioning the young policeman for a few minutes as they waited for the elevator car, gleaning whatever he could about the crime scene.

"Thanks, Rick," Arthur said to Lassen, patting the patrolman on the arm. "We'll get it sorted out."

The young cop smiled awkwardly and nodded.

Lorenzo drove himself and Art back to the Coral Cab dispatch office. They found a different dispatcher working than the one they had questioned almost a week prior. Lorenzo found the new one to be a suspicious yet forthcoming woman with highly damaged peroxide blonde hair; a face with a network of deep wrinkles and dark circles that suggested hard living beyond her years; and a dress that revealed an unpleasant amount of the middle-aged woman's ample cleavage. A freshly lit Camel 100 smoldered between her fingers with about an inch's worth of ash clinging to the tip.

"What can I do for you gentleman?" said the woman, whose desk plate read Sharona Pyle, as the two detectives approached her desk. "I hope it's something pleasurable."

Lorenzo flashed his shield. "My partner and I are looking for one of your drivers," Arthur said, looking down at Lassen's report, "one...Ronnie Vikram."

The dispatcher typed a few words into her computer. Lorenzo noticed the long, hot pink, press-on nails as they clacked over the keyboard with an unnerving clicking sound. "You're in luck, boys. Ronnie's on his way back here now. What do you need to talk to *him* about? He in trouble?"

"No, ma'am," Lorenzo reassured the dispatcher. "We just need to ask him a couple questions about some men he picked up the other night." He and Arthur took a seat, as far from the dispatcher's desk as they could, doing their best to avoid awkward conversation with the woman until the cab driver arrived, ten or twelve minutes later.

"Did you get the biopsy results yet?" Arthur asked.

"Tomorrow," Lorenzo said. "I'm supposed to get a call tomorrow."

"Any idea?" Arthur said, his eyes wide with concern.

Lorenzo shrugged. "Doctor's got one o' the best poker faces I ever seen. Didn't give away nothing."

"But what do you think? You got a gut feeling or anything?"

"Until I hear otherwise," Lorenzo said, folding his arms and leaning back in his chair, "it's just a mass."

"Ronnie. These cops—police officers—would like to speak with you," the dispatcher said when the dark-skinned, obviously Indian, turban-headed taxi driver entered the shabby dispatch office.

For a second, it looked as though Ronnie Vikram might make a run for it. Lorenzo saw the internal conflict in his eyes. The frightened cab driver likely processed the situation in less than a second. *Two detectives want to question me, I should bolt. No, wait, I didn't do anything wrong, did I?* was sort of how Lorenzo expected the internal dialogue might have gone in the immigrant cabbie's head. He'd seen it hundreds of times before in otherwise innocent people.

"We would just like to know a little about two men you picked up last Saturday, early," Arthur said, sounding sympathetic. Art played the good cop so well. But Lorenzo knew that if his partner's good nature couldn't win a person over, it would be time for Lorenzo to up the ante. He wasn't a bad cop, really. He just didn't dick around with people.

"Tell us about these two men you picked up in front of the tiki bar near Lemon Street," Arthur continued. "I understand someone was shooting at you when you picked them up."

"I did not ask for this trouble," Ronnie said, his voice tightening into a high-pitched rant, thick with a Mumbai accent. His mouth was small, his lips purple. "I did not even offer them my services.

I was only driving by at the wrong time. They stopped me. They forced their way into my cab. They brought me trouble that I do not ask for."

"Easy, friend," Arthur said. "Why don't you sit down, you'll be more comfortable."

Ronnie Vikram took a seat in one of the ripped, padded vinyl chairs that must have been new in the mid-seventies.

"Describe these men, the ones who got into the cab," Lorenzo said, stuffing a stick of Big Red into his cheek. He offered the pack to Ronnie, who gladly took three sticks. He tucked the foil-wrapped gum sticks into his shirt pocket for later enjoyment.

"They are crazy!" Ronnie said, turning his attention back to his high-strung tirade. "These men are magnets for bullets. They climbed into my cab. Bullets rained down upon it like fire from Naraka. I see my whole life flashing in my eyes. It was terrifying!

"Mother told me I could someday be the world's greatest proctologist," the worked-up cab driver said, his eyes beginning to bulge more the longer his tirade continued. "I studied in medical school for two years before I quit, to come to America, to become a cab driver."

Arthur nodded and grinned magnanimously. Lorenzo thought his partner looked like a patronizing prick. But he knew it was part of the amiable cop package.

"During my training to become a doctor, I performed nearly twenty examinations on different men in my village, to inspect the health of their prostate glands. How would you feel if you had done this, only to go on to become a cab driver?

"No wealth to speak of, no voluptuous blonde wife, no penthouse condominium in Bandra. Just a filthy apartment in a Little Havana slum; a blind cat that pees on my shoes; and Chinese takeout on Fridays.

"I wake up in a cold sweat because I remember the anus of the man my father used to play marbles with. I wake up screaming!

This is not the life I wanted, and now men are shooting their guns at me, just for driving into the wrong street."

"Easy, Ronnie," Arthur said, standing and placing a hand on each of the anxious cab driver's shoulders. "It's okay, man. It'll get better. Just take it easy."

Lorenzo rolled his eyes and checked his email on his iPhone.

"The thing that would help us most would be for you to describe the physical features of the two men who got into your cab Saturday morning," Art continued, his voice calm and soothing. Lorenzo thought his partner should have been a psychiatrist—or a horse whisperer, or something. "What did these two look like?"

"It's like I told the other officer," Ronnie said, his eyes flashing from side to side, wildly as he spoke. "One man was a black man, young, maybe twenty. He wore long black short pants and a dirty and ripped white t-shirt that smelled like dead people. I might have forgotten to tell the officer that I did notice a silver chain hanging around the young man's neck—it looked like a Catholic idol or something."

"What about this other guy?" Arthur asked, his fingers locked together except for both of his index fingers, which were pressed together and touching his lips.

"The other man was a white man, he looked drunk," the colorful cabbie said. "He had messy hair. Short, blond, light brown maybe. He was wearing a navy blue blazer and gray pants. And now that I recall...there was one thing I did not remember to say before about the man's face. His ear was scarred and scabbed—it looked like he'd been wearing a large earring that had been ripped out. The sight of it made me feel sick in my stomach."

"Which ear?" Lorenzo asked, expectantly, thinking Ronnie Vikram would have made a terrible doctor.

"The left."

"Art," Lorenzo said, sitting upright in his chair, "who does that sound like to you? The dirty-blond with the blazer and the ripped ear?"

Arthur thought for a moment, his mind working to assemble the pieces of the last week or so together in his mind. "It can't be..." His mouth hung open for a second in disbelief. "The dead guy?"

"Exactly," Lorenzo said. "I would bet you a pallet of Juicy Fruit the guy Vikram picked up was the same guy we found in the gutter that day. I would bet you."

Arthur nodded.

"You look like a famous tennis player I remember," Ronnie said. "I would think that you are him, but I know that he passed away some time ago. He suffered from the AIDS virus which he encountered from a blood transfusion. You look very much like this man. His name was Arthur Ashe."

"Thank you for your time," Arthur said to the animated cabbie. He and Lorenzo walked out into the bright sunlight of the parking lot.

"What do you think it means?" Arthur asked.

"It means our Haitian refugee, just off the boat, somehow hooked up with the dead guy," Lorenzo said, scratching his arm. "It means that wherever they are, for whatever reason, they're probably together. It means we're not looking for a black male youth. We're looking for a black male youth accompanied by a white male drunk, mid-thirties to forty."

Arthur opened the passenger door to the black Dodge, a sly half grin on his lips. "That sure as hell narrows down the pool."

CHAPTER 29

"HEY, MOMO," THE VOICE ON the phone said, "it's Hazy Junior."

"Yo, what up, Junior," Momo said, feeling perturbed that the youngest member of the gang would call during the construction of a monster hoagie. Momo had lunchmeat, sliced cheese, and jars of pickles, mustard, and jalapeños strewn all over the small kitchen counter. "Somethin' you need?"

"Hey, brother man, I know y'all been lookin' for that loser, Josue Remy," Hazy Junior said, blissfully unaware that his own brother had been murdered by the leader of the gang the young man had chosen to be part of. Momo sure as hell wasn't going to be the one to tell him. "Well, I think I spotted him! He's here, right inside. If'n it's him. Pretty sure it's him."

"Yo, where you at?" Momo said, dropping his mayonnaise-covered butter knife and drawing the bulky Desert Eagle fifty cal from his waistband. He pulled back on the slide of the powerful hand weapon and double-checked it had a round in the chamber. "I'll come directly."

"Yo, man, I came down to Little Havana, 'cause I wanted to go to Bongo's to get some new pipes. You know Bongo's, close to the casino down by the river where they play that weird game, throw the ball at the rock wall."

"Jai alai?" Momo asked, wondering how much longer until the young gangbanger might get to the point and tell him where to find the traitor, Josue.

"Yeah, yeah, that's it, Momo," Junior said, sounding animated. Momo guessed he was already tweakin'. "Well I went into Bongo's, bought me some glass pipes and a sweet-ass bong, you gotta see it, man—looks like an old-timey wizard bong from Middle Earth or somethin' like dat."

"Time you got to the point, young gun," Momo said, out of patience.

"Well, after Bongo's, I came down to Shakey Redbone's, 'cause I needed me some chicken. An' guess what. I seen that chump, Josue, at the counter orderin' everything off the menu. Soon as I recognized him, I came outside ta call you, brother. Dig?"

"Shakey Redbone's?" Momo asked, with urgency. "The one in Little Havana?"

"Yeah, man," Junior said. "He here *right now*."

"Keep yo' eyes on him, Junior," Momo ordered. "Feel me? He leaves, you don't confront, but you follow. Dig?"

"Yeah, I dig."

Momo sprinted from the kitchen, running back to Tiny Deege's room. He found the little man curled up on his bed, staring at the forty-two-inch flat screen on his bedroom wall. He was watching a reality show about a couple of bikers who were building a jet-powered Harley Davidson Electra Glide using an engine from a scrapped Learjet. "Yo, Deege, I know you had your car scrapped last night, but I gotta know, you replace it yet? You got somethin' else ta drive?"

Momo had never felt like he needed to have a car of his own. There were so many guys around him that drove sweet rides, that Momo always happily rode shotgun with someone. Now that he found himself desperate to get way down to Little Havana in a flash, he regretted not owning some kind of vehicle.

Wily Beeve had had a gorgeous '69 Lincoln, painted with metallic purple flake paint; but the flamboyant vehicle had been dumped in the river, along with his body.

Zann drove a tight '83 Monte Carlo, but he wasn't around.

"No," Tiny Deege said, an awkward pitch to his voice. "I ain't replaced it yet."

"Listen, I gotta get down ta Little Havana, and I got no time to wait around fo' a cab, so I'm open to suggestions. This is an emergency, man. Your cousins around? One of them gotta car?"

"I...I gotta way we can get down there," Tiny Deege said, speaking tentatively. "I didn't dump my whip last night. It's under a tarp down by Chester's house, the end'a the block. Just couldn't bring myself to do it, Momo. I tried, but I seen my grandma's face the whole time, like she was waggin' her finger in my face, saying 'no, Deege, don't you do that to my donk. Don' you crush it, little man.'"

"We'll talk about me pistol-whippin' yo' ass later, Tiny," Momo said, grabbing the smaller man by the shirt and pulling him toward the door. "We gotta go. Now!"

The two men ran down the street until they reached a house that looked as if it had been condemned, a rusty chain link fence containing it like a crime scene. Outside, a moldy tarp sat like a big lumpy rock next to a tall denuded pine tree out front.

Momo gave the tarp a good yank and exposed the bright, candy orange paint. It would be a flagrant risk, driving the suspicious car downtown. But Momo didn't have a lot of options.

Momo tried to wriggle into the driver's seat. Tiny Deege's custom-raised seat and pedals made it virtually impossible. The hulking man finally gave up and ran around to the passenger side. "You drivin', Tiny!"

The Cutlass peeled out and was tearing down North Miami Avenue in no time. Tiny Deege fiddled with the knobs on his CD player, trying to adjust the output for the two twelve-inch subwoofers that resided in a sealed box inside his trunk. Waves of deep bass pulsated through Momo's body, giving him a tingling sensation over the skin on the back of his neck.

"Watch what you doin', fool!" Momo said, giving the steering wheel a good yank to keep the distracted driver from plowing into the back of a fuel tanker truck. "Gonna blow us all to smithereens."

Momo turned the knob to kill the volume on the stereo.

Tiny Deege reached for the knob to turn it back up, and Momo slapped his hand. "Ow, man," the pint-sized gangbanger said, recoiling his hand with a mortified look on his face.

"Cops already lookin' for this ride, Tiny," Momo said. "No need to make their job easier by drawin' even more attention to us."

The two men traveled the remainder of the way to the Little Havana neighborhood of Miami in silence. Momo thought it was nice. He'd been looking for a few moments of peace with all the chaotic events the gang had encountered as of late: taking in new unvetted members; the haywire job on the river that resulted in five people dead; watching Big Flow kill one of the gang's newest members; and chasing after one of the other new members who had betrayed the gang and fled.

Momo knew he couldn't make all of it seem right in his mind, but he knew there was at least one loose end he could fix—he could kill Josue Remy, before he said one word to the cops about Ti Flow, and their involvement in the murders of their fellow officers.

"Turn here. Turn here!" Momo said excitedly, as he stabbed his finger toward the road ahead.

"Where we goin' anyhow?" Tiny Deege asked.

"Hazy J seen Josue at Shakey Redbone's," Momo said, keeping his eyes peeled as Tiny turned the wheel to navigate the corner.

"Oooh, man. I gotta get me some," Tiny Deege said, his face lighting up like an excited puppy. "Shakey Redbone's? Man, I'm gonna get me some o' them Crispy Chicken Hands. Things creep the crap out o' me, but—"

"Shut up, Tiny!" Momo ordered, as the flamboyant orange

car turned a corner and approached Shakey Redbone's Southern Fried Chicken on the left, and a big, bright orange, Spanish-themed motel on the right, its roof missing a bunch of its faded red clay tiles. "Slow down, park over here on the side'a the road!"

Tiny Deege flipped on his turn signal and pulled forward into a space against the curb in front of Paradiso Inn. Both men gazed a short way down the street toward the chicken restaurant, its bright neon chicken glowing in the front window beside the Always Open sign.

"Yo, man, you see Josue?" Momo asked, his hand on the dashboard as he leaned far forward in the Oldsmobile to get a better look through the front windshield.

Tiny Deege scrunched up his diminutive face and squinted, trying to get a glimpse through the front windows of the fast food restaurant. "Don't see him," the little man said, "but is that Hazy J out front?"

Momo spotted the young twin standing at the outside corner of the restaurant. He stood poised to look through one of the windows, and he seemed to keep a vigilant watch, just as Momo had ordered him to.

Good man, Momo thought. *Sorry about your brother.*

"Tell you what, Deege," Momo said, checking his fifty caliber pistol. "When Josue come out, we get the chance, we gonna run him down. Dig? We cut him down like a dog. You drive quick, right over him, you get the chance."

"That's him! That's him! That's Josue!" Tiny Deege screamed hysterically, as the door to Shakey Redbone's swung open. The young Haitian refugee was heavily laden with three big plastic bags that bore the angular bulge of many cardboard boxes stuffed into each one. Josue walked out the front door and strode directly toward the street.

"Where he goin'?" Momo said, sounding somewhat flummoxed.

"An' why he got so much food, Momo?" Tiny Deege asked. "He goin' to a party or somethin'?"

The two men fixed their gaze on the displaced refugee as he glanced side to side before stepping forward to cross the street toward the Paradiso Inn.

"Looks like he headin' to the motel," Momo said. "Must be stayin' there with someone. Wonder if it's that chump who tried to gun us down the other night in our own 'hood. I tell you what, Tiny, I get hold o' that fool, I gonna—"

Momo didn't finish his thought.

A small car, looked like an old Honda Civic from the nineties—halfway primered up, and booming with throbbing bass—zipped around the corner in front of Shakey Redbone's.

The driver spun around the corner so fast he couldn't have had time to see Josue Remy in the middle of the street. Dude hadn't even had time to hit the brake pedal.

The car plowed into the young Haitian. Then the Civic's tires screeched. The car skidded to a stop, enrobed in thick, white rubber smoke.

Momo's mouth hung agape as he watched the Civic strike Josue, sending his body hurtling into the air, before it crashed down, landing in a twisted heap in the middle of the road. Josue's bags and boxes of chicken scattered everywhere.

Two seconds later a large Styrofoam container of commingled mashed potatoes and gravy splattered onto the windshield of Tiny Deege's bright orange car.

"What?" Momo croaked. "Did you see…?"

Tiny Deege reached for the windshield wiper control next to the steering wheel.

"No, wait," Momo protested, but it was too late. Tiny Deege turned on the wipers, smearing white mashed potatoes streaked with brown lines of savory gravy all over the windshield.

"Fool!" Momo shouted, as he threw open his door and gazed

down the street toward the unmoving man laying in the street. The driver of the Civic took one look at the lump in the middle of the road, and he took off. His whiny old engine revved up high as he popped the clutch. His tires chirped, and the driver sped past Shakey Redbone's, passing right by Momo and Tiny Deege. Momo looked at him, making eye contact with the red-haired, red-bearded man who now fled the scene of the shocking collision.

Momo noticed the long cracks in the Honda's windshield, and the crumpled metal of the car's hood.

"What?" he said again, dumbfounded, as he struggled to take in the shock of what he had just witnessed. It surprised Momo how rattled he felt at watching someone do the very thing to Josue he had intended to do himself. Now, he tried to snap his mind back into reality.

Momo reached into the backseat of Tiny Deege's car and grabbed a black hoodie, which he used to wipe the smeared side dish off of the car's windshield.

"Man, that was my favorite hoodie too," Tiny Deege protested.

"We gotta run him down," Momo said, tossing the hoodie onto the sidewalk. "Gotta make sure he don't get back up."

Momo sat back down in the passenger seat and secured his seatbelt over his massive chest. "Gotta finish it, Tiny. Go! Just think 'o him as one big speed bump!"

"Momo, I don't know if I can—" Tiny Deege started to say, but stopped when Momo mashed his foot on top of Tiny's to press the gas pedal to the floor. "Ow, man!"

But Momo hit the brake pedal just as quickly as he had stomped on the gas. A white ambulance, with orange and turquoise stripes on the front and sides, negotiated the corner, coming to a stop directly in front of Josue's body, where it lay in the street, the vehicle's lights flashing, its siren wailing.

"How they get here so fast?" Momo asked.

"Ambulance drivers like chicken too," Tiny Deege said.

Momo watched for another couple of minutes, until a fire truck arrived, followed by another ambulance, and a City of Miami squad car. It seemed to Momo like virtually no time had passed by at all, and the scene had become one of utter chaos.

"Yo, we gotta get outta here," Momo shouted to Tiny Deege. "Back away. Back outta here slow!"

Tiny Deege reversed the vivid orange car from the crime scene with caution, dissolving into traffic on a busy boulevard heading east towards downtown. The two men continued on for a time in silence again, before Momo said, "Hey, Tiny, I think maybe our work been done for us. Let's head back and tell Big the job is done."

CHAPTER 30

T HE SOUND OF A SIREN howled outside as Max stepped out of the shower, toweling himself off inside the steamy bathroom. He dressed quickly, and opened the door to step out into the murky room. He'd heard sirens passing by outside all week. Max conceded to himself that his motel choice had not placed him into the greatest neighborhood of Miami.

Max threw open the curtains, bathing the room in the brilliance of midday sunlight. His pupils dilated instinctively, and his eyes struggled to adjust to the influx of bright light.

As he squinted against the scene outside, Max thought it peculiar that the sirens hadn't passed by, as so many others before had done. If anything, they had increased in intensity, as the high-strung wail of two more emergency vehicles joined the chorus of urgent bawling.

"What is going *on?*" Max asked himself aloud. He placed a hand just above his eyes, giving them just enough shade to focus on the spectacle outside. As his eyes focused, Max saw two ambulances, a big fluorescent green and white fire truck, as well as two white police cars with blue lettering and decals adorned with palm trees plastered across the side, City of Miami Police.

A large EMT with blond hair and powder blue latex gloves pushed a gurney toward an ambulance, its rear doors ajar, as another EMT, this one short, black, and bald, pulled the rolling stretcher, guiding it.

"Poor guy," Max thought, looking at the guy on the gurney.

Next thing Max noticed was the red and white Shakey Redbone's boxes scattered about the street and the wounded man's—or dead man's—dark complexion.

Max's heart leapt into his throat. For the first time, he wondered if the guy on the gurney could be Josue?

What had he been wearing when he left the room? Max found himself asking, feeling terrified—like a person whose child had just been involved in a horrible accident. He recalled the turquoise button-up shirt, the khaki shorts, the red and white sneakers he had just bought Josue.

Max spotted turquoise fabric peeking out from the white sheet placed over the unfortunate man, as well as the blood that soaked through, staining it. A red and white shoe lay in the street nearby.

No, Max thought. *No, not now. Not after everything that's happened.*

Max threw open the motel room's door and bolted to the end of the second floor balcony. He took the rusted steps down, two at a time. He ran straight for the ambulance where the two EMTs loaded Josue into the back.

"What happened?" Max asked urgently. "Is he all right? Is he alive?"

"Who are you?" the bald EMT asked.

"I'm his…brother," Max said, hoping a little white lie might help, as preposterous as it was.

"Yeah, right," the big blond said with a knowing smirk. "Sorry, man. Can't let you ride along."

"Look," the bald guy said, "he's alive. Pulse is weak, but he's alive."

"Where are you taking him?" Max asked.

"Reed Memorial," the bald guy said. Then the other man shut the doors behind Josue and the other EMT, before rushing around to the driver's side. The ambulance raced from the scene, sirens ablaze, leaving Max standing in the middle of the street before a large crowd of chicken-eating gawkers.

He noticed the police, poring over every bit of debris in the street, whether it was a tumbled-aside sneaker or a buttermilk biscuit. Max turned away from the street and made a beeline for his motel room, before the cops had a chance to turn their attention in his direction.

Max was about to enter his room when he observed the black car parking in front of the Paradiso Inn's office. The car was obviously an unmarked police car. Painted black, with tinted windows, and adorned with all those weird little antennas.

The two men who stepped out of the car were detectives— Max spotted the holstered pistols and gold detective shields, which one man wore clipped to his belt, the other slung around his neck on a silver chain.

But there was something more. Max felt familiarity with these two men, and it bothered him. He had seen these two men somewhere, but for the life of him, he could not remember where, or in what context.

They would ask about Josue; the manager would lead them to Max's room, where he would be peppered with questions. They might be able to make the connection between Josue and the violent gang that had recruited him. They may suspect him of involvement in the shooting that killed those two police officers; indeed, Josue *had* been there.

The detectives would wonder what Max was doing with Josue. They would expect the worst, of course. No matter what Max might tell them, they would not believe he only wished to see the young man looked after, to help him, after all the trauma and pain he had experienced in such a short period of time.

Max knew he had maybe two minutes. He gathered up everything he could: toiletries, dirty clothes, his laptop, any other personal effects in the room. Max stuffed it all into Josue's duffel bag and backpack, as well as his own Tampa Bay Buccaneers bag. Max left the empty and partially-filled rum bottles, and all of the leftover chicken and sides in the room's tiny mini-fridge. He grabbed everything he could and tucked the Smith & Wesson pistol into his front waistband. Then he bolted down the balcony, heading away from the motel office. Max descended the rickety steps at the far end.

Once he cleared the side of the building, and the sprawling crime scene in front of Shakey Redbone's was out of view, Max ran. He ran as fast as he could run wearing a backpack and clutching two thick duffel bags. Max didn't stop for five or six blocks, where he had to plunk himself down onto a bus stop bench and pant until he had caught his breath.

Max used his iPhone to call a cab to take him to the hospital. He entered the Emergency Room through the sliding automatic doors, and made a beeline for the ER's check-in counter. A young redheaded woman with black glasses and four silver hoop earrings stepping up her left ear sat behind the desk, punching away at her computer keyboard. Max paused, waiting for her to stop and give him her attention.

"Yes?" the woman said, as she continued to type.

"My friend, he was brought in here a little bit ago by ambulance. He was hit by a car. Can I see him?" Max tried to remain calm, but the stress and fear arose in his tone.

"Name?" the typing woman asked, not looking up.

"Josue," Max said. He didn't give a last name.

"I believe he was taken into surgery," the woman said. "What is your relationship with the patient?"

Max felt a great heaviness inside him. "He is my friend. My best friend."

"I'm sorry," the typing woman said. "You are welcome to have a seat and we can allow you to visit him when he is able to consent to you doing so."

"When is that going to be?" Max asked. "I don't even know what's happened to him. Is he hurt bad?"

"I'm sorry, sir," the receptionist said, looking up from her computer, but still continuing to type. "But I can't share that information with anyone who's not a family member. Go ahead, take a seat. I'll let you know anything I can."

"Thank you," Max said, feeling bewildered by the woman's ability to multitask so efficiently. Max couldn't even walk and chew bubblegum at the same time.

He wanted to take a seat. Max wanted to sit down and wait for Josue, to be the first to know when his surgery was successful, whatever they were doing to him. But he knew that here, like at the scene of the crime, there would be a lot of questions. So Max took Josue's backpack and the duffel bags, and he walked back toward the ER's automatic doors.

Max observed the two detectives he'd seen walking into the manager's office at the Paradiso Inn. The context of their prior meeting still seemed fuzzy in his mind, almost as if it had been a dream.

As the two men approached the opposite side of the automatic sliding doors, Max recognized that one of the men was a police detective he remembered to resemble the late tennis star, Arthur Ashe.

A pang of fear washed over Max, and he felt an urge to disappear before these men had a chance to recognize him. After all, they *had* spoken with the motel manager. She would have described both Max and Josue.

Feeling panicked, Max wandered away from the ER's exit, veering down a hallway so long Max couldn't see the end of it. It appeared to be the main artery of the building, with doorways and side hallways shooting off left and right for its whole length.

As the ER doors swung open with a whoosh, Max reached for the first doorknob he saw. He leaned against the door and twisted the knob, letting his weight carry him to the other side. Max stumbled into a surprisingly large space with a low ceiling. He was surrounded by rack after rack of clothing on hangers.

"What can I help you find today?" a kind-faced woman in her sixties asked. Max peered in the direction of her voice, and turned around to spot a checkout counter with a cash register behind him, just to the left of the doorway.

Max's mind reeled as he gave a quick spin, taking in all the sights of the room. *These are all scrubs*, Max thought. The hospital had a store that sold scrubs for hospital employees, and Max had just stumbled into it. He seemed to be the only customer in the store.

Max's mind raced to make sense of his situation, to sort it all out as quickly as he could. By looking at the signage behind the clerk, Max ascertained the store was called Scrubs 'n Stuff. It occurred to Max that virtually everyone at work in the hospital wore scrubs, no matter what their job: from x-ray technicians, to nurses, to rich plastic surgeons.

The rainbow of scrubs on display around him was impressive: pale blue, bright blue, dull green, vibrant yellow-green, bright pink, maroon, or for pediatric doctors and nurses, they might be bright blue or pink and covered with colorful cartoon elephants or giraffes, and so many more.

Max found the men's section as quickly as possible.

"Hi," Max said to the clerk. She appeared to be an elegant woman, like someone you might meet behind the counter at a country club, or posh hotel, "I'd just like to browse for a bit, if that's okay."

"Certainly, young man," said the clerk, whose nametag read Lois. "I'm here if you have any questions. And I hope you like blue, because we're are having a blue sale. Anything blue is twenty-five percent off until the end of the month."

"Sounds good," Max said, tipping his head down toward the

clothes on one of the racks as if he were a fugitive from justice. Maybe he *was* a fugitive from justice. Josue's involvement in the river robbery made him an accessory or a witness to a very serious crime, no matter his intentions. And Max was harboring him. Like it or not, he was involved.

Max had no idea what he was going to do. He admitted to himself that he was winging it with each move that he made. Seeing all of the racks of scrubs gave him an idea; if he could make himself look as if he belonged in the hospital, it might give him more time to figure out a plan.

"I'm new at the hospital," Max said to the kind clerk, finding that his little fibs were coming even easier now. "I just got hired on as an x-ray tech and I'm starting work on Monday. I need everything. Can you help me?"

"You're in good hands, darling," Lois said, stepping out from behind the counter and coming to stand beside Max. She flipped through some of the clothes on the rack with her right hand, and Max felt her left come to rest in the middle of his back. "I'll take good care of you."

Lois helped Max choose a few different outfits consisting of scrub pants, shirts, and matching caps. He knew he would only need one outfit for his plan to work, but Max bought several to make his new-hire story seem more believable.

Max paid for the scrubs and found himself back in the hallway, toting a big shopping bag, Josue's backpack, and the two duffel bags. He ducked into the nearest men's room and changed into a suit of scrubs.

Max had spent enough time in the hospital after he'd been shot to know his way around one. The scrubs would allow him to blend in. There was just one more accessory he needed to give him unlimited access to most of the hospital's rooms.

Outside the bathroom, Max found a supply room where he

was able to stash his bags, at least for a while. Then he headed for the cafeteria.

It only took about two minutes of observation for Max to realize which of the employees sitting at the tables were on a short break, which were on lunch, and which were finished for the day, partially by their demeanor, and partially by what they were eating, drinking, or wearing.

Max ordered himself an iced coffee and sat down at a table, directly behind a trio of giggling nurses, who looked to Max as though they had just finished their shifts, and were enjoying a latte before going out on the town. One of the women had already taken off her scrub top, and she sat at the table in a bright pink tank top. Another of the women looked into a hand mirror as she applied a smoky application of makeup around her eyes.

As he sat, Max intentionally slammed his chair back hard into one of the nurses' chairs. He reached back to grab the back of his chair and scoot it back in to his table. Max turned his head, "I'm really sorry," he said. "I'm a total klutz. Forgive me."

The nurses giggled again, and Max distinctly heard one of them say, "He's cute."

"Would you like to join us?" one of the other nurses asked. She looked at Max with a smile that said to Max, "I would *really* like you to join us."

"Thanks, but I'll have to take a rain check on that," Max said, looking over his shoulder at the women. "I've barely got time to slam my coffee before I've got to get back up to Radiology." Max remembered that the hospital directory placed the Radiology department on the south side of the second floor.

"You must be new here," one of the other nurses said, the one with the heavy eye makeup. "I'm Lorraine."

"I'm Chrissie," said the nurse in the pink tank top. She wore her hair in a short platinum-blonde bob.

"He doesn't care about that," Lorraine said, and the three women giggled again.

"Shut *up!*" Chrissie said. "And this pathetic, lonely thing here is Tina," referring to the third woman at the table, a black-haired Asian girl with a great smile. "What's your name?"

"I'm...Max," Max said.

"Oh, had to think about it first," Lorraine said, and the three women snickered. "Well, we'd better see you around, Max. You promise?"

"Promise," Max said, standing up from his table, clutching his icy cup of coffee in his right hand. He felt Chrissie's laminated badge, which he had snatched right off of the pink sweater she had draped over the back of her chair. It was now pressed between his palm and the coffee cup. "Now, I gotta run, or I'll be late."

"Shame," Lorraine said.

Max felt all six of the women's eyes burrowing into him as he walked out of the cafeteria, toting the purloined badge. He self-consciously wondered if he'd bought his pants a little too snug. In the long hallway, Max tossed his coffee cup into a trash can, and clipped the badge to his blue scrubs top, making sure the side with the photo was turned against his chest.

Max stopped to study the hospital directory with great intensity. He wanted to get his bearings, and learn the most efficient routes all around the huge building. It wasn't likely that Josue would be out of surgery yet, so Max took his time.

As he stared at the huge directory, with its hundreds of carefully placed tiny plastic letters and numbers, Max felt overwhelmed. He didn't know what he should do.

Two men, one of them decked out in blue scrubs similar to Max's, and one wearing a long white lab coat, walked past Max. His weeks spent in the hospital told him that one man was probably a senior resident, or perhaps the chief resident of the hospital, while the other was probably a first-year intern. The men were engaged in deep discussion, and it sounded a bit like the intern was getting chewed out by the more senior physician, who held an aluminum clipboard and repeatedly stabbed his finger onto a chart as the men spoke. They walked past Max without even glancing up at him.

Max watched after them until they reached the end of the long hallway, emerging into the airy waiting room of the ER. Neither one of the men looked back or gave Max a single indication they had even noticed him.

Max looked down at the bright blue scrubs. Out on the street, he would have felt like a clown wearing the brightly colored garb. But here, inside the hospital, it was a far different situation.

"I'm invisible," Max said.

CHAPTER 31

MAX COULDN'T STOP LOOKING DOWN at the cornflower blue scrubs. He smoothed out his top and silently wondered why he had chosen a v-neck. Max lowered his head and made his way, slowly, back toward the check-in desk at the ER, where the two detectives he had spotted coming in the door were making no headway in getting past the cute red-haired dynamo behind the counter.

"So, just to be clear, you're sayin' we *can't* go back into the ER and wait 'til he's out of surgery," the first detective said. Max remembered him as the one who seemed like a displaced New Yorker, still wearing the familiar black jacket over his green shirt and black and blue striped tie.

Max had positioned himself against the wall, just around the corner from the check-in counter. He held his iPhone, tapping the screen inattentively, while he stared blankly at the glowing face. If anyone noticed him, they wouldn't think he was a guy just standing there, eavesdropping.

"I don't see what good it would do you," the receptionist said, now clicking away with her mouse. "Since he's not going to be in the ER."

"Can we wait in ICU?" the black detective asked, and Max remembered that his name was Arthur, like the tennis player. "So we can be there when he wakes up?"

"I would prefer that you wait out here," the redhead said. "When the patient is out of surgery, I can have his surgeon come down and talk to you about his condition. The doctor will make the final say on whether you can see him or not."

"We need to post an officer by the room he'll be in," the New Yorker said. "This guy could be dangerous."

"What has he been charged with?" the receptionist asked, and Max heard the sound of shuffling papers. She must have moved on to some filing as she spoke to the detectives.

"Nothing...not yet anyhow," Arthur said. "But we really need to speak to him as soon as possible. He—"

"Is he considered a suspect in a crime?" the tenacious receptionist asked.

"He's a person of interest," the gruff, leather-clad detective said, sounding irritated. "We need to question him about a killing spree that occurred not far from here, on the Miami River. Couple of my friends were killed on the job. This is serious, young lady."

"Sorry about your friends. But hospital admin has been cracking down on this kind of access. People coming and going, even if they have a badge. If you have a warrant or something, I'm sure that would help your case, but I can't let you through at this time," the receptionist said, her quick fingers now clacking against the keys of her computer keyboard again. "I'll notify hospital security, and we'll post a guard outside the man's door. You'll be called as soon as the patient is in a condition to submit to an interview."

Max heard a long pause, and peeked around the corner to see the detectives' exasperated faces.

After the awkward moment of silence, the receptionist said, "I watch a lot of cop shows. Have you guys been watching the *MCS* marathon on the Citrus Channel?"

"Look, Miss," Arthur said, removing a card from his wallet and sliding it across the counter to the receptionist, "that's my card. Please call me if he wakes up and can speak. Okay? It's quite urgent we speak with him."

Lorenzo slapped his own card on the counter. "Call me first."

"If you have no further questions, please step aside so I can help this lady," the receptionist said.

Max turned back toward the hall and lowered his head as he watched the detectives leave through the automatic doors of the ER. They would be back, and as soon as Josue was able to talk, they would press him for everything he knew about Ti Flow, the murders down by the river, his illegal arrival in the country.

Josue's situation was very sadly and suddenly about to unravel. The kid might end up in prison. He might be deported to Port au Prince.

Either way, he's screwed, Max thought.

When Max had given the detectives a good five minutes to leave, he walked out into the parking lot, settling into the backseat of one of the half-dozen or so Coral Cabs waiting in the circular driveway at the end of a concrete path not far from the ER's entrance.

Max had the driver take him to a nearby hotel. When the driver, a quiet Eastern European man, asked which one, Max simply replied, "A nice one." He had had about enough of sleeping in questionable motels; there was a good chance he was starting to develop scabies.

The cabbie dropped Max at a very modern five-story hotel near Miami International, and he checked into a king suite overlooking a small man-made lake connected to the Miami River. Max dropped his bags on the floor and gazed out across the room's wide picture window. It was a great view. But Max didn't much care.

He dropped himself onto the sofa in the cozy living area, and kicked his feet up onto the rock maple coffee table, accidentally kicking over a small vase of flowers. Max stared out at the busy city in the sunshine of late afternoon.

Max pondered his next move. *How could he even get in to*

see Josue if the hospital was guarding him? Max was at a loss. He simply didn't know what to do next.

Max fell asleep almost instantly, right there on the sofa overlooking the lake. He must have slept for a couple of hours. He awoke feeling groggy, and as though he needed a drink. Max got to his feet and made his way to the kitchenette, finding a well-stocked mini-bar with several mini-bottles of very fine rum, along with top-shelf vodkas, gins, whiskeys, and tequilas. He considered mixing himself a diluted cocktail, keeping with the program of weaning off alcohol over time. But in a moment of great clarity, Max decided he didn't need it. Not anymore. It wouldn't help him, and it wouldn't help Josue.

Max remembered that the cab that had brought him to the hotel had driven him past Casino Miami, where jai alai was played. He'd seen it on TV when he was a kid growing up in Orlando, and he'd always wanted to watch the game played. He needed to clear his head. He wondered if sitting and watching a game might help him formulate a plan.

Max walked about a mile to get to the casino, skirting around the little lake, and crossing the Miami River on an old, green train bridge that raised and lowered to let boats pass along the river. The walk was good; at about seventy degrees it was the warmest part of the day, and it felt nice to stretch his legs.

Max stepped into the casino's front doors, inundated by the bright flashing lights of the gaming floor and the busy, ear-assaulting blips and beeps from long rows of slot and video poker machines. Max crinkled his nose as he breathed the air, blue with cigar and cigarette smoke.

He bought a bottled water from the bar and made his way to the fronton, where the jai alai games were played. Entering the doors to the sports arena, Max found himself immediately disappointed.

He'd expected a packed house: spectators filling the six-thousand plus seats in the arena, eagerly watching the fast-paced action. Maybe twenty spectators now watched the athletes play, sitting in scattered pairs or singles, here and there throughout the ocean of empty seats.

Max imagined it must have been something to behold, to have come into the fronton in the seventies or eighties, during the apex of the sport's popularity. But now, the great game seemed only to be played for those placing pari-mutuel wagers.

Max settled into a seat, not too far from an elderly couple who argued about what kind of fish to eat for dinner, but close enough so he could get a good glimpse of the action. It was only then that Max realized that, while the game had fascinated him as a kid, he really didn't know the rules.

A guy threw the hard, little, white goatskin ball, called a pelota, lightning fast at the far wall from an oblong wicker basket attached to his arm, called a cesta. A deafening crack erupted each time the ball hit the granite wall, hurtling through the air at over 150 miles per hour. Then one of the other players would catch the ball and hurl it back at the wall, all in one fluid motion.

Staring blankly at the players, and placing a great deal of confidence in the chain link fence that protected the spectators from an errant pelota, Max's mind drifted as he considered what to do about Josue's situation.

Max knew the kid was innocent. That was why he had fled. He'd never wanted to be a part of Ti Flow. He had just gotten caught up in it.

Max recalled one of his favorite episodes of *Miami Crime Squad*. Palomar Teete had gone undercover as a jai alai player in an effort to infiltrate Chico Cabrera's organization. But Teete, as it turned out, had been a terrible jai alai player. During his first game he had been struck in the middle of his forehead by a surging pelota, and had been knocked out cold.

The Jamaican detective had awoken in the hospital, unable to recall exactly who he was. In the aftermath of the accident, one of

Cabrera's men would identify Palomar Teete as a cop. Later, when the organized crime boss had sent some of his men to go into Teete's hospital room to finish him off, Charleston Corbin had taken the drastic measure of loading his best friend and partner into a wheelchair and sneaking him out of the hospital.

Sure, Cabrera's men had caught up to Corbin and Teete in the parking lot. But somehow Detective Corbin had been able to shoot six of Cabrera's men with his 9mm pistol and blow up a white Cadillac limousine for good measure.

Max smirked as he remembered the episode. Life had been so much more fun when he'd been a kid. As long as he was the hero, the guy with the pistol could somehow always manage to overcome the guys with automatic rifles, no matter their number.

Another loud crack against the wall. The idea hit Max like the hard pelota striking like a thunderclap against the granite. He suddenly knew what he would do. The plan only required a desperate man with nothing left to lose; one who was at least a little bit crazy. Max suddenly felt fortunate that recent circumstances in his life had quickly changed him into both.

CHAPTER 32

MAX USED CHRISSIE'S PURLOINED HOSPITAL badge, swiping it over a card reader to gain entry into one of the more discreet, out-of-the-way security doors. The hospital directory told Max the door would open into a hallway lined with utility rooms. He would be far less likely to run into hospital staff members there than he would in a hallway populated by patient rooms or doctors' offices. Max liked the hallway most, though, for its stairway at the end; it would take him right up to ICU on the second floor.

At the top of the steps, Max strode through the ICU area with purpose, as if he belonged there. He walked past several of the dozen or so glass-fronted rooms, all situated in a big rectangle around an oval-shaped central nurses' station. Max walked through the ward, taking furtive peeks inside each room, hoping to see his friend. He felt his heart flutter once as he spotted a black man with tubes sticking out of what seemed like every orifice of his body. But the man's gray hair told Max he wasn't the patient he'd been looking for.

Max had reached the last room when he peered through and saw Josue. An eagle-eyed nurse with dark brown hair and a nice, lightly-tanned face stood behind the high counter at the nurse's station glaring at Max.

He stepped over toward the counter, noticing a couple of other nurses sitting behind the counter as well, their backs toward Max as they stared at expansive computer monitors. Max observed two more people sitting behind the big oval-shaped counter, likely doctors, one of whom seemed to be comparing some paperwork to data on a computer screen in front of him. The brunette, probably the charge nurse of the ICU, was the only one who seemed to be paying any attention to passersby.

"Can I help you?" the nurse said, her voice soft and with a hint of a southern accent, while her tone was no-nonsense. She had shoulder-length hair the color of dark chocolate, highlighted with streaks of dirty blonde. Max noticed that her nametag read Crenshaw. She was attractive in an unconventional manner, maybe thirty years of age, with a slightly rounded face, particularly around her chin.

"I'm new here," Max said, placing his palms on the counter as he stood before the forthright nurse. "Crenshaw, is it? I'm just trying to get the lay of the land before I start work in Radiology on Monday."

"You know this is ICU, right?" the woman said, her big brown eyes locking onto Max's with a steely gaze as she drummed her long, painted fingernails on the countertop. "And yes, I'm Crenshaw. Crenshaw Stubbins."

"Lovely name," Max said, wondering if he was actually going over to the dark side with his little fibs. He noticed Crenshaw had a tiny pill or tablet carefully painted onto each one of her fingernails. He recognized Vicodin, valium, percocet. *But what were these others?* Max thought to himself. *Viagra? The party drug MDMA? Quaaludes? Who was this person?*

"I'm...Nubbie," Max said, quickly thinking of the first phony name that popped into his mind. He had suddenly recalled the name of the quirky Swedish informant whom Corbin and Teete had frequently pressed for important street-level information on *Miami Crime Squad*. He kicked himself mentally for not having thought of an alias earlier.

"Nubbie?" Crenshaw asked. "I thought my name was bad."

"Well...it's short for Nubbington," Max said. "I'm Alexander Nubbington," he continued, "of the Manhattan Nubbingtons." The audacity of this white lie made him cringe inwardly.

"Well, it's really nice to meet you...Nubbie," Crenshaw said. "Welcome to the Reed family. I'm looking forward to seeing your face around here a lot more."

"You know, Crenshaw," Max said, taking a quick glance down at his chest to make sure his laminate was still turned backwards, "I don't know if this is my business, but I thought you should know: as I walked past room eleven, the elderly woman inside called me in, told me I should tell the nurse at the front desk that she never got her lunch."

"Right. I'll go and check on Mrs. Klein," Crenshaw said, smiling, and Max observed that she had a lovely smile once one chipped through the initial iciness of her personality. "The poor li'l dear has pretty advanced Alzheimer's; she probably truly believes she hasn't actually eaten, even though she has."

Crenshaw left the counter to go and speak to Mrs. Klein, whom Max hadn't actually spoken with. He hoped a small argument might ensue about the lunch, giving him ample time to check on Josue.

As Crenshaw Stubbins disappeared into Mrs. Klein's room, Max found his way back to Josue's, and he slipped inside. He crouched in close to the wall, near the head of the elevated hospital bed. Josue lay, eyes closed, head wrapped in gauzy bandages. His leg was propped up on pillows, and encased in a thick cast that reached just below his left knee. He looked to be in rough shape.

Besides his more traumatic injuries, clear bandages covered big patches of abrasion on his arms and right cheek. An oxygen mask covered Josue's nose and mouth, and a cluster of complex machines kept track of the busted-up Haitian's vitals, making consistent beeping sounds at regular intervals.

Josue looked like a mad scientist's experiment: an EEG

meter with a tangle of wires was connected to the unconscious man's gauze-wrapped head to monitor his brain waves; an IV pump delivered fluids and medication into the unconscious man's bloodstream; a pulse oximeter clamped onto his right index finger to measure the oxygen in his blood; an air-filled compression boot wrapped his right leg to discourage blood clots from forming; the bag of a Foley catheter hung on the side of his bed, along with several more devices Max didn't recognize.

Max picked up the big clipboard with Josue's chart from an acrylic holder at the foot of his bed. His eyes skimmed the chart, and he struggled to pick out the words he understood—concussion, mild subdural hematoma, oblique fracture of left tibia—while he ignored the words he didn't. He snapped photos of all of the monitoring devices' screens with his iPhone; he would later perform internet searches on the readouts, and try to make sense of them, despite not actually being a medical professional.

Looking down at the unconscious man, Max felt sick inside. *None of this should have happened to my friend*, Max thought. He wanted to load him up into a wheelchair now and make a break for it. But he knew such rash action would likely cause more harm than good.

"Josue," Max said. "Josue, can you hear me? It's Max."

Josue stirred and opened his eyes. "Maxwell?" he said, trying hard to sit up. He reached his hand up to pull the oxygen mask off his face. "Maxwell. You take me out from here. Take me out."

"It's okay," Max said, pressing his hand into the other man's chest to restrain him, to keep him from ripping his support wires and tubes from his body. "You're in the hospital, Josue. I don't know how much you recall, but you were hit by a car. Looks like your leg is pretty badly broken. And you have a concussion."

Josue looked down at his leg with terror in his eyes. "How this happen? How do I get here? Please, Maxwell, take me out from here."

"You're going to be okay, Josue," Max said. "But I need you to stay in bed. Okay? Just stay here, in bed. When the police, or anyone else, comes through that door to talk to you, pretend you're still asleep. Can you do that? Just pretend you're asleep. They'll keep you in here where you're safe, the police won't be able to question you."

Josue still looked terrified. But he nodded.

"I've got to get out of here, or I'm going to be arrested," Max said, grabbing his friend's right hand and squeezing it tightly. "I'll be back for you, Josue. I promise you I'll be back. I won't leave you behind. Not again."

Josue nodded. Trepidation showed in his eyes. Max didn't blame him. His own time spent in the hospital had been almost as traumatizing as the gunshot wounds themselves: waking up in a strange place; the odd noises and smells; the strangers constantly milling around. He had spent nearly a month in the hospital before being discharged.

"Just stay in bed and rest," Max reiterated. "Take care, my friend."

Max slipped out through the big glass door that separated Josue's ICU room from the rectangular hallway loop. Max watched the automatic door close behind him, just as Crenshaw stepped out of Mrs. Klein's room, and walked over to him.

"What happened to this poor guy?" Max said, doing his best to sound oblivious. "He looks like he got pretty badly mangled."

"Hit and run," Crenshaw said, looking through the glass at Josue, who lay back on his bed, his eyes closed.

Good man, Max thought.

"It's a sad deal," Crenshaw continued. "I think he's an illegal or something, maybe from Haiti. Don't know if he came here before or after the quake, but could you imagine escaping a third-world country, only to make it to the States and get slammed by a car in the street? Broke his leg pretty bad, compound fracture.

"But the real reason he's in *here* is his head wound. Looks like his noggin bounced off the pavement, got a concussion. He has a slight subdural hematoma, and that's what we're keeping an eye on—we expect the swelling in his brain to subside over the next twelve hours or so. If so, and all the vitals are good, we'll move him to a regular room. Of course, the cops want to talk to him, so I bet they'll take him to jail or something at some point."

"Thanks, Crenshaw," Max said, looking at the nurse with a new sense of respect. Sure, she had shared a great deal of confidential patient information with a total stranger. But Max could tell she cared about the patients brought into ICU, no matter their situation. "I'll see you around. I'm gonna go figure out my way around, you know? I feel like I'm getting ready for my first day of high school or something."

"You'll do fine," the kind nurse said, placing her hand on Max's shoulder. "And if you have any questions about anything, come back in here and ask, okay?"

Max was relieved to hear that Josue's head injury did not seem to be as serious as it could have been, or as bad as the bandaged head looked. But the idea of Josue healing up in ICU, getting better, and then being transferred to another room wasn't going to work. Josue would soon find himself wrapped up in a legal system he'd probably never find his way out of.

Max knew what would come next would be crazy. And it would all unfold before he knew it.

CHAPTER 33

MAX OPENED THE DOOR TO Mighty Morty's Surplus and Pawn on Sugarpalm Street, only a few blocks away from Biscayne Boulevard in Little Haiti. The structure was a big metal warehouse converted into a retail space.

Mighty Morty's was situated on a distinct line of demarcation: the buildings neighboring the questionable pawn shop ranged from shabby industrial to just plain dilapidated, while those across the nearby railroad tracks made up an upscale office park recently built in a refined Spanish style, and looking like part of a whole different world.

Max had been here before. It was where he'd bought the Smith & Wesson pistol and all of the extra magazines he'd thought were empty. He approached the counter, constructed out of wooden pallets, and some kind of hardwood-faced plywood, centrally located in the middle of all the shop's wares: clothing racks filled with military body armor; olive drab coats and pants; desert print camouflage clothing; countless shelves of survival gear, emergency food, and supplies; bladed weapons; along with the usual pawn shop fare of guns, guitars, amplifiers, memorabilia, power tools, televisions, and video games.

"Hey, man," the skinny blond man behind the counter said. His long pale mullet reminded Max of David Bowie from the late eighties. The man looked familiar. "I remember you. I sold you that 6906 a few weeks ago. I never forget a piece. What do you need, brother? Ammo? Another pistol? Maybe a long gun to go with the pistol? Somethin' a little more...heavy?"

Max noticed the man's nametag said Shreeve, and for some reason the name gave Max the creeps. "What I really need," Max said, glancing furtively from side to side, "is information. I need a new ID, and I need it quickly."

"The DMV is over by the mall, off the Palmetto Expressway," Shreeve said. "Not sure if they're still open," the pallid pawnbroker said with a big sardonic grin and a breathy laugh, "but if you hurry..."

"That's not the kind of ID I need," Max said, feeling his heart thumping in his chest. He wasn't used to dipping his toe into the unfamiliar waters on the shadier side of the law. "I need the kind that comes with its own identity. A fresh, new identity."

"You got me mistaken, brother," Shreeve said, still showing an overly toothy grin. "I don't sell phony IDs. I sell only legitimate military surplus and the highest quality pre-owned goods." The man spoke with an almost robotic, pre-scripted spiel.

Max dug into his pocket and counted out a thousand dollars. He slapped it down on the counter. "All I want is a name," Max said, "and maybe an address. And there's a grand in it for you, Shreeve."

"I don't know, officer," Shreeve said, his eyes watering as he glared at Max with suppressed laughter, "if I can help you. That might put a damper on my legitimate business enterprises, if you were to arrest me today."

"I'm not a cop, Shreeve," Max said, impatiently. "I'm just a guy who came to Miami to drink myself to death. But I've...had a last-minute change of plans."

"How the hell do I know that?" Shreeve said, and he suddenly wasn't laughing or smiling anymore.

Max walked away from the counter, heading back toward the front door. He grabbed a baseball bat from a barrel that looked like it might have once contained powdered eggs, and then he pushed open the door and walked out into the parking lot.

"Hey, man," Shreeve shouted after him. "Gotta pay for that."

Max strode to the finest car in the parking lot, a 1969 Camaro SS/RS with fresh British Racing Green paint and two silver stripes. He stopped for a moment to appraise the exquisiteness of the lovingly restored classic.

Then Max bashed the Camaro's windshield with the bat. He beat the glass ferociously, over and over, until it had shattered into a network of thousands of tiny white bits, connected by a layer of laminating film.

Max strode back inside the pawn shop. He tossed the baseball bat onto the floor and approached the counter again, where Shreeve stood, looking dumbfounded.

"Would a cop do that?" Max asked the pawn broker.

"No. No, I don't believe a cop would do such a thing," Shreeve said, gazing past Max out into the parking lot. "But there's just *one problem*, man."

"What's that?" Max asked.

"That's *my* Camaro," Shreeve said, his forehead crinkled into an angry expression that suggested he'd grab a sawed-off shotgun or an antique sword from behind the counter, and waste Max for so much as looking at his beautifully rebuilt classic, let alone defacing it.

Max counted off more money from the roll of bills in his pocket. "And another thousand for the windshield," Max said, offering a nervous, but polite, smile.

Shreeve gathered up the money and stuffed it into his shirt pocket. He shook his head. "You're crazy, man. But you're looking for Bongo. Bongo Peppitone. Owns a little head shop in Little Havana, sells all kinds of smoking gear."

Max thanked Shreeve for the information, and he apologized for his car. Then he took a cab downtown to the same bank branch where he'd been making withdrawals from his account for weeks. He walked into the modern glass and steel building. It surprised him what a nice bank it was, almost as if he were seeing the place for the first time.

A man with a name tag, likely the branch manager, frowned as he made eye contact with Max, but then forced himself to smile. The guy looked vaguely familiar, with his short-sleeved, white button-up and blue tie, and his paradoxically wild yet thinning hair. The stern look on the bank manager's face made Max wonder what exactly he had done last time he'd been inside the branch to earn such passive-aggressive glances of disdain.

"Next, please," a sweet voice called, and next thing Max knew, he was face to face with the angelic blue-eyed teller called Chloe.

"Hi," Max said, handing the teller his ID. "Before you say *anything*, I want to apologize for whatever offensive things I might have said or done to you, or anyone else inside the bank, last time I was in here. Up until very recently, I was going through a dark time in my life; not that it's completely over or anything..."

Chloe gazed up to look Max full in the face. Her skin glowed, and her eyes were like deep pools one could get lost in. "I do remember you being in here before. You look...better. Healthier. It's good to see."

Max smiled. "Could you please check my account balance? I need to know what I've got left."

Chloe picked up Max's ID and began punching away at her keyboard. "It looks like your current account balance...is...two hundred and seventy-nine thousand, forty-three dollars, and sixty-two cents."

"That's kind of a lot," Max said thoughtfully.

Chloe laughed. "Yes, indeed it is."

"Do you have enough cash in the branch to close out my account?" Max asked.

The sweet bank teller looked at him at first as if he wasn't serious. "You want it all now? In cash?"

Max nodded.

"Can I just ask you something?" Chloe said, "And I know it really isn't my business, so you can tell me to shut my face if you want to, but I'm really curious…"

"Why do I, a man with all the great qualities of a wino, have so much cash in my account?" Max asked.

The bank teller nodded, and flipped her platinum hair off her shoulder. She smiled, and Max felt a flutter in his stomach.

"My wife and I had just sold our house up north, close to Disney World," Max said, pausing to swallow, "and we were about to purchase another one. Part of that money is the equity from the sale of our house."

"What's the rest?" Chloe asked. "If you don't mind me prying."

Max felt a wave of sorrow wash over him like a breaking wave on a desolate shore. He felt his breath catch in his throat, and his eyes wandered. He exhaled sharply, to keep himself from cracking.

Chloe handed him a tissue from the silver box on the counter in front of her.

"Thanks," Max said, dabbing his eyes and doing his best to control his breathing. "The rest…the rest is a life insurance settlement."

Chloe's deep blue eyes were huge.

"For my wife, my son, and my daughter," Max said, choking the words out with great effort.

Chloe's chin quivered, and tears began to smudge her mascara. Max reached for the silver box and handed her a tissue.

"I'm sorry," she said. "I'll…just go get Mr. Mordecai, to find out if we have enough cash in the branch."

Chloe conferred with the ill-kempt bank manager at his desk, while Max stood awkwardly in the teller window. He considered grabbing a whole handful of the wrapped chocolate mint candies from the dish in front of him and stuffing them into his pants pockets, but he decided against it. Max watched the bank manager pick up the phone and start dialing. At first, he wondered if he should bolt. But he hadn't done anything illegal.

The attractive bank teller came back just as Max took a single candy from the dish and carefully unwrapped its thick foil wrapping. "Mr. Mordecai said that we can give you a hundred and eighty-five thousand in cash, and he's on the phone now with our Key Biscayne branch. If you don't mind driving over there, you should be able to pick up the rest of your cash and close your account there."

"Thanks, Chloe," Max said, feeling suddenly very comfortable with the lovely young bank teller. Maybe it was the fact that Max knew he had plans to quickly leave the country and not come back. "You know, when I came in here and I was wrecked, you were nice to me, and you treated me with a lot of respect that I didn't deserve. I mean, I don't remember everything, but I do remember your kindness. Thank you for that."

Chloe grabbed a deposit slip and flipped it over. She scribbled something on the back and slid it over to Max. He lifted the small white rectangle of paper from the tall counter. Chloe had written her name and phone number. Max glanced at her, feeling surprised.

The charming bank teller's lips curled into a lovely, charismatic smile that warmed Max's heart. It made him feel like a piece of hard candy with a soft, gooey center. Max folded the paper and tucked it into the inside pocket of the blazer he'd recently had dry-cleaned at the launderette near the Paradioso Inn. "Thanks."

Max collected his cash, stuffing the paper-wrapped bundles inside the backpack he had bought Josue at Kmart. He called a cab and waited by the curb outside, suddenly feeling very exposed with almost two hundred grand slung over his shoulder. At last the cab came and picked up the determined man, taking him to Key Biscayne, to collect the rest of his money and close out his account.

It was only when he returned to the cab after leaving the second bank branch, and sitting down in the back, that the finality of his plan fully sunk in for the first time. Once Max had committed, there would be no turning back. He would either succeed and be free, or he would likely spend a very long time inside a prison cell.

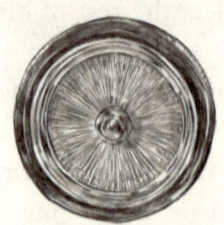

CHAPTER 34

"Yo, my brothers," Hazy Junior said, as he plunked himself down onto Big Flow's sofa and reached for a bowl of pretzels on the worn coffee table in the middle of the room, "has anybody seen Wily? Boy ain't answerin' my texts. Kinda gotta bad feelin' about it."

Momo, Tiny Deege, and Zann exchanged glances, but held quiet. As far as Momo was concerned, the news of young Wily Beeve's death was not his to break to the rightfully concerned, murdered man's twin brother. And Momo knew as far as Zann and Tiny Deege were concerned, the two gangbangers were likely too terrified about the whole situation to either say a word.

Momo looked at Big Flow, wondering if the gang's brutal leader would admit to killing the young man's brother, which he had done for no greater reason than to simply make a point. Big Flow pulled his needle-sharp screwdriver out of his pants pocket and glared back at Momo. Momo didn't flinch.

"Tell me everything that happened in Little Havana," Big Flow ordered, as he began to pick at his fingernails with the menacing point of the modified screwdriver. "You said Tiny Deege hit Josue Remy with his car? I thought our tiny kinsman here disposed of that vehicle. Is that not correct?"

Momo was not even about to broach the subject of the Cutlass Surpreme. "No, no, no," Momo said. "We gotta call from Hazy J, said he seen Josue down by Shakey Redbone's. We drove down, spotted him comin' out, then some bottom feeder in a Honda

P.O.S. come rippin' around the corner, cut Josue down afore we even got the chance."

"Did you make certain Josue was dead?" Big Flow asked. He peered through the front curtains of his living room suspiciously.

"Cops showed up, firemen, ambulances; we lit outta there," Momo said. He absentmindedly placed his hand on the grip of the tiny Kahr pistol inside his pocket.

Tiny Deege produced a small glass pipe from his pants pocket. He dropped a small rock of crack cocaine into the bowl and held his torch lighter underneath. Momo noticed that his hands trembled.

A siren wailed outside, and Momo heard it grow distinctly louder, much louder than the typical passing wail of sirens he was used to hearing on nearby Stonecrab Avenue. He frowned as Big Flow held aside one of the dirty lace curtains to glare outside. The dangerous gang leader turned toward Momo, screwdriver tip pointed toward the larger man's throat.

"Did you bring the 5-0 back to my house, Momo?" Big Flow asked, a menacing, feral look in his eyes. "Did you lead the cops back here to Lemon Street?"

"Naw, man," Momo said, showing Big Flow his palms as he peeked past him. The howling siren grew to be piercingly loud.

"Guns up, my brothers," Big Flow ordered, as he slid the window open and pushed back the curtains. He reached for a MAC-10 he kept stored behind a waist-high stereo speaker. The vicious gang leader charged the 9mm machine pistol and pointed it out the window.

Momo grabbed a Benelli semi-automatic twelve-gauge leaning against a wall in the corner of the room. He stood beside Big Flow, pointing the shotgun out the window. The rest of the gang members stood by, pistols in hand.

A collective groan of relief erupted from the crowd, as the familiar fluorescent yellow-green paint of an ambulance whizzed by on the street. Gang orders were to light up any cop car on sight. But ambulances and fire trucks were allowed through; Lemon Street had a great many elderly residents, and emergency calls were fairly common.

"What should we do about Josue?" Zann asked, tucking his nickel-plated pistol inside his waistband, and rubbing his fingers over his bright, carrot-colored hair.

"Want for us to go and check the hospitals, maybe go back to Shakey Redbone's, ask if anybody know anythin'?" Momo asked.

"No," Big Flow said with resolve. "We ask too many questions, we bring too much heat back to the Flow. We gotta play this cool. But we also gotta know where to find that back-stabbing traitor, Josue Remy."

"Yo, yo, Big Flow," Hazy Junior said, stepping in front of the dreadlocked gang leader with his hands in his pockets. He bobbed back and forth nervously as he spoke. "My cousin works, drivin' ambulances down in Coral Gables. I'm thinkin' he might know where they took Josue, or maybe he can figure out where they woulda took him, based on where he was hit by that car, or somethin.'"

Big Flow handed Hazy Junior his cell phone, and stood, staring at the younger man as he placed his call. Hazy dialed, and many tense seconds passed in the quiet room as everyone waited expectantly for the call to connect.

"Marvin?" Hazy Junior said. "Yo man, this is yo' cousin, Hazy. Don't know if you know about that kid got run down in Little Havana by the Shakey Redbone's there, do you? Well, if someone was mowed down by a car, and a ambulance came and took 'em outta there, do you know where they woulda took him?"

Fire seemed to flicker in Big Flow's eyes as he glared at the slender young gang member.

"Reed Memorial definitely?" Hazy Junior said. "Brother, that helps out a lot. Thanks, man." He hung up the call and handed the phone back to Big Flow. "My cousin said they woulda certainly taken Josue to Reed Memorial Hospital. Close by where he was hit, and it's where they woulda took someone they thought had no insurance."

"Thank you, Hazy J," Big Flow said, slipping his cell phone back into his pocket. Big Flow produced a small pistol, a .22 caliber made by Ruger, and he placed it to the side of Hazy Junior's head. He pulled the trigger without hesitation.

The small caliber bullet pierced the young man's skull with a sickening, muffled sound. The bullet must have lodged deep into his brain, for it never exited out the other side.

Hazy Junior's body crumpled to the floor in a sad heap, as blood trickled out the side of the small hole in his head, punctuated by a shocking singe of gunpowder burns around the wound.

"What?" Tiny Deege screamed, standing up from the couch, where he had just made himself comfortable. Zann's mouth hung open. Momo frowned angrily.

Big Flow didn't say a word. He walked into the kitchen, smoking pistol swinging in his hand by his side. The sound of stretching latex rubber squealed from the kitchen, and a moment later, Big Flow walked back into the living room, gloved-up, and wiping the pistol down with a rag. He even dropped out the magazine and wiped that down as well before replacing it.

Then the charismatic gang leader placed the pistol in the hand of the dead man, curling his lifeless finger over the trigger.

"Whoa!" Tiny Deege shouted, when he noticed the pistol's barrel was pointed toward the middle of his chest. He jumped out of the way, and the other gang members scattered to the sides of the room. Big Flow forced Hazy Junior's lifeless finger to pull the trigger, firing a round into the wall.

"What's that all about, Big?" Zann asked, showing his shiny silver grill through a terrified grimace.

"If our late friend, Hazy J, truly killed himself," Big Flow said, sounding nonchalant, "there would certainly be gunshot residue on his hand. And the police like to check for that sort of thing."

"Yo, but why you gotta kill him, though?" Tiny Deege dared ask. "He was one of us."

"The organization is taking too much heat, my undersized friend," Big Flow said, slipping the pistol into a gallon-sized Ziploc bag. "We need to spread the suspicion, so it doesn't fall entirely upon our shoulders."

Shoulda thought of that afore you started cuttin' people down like animals, Momo thought. *You the one bringin' all the heat, Big Flow.*

"Zann," Big Flow ordered, "go to Walmart and buy another box of dominoes, take out the double zero so we can slip it into Hazy J's pocket."

"Mannn, what?" Zann protested. "We gonna make the 5-0 think another one o' our brothers was one of them chump Cuban bangers?"

"This will be the second body they'll find that links the murders on the river to Code 31," Big Flow said. "That should be more than enough evidence to cast the heat off of ourselves, and place it upon the Cubans. Do you disagree? Or do you think we need a third body to convince them?"

Momo saw the terrified look in Zann's eyes. Based on the gang leader's alarming actions of late, he knew the dreadlocked firebrand wouldn't hesitate to terminate even a longtime member of the gang like Zann, any longer than he had for a pair of rookies like Wily Beeve and Hazy Junior. Zann shook his head.

Big Flow gave Zann specific orders to steal a car from somewhere in Little Havana. The idea was to place the body with the gun in the stolen car, and dump it in a vacant lot someplace along the river.

"Cops will think it's just a suicide," Big Flow explained, pulling a handwritten note out of his pants pocket with his still-gloved fingers. "Especially after reading about how depressed Hazy J has been these past few months, and the great remorse he felt over shooting those cops for his gang, Code 31."

"Man, you gonna let our own brothers hang out to dry to cover yo' ass?" Momo asked. Rage seethed through him. He thought about grasping Big Flow's throat and choking him out. "What you thinkin', man?"

"Momo," Big Flow said, an unnerving, calm tone apparent in his voice, "I'd like to speak with you privately for a moment, if that is all right with you."

Momo thought about pulling his petite pistol and smoking Big Flow right there in his own living room. But he was curious. Curious to see how the gang's leader might try to justify his unpredictable behavior

Momo followed Big Flow down the hall, keeping a few feet of space between himself and the bobbing dreadlocks that reached the middle of the gang leader's back. He stepped into Big Flow's master bedroom, finding it cramped with his California king-sized bed, onyx black headboard and footboard with matching dresser, all taking up most of the floor space in the small room.

Big Flow stopped into the few feet of space between the foot of his bed and the wall, and turned to face Momo. Momo kept his hand in his pocket, his finger on the trigger of his pint-sized pistol, as he waited for Big Flow to make his next move.

CHAPTER 35

B ONGO PEPPITONE'S HOUSE WAS JUST a small cottage out behind his storefront, which was a well-known head shop in Little Havana, called Bongo's Glassworks and Sundry. At first, Max had thought the diminutive building was just a garage or a storage shed, but as he drew closer, led by the shopkeeper himself, Max realized the little building was actually a very well-maintained and cozy home.

The landscaping between the store and cottage included a row of miniature roses and some scattered Japanese maple trees, and the area directly in front of the cottage door contained a purposefully raked sandpit with deliberately placed smooth river stones here and there. Max had seen these in magazines before, and recognized it to be a Zen garden.

He followed Bongo over stone steps toward the front door, and the cautious shop owner unlocked three or four locks before opening the door and holding out his hand, allowing Max to enter first.

"Please, take a seat," Bongo said, locking the door behind them. He picked up a black remote control from a side table and used it to turn on a couple of lamps to illuminate the room with warm, even light.

Max sat on a cushy brown leather sofa, while Bongo sat cross-legged in a sort of yoga pose in a high-backed wicker chair. Max looked at the eccentric man, sizing him up the best he could: Bongo Peppitone was maybe fifty to fifty-five years old, and he wore a pair of wildly grown mutton chops, long camel-colored hair that settled into a tidy braid on his left shoulder. His eyes appeared large through the clear lenses of his frameless glasses, and they glared back at Max, likely wondering what such a clean-cut fellow was doing in such a place as this.

"So, what can I do for you, my friend," Bongo asked. "Shreeve sent you over, so he must trust you. What was your name again?"

"Max," Max said. "Maxwell, actually. I normally wouldn't need something like this, but recent circumstances in my life have found me needing a whole new identity, as well as one for a friend and colleague of mine."

"Tryin' to get away from the wife?" Bongo asked, looking down at the wedding ring on Max's hand.

Despite the pain he still felt every time he thought of his wife, Max could not help but chuckle at the suggestion. "No, nothing like that, Bongo. How much do you really need to know about my situation? Is it important for us to do business?"

"No, no, it really isn't," Bongo said. He used his remote control, clicking a series of buttons before Creedence Clearwater Revival started playing *Lookin' Out My Back Door* from hidden speakers, and Max immediately noted the exceptional sound quality; Bongo was a true audiophile. Max also noticed an odd smell in the room, and the air in front of his eyes grew increasingly hazy.

"I just like to get to know my clients before I start working for them," Bongo said. "I don't wanna just sell a product, you know. I prefer to establish a relationship. But there's also something to be said for plausible deniability too." Bongo chuckled, and Max was somehow surprised to see the head shop owner's perfectly straight, bright white teeth. *Must go to the same dentist as Josue,* Max thought.

"Pardon me for saying so," Max said, continuing to look the other man up and down, noticing his white button-up shirt that draped open to the man's navel, as well as the black leather pants, and the unbuttoned suede vest; he was a cross between an aging rock star and a too-young hippie, "You strike me as sort of a Woodstocky kind of guy. Aren't you a bit young to have experienced the sixties and all that?"

Bongo laughed. "You're right, man. I sort of missed the party. But my brother was much older than me. He was the real deal, you know? He was actually at the Stones Altamont Free Concert. You know, *Sympathy for the Devil*, dude got stabbed by Hell's Angels, all of that. It was a bad scene, man.

"We grew up in East Palo Alto, me being born about twenty years after my brother. I suppose I looked up to him a lot, was influenced by him. I also grew up in the glory days of Silicon Valley, fueling some of my other passions. Like adopting new technologies early on." Bongo inhaled deeply, held his breath for about thirty seconds, and then exhaled.

Max noticed himself starting to feel lightheaded. "Is there some sort of…smoke…being pumped in here or something?"

"Oh, sorry, man," Bongo said, flipping a button on his house-controlling remote. "I should have asked you first if you were down. See, I used to hit the bong pretty hard—that's where my nickname came from—but when vaping came onto the scene, I was fully onboard with combining my love of the leaf with my love of tech. You may have central air-conditioning in your house. I got that too, but I also built a central vaping system. Every fifteen minutes or so, a burst of vapor from some really good Jamaican White Tiger concentrate is expelled out into the room."

"Wow," Max said. "That's…innovative."

"Thanks, man," Bongo said. "So you need two IDs. I'm assuming you need full backgrounds and histories too. That's kinda my specialty—and why I cost a lot more than the other guys.

"Somebody starts looking into your past, they're gonna find out you have a history, you went to a certain high school, you used to work for so and so, etc. I can do all that; it just takes a little time. I usually charge ten grand apiece for a full background. And it'll take about a week or so to get it done."

"I need them by tomorrow night," Max said. "And I'll give you twenty apiece."

"Tomorrow? Really? Twenty each?" The gears seemed to turn in Bongo's mind, as he likely considered if such a truncated timetable was even possible. He closed his eyes and inhaled deeply again, holding his breath.

It seemed like a long time before the unique forger exhaled and said, "I'll do it, man. You got cash?"

Max nodded. He reached into his bag and pulled out four $10,000 bundles and set them on the little square coffee table between him and Bongo.

Bongo looked down at the stack of cash in front of him. "Well, all right, man."

Max followed Bongo to the next room, and the oddball forger took a seat at an ergonomic task chair—the kind they don't make anymore—in front of a computer desk with a mouse, keyboard, and about a dozen monitors, ranging from fourteen-inch square to about thirty-inch widescreen. All of them were on; a few flashed monochromatic streams of numbers and other data feeds, while a couple of them were all black, with a white cursor blinking in the upper left corner. Bongo offered Max a stool nearby and cracked his knuckles before clicking his mouse and beginning to type on the keyboard.

"I'll need to know a few things to get your background ID going. Then, you are free to go, and I'll deliver the IDs to you tomorrow night. You can just stop by the store. Unless you want to meet me someplace."

Max agreed to stop by the following day. Bongo began the questionnaire, asking questions like: Where were you born? What states have you lived? How old are you?

"Don't want to set up an ID that's too close to the real one;

might cause some red flags to go off." Bongo typed quickly as Max spoke. He also asked questions about Josue, though Max did not know the answers to many of the questions. He didn't think it mattered much, since Josue had never been a United States citizen before. And he figured that records in Haiti were probably not very thorough.

Bongo opened a mini-fridge beside him and twisted the cap off a Belgian IPA. "Like one?"

Max shook his head. As far as he was concerned, until further notice, he was finished with drinking any kind of alcohol. "But I'd love one of those bottles of water you've got there."

Bongo handed Max a green glass bottle of chilled San Pellegrino from the fridge. "What do you want your friend's alias to be?"

"Alias?" Max asked.

"I'm assuming you don't want his real name used on his bogus passport," the forger said, a serious look on his face. Max wondered if the shady criminal was sizing him up, secretly judging Max on his lack of criminal savvy.

"Hmm," Max said. He had not considered what he or Josue would use for aliases. He supposed he might have thought Bongo would just "assign" him one. But he pondered the question for a long moment, thinking of how much it reminded him of naming one of his own children.

Max picked up a legal pad on the desk next to Bongo and printed a name. The forger put on reading glasses and looked at the paper. "José Dumbass? That's what you want your friend's name to be?"

Max laughed hard. "No, Bongo. It's Josue." Max spelled it aloud for the confused counterfeiter. "And it's Dumas, not Dumbass. I was thinking of Alexandre Dumas, author of *The Three Musketeers, Man in the Iron Mask, The Count of Monte Cristo*. He is one of Josue's favorite authors, and I thought he'd like to be named after him. His name isn't that important to me, I'd just like for him have a legitimate US passport and work history—at least one that looks legit."

"Well, that's a lot better," Bongo said, looking back at his computer screen. Max made certain he typed out the name correctly, Josue Dumas. Then the forger looked at Max.

"Do you know what you'd like *your* alias to be," Bongo asked, having twisted in his ergonomic chair to face Max. He kneaded his long ponytail, and Max noticed for the first time that his light tan hair was dappled with streaks of pure white.

Max considered the question for a long moment. It *was* important. Whatever name he chose would likely become his name for a long time, maybe for good.

"There's a story that's been told in my family for generations," Max said, noticing his hand beginning to shake slightly. Maybe he wasn't completely free of his withdrawal symptoms. He stuffed it into his pocket. "It's about my great-great-grandfather."

Bongo looked interested. He took off his reading glasses and sat back in his chair, taking a long sip from his beer. Max wondered if the forger got much company inside his virtual walk-in bong.

"My great-great-grandfather was a hunter and skinner living in a rustic cabin he had built with his own hands in the Cuillin, a range of jagged mountains located on the Isle of Skye in Scotland.

"This would have been around the turn of the twentieth century," Max said. "Or so the story goes. Few understood why my relative had chosen to live the reclusive life of a hermit. But he lived in the foreboding mountains above a quickly modernizing village situated beside a beautiful, picturesque loch down in the valley below.

"I think he probably liked the company of the red deer and majestic elk up there more than he liked the company of people. The deer, they pranced amongst the jagged black basalt rocks that jutted up through the sparse glens, close to the summits of the mountain range. Must have been a beautiful place, like a postcard." Max was careful to tell the story exactly like he had heard it, a dozen or so times when he was growing up.

"The grizzled highlander kept to himself, for the most part, spending his days hunting, skinning the animals, and tanning their hides into supple and sought-after leather."

Bongo rubbed the black bonded leather that wrapped the arms of his chair, eyebrows raised, as he listened intently to Max's account.

"One especially cold February day—I mean a bitterly cold, freeze-your-spit-before-it-hits-the-ground kind of day—in the small hours of the morning, a fire broke out inside the cabin. It was later decided that a smoldering log must have rolled out of the fireplace when the burned ones underneath it had shifted. The flaming log rolled out, causing a kerosene lantern on the floor to explode."

"Whoa, man," Bongo said, looking up at Max with huge, moon-sized eyes with dilated pupils. "That's heavy duty." The forger took another deep breath of the thin THC-laced vapor that permeated the room.

"My grandfather had been asleep at the time, supposedly after a long evening swilling large amounts of Highland Scotch, and stuffing himself until round with venison stew. The tenacious trapper awoke to find his cabin fully ablaze, engulfed in flames that licked like flickering tongues onto the walls all around him.

"The cabin's only exits were the front door and the side window. Both were blocked by sheets of fire fueled by the buckets of lard my grandpa had rendered from the carcasses he hunted, or by the piles of dried wood he had stacked under the window to feed the hungry fireplace."

"Good heavens," the forger said, literally biting one of his fingernails as he listened. "What happened next?"

"Two or three times my grandfather tried to get close enough to run through the fire to reach the door, finding himself singed each time just by the radiant heat of the fire—he knew there would be no chance of getting close to the door or window without being burned alive."

Bongo gasped.

"In a desperate measure to preserve his life, my grandfather grabbed several of his freshly tanned red deer pelts and dunked them into a bucket of water. He picked up one of his sharp skinning knives, and covered himself over with the wet pelts. For hours, he dug that blade into the soft loamy earth that made up the floor of the cabin. He didn't know at the time whether he was creating a safe refuge for himself, or if he was literally digging his own tomb.

"The next morning, some of the folks from down below in the village—no doubt drawn by the billowing smoke that rose from the jagged cliffs above, near the site of my grandfather's cabin—gathered around the smoldering remains of the burnt structure. Some stood by, hats in hand, others wept.

"When my grandfather climbed up out of his earthen recess, beneath a mound of wet buckskins, folks gasped. One or two of them wailed, as if they were actually seeing the ghostly remains of a dead man, reanimated.

"When the stubborn skinner stumbled into the Presbyterian church house in the village later that morning, still smoking by some accounts, members of the congregation began to murmur among themselves. They said that Wallace Craig had spent an evening in hell, and he had crawled out of the ashes like a phoenix."

"Damn," Bongo said in a breathy whisper.

"All that being said, Bongo," Max said to the quirky forger, "I would like to be called Craig. Maxwell Craig."

The enraptured forger furrowed his brow and pursed his lips in a gesture that suggested deep reverence for Maxwell's ancestor.

The young hippie nodded once, as if he approved of Max's choice. "It's a good name."

Max rubbed his eyes and exhaled a long breath, slowly. Then he turned toward Bongo, who still looked at him. "You got anything to munch around here?"

CHAPTER 36

ARTHUR PLACED HIS HANDS ON the countertop directly in front of the charge nurse in the ICU at Reed Memorial Hospital. He squinted his eyes through his Ray Bans, scrutinizing the thirty-ish brunette's nametag.

"Hi...Crenshaw? Like the melon? I'm Detective Parks from Miami PD and this is my partner, Seargent Ferrigno. Yeah, like the Hulk, Ferrigno. We're here to check on the condition of a young male black you have recovering in one of your ICU rooms. It is paramount that we interview him as soon as possible; he may have been involved in a violent robbery, not far from here, about a week ago, which resulted in the deaths of two of our fellow officers, as well as three civilians."

Lorenzo leaned his elbow against the counter and watched Arthur speak as if it amused him, while he held quiet.

"You must mean this young man, maybe eighteen to twenty, brought up with a broken left femur and a nasty bump to his noggin. Josue is all we've got for a name—from a torn envelope we found in his pocket. I think it's here somewhere," the brown-eyed nurse said, shuffling through some scattered papers, until she had located a manila folder. She pulled out the tatty envelope.

"See how it's ripped? You can make out his first name, and his town in Haiti, but the sender's name and address is completely gone."

Arthur scrutinized the envelope, and passed it to Zo. "Haitian.

You think he just got off the boat and fell right in with Ti Flow? Maybe he already had a connection in the gang."

Lorenzo shrugged.

Arthur noted how tired his partner's eyes looked. He wondered if it was the physical manifestation of his undiagnosed illness, or just the stress of the job, compounded by *not knowing.*

"What else?" Lorenzo asked.

Nurse Crenshaw reached into the envelope and slipped out a long, snakelike silver chain with a quarter-sized pendant. She handed it to Lorenzo, who held the pendant close to his eyes. "Catholic. One of the saints, or something."

Arthur took the necklace from his partner. "Our Lady of Perpetual Help. Also known as the Blessed Virgin Mary, mother of Jesus Christ, and designated patron saint of Haiti."

"Well this was clutched in his left hand when the ambulance brought him in," Crenshaw said. "Must have meant a lot to him. I mean, he'd been carrying a couple of big bags of takeout chicken, and clinging to this at the same time. Poor guy probably didn't see it coming."

"Poor guy may have killed a friend of mine," Lorenzo said, glaring at the charge nurse. Arthur thought it looked as if Zo were leaning on the counter for support. It concerned him. "We need to see the kid, now."

"He's in room thirteen," the charge nurse said, looking down at her computer screen. "I'll take you in to see him. Please keep quiet when we go in. If he is conscious, I'm going to take his vitals and determine if he's stable enough for questioning. If he's coherent, you may ask him a few questions for now, but serious questioning will have to wait, at least until tomorrow. This guy's been through a lot."

Art and Zo followed Crenshaw into the room. The young immigrant might have been a robot, connected to so many machines with tubes, wires, electrodes, sensors, and some strange devices that Arthur did not recognize. The kid's leg had been placed in a thick cast up to his knee, while his other leg was wrapped in some kind of orthopedic sock, probably something to stave off blood clots. His head had been partially wrapped with white gauze, and small electrodes had been placed all around his skull to monitor brain activity.

Lorenzo gazed suspiciously at the computer screen that monitored the kid's brainwaves. "Is this normal activity for a guy that's asleep?"

"Shhh," Crenshaw shushed. She continued about her procedures of checking Josue's vitals, lifting his eyelid and shining a light at his pupil. She checked his blood pressure, writing all the data on a chart, before she performed a couple more tests, and then stepped out of the room, waving for the two officers to follow.

"His vital signs look very promising, considering all the trauma he's experienced," Crenshaw said, looking down at her notes.

"His brain activity looked like it was from a guy that was wide awake," Lorenzo said. "How come he's still not conscious?"

"He might be partially conscious, but the lingering anesthetic is keeping him from waking up fully for now," Crenshaw said. "It's obviously not a good time for you to question him. If you're really that adamant, I would suggest you come by in a few hours. Maybe he'll have woken up by then. But there's no use in your staying here now. He's not going anywhere."

"Where's the guard?" Lorenzo asked. "I told the ER receptionist to have a guard posted on his room."

"Charlie's been in and out of here all day," Crenshaw said. "He checks in regularly. There's just no need to keep him posted if the kid is unconscious. He wakes up, I'll call Charlie to stand guard over him."

Lorenzo shook his head. He seemed unable to disguise

his disgust with the entire situation. Arthur recognized this, and thought he should intervene before Zo got into it with the charge nurse.

"I think we'll go and catch dinner, and then be back," Arthur said, forcing a polite grin. "Thanks a lot, Crenshaw. See you later."

"I'll be here," she replied. "Until two a.m."

Lorenzo took one last look through the glass wall of room thirteen. He glared at the unconscious patient. Art wondered if the other man suspected the kid of faking sleep. After a few seconds, Art placed a hand on his partner's shoulder and pushed him in the direction of the elevator. "What you want? Ribs? Steak?"

"Funny," Lorenzo said, taking one last glance at the sleeping Haitian. "But I suddenly got a hankerin' for Shakey Redbone's chicken."

Max slipped out of the elevator and adjusted his badge on his scrubs top. He looked down at the photo; he thought he resembled a criminal posing for a mug shot. He supposed it was fitting, though. He was a criminal. Or at least he would be soon.

Before he had left Bongo Peppitone's house, Max had asked the eccentric forger about the possibility of getting a more authentic badge made, using the purloined identity from the hospital cafeteria. The tech-savvy hippie had told Max he would gladly do him one better: Bongo had hacked into the hospital's database, and added Max as a bona fide member of hospital staff, printing him off an authentic-looking laminate with a scannable barcode.

Through the glass partitions that surrounded the ICU's centralized nurses' station, where a trio of doctors, four nurses, and another guy, maybe some kind of lab technician, sat at various stations, staring almost blankly at computer screens while they monitored their patients' vital statistics, Max spotted the two police detectives he had earlier seen at the Paradiso Inn.

The pair followed Crenshaw, the head ICU nurse, into Josue's room. Max tried to be furtive as he made his way to a men's room on the opposite side of the rectangular ward from his friend's glass-fronted ICU room.

Max slipped inside and quickly checked the two-stall bathroom, finding it deserted. He switched off the light and opened the door a crack, just enough that he could watch the two cops as they stood, waiting inside Josue's room, as the nurse checked the young man's vitals.

Max saw that Josue kept his eyes shut the entire time the nurse worked on him. *Good man, Josue*, Max thought. He guessed that Josue must have regained consciousness by now, as semi-coherent as he had been earlier.

When the detectives disappeared into the elevator, Max watched the charge nurse, as she unlocked her smartphone on her desk, toggled through an app or something with her finger, and then set the phone back down, before leaving the ICU counter for the ladies' room.

Max did not waste another second. He stepped out of the men's room, smiled and nodded back at a lovely black-haired nurse with pale skin who looked up at him from her computer station behind the big oval counter, and then strode toward Josue's room. Max slipped inside and found the young Haitian asleep, his head cocked to the left of the elevated head of his mattress.

"Josue," Max whispered. "It's me, Max."

Josue's eyes opened, and he lifted his head, staring at Max with a piercing gaze. "Maxwell, you come back."

"Of course I came back," Max said, stepping over to the bedside and grasping his friend's left hand, gripping it tightly into his own. "Listen, I don't have much time. I'm working on a plan to get you out of here, get us both out of here. All I need you to do is rest up and be ready when I come and get you. I don't have it all worked out, but when the time comes, we're going to have to quickly disconnect you from all this crap and flee the building. Okay?"

Josue nodded. Max thought his friend looked as if he were in a lot of pain, but Josue still smiled through his grimace. The young Haitian held up both of his thumbs, just like Palomar Teete. Max chuckled.

Max pulled his iPhone 3GS out of his scrubs pocket and flipped open the camera app. "Hold still and smile big," he said, taking a photo of the bandaged man.

"It may be tomorrow night when I come back, or it may be the following morning," Max said. "But I'll need you to be ready."

"I'll be ready, Maxwell."

Max nodded and slipped back out through the sliding glass door to exit the room. As he stepped out into the hallway, he found Crenshaw waiting for him.

She snatched the badge off of Max's chest and made a beeline for her computer behind the nurse's counter. "Who the hell are you really?" the fired-up nurse asked, as she waved Max's laminate under a barcode scanner. "I'm supposed to believe your name is Nubbie? That's the fakest name I've ever heard. It's like you didn't even try to come up with a fake name that sounded real. And you're a new-hire x-ray tech who just happens to wander around the ICU ward for fun? I'm supposed to believe that?"

"I..." Max didn't even know what to say. He considered making a run for it.

The charge nurse's scanner made a bright blipping sound, and she glared at Maxwell for a second before glancing down at her computer monitor. "According to the hospital computer," Crenshaw said, garnering the attention of the ICU doctors and the other nurses who now stood assembled behind her, "your name is...Alexander Nubbington. It says you're an...x-ray technician, and your first scheduled day is...next Monday."

Max shrugged his shoulders and frowned. He folded his arms and glared back at Crenshaw.

"If you're in the Radiology department, you must have been hired by Dr. Macy," Crenshaw said. "Terry Macy, right? He's a sweetheart."

An alarm went off in Max's brain. He wasn't sure, at first, what was wrong, but something about what the vigilant charge nurse had said wasn't right. Max's mind went back to the hospital directory he had scanned earlier when he had studied it to learn the layout of the hospital.

"That is all true, Crenshaw," Max said. "May I call you Crenshaw? Except that I've only met Dr. Macy once. And he told me his name was Tony, not Terry."

Crenshaw Stubbins looked surprised, even embarrassed, as her slightly plump cheeks reddened a bit. She glanced around herself, seeing the judgmental faces of the other nurses looking back at her. Then she looked at Max.

"I am so sorry, Alexander...Nubbie. You have to be able to see how suspicious it looks, though. I mean, why have you been spending so much time walking around in the ICU?"

"I'm new to Miami," Max explained. "I parked my car in the southeast parking lot, and I found that if I take the stairs near the gift shop, I can then cut through ICU to Radiology, and save around ten minutes, versus taking the elevator and following the main hallway. I suppose I *have* been spending a lot of time loitering in different departments around the hospital, you've got me there. I'm taking night classes—it's my dream to be an RN— and I just want to pick up anything I can. I've really got nothing better to do. I don't know anybody in town. And I don't have any friends here—I suppose my prospects here at the hospital are looking pretty bleak as well."

Crenshaw's big brown eyes welled up with tears.

"Is this what it's going to be like here at Reed?" Max asked, doing his best to sound crestfallen. "You know, I worked at Johns Hopkins in Baltimore, for almost a year. I gotta tell you, the people there were *nice*, they never made fun of my name, and they all seemed to be able to accept me just the way I am." Max wondered if his latter remark might be pushing it, just a bit.

The raven-haired nurse who had earlier smiled at Max looked at Crenshaw with a bitter expression. Crenshaw turned her head to look at one of the doctors, who had a face that said, "Don't look at *me*."

"I'm soooo sorry, Nubbie," Crenshaw said, her chin beginning to quiver, and her charming southern accent becoming much more pronounced. "Would it be all right if I gave you a hug, sweetie?"

"Sure," Max said, holding his palms up by his sides. The charge nurse latched onto him with a powerful embrace. Max cautiously reached his arms around the nurse and allowed his hands to settle on her back. He looked past her, noticing something glinting on the nurse's cluttered counter. It was a long silver chain and pendant. It was Josue's mother's necklace—going back to retrieve it had almost gotten the kid executed in the middle of Lemon Street.

"If you need anything, honey, you come and ask me, all right?" Crenshaw said, snatching a tissue from a box on the counter and dabbing the tears from her eyes, being careful not to smudge her thick mascara and eye liner. "Sorry we got off on the wrong foot here, hon. How about if we just start over. Hi, I'm Crenshaw Stubbins. Welcome to the Reed Memorial family."

"Thanks," Max said, feeling about as surprised as Crenshaw that his credentials appeared to be legitimate as far as the hospital computer was concerned. *This is going to be easier than I thought.*

After that sweet new x-ray tech left the ward—Crenshaw had made sure to watch him leave, as good as he looked in his tight scrubs pants—and everyone had turned their attention back to their workstations, Crenshaw took a furtive glance around her, and then picked up her phone and began to tap through her list of contacts. It was a bit of a chore, navigating the contacts with her ostentatious nails, but as the long gels clacked on the glass screen of her smartphone, she finally found the right name and tapped on the "call now" button.

"Hello? Big?" Crenshaw asked, keeping her voice low, as she took another glance around her. "How you doin', sweetie? It's Crenshaw. Yeah, I know it's been a long time. Sorry I haven't called or come around, but work has been *crazy* the last couple months. Anyway, I'm calling now because I talked to Tonya at Good Vibez last night. She said she'd run into Momo in the old neighborhood; he told her about the kid who crossed you guys and ran away from the gang, that 'running man' the police said they were looking for on the news. She told me you guys had a bounty on the kid's head, and would pay five large for any tips on where to find him. Well, baby, how about this for a tip? He's here, right now. In the ICU."

CHAPTER 37

MAX HAD USED AN INTERNET search engine to find the boat dealership, called Sherman's Marine Menagerie, which specialized in all manner of new and used seagoing vessels. The place was located in the Upper East Side of Miami, not far from the bridge that connected the mainland with tiny Pelican Island, where early morning boaters shoved off from a small marina. The boats would be heading offshore to nail as many marlin, sailfish, or mahi mahi as they could.

Max had caught a cab to take him to the dealership, arriving just a few minutes before the place opened. He stood outside the prison-like wrought iron fence that surrounded the dealership's expansive yard, peering in at the wide selection of inventory on display within. Big industrial racks built from stout steel I-beams were heavy-laden with boats of varying size and manufacturer, all stacked four levels high. Everything from small inflatable rafts with outboard motors to high-end center console offshore fishing boats, compact cabin cruisers, and fast water-ski boats, were all on display on the lot.

Through the gate, Max spotted the more impressive vessels, fifty to seventy-plus foot luxury yachts, docked at the far end of the boat yard, sitting still in the protected water of the intracoastal waterway that stretched, snakelike, far inland from the bay.

Max approached the gate and gave it a tug, finding it to be locked.

"Ahoy there, sailor," a gangly man behind the fence shouted

in Max's direction. The man's anachronistic style of dress surprised Max. He supposed he might simply have described it as unique. The lean man, obviously a salesman, wore a black captain's hat, cocked slightly sideways as the skipper always wore on *Gilligan's Island*. His navy blue blazer featured large brass anchor-embellished buttons and partially covered an untucked Hawaiian shirt of many colors. But the strangest thing about the salesman's appearance was his pants: white and green plaid polyester slacks that looked as though they must have been stolen from his grandfather's dresser.

"Hey, listen," the man shouted through the iron fence, "we're not officially open for another..." the man looked at his watch, "seven minutes. But I'll tell you what. I can tell you are a serious buyer, and I'm just going to let you in early."

The colorfully dressed man pulled a key ring, heavy with about two hundred keys, from his pants pocket and used what looked to Max like an old-fashioned jail cell key to open the gate to the boat dealership's sales yard.

"I'm Stanley," the man said in a bright voice Max would describe as somewhere between a tenor and a soprano. "Stanley Fump. I'm the regional sales manager here at Sherman's, so if you have any questions, I'm your guy."

"I'm Maxwell. Maxwell...Craig."

"Great to meet you, Max," Stanley said, grabbing hold of Max's hand and shaking it vigorously. "Here's my card. If you flip that over you'll see it's also a coupon: you take that down to the nearest Monty Maximus, flash 'em the card, tell 'em Stanley Fump sent you, and you get free marinara dipping sauce with your breadsticks. No joke, I worked out the deal with 'em to treat my best customers. Anyhow, what type of vessel can we get you into today? You look like a fisherman to me. Marlin? Swordfish? You just look like a billfish fighter to me. Am I right?" Stanley felt Max's bicep and made an expression of amazement. "Tell you what, I'll show you around, you just nudge me when something grabs you, okay? Don't let me get in the way of *your* dreams."

Max was about to tell the salesman exactly what he was looking for when he was interrupted.

"I bet you water-ski," Stanley said, waving his hand toward a long, pointy vessel that must have been over forty feet long. "You probably tear it up on the water, don't you? Backflips over the wake and whatnot? Over two thousand horsepower in this one. Of course, you might pull someone's arms off trying to get them up out of the water, it's that fast. But a beauty nonetheless."

Max noticed that in addition to all of the boats in the yard, about a half-dozen cars and pickups were on display in front of a gray building with a sliding glass door that housed the dealership's office. The cars and trucks featured bright orange and red adhesive price numbers pressed onto their windshields.

"Didn't know you sold cars too," Max said, as he and Stanley walked past the used cars.

"We sometimes make trades for some of our boats," the slick boat dealer explained, "and sometimes we end up with some really fine low-mileage examples of late model automobiles. We only offer up the best of the best of these for sale."

Max considered the cars as he walked: an early eighties jacked-up, four-by-four GMC Sierra pickup with a roll bar; a late seventies Pontiac Firebird with highly oxidized maroon paint, torn seats, and t-tops; a couple of bland-looking Ford Tempos; a 1990 cherry red 5.0L Mustang convertible; an especially long canary yellow Cadillac from the seventies; and a shiny black and silver 2011 Smart Fortwo. Max stopped to scrutinize the latter a little closer.

"A real honey, isn't she?" Stanley asked. "My personal vehicle, if you must know. Only had her for about six months, only driven between here and my home in Coral Gables. Sure do hate to see her go. But out with the old, you know."

"What's wrong with it?" Max asked.

Stanley doubled over in laughter. "Wrong? What's wrong with Sheena, here? There *ain't nothing* wrong with her, my friend. She's in showroom condition, though this overcast lighting doesn't do her justice. Come to think of it, you've just convinced me. I'm not selling her. She just means too much to me to let her go."

Stanley took hold of Max's arm. "Lemme show you a catamaran over here that the previous owner had retrofitted with two Porsche 911 engines. Okay, I'll spill; she used to belong to Ernest Borgnine."

Max shook off the boat dealer's grasp. "Look, Mr. Fump…"

"Stan."

"Look, Stan," Max continued. "I'm going to make this really easy for you. I need a cabin cruiser with sleeping quarters to accommodate two men, and is capable of cruising the open sea, mostly between the islands of the Caribbean. And I need it today."

Stanley Fump's eyes sparked to life like the lights on a pinball machine. "Hey, I'm here to make your wildest dreams become reality, Maxwell, and I won't be able to sleep tonight if I don't send you home with the perfect vessel for your needs." The boat dealer seemed to stare for a moment at the ring on Max's left ring finger. "You said you needed accommodations for two men. Why didn't you bring your husband with you today?"

"No," Max said, looking down at his own wedding ring, and then stuffing his hands into his pants pockets, "it's not like that. Josue's my…brother."

"Of course, of course," Stanley said. "Tell you what. Let's head over to the dock, and I'll show you a few of the more comfortable vessels we have that feature overnight accommodations."

The fast-talking salesman made a beeline for what must have been the most expensive and luxurious vessel at the dealership, moored to some pilings beside the blue-green intracoastal water that opened up to the bay about two hundred yards to the east.

"Isn't she a sight to behold," Stanley said, laying his right arm against the convertible yacht's gunwale, near the stern, and then laying his head down on his arm as if he was going to sleep. "Seventy feet of brand-new Viking yacht glory. It's the 2010 model. Her salon will be like your home away from home when you're at sea, and the extravagant galley has only the best appliances, walk-in pantry, and granite countertops. She's got satin-finished teak wood cabinetry, three well-appointed staterooms, as well as two crew rooms with bunks; and for the fisherman I know you are, there's a fighting chair, in-deck livewell for all those helpless fish you're going to land, as well as mezzanine-level bait stowage, and a generous freezer to preserve the haul. And she's ready for you to shove off today for just five point four mil."

"Sorry, Stan," Max said, rubbing his forehead with his thumb and forefinger, as he felt the first semblance of a headache coming on, "but that's a little bit out of my price range."

"Hey, that's okay," Stan said, smiling broadly to reveal what must have been a mouthful of expensive capped teeth. "'Cause I gotta be straight with you, Max. We need to make room for the 2011s which are on the way *as we speak*. And just between you and me, you can have her today for just five point one."

"As good of a deal as that obviously is, Stan, I'm afraid I'm looking to spend not much more than a hundred K." Max slipped his thumbs through the straps of his backpack, adjusting it over his back. It felt weird wearing so much cash.

"Well, okay," Stan said, his voice rising about an octave. He strode down the dock toward another, much older-looking vessel tied off to some more dock pilings. "Now we're getting somewhere. Check out this 1988 convertible, also by Viking. This one's a forty-eight footer. She's got the high-end features, and the economical price tag you're looking for."

The salesman stepped over the bow rail and grabbed the handle to the rear salon door. Max clutched the safety railing that ran around most of the vessel's deck, meaning to pull himself over the vessel's gunwale. Part of the railing broke off, and Max nearly fell into the gap between the yacht and the dock.

"Woah," Stan said. "Easy, sailor."

"No offense, Stan," Max said, dropping the broken piece of bow railing into the vessel's stern, "but this one's a little 'run down' for my taste. You know, I'm really not sure exactly what I'm looking for, but it's got to be brand-new. I don't know how to fix anything on boats, and I just need something that's not going to break down or wear out right away."

"Hmmm," Stan said, crossing his arms, and then touching his bottom lip with his index finger. "That really paints me into a corner, Maxwell. I don't know. I don't know." And then, as if a light bulb had burst into brilliance over his head, he said, "Now there just might be one boat that could fit your needs. Come this way, my friend."

The salesman led Max to a good-sized vessel that must have been around thirty feet in length, and appeared rather tall and stocky. It rested on a triple-axle trailer and was completely wrapped in thick white shrink wrap. "It's a Bayliner thirty-three footer, and it's just arrived. If you're really serious about buying something today, I can get Paco and Fabio over here to unwrap it so you can have a look."

"How much?" Max asked.

"Just between you and me, Max," Stanley said in a low voice, as he glanced furtively from side to side. "It's one twenty-five. Zero hours. Haven't even put it out on the lot yet. But I heard a rumor about this older fellow from Cocoa Beach who might be coming down this afternoon to take a look at her, so I wouldn't dawdle if I were you."

"Yeah. Get it unwrapped. Let's have a look. You think a Bayliner would be okay to take out onto the open ocean?"

"Don't let the name fool you, Max," Stan said, waving over

another employee in a dirty white tank top. Stan stabbed his thumb toward the wrapped vessel, and the other man nodded. In no time, two men were peeling away the shrink wrap to unveil a beautiful white and blue vessel with a stylish forward slanted spoiler.

"Thanks Paco, Fabio," Stan said. "You guys are the best." He turned toward Max. "She's not just built for the bay. But she's also not built specifically for open water. So, I think if you want to cruise the Caribbean, and can avoid the really heavy chop, this might just be the perfect vessel for you. But you'll really want to check the weather before you leave port; only head out into calm seas."

"And it can carry enough fuel to get me between the islands?" Max asked.

Stan's lips tightened. "That's where you might have a bit of trouble, Max. She'll hold somewhere in the neighborhood of a hundred and twenty gallons. Not gonna get you that far. Not with the twin Mercruiser five point oh's. She's got the upgraded motors, and she'll make over five hundred screaming ponies."

The dealer climbed a stepladder one of the lot attendants had placed against the swim platform at the rear of the vessel, and Stan stepped aboard before reaching his hand down to help Max. Stan showed Max the vessel's control console in the open cockpit, which featured ample seating, a small sink, and a fridge, before moving forward to open a companionway door.

Max followed Stan down a few steps to where a kitchenette was situated beside a cozy-looking double bed tucked into the bow. "Flat screen TV here," Stan said, as he opened a door, "full head with chemical crapper, sink, and shower." He opened another door. Here's a private stateroom with a queen-sized bed."

Max poked his head inside. It wasn't much of a stateroom, but it was an enclosed space with a built-in dresser and a comfortable bed, though only part of the space was standing height. The roof over the lower part of the bed must have only been around three feet above the bed.

"Can I add an extra tank or something to increase my fuel capacity?" Max asked. "It does seem like just the right boat, but I need to be able to travel six or seven hundred miles at a time."

"You know," Stan said with a knowing grin, "we just might be able to make this work. One of the accessories we sell now is called a fuel bladder. Think of it as just like a big water balloon filled with gasoline that sits on the deck. They'll strap down securely and increase your fuel payload. I think if we attached a four-hundred-gallon bladder on the bow deck, and two hundreds underneath the seats in the stern, it would give you a very nice range without adding too much weight, especially if it's just the two of you onboard."

"How much, for everything?" Max asked.

"With the boat, the fuel bladders, delivery fees, the special 'friends and family' discount that I'm going to extend to you, Max, etc.," Stan said, and he seemed to be crunching numbers in his head. "I think we're looking at the one thirty-two range."

"Tell you what, Stan. If you can deliver the boat—fuel bladders installed and filled—to a particular dock in Islamorada by tonight, tomorrow at 6 a.m. latest, then I'll give you an extra ten grand. I'll also need the registration handled today."

"One forty-two? I think we've got a deal, Maxwell." Stan extended his hand for a shake.

Max shook the slick boat salesman's hand.

"How about we go back to my office, I'll punch your info into my old computron, and we'll see about getting you pre-approved for this tasty little eclair?"

"How about we go back to your office and I pull the full amount in cash from my backpack and hand it to you?" Max said.

"Hey, whatever works best for you, Maxwell," Stan said. "Are you sure there isn't anything else you need today? Maybe a dinghy to tow behind your flagship? Maybe some water-skis or one of those big inflatable bananas so you can drag the kids around?"

"Maybe," Max interjected. "I think I need a few of those cars you've got out front."

Stanley Fump looked at Max with a sideways glance. "Now, Max. My prices aren't *so low* that you're going to go and resell those cars now, are you?"

"Of course not," Max said. "I'll take the 4x4, the Firebird, the convertible Mustang, and the Smart car. I'll give you another…twenty-five grand."

"Deal," Stan said, offering his hand for another shake so fast Max wondered how he had even had time to consider the offer.

Max and Stanley Fump entered the salesman's office, and Max thought it smelled like mushrooms. The thick blue carpet had transformed over time to a nearly brown color, and a cluttered desk sat opposite the sliding glass door. Max sat down across from the boat dealer and placed his backpack on the chair next to him. He unzipped the pack and noticed that Stan's face had suddenly gone white.

"What is it?" Max asked, confused.

"What's with the gun, Max?" Stan said. He stared down at Max's waist.

Max looked down and saw that his shirt had pulled completely away from the Smith & Wesson pistol tucked into his waistband, leaving the weapon exposed. He had carried the weapon with him everywhere since the dangerous encounter with the gang members.

Max was about to dismiss the sight of the gun with an apology, telling the boat dealer he carried it for his own protection, when he suddenly changed his mind. He pulled the pistol from his waistband and placed it on the desk in front of him.

"I carry this to make sure no one jerks me around, Stanley. Now we've got a deal, and you are going to honor that deal, and you aren't going to tell anyone that I was ever here, or you and I are going to have some friction between us. Is that understood?"

Stanley Fump swallowed dryly. His head bobbed up and down slowly.

Max felt bad. He hated being the type of man who would intimidate another. But he knew he had already tiptoed into the life of a criminal. He needed to ensure he would have no trouble securing the boat. And the cars he was buying were just the latest part of a plan that seemed to be in constant flux.

Max counted out $167 thousand, mostly in $10,000 bundles of hundreds, stacking the money high on the desk in front of Stanley Fump's wide, seemingly mesmerized eyes. Then Max grabbed a pad of paper and wrote down the name of the marina where he wanted the boat delivered. He also made a list of items he wanted the slick boat dealer to procure for him. He slid the list across the desk to the salesman. He also told Stan a photocopy of his new Florida driver's license, which Bongo had procured for him, would be emailed to him today, for the boat's registration. Max told the salesman not to bother with the registrations for the cars; he wouldn't need them for more than a day or two anyway. "If the police come back here asking about these cars, you can just tell them they were stolen off the lot. You can take them back if you like and keep the money I paid for them. Just don't mention my name.

"I'll also need everything on that list, Stan," Max said. "I need it left on the boat. You get all that, there's an extra two grand in it for you."

Stanley Fump put on a pair of reading glasses and scrutinized the list.

"I'll be at this location tomorrow morning by six a.m.," Max said, glaring at the boat dealer with a menacing gaze. "If this boat isn't there, and ready to go. I'll be coming back here looking for you to ask why. Do you understand?"

Stanley Fump nodded again. Max considered the man's odd facial expression. He supposed it was the look a man gave when it was both the best day of his life, and the worst, all at the same time.

"Six a.m."

Stanley swallowed. He nodded.

CHAPTER 38

B IG FLOW'S EYES BLAZED WITH fire. He glared at Momo, and his hand fiddled in his right pants pocket.

Momo's heart pounded in a palpable way; he could count his own pulse without even touching his wrist or neck. The imposing second-in-command of the gang did his best to keep his breathing deep and even. He didn't want to get lightheaded. Not now.

"Yo, what is it?" Momo asked. He felt beads of sweat forming on his forehead as he stood, facing the leader of Ti Flow.

"You challenge my leadership, Momo?" Big Flow said. The vicious man actually appeared to Momo to have a disappointed expression, as if Momo's doubt had somehow hurt the other man.

Momo considered telling Big Flow exactly what he expected the gang leader wanted to hear. That no, he did not challenge him, that he would follow any directive the other man put forth. But Momo knew he couldn't do that. Taking even one more step down the dangerous path Big Flow was leading the entire gang down would almost certainly see even more of Ti Flow's members dead. First Wily Beeve, then Hazy Junior. *No more*, Momo said to himself.

"Man, you're outta line," Momo said, tucking his right index finger inside the trigger guard of his pistol in his pants pocket. "Can't let you lead this gang to its own destruction. And I can't let you kill any mo' of its members. We ain't gonna have no gang left, you keep killin' everyone. Dig?"

Momo wasn't sure what would come next, if it was all about to go down, or what. He only wondered if he'd have time to get a shot or two off from his pistol before the dreadlocked menace had a chance to strike with his furiously lethal hand weapon.

And then Big Flow said something that floored Momo.

"I'm so pleased you've risen up to stand up to me, Momo." Big Flow stepped past Momo and walked around to the side of his huge bed. He plopped down on the edge of the soft memory foam mattress. He crossed one leg over the other.

Momo was dumbfounded. His mouth dropped open, but his brain was unable to transmit words to his lips. *He was pleased?*

"I know it's taken a lotta guts to confront me, my friend. I know you know that some others before you have done so, and they might have paid for it with their lives. But it's a timely thing you do. Timely. For I've been starting to wonder if it isn't time to begin the grooming of this organization's next heir apparent."

"Yo, man, I don't know about all that," Momo said, still feeling greatly uneasy about the present confrontation, "but I gotta call you out on your erratic behavior of late. You killin' that guard in the marina without regard; killin' that old couple on they yacht; killin' them cops. You killed the twins in cold blood. I gotta say, brother, if this is what the Flow has become, I don't know that I wanna be in it, let alone be leadin' it."

"I realize that, at a glance, my actions of late might have appeared impulsive, my friend," Big Flow said, taking his sharp, pointed screwdriver out of his pocket and setting it down on his nightstand.

Momo wondered if he were sending a message, that he was effectively "disarming" himself.

"But if you look closer," Big continued, "you will see that I've made one difficult decision after the next, and I've done it for the health and preservation of our precious organization. What you don't see, my friend, is how I agonized over each of these decisions. How they tormented me.

"The guard in the marina, Momo," Big Flow said, looking up at the larger man with sincerity in his eyes. "I watched him through the scope of my rifle. He raised a pair of binoculars. He looked right at me, Momo. I am sure he spotted my rifle. Through the crosshairs I saw him reach for the radio handset attached to his shoulder. He was going to alert others, Momo. I shot him before he could raise the alarm."

Momo was still skeptical. It was a hard thing, to justify such brutality. But he held quiet while Big Flow continued.

"I know you didn't see the fighting knife the old man on the yacht clutched in his grip, or the small pistol in the hand of the vicious old woman. I shot her, Momo. I killed her, because she would have killed one of us. She had actually taken a single shot that had passed close by my head.

"Later, when the police caught up to us on the Miami River, I know you didn't see it all unfold, as you were in and out of the salon, piloting the vessel," Big Flow continued, an earnest tone apparent in his voice. "A police woman had an AR rifle pointed at Zann's chest. I saw the red laser dot crawling over his body like a bug. My instincts were fatherly, even if they *were* rash. I knew I had to kill her before she could kill my brother, my friend, my surrogate son, Zann Manning.

"So I opened fire," the larger-than-life gang leader said, speaking with a tone of lamentation. "An unfortunate situation. To have taken those lives when I would have much rather allowed them to live. But I brought all of my brothers home alive that night. And I will not apologize for that, Momo."

"What about the twins?" Momo asked. "That was messed up, you ask me. Why *they* gotta die?"

"Both of them spies," Big Flow said bluntly. "They belonged to Code 31. Planted in our gang by 31's leadership, to infiltrate us, find out what they could about the Flow's moves. They aimed to tear us down from within. Again, I made a tough call to protect our organization, as some day, I hope you will do."

Momo just stared at Big Flow, speechless. His brain struggled to connect all the dots. It was as if he had built a huge puzzle that was missing half a dozen pieces, and he had now just found them on the floor, under the couch.

"I do not relish taking lives, Momo. That it's become my reputation is merely an asset I regard highly, and protect fiercely. Perhaps my reputation for viciousness could prevent me from having to take other lives in the future."

"So you didn't..." Momo started to say, but still felt completely taken aback. "You aren't...a complete lunatic?"

Big Flow laughed. He stood up and put his hands on Momo's shoulders. Momo dared to relax his grip on the pistol in his pants pocket. Big Flow put his arms around Momo and hugged him tightly. "No, brother. I'm not a complete lunatic."

"An' everything you done, you done for a good reason?" Momo asked. He seemed to want to reassure himself of the gang leader's veracity.

"Everything I've done, and everything I will do, will only be to protect our precious brotherhood, Momo," Big Flow said reassuringly. "Ti Flow is so much larger than any one of us. It's worth protecting, Momo. I hope that, in time, you too will stand up to protect it with your own life."

Momo nodded. He felt better. Even if he still felt dazed by Big Flow's revelations.

"Are things all right between us then, brother?" Big Flow asked, holding out his hand for a shake.

Momo took Big Flow's hand. He nodded and shook the hand of the gang leader. "Yeah, man. We good."

"But you *did* challenge me in front of other members of the gang," Big Flow said, slapping Momo good-naturedly on the shoulder. "And for the good of the organization, my dear friend, I must now beat your ass."

Momo chuckled. But it only took a second for him to realize that Big Flow wasn't joking. Momo knew it would be crazy to allow another man to assault him. But he also knew the example such a beating would set for the other members of the gang. And Momo knew that, like Big Flow, he was willing to do what was right for the gang. So he supplicated himself.

Momo held his hands into fists by his sides and he leaned forward toward Big Flow, who had just stood up from the bed and cracked his knuckles. "All right, man. Get it over with."

"I'm sorry, brother," Big Flow said, shaking his head. He threw a punch to Momo's midsection that made the big man feel like he might puke. He gasped for breath, doubled over. The dreadlocked boss of Ti Flow pounded his fist into Momo's eye.

And then Big Flow unloaded on him.

CHAPTER 39

MAX PARKED THE SMART CAR against the curb in front of Max's Hardware and Paint, thankful he'd gotten such a good parking space. Max had turned the key in the ignition of the pint-sized two-seater outside of Stanley's office at the boat dealership, only to be blasted by the sounds of Barry Manilow singing *Ready to Take a Chance Again*. The song had reminded Max of an old Chevy Chase movie he'd watched a lot when he was a kid. But none of the buttons or knobs worked on the CD player on the dash, and Max couldn't turn off or change the song, so he just allowed Barry's soft rock stylings to serenade him as he drove the tiny car, navigating it swiftly through Miami's busy morning traffic.

The diminutive two-seater had taken a bit for Max to get used to. The shifter was able to switch between automatic mode and a sort of "manual" mode, although Max found it rather unconventional. He ultimately chose to use the flippy little paddle shifters on either side of the steering wheel. Max had found the inside of the vehicle to be much more spacious than he'd expected, and he knew that when the time came, he and Josue would both fit comfortably inside.

As he slammed the unnervingly flexible plastic door behind him, Max noticed he had almost left his backpack sitting on the passenger side seat. Even having paid more than $167 thousand to Stanley Fump for the brand-new boat and the used cars, Max's pack still bulged under the weight of more than a hundred thousand bucks. He'd decided to keep the backpack with him, rather than leaving it at his hotel room. He simply didn't feel secure leaving the money there, even in the room's safe. But he stopped, shook his head, and snatched the backpack out of the car, lest he have it stolen while he was shopping twenty feet away.

Max pushed open the door to the hardware store, thinking the old stucco and glass-fronted building must have looked really nice in the 1960s. Now, though, the smell of paint, cleaning supplies, cut metal, and freshly sawn lumber met his nostrils in a familiar way. But Max knew his mind had been so foggy the last time he'd been in the store that it now felt like his first time there.

"Well, hello," a weak, yet hopeful male voice called from Max's left. "You're back. Hope your project went well. What can I help you with today?"

Max looked at the old man behind the counter. He sat on a stool, probably necessary to make it through the whole day on his feet at his age. But the man stood up and smiled at Max.

"Hi," Max said, trying to recall what exactly he had said to the man before. Had he told him that he needed tools to file the sight off his pistol so that it would feel better in his mouth when he killed himself? The mere thought of such an exchange gave Max a shudder. "How are you? It's...good to see you again."

"Likewise, young man," the kind store clerk said. "What can I help you find?"

Max didn't actually know what he needed. His intention had been to look around the store, and try to figure out what he needed to aid his burgeoning plan to free Josue from the hospital, and to tip the possibility of a successful escape from the law in his favor. "I think I'd just like to look around, if that's all right."

The old man nodded. "Take your time."

Max grabbed a cart and began to circumnavigate the outer aisle of the small store. He grabbed things off the shelf, dropping them into his cart; things that might have seemed to an uninformed observer to be completely random stuff. But as Max gazed down at the mixed contents he'd assembled, his plan solidified more in his mind with each item he grabbed: boxes of nails and sharp-pointed screws; Ziploc bags; angular galvanized steel joist hangers; duct tape; panes of thick glass shelving; a couple of hammers.

Max found a selection of dimensional lumber leaning between steel dividers up against one of the outer walls. He picked up a spruce two-by-four. "Could you chop this in half here?" Max said, making a chopping gesture with his hand. "At a forty-five degree angle?"

"Sure," Roy said, taking the board from Max. In no time, he had lopped the stud in half with a compound miter saw and placed both pieces into Max's cart.

Max's mind whirled when he turned a corner and found the little store's "marine" section. Something about the sharp prongs of a boat anchor on display, with its triangular galvanized steel flukes, activated Max's imagination. He loaded four of them into his cart, along with about a dozen long u-bolts with threaded ends. Max didn't know if any of the stuff would work the way he imagined, but he felt as though he had to try.

Max noticed the old man following him around the store. Probably just standing by, ready to be helpful. "I need some paint," Max said, looking at the embroidered name patch on the man's red vest that said Roy.

"Right this way," the elderly shopkeeper said, leading Max down the store's center aisle. He turned to face Max and his cart. "What color?"

"Oh, I don't care," Max said.

Max found himself challenged with loading all of his purchases inside the Smart Fortwo. *Should've brought my new pickup*, Max thought. But the jacked-up Sierra had been parked on the street by Stan, Paco, or Fabio in front of an import warehouse near the Miami River in Little Havana, specifically where Max had indicated.

Presently, Max drove the zippy little Smart over to Bongo's shop, so that he could pick up his and Josue's new IDs. Max entered the little storefront, which was a shabby little building situated just off a newer strip mall. At a glance, one might have thought the buildings were connected, but closer inspection revealed the schism between them. And from the parking lot, no one would have suspected the magnificent garden and cottage would have existed out back, in the epicenter of such a time-worn commercial district.

Max opened the door and passed shelves of beautiful hand-blown glass pipes, colorful and creatively crafted, but obviously made for smoking weed. Max chuckled as he looked at the sign on top of one of the racks; it said Handmade Tobacco Pipes. Max approached the counter where a guy in his twenties, with long wavy hair tied up in a bun at the back of his head, and wearing flip-flops, and a tight-fitting Alice in Chains t-shirt, stood leaning on the counter, scrutinizing a catalog of guitar amplifiers.

"You Maxwell?" the kid asked.

"Yeah," Max said, surprised. "Why?"

"Bongo's expecting you," the head shop clerk said, glancing up at Max. "You can go on back, man."

Max walked through the back door of the shop and found his way past the stone steps of Bongo's Zen garden, and knocked on the door. As soon as his knuckles hit the wood, Max heard the first lock being undone. Another three or four latches articulated next, and Bongo opened the door. "Hey, Max."

Max took a seat in the cottage's cozy living room, and almost immediately noticed the hazy vapor in the air, and soon felt the relaxing effects of the drug's potent active ingredients working their way into his bloodstream.

"Oh, I can turn this down if it's too much for you, Max," Bongo said, reaching for the remote control that operated his centralized vaping system. He sat in an arm chair across from Max.

"No, it's okay," Max said. "I hate to be that guy, but I gotta ask. Are my IDs finished?"

Bongo handed Max a small zippered bag, like the kind a business would drop off at the bank's night deposit filled with all their cash and checks for the day. Max zipped the bag open and pulled out a passport. He opened it and saw the photo Max had taken of Josue in the hospital.

"Did my best to make him look a bit more naturally posed," Bongo said, and Max detected a hint of pride in his voice.

Indeed Max noticed that Bongo had digitally altered the photo, removing the bandage on Josue's injured head and giving him a normal, natural pate with a short afro. It was superior work. Max flipped open his own passport, featuring a photo Bongo had snapped himself.

Max looked down at his name. Maxwell Craig. It sounded like a stranger to him.

Max felt weird about the idea of completely changing his identity. But he now believed it was the only way to see his friend freed from his dire situation. *Besides*, Max thought, *I don't have anything left to lose.*

"There's also library cards, a few grocery store rewards cards, social security numbers, and car insurance policies," Bongo said, interlocking his fingers and placing them on top of his knee, which was crossed over his other leg. "Don't worry about the cars linked to the policies, they've already been junked. The insurance agent is a friend of mine, and he helps out. I also recommend that you apply for a bunch of credit cards—I've made sure you and Josue both have excellent credit—just be extremely careful how and when you use the cards you get; you'll be traceable. But I encourage you both to take some time, investigate yourselves. I've given each of you a rich and highly credible history."

"Look, Bongo," Max said. "I don't usually do this type of thing: hiring a forger to create a false history. It doesn't feel like me. It doesn't feel like the person I think of myself as at all.

"I've never before stepped into the criminal underworld. It feels like the desperate act another man might take; a creature of a lower life form or something like that. Yet here I am now, among them, one of them. I suppose it says something about me.

"Maybe I'm not really above it all. Maybe I'm not as much of a 'good guy' as I once thought I was. I really am just as depraved as all those other guys."

"I don't know about all of that, Max," Bongo said, "but I can tell you this: A lot of different guys come to me for a lotta different reasons. Whether they're right or wrong is something I've decided not to get into. Obviously I'm no better either. But if anything, I just hope I can help. Whatever situation a guy is in, it can't be good if he comes to me. At the end of the day, I just want to do whatever I can."

"Thanks, Bongo," Max said, standing and shaking the other man's hand. "I appreciate all you've done to help me and Josue. You've given us something…a chance, I guess."

"It's my pleasure, Max," Bongo said. His eyes wandered to a wall behind Max, and a serious look of grave concern overwhelmed the hippie forger's face. "Sorry, Max, but I think it's time that you go."

"What is it?" Max asked, feeling fearful. He turned around and saw two flat computer monitors bolted to the wall near the ceiling. One of them showed the feed from a surveillance camera inside Bongo's shop. Presently, the store was being swarmed by police officers. One cop held the slacker with the Alice in Chains t-shirt up against a wall, his face pressed uncomfortably against the wallpaper.

"They raid me all the time," Bongo said. "If you sneak out the back door now, and slip over the fence, you can probably get free of this unscathed." The forger slammed his hand into a red button on a wall. Max heard a bright hissing sound coming from the next room, where Bongo kept his office. A thick cloud of some kind of vapor crept smoke-like into the hallway.

"HCL. Hydrochloric acid. I use it to destroy my computers. I go through about ten of 'em a year. But the cops haven't lifted a single byte of data off one of 'em yet. Your details are safe, Max. Don't fret."

"Thanks again, Bongo," Max said. "You're a good guy."

Bongo nodded and smiled. "Cover your nose and mouth, don't breath in those fumes. Head straight out the back and through that door."

Max nodded.

"And if you'll excuse me," Bongo said, stretching the straps on a military-style gas mask and placing it over his head. He lifted up his couch cushions and started to dig for something. "I've got to flush the toilet a few times before Miami's finest breaches my front door."

Max bolted through the forger's back door, finding himself in a small grassy yard, facing the seven-foot-high cedar fence that wrapped the property. Max approached the fence between a couple of Japanese maple trees, grabbing hold of the top of the fence and jumping, trying to lock his arms above the fence so that he could kick a leg over and hoist himself the rest of the way up. It took a few tries, and Max ultimately kicked his foot awkwardly off one of the maple trees, but he was able to hurl his body over the top of the fence. He landed in a heap on the sidewalk beside an avenue, busy with speedy traffic.

Max picked up his backpack and walked, as nonchalantly as he could, just as a squad car squealed to a stop by Bongo's fence. Max was about to put up his hands when he watched the cop get out of his car wearing full body armor, and holding his Glock pistol at the low ready position in front of him. He stepped right past Max as if he didn't see him.

Must have assumed I'm just a passerby, Max thought. He continued walking all the way around the block, back to the front of Bongo's Glassworks and Sundry, where he had parked the Smart car. Max found three police cars, white with city of Miami police insignias, lights flashing.

One officer, a tall black man built like a brick house, leaned against his cruiser and watched the front door of Bongo's shop, clutching a Mossberg twelve gauge.

The officer looked at Max suspiciously as he approached the little black and silver car. Max simply smiled and nodded, and at the last second thought to salute the muscular cop.

The officer smiled back awkwardly and nodded.

Max pressed a button on his keychain to unlock the Smart Fortwo, and he opened the door. Before he climbed in, he heard the cop's intimidating baritone voice, calling to him.

"Hey, man," the officer said, "why you got all that crap in your car? If you don't mind me asking."

Max considered his load: he had two-by-fours, joist-hanging brackets, nuts, bolts, boat anchors, hammers, a file, cans of paint. It was an odd assortment of objects to find crammed into every available crevice inside a Smart Fortwo. Max thought quickly.

"I'm a contractor," he said. "My F-350's in the shop, blown head gasket. Got my wife's car, you know how it is."

The stern black police officer could not suppress a light chuckle. "Yeah, man. I know how it is. Take it easy."

Max turned the key and Barry's voice belted out the chorus to *Somewhere in the Night. Thanks, Stan*, he thought. Max wondered if the broken stereo was the only reason the slick salesman had wanted to sell the car, to stop the incessant easy-listening vibe that burrowed into his brain every time he drove it.

Max fired up the Smart and drove away quickly from the curb, happy to put the flashing police lights in his rearview mirror, and hoping the best for Bongo the forger.

CHAPTER 40

ARTHUR GRIMACED AS HE WATCHED Trina pour the thick light gray gravy over two six-inch buttermilk biscuit halves on a hubcap-sized plate. The ladle must have held about two cups of the gravy, chock full of bits of browned pork sausage and crispy bacon. The young black-haired cook had too many ear piercings to count, as well as others in her nose, lip, and eyebrow, and so many tattoos she appeared to be wearing a colorful, tapestry-like long sleeve shirt. She handed the finished plate over a short glass wall that separated *Trina's Diner*'s food prep counter from the eagerly waiting customers.

Zo took the plate and sniffed its steaming contents. "Thanks, Trina, sweetie. You are God's gift to those of us who like food that tastes good."

The young chef smiled at the veteran detective. "Zo, you're such a doll. When are you gonna leave that wife and whisk me away to Morocco?"

"The day is coming," Zo said, with a maniacal chuckle. "It's coming." He set his plate down at the table he and Art frequented, the one looking out the front window of the six-table establishment.

"You know she makes other stuff too," Art said, sitting down and beginning to shake pepper onto his scrambled eggs.

"Like what?" Zo asked, sounding perturbed. "Egg white omelettes? Vegan waffles? Fresh fruit medley?"

"Just sayin', scrambled eggs and some mixed berries are

gonna be a lot better for you in the long run than that plate of cholesterol," Art said, tucking his napkin into his collar.

"This is the first time you've ever busted my chops over what I eat, Art," Zo said, looking up from his plate, a stone-cold expression on his face. "What is this about?"

Arthur didn't look up from his eggs. He shoveled a mouthful and chewed it before speaking. "Maybe you should think about taking some leave, Zo. You and Shelley could go up to Beantown or something. Take a little trip to get away, clear your head."

"Oh, so that's what this is about," Zo said, taking a huge mouthful of biscuits and gravy. He chewed deliberately. His mind seemed to be spinning as his expression betrayed a man who was growing increasingly agitated. "You know I've not been diagnosed with any illness, and here you are, already planning my funeral."

"Zo—"

"No, man. It really pisses me off." The bristly detective glared at his partner. "I thought you'd be the one person in the world I could count on just cutting me some slack."

"I'm tryin' man," Arthur said, setting down his fork and taking a swill of hot coffee to cleanse his mouth. "I'm tryin' real hard to just keep working with you. To act like there isn't anything going on that's gonna change us. But what do you think, man? It's gonna turn out to be nothing?"

"Damn," Zo said, lowering his head. He took a series of deep breaths, almost as if he were panting like a dog. He lifted his head, and Art saw the slight glistening in his eyes. "Gotta say that hurts," Zo said in a voice like a gruff whisper.

"Man, I'm sorry," Art said, taking off his Ray Bans and rubbing his eyes. "I didn't want things to go this way." He thought about the results Lorenzo's doctor had given a day earlier: inconclusive. But he had quickly ordered another biopsy. Art thought that was rather telling.

"I suppose you're also wondering if I can still handle the job."

"Man, I did not *even* say that." Art hoped his expression didn't look as defensive as he felt. "You're my partner, Zo. I trust you without reservation. *Without reservation.* And I'm talking with my life here. But what you got going on could be really serious. I just don't want to see you trying to tiptoe around it, pretending like there ain't nothing going on when there is. Understand?"

Zo nodded. It broke Art's heart to see his partner so tormented. Not knowing what it was that grew inside his chest must have been even worse than knowing. More than anything Art just wanted to be the friend and brother who was there for his partner. But he struggled seeing the other man gloss over his perilous reality.

"What do you think about the suicide?" Art said, turning on a dime to change the subject now that everything that needed to be said had been vented. "I mean, you got me up before the butt crack of dawn to come to this slippery grease pit—you must be up to something."

Lorenzo swallowed another bite of his food and laughed. "Yeah. Suicide."

"Think it's a setup?" Art asked.

"Peculiar. Second Code 31 guy shows up dead inside a week. And what of the fact that the other guy, the floater they found in the river, was this guy's twin?"

The two lawmen had just been at the crime scene where a fisherman had found the body. Kid must have been seventeen or eighteen, dead in a stolen Mazda RX-7, Ruger Mark III on the passenger seat. The car had been found under the bridge, right beside the marina where the two cops, Josephine Fuentes and Reggie Van Camp, had been killed.

Art thought it seemed clear that these two gangbangers had been involved in the original heist, and this one couldn't live with the remorse at having killed two cops.

"Suppose we find GSR on this guy's hand," Art asked. "Are you gonna believe that he smoked himself then?"

"I don't know," Zo said, glancing up at his partner suspiciously.

"What?" Art asked, wondering if his partner possessed some shred of evidence he had missed. "There was a note, Zo."

"Yeah, typical," Zo said, rolling his eyes. "I'm so sorry for the pain I've caused, I don't think I can go on living knowing what I've done, blah, blah, blah. That sure would be tough to fake. Bet we've got a really good chance of getting a handwriting analysis done for the kid too."

"So you're one hundred percent certain then, this is a Ti Flow hit?" Art asked.

"The first brother," Zo said. "Street name Wily Beeve. Guerrero from the Gang Unit thinks this guy's with Code 31, the Cubans. His murder fits the m.o. of Big Flow, who leads Ti Flow, the Haitians. Who else do you know that kills a guy with a sharpened screwdriver, I mean, outside of prison bars?"

"So this Wily guy somehow gets mixed up with the Haitians, rubs 'em the wrong way, Big Flow takes him out," Art said. "This stuff happens every day. Kid probably just walked down the wrong street. Doesn't mean much."

"Means he probably wasn't on the River job," Zo said. "Maybe Big did this, or maybe someone *else* did this kid to make it look like it was Big that done it."

"So you're saying that someone killed the kid, trying to make it look like Big Flow did this?" Art said. "Who would do that? Why?"

Lorenzo shook his head and looked out the window. He appeared to be lost in deep thought for a moment.

"I'm wondering if these twins really *are* Code 31, and they got sent to Lemon Street to join Ti Flow, dig around, find out what they can about the Haitians' movements," Zo said. "Then, maybe Big Flow finds out they're loyal to the other gang, took the first guy out, made an example of him. Then he smoked the brother, dumped his body to look like a suicide, knowing that if we believed this Code 31 kid was really so wracked with guilt for killing cops on the river that he killed himself over it, that it would cast the blame onto the Cubans."

"Wow, that's complex, Zo," Art said, forking a half strawberry into his mouth. "Now you're getting layers deep, like that Christopher Nolan movie. What was that called, *Conception*?

"So, you're saying you like Ti Flow for the river job? And definitely not Code 31, despite the mounting evidence?"

"The running man went straight back to Lemon Street, Art. What do *you* think? I just don't know how the dead guy factors into all of this. I mean, how does he know the running man? What are they doing together? They gay? They're probably not related, am I right?"

Art laughed. "No man, probably not. So what's our move?"

Zo wiped his mouth with a napkin and dropped it on his plate. "We're gonna go back to Reed and talk to this kid, Josue. We've gotta interview this kid. He's asleep, we gotta wake him up. He don't feel like talking, we gotta make him feel like talking. No more messing around, Art. It's time we talk to him and get to the bottom of all this. Today. This morning."

"All right then," Art said, placing his glasses back on his face. He slipped a few singles out of his wallet, dropping them onto the tabletop. "Let's go."

CHAPTER 41

MAX SAT IN THE SMART car at the edge of Reed Memorial's southeast parking lot, facing the automatic doors to the hospital's Emergency Room entrance. He'd been able to park in the space nearest the door, and Max had parked the undersized automobile facing outward. He would need every advantage he could get for a speedy getaway.

Loading Josue into the car would be a rodeo. Max only hoped he could do it without hurting the other man. He didn't want to worsen Josue's concussion or harm his severely broken left leg.

Max clutched the wheel and gazed at the sliding doors in front of him. They swished open, and a old man hobbled out behind a walker, assisted by a much younger woman, likely a daughter or a granddaughter. Max's vision blurred and his mind wandered.

He'd been awake since two a.m. He hadn't been able to sleep, not even in the cozy room by the airport. But he'd done his best to get three or four hours before he'd had to get up, to make all of his preparations for the big getaway.

Stealing another man from ICU was generally frowned upon, and there was a strong likelihood Max would get caught. He'd almost certainly be pursued. He hoped it would only be by one or two squad cars. He didn't intend for any pursuit to last long, just long enough for him and Josue to get away, hopefully enough time for them leave Miami, and the country, for good.

In his hotel room, Max had run through as many possible permutations as he could imagine. Some of them seemed downright farfetched, and included images of every cop in Miami making chase. But as he had considered everything likely to go wrong, Max had made some preparations.

Sitting in the posh hotel room, looking out over the city lights twinkling off the black water of the small lake nearby, Max had stuffed Ziploc bags full of jagged pieces of the metal hardware he'd bought at Max's Hardware and Paint. He had also filed the corners of the galvanized steel joist hangers into razor-sharp edges before loading them into the plastic bags and zipping them closed. And he'd also filled a few of the polyethylene bags full of latex house paint.

Then Max had transferred some essential clothing items he and Josue would need to the Tampa Bay Buccaneers duffel bag, which he had thrown into the trunk of one of the cars he'd purchased from Stanley Fump. He'd used the screwdriver on his Swiss Army knife to remove the hard drive from his laptop, and then dumped the laptop in a trash can. He could buy a new one later. He even dumped the new duffel bag he had bought for Josue, along with most of his clothes and the other personal belongings he didn't need, in a trash bin at the hotel, and then he'd checked out.

Now Max needed to travel light. Extremely light. Whatever wouldn't fit into Josue's backpack he did not need. He'd replace it all later.

Under a dark blanket of predawn sky, with the hospital parking lot's white LED lights bathing the lot with a cool, uninviting fog of light, Max felt groggy and disoriented. He certainly felt in no condition to be executing such a delicate rescue operation.

But it had to be now. Max truly believed that if he delayed, even half a day, Josue would be moved out of ICU, and processed into the criminal justice system before he could say the word *deportation*.

Max had driven the Smart car all around Little Havana,

practicing his getaway route, and looking for a good location to install the flagship booby trap in his erratic getaway scheme.

Max had driven for maybe an hour before he had spotted the very site he'd been hoping to find. Ironically, just a short distance from Casino Miami, where he had watched the lightning-fast jai alai game, as he had daydreamed his ideas into a cogent plan to rescue Josue.

When Max had walked across the train bridge to cross the Miami River, he had observed that the train tracks entered a wide, sandy, fenced-in lot beside the Metrorail overpass, as the train tracks terminated at Miami Central Station, right beside the airport. This would be the place for Max's Hail Mary play, should it come to that.

It had taken about twenty minutes to set it up, unloading the supplies from the Smart car, and hammering the u-shaped bolts into the dirt, before placing a discreet marker—a stake with a bright orange ribbon tied onto it—to keep himself from running over his own trap. All the while, Max felt wracked with anxiety, hoping no one, particularly a police officer, spotted him in the throes of such blatantly suspicious activity right by the train tracks so close to Miami International.

Now, in the driver's seat of the Smart car, hands on the steering wheel, Max willed himself to move, to begin to set his plan in motion. He wanted to get things rolling while darkness still covered the city.

But something nagged inside him, a small detail he realized he hadn't addressed before. His wife was gone. His kids were gone. And yet he wondered. What would Lovelle think of him—a man who had worked as an accountant for a TV ministry for so many years—now preparing to thwart the police, to initiate a plan to free a man they seemed to want to hold accountable for murder?

Would she be ashamed of him, the man he had quickly

become? What would she say about the phony IDs he'd had made? What about all of the little white lies he had told along the way?

As he sat still, willing himself to move, Max heard his wife's voice speaking inside his head as clearly as if she had been sitting beside him.

Max, I know what you're thinking about doing, Lovelle's sweet voice said. He closed his eyes and saw her glistening dark eyes in front of him. *It's a crazy thing you have planned. But I could not be more proud of you. I love you.* Tears flooded Max's eyes. He wiped them away with the sleeve of the Henley shirt he wore under his bright blue scrubs top.

Max grabbed the door handle and opened the Smart car's door.

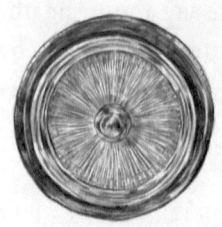

CHAPTER 42

"Zann," Big Flow said, pulling a long green car coat over himself to cover the AR-15 carbine, which he wore on a one point sling, "pull your car around out front and we'll all get loaded in."

"Ain't got my car no mo," Zann said, and Momo detected the reticence in his voice. "Damn thing broke, I sold it to my cousin." The orange-haired member of the gang flashed a sheepish, shiny platinum smile.

Big Flow looked at Momo, who just shrugged. "You know I ain't got no ride, brother. Just the way I roll."

The gang's dreadlocked leader looked agitated. The four men had assembled in the front yard of his house just before four a.m., determined to implement their assassination plot against Josue at the best possible time. Crenshaw Stubbins had told Big Flow that between four thirty and five would be the best time. The ICU would be manned by a skeleton crew at that time. She'd be in charge, meaning it would be quite easy for her to divert the attention of the other nurses, doctors, and security guards on staff at the time. The ICU would be virtually empty when they came to take out Josue Remy.

Though Big was prepared for World War III—they had an AR-15, a shotgun, four pistols, and a 9mm submachine gun—Momo knew the gang's leader really wanted an easy in-and-out incursion, blowing away Josue where he lay in his bed, and then slipping out clean.

"Ain't nobody in this gang have an automobile?" Big Flow shouted, his speech's inflection saturating heavily with his native Creole. Momo knew that happened when their leader got angry. The polished veneer he had worked so hard to put on, his efforts to present himself as eloquent and articulate, sort of went right out the window. "Call somebody! Wake up Jean Pike, Chad, P-Throne. One 'a them's gotta have a car!"

Zann cleared his throat. "P-throne and Jean Pike wen' up ta Orlando, wanted to check out that new Indian casino up there. Ain't gonna be back 'til tomorrow."

Big Flow reached under his coat and drew a pistol from a holster positioned on his left front hip for a crossdraw. Momo recognized the weapon to be a new Heckler & Koch VP-9 the gang leader had had fitted with a suppressor. He pointed the 9mm pistol at Momo's face, then Tiny Deege's, then Zann's, and then back at Momo's. Clearly the gang leader was coming unhinged.

Momo waited until Big Flow, in his erratic state of mind, pointed his pistol back at Zann. He drew his own pistol, the massive Desert Eagle .50 AE, from his waistband, and pointed it at Big Flow's face.

The dreadlocked leader pointed the H&K pistol at Momo again, and the two men stared each other down in a deadly face-off.

"Yo, man," Momo said, sounding more irritated than frightened, "what the hell we doin'? Turnin' on each other. This ain't right."

Big Flow glared into Momo's eyes, blinked a couple of times, and lowered his pistol. He shook his head vigorously, causing his snake-like dreads to dance around his shoulders. "You're right, Momo. You are becoming a strong second-in-command, and I am proud of you."

Momo tucked his pistol back into the front of his long black basketball shorts.

"Where Deege go?" Zann said, himself looking terrified.

Momo looked around, wondering where the gang's smallest member had disappeared to. It surprised Momo when Tiny Deege's candy orange Cutlass Supreme turned the corner at the end of the block and drove up, stopping directly in front of the bickering gangbangers.

Big Flow's eyes bulged. He looked like a madman.

He glared at the little man, who opened his door, stepped out, turned to face the others, throwing his hands in the air with a sheepish grin. "Sorry, my brothers, but I ain't had a chance to get rid o' my whip just yet. Still got it if'n you all wanna take it."

Momo wondered if Big Flow would put a bullet in Tiny Deege's forehead. Instead, he tucked the suppressed pistol back into his holster under the olive green coat and opened the passenger side door. Big Flow pushed the seat forward and took a place in the backseat, behind the driver's seat. Zann sat next to him, while Momo took the front passenger seat, as Tiny Deege settled into his special, boosted driver seat.

"Well, all right then," Tiny Deege said with a nervous laugh. "Guess we all gonna go an' smoke Josue then. Buckle up now, y'all."

CHAPTER 43

MAX WALKED THE MAIN HALLWAY of the hospital until he reached the doorway leading to a narrow hallway that split off from the main one, the one occupied mostly by supply or utility rooms. He swiped his badge and slipped into the supply hallway.

Max recalled the location of a particular supply room from the mental map of the building he'd stored in his brain, and he now found the room, situated about halfway down the hall. The heavy steel door featured a narrow glass window embedded with steel mesh to discourage someone from smashing the glass and turning the knob from the inside. Through the tiny window, Max saw that the room was dark and unattended.

Max needed to grab some supplies he would need to execute his plan, and to patch up Josue temporarily, if needed.

Forcing the door would sound an alarm. The last thing Max needed was to be caught before he had even reached Josue, arrested for grabbing some gloves and syringes

Max had realized from his own time spent in the hospital, seeing the extreme measures the doctors and nurses had taken to secure the pharmaceuticals, that trying to steal drugs from the hospital supply would be the fastest way to get himself locked up. So the previous evening he had called Bongo to ask if he knew anyone who could get him a lot of the stuff he knew Josue might need: Vicodin, Percocet, amoxicillin; packages of azithromycin; vials of Heparin, Dilaudid, Fentanyl. He didn't know exactly what the wounded man would need, but he wanted to have his bases covered.

Amazingly, Bongo had said, "No problem, Max." An hour later, a messenger had arrived at Max's hotel, handing him a zippered pouch, like the one the forger had delivered the phony IDs and other credentials in. Inside, Max found bottles of all the meds he'd requested, along with a few others. Max paid the courier two grand and watched him disappear down the hallway like a ghost.

Now Max really just needed a couple of syringes with needles, some saline solution, and maybe a Foley catheter kit. None of these things would be held under tight security, and should be easy to grab. Everything else he needed he had bought at a Walgreens store in Little Havana: adhesive bandages, gauze, medical tape, and ACE bandages.

Max looked at the card reader on the wall beside the doorknob, its bright red LED bulb taunting him. He unclipped his laminated badge, the one Bongo had forged him—the one that showed him as a legitimate hospital staff member. Below the badge's barcode, Max noticed a magnetic strip.

"Why not?" Max asked, swiping the card in the slot on the wall. The LED light flashed green, and Max heard the electronic solenoid unlocking the door. He turned the knob and quickly slipped inside.

Max found the narrow room to be crowded on both sides with dozens of drawers. He started trying them, finding the unlocked drawers to be stuffed with everything he needed.

Max stuffed the supplies into his backpack already laden with cash and the few other possessions he had chosen to keep with him. At Walgreens, Max had also bought red food coloring, a food-preparation squeeze bottle, and some corn syrup to make a simple concoction he hoped would create a bit of chaos in the

ICU. He now fished his hand into the bottom of the pack to make sure he had it with him.

Then Max walked back toward Reed Memorial's main hallway, grabbing the handles of a wheelchair he'd seen unattended a short distance from the ER reception counter. He pushed it toward the elevator and smacked the up button.

The elevator lifted Max to a small foyer facing the main doors to the ICU. A window overlooking the parking loomed to the left, while another long hallway stretched down to the right. Max hooked the straps of his backpack over the push handles at the back of the wheelchair, and he fished out the squeeze bottle, stuffing it into the pants pocket of his blue scrubs. He also removed a special syringe and stuffed it into his other pocket.

Max took a deep breath. It was all going down in the next five minutes or so. His cover story would be that he was transferring Josue to Radiology for a series of x-rays. If anything went wrong, Max would go to jail. Josue would also face jail, maybe deportation.

Max exhaled.

He pushed open the door to ICU.

No one noticed Max enter the ward. At least, he saw no indication that anyone had reacted to his presence. Max saw Crenshaw's lovely round face behind the main counter, her head turned away from him. He slipped around the counter, moving in the opposite direction she was facing, stepping inside the last room in the corner of the ward.

Mrs. Klein, the elderly woman with Alzheimer's, whom Max had fibbed about to the charge nurse, telling her the patient had complained about not getting her lunch, lay asleep in her bed. The elderly woman's face was pale, and Max noticed a tube installed into her throat, connecting her to a ventilator that forced air into her lungs with a sound that reminded Max of a famous black-helmeted movie villain.

Max approached the old woman, hoping he wouldn't

startle her too much. The last thing he needed was to wake her up screaming.

"Mrs. Klein?" Max said gently.

It took a few seconds, but the woman awoke. She strained her eyes, trying to focus on Max's face. She reached her hand into the space beside her, and Max wondered what she might be doing. Then he spotted a pair of glasses on the table beside the bed. Max handed the woman the glasses, and she put them on her face.

"Roger?" she said, squinting up at Max. "Is that you?"

"No, ma'am. I'm Max. You don't know me. But listen, I could really use your help." Max picked up the woman's chart from its cradle at the foot of her bed and glanced over it. He spotted the words Alzheimer's, hip fracture, blood clot, and figured he understood why she was presently in ICU. In her frail condition, Max wondered how much longer she could last.

"Look, Mrs. Klein," Max implored the elderly woman, "I don't have much time. But if I can't get just a little bit of help, there's a good chance my best friend, Josue, will go to jail for something he didn't do. Maybe he'll even be sent back to the hellhole he just escaped from.

"Are you my son?" the old woman asked.

"What?" Max replied, taken aback.

"I just want to know if you're my son, Roger," the delicate woman said. "I don't always recognize him when I see him. But you look like him."

"No, ma'am. I'm not your son."

"You remind me of him. He's a hero. He went to fight in Afghanistan. Bagman, Bagram, can't remember the name of the place." The woman stared blankly at the wall in front of her. "I don't know if he's come back or not. I certainly hope he has. I hope he's safe."

"I'm no hero," Max said. "But I have a chance to do something right now. Something that feels right to me. If you'll help me."

Mrs. Klein nodded. Her face lit up in an overwhelming smile that almost broke Max's heart. To see such an old woman, so broken and frail, and not knowing whether her soldier son had made it back alive or not—to even be capable of such an expression touched Max to his core.

Max grabbed hold of the corded remote that one used to alert a nurse without having to leave their bed. He handed it to Mrs. Klein. "When I leave the room, I need you to count to twenty, and then push this button, to call one of the nurses in here. That's all I need, ma'am. It will help me, and it will help Josue."

The infirm woman nodded.

Max pulled the squeeze bottle out of his pocket and gave it a good shake. "This is some fake blood I made. I'm gonna squirt some on you, okay? It will create a diversion to allow me to get my friend out of the hospital. To get him safe."

Mrs. Klein looked up at Max with soft, kind eyes. She nodded. "I'll help you, because you look like Roger. And because I can tell you are a kind-hearted man."

Max's lips tightened, and he nodded back at the elderly patient. "This will feel weird. But they should get your bed linens changed in no time, after they figure out you're not hurt. Thank you so much for your help, Mrs. Klein. Thank you."

Max flipped the cap off of the squeeze bottle and began to squirt the phony blood all around Mrs. Klein's hips and over her abdomen. It wouldn't take long to figure out that nothing was actually wrong with the woman. But one of the nurses would almost certainly hit the code blue button on the wall, and the ensuing chaos would buy Max a few precious minutes.

Mrs. Klein giggled as Max poured on the fake blood. "It's cold," she said, unable to contain her laughter.

"Remember, Mrs. Klein," Max said, stepping toward the room's sliding glass door, "count to twenty and push the button."

The elderly woman nodded again. "If you see Roger, would you tell him I'd love to see him?"

Max nodded and wiped his eyes. "Yeah," he said before clearing his throat. He slipped out into the rectangular hallway of the ICU ward. Then Max made a beeline around the tall nurse's counter, heading straight for the men's room. He pushed open the door and stepped inside, hoping he hadn't been noticed.

Max waited for a what seemed like a long time, maybe a full minute, without hearing anything. Chilly beads of perspiration formed on his forehead. He wiped his face with his sleeve and gazed through the crack in the door.

A toilet flushed behind him, startling him. Max had thought he'd been alone in the men's room. As he heard the latch on the stall door clicking open, Max clung to the door handle, ready to pounce into action.

And then all hell broke loose.

"Code Blue. Room three," a pre-recorded voice declared over a loudspeaker. The tinny voice resounded loudly throughout the ICU ward. "Code Blue. Room three." The message repeated several more times.

Max pushed the bathroom door open, just in time to see the entire skeleton crew of one doctor and two nurses rise up from their positions behind their computers, seemingly as one, rushing in formation into Mrs. Klein's room.

Max crept back around the long oval counter, toward room thirteen. On his way, he heard voices speaking loudly inside Mrs. Klein's room.

"Where is all of this blood coming from?" one of the nurses said in a high voice on the verge of panic.

"Why is this blood so cold?" a male voice said. "What...?"

Max entered room thirteen quickly, dropping his backpack on the ground beside his friend's bed. "Josue, it's Max," he said, gently shoving the sleeping man's shoulder. "Wake up, Josue. It's Max."

Josue stirred and opened his eyes. They bulged wide when they saw Max's face. "Maxwell! You not forget about me."

"Never," Max said, clutching his friend's hand in a tight handshake. "We're going to get out of here, my friend. But first I've got to get you disconnected from all this stuff. It's going to be uncomfortable, but I'll do the best I can."

Josue just nodded. Max knew the young Haitian trusted him.

Max turned off the small machine that filled the compression sock on Josue's right leg. "Wait here," Max said.

He bolted out the door, pushing open the door leading out of the ICU, and into the long second floor main hallway. Max grabbed the handles of the waiting wheelchair and tugged it back into the ICU, spinning it and pushing it into room thirteen, locking its wheels down right beside Josue's bed.

"I need to take out your IV," Max said. He peeled away the clear adhesive tape holding the IV needle and its tubing to Josue's arm, and then he dug into his backpack for a wrapped piece of gauze and some tape. Max deftly slipped out the IV needle, applying pressure with the gauze, which he taped down to Josue's wrist.

"Okay," Max said. "Let's try to get you into the wheelchair before we disconnect you from anything else; that's when the alarms will start going off."

Max had to wheel the EKG monitor around to the opposite side of the bed. He lowered the thick cast on Josue's left leg down to the floor. "Lift your weight with your right leg. That's it. Careful of your cast." Max gingerly helped Josue into the chair. The young man winced as his cast bumped the floor, and Max adjusted the left side leg support on the chair to raise up his left leg.

"All right," Max said, glancing at all the flashing lights, colorful LED screen monitors, and vital signs readouts. "No turning back now. Are you ready to get out of here?"

Josue looked up at Max with eager eyes. He nodded his head as vigorously as he could, bandaged and hurting as it was.

"Okay," Max said. He picked up Josue's catheter bag and clipped it onto the back of the wheelchair; he'd remove the tube later. Then he quickly yanked the oxygen sensor off Josue's index finger, disconnected the ECG pads from his chest, and the EEG electrodes from his scalp. The obnoxious beeping sounds started immediately. Now free from all encumbrances, Max zipped up his backpack, slung it on his back, and positioned himself behind the wheelchair.

Without another thought, Max pushed the wheelchair toward the glass door, which dutifully slid aside. Max turned the corner and pushed Josue toward the door to the hallway. He pushed a button on the wall to open the door electronically, and then he pushed his friend through, making a beeline toward the elevator.

Max stood by Josue for what felt like an eternity, waiting for the elevator car to return. But at last the tone beeped and the elevator doors opened, and Max pushed Josue inside.

"I've got to remove your catheter, and it won't be fun," Max said as the doors closed behind them. He pulled a syringe out of his backpack and connected it to the port on the Foley catheter. Max peeled off the adhesive tape that attached the catheter's tubing to Josue's right thigh. Then Max drew back on the syringe to deflate the saline-filled balloon that was inside his friend's bladder. Max disconnected the syringe and dumped out some of the fluid before reattaching it and drawing it back once more, to ensure that there was no fluid left in the balloon. Max must have had this same procedure done to him a dozen times when he was in the hospital to treat his gunshot wounds, only a couple of months past. Now confident he had withdrawn all the fluid, Max nodded at Josue. "Go ahead and pull it out." Max stood up and looked at the elevator door to give the other man a hint of privacy.

"Ahh," Josue groaned as the tubing slipped free from his

body. He let go of the tube, and Max dropped the entire catheter assembly onto the floor of the elevator: an unfortunate surprise for whoever stepped inside next.

The two men exited the elevator to find the main hallway virtually empty. Max moved quickly, pushing the wheelchair ahead of him, hoping not to draw any attention to himself or the bandaged man as they were speeding toward the automatic doors of the ER's entrance.

They made it to the parking lot. Max's heart pumped hard as he spotted the Smart car. His plan had worked so far. They were almost free.

He pushed the wheelchair to the passenger side and grabbed hold of Josue under the arms, easing him out of the chair and into the car, being extra careful of the man's wounded leg, and minding his injured head.

Max secured Josue's seat belt. Then he took his own seat behind the wheel, and strapped himself in. "You're gonna need to hold on tight," Max said. "This could be a wild ride. Not sure how long it's gonna last, but you gotta protect your leg and your head, so brace yourself."

Max started the car, surprised he'd not met with any resistance. He revved up the Smart car, about to shift from neutral into first, to tear out of the hospital parking lot, when he spotted a man rushing the driver's side door.

The sun had not yet peeked over the horizon, but the man's features shone clearly in the sterile light of the bright parking lot. The runner was one of the detectives from the Paradiso Inn, whom Max had spoken with once, after he had woken up facedown in that Little Haiti gutter.

He was the police detective who resembled Arthur Ashe. He now strode toward the tiny car, badge displayed in one hand, his Beretta pistol, pointed toward Max's face, gripped in the other.

Max started to lift his hands from the steering wheel. He

would hold them in the air, showing his clammy palms so the detective would know Max would not resist.

The jig was up. Max was caught. He'd be going to prison. Josue would go back to Haiti. The entire plot had been for naught.

A bright blur of shiny orange paint whisked against Max's door, striking it. The violent abrasion ripped off a shower of plastic bits that had once made up the door's outer skin.

The flamboyant car, an old Oldsmobile or Buick from the eighties and highly customized, screeched to a halt about fifty feet ahead of Max. The car's tires squealed and smoked in a violent stop that assaulted Max's nose with the sharp smell of melted rubber.

Then Max spotted him again. The police detective who had just been standing beside Max's car door, about to arrest him, now lay on his side on the hospital sidewalk, halfway between the stopped orange car and the sliding doors to the ER's entrance.

Max had seen enough death in recent months to know the detective's life had left his body. The mangled, bloodied man lay still, his left leg twisted behind him in a completely unnatural way that made Max's stomach lurch. A bone protruded through the man's right coat sleeve. The detective's eyes gazed toward Max in a horrifying, yet unmistakable death stare.

Max felt sick. He gripped the door handle.

He knew he had to at least go and check on the man who had been, a moment earlier, alive by Max's car door. That was when Max spotted the other detective, the older cop with graying black hair and the black leather jacket: Arthur Ashe's partner, the New Yorker.

The gruff detective rushed to his partner's side, kneeling beside the other man's body. He looked frantic, mortified.

An arm reached out of the orange car's passenger side window. Max spotted a small silver object glinting in the black passenger's meaty hand.

The gun went off with three sharp stabs of bright yellow-orange flame as the car's passenger fired the pistol point blank into the second detective's back. The leather-clad man slumped down on top of his partner's body.

He was almost certainly dead.

Max's mouth gaped open as the scene unfolded before him. It was like a scene from a disturbing movie, one he wished he could un-watch. But as he turned his head to get a glimpse of the bandaged man beside him, freshly absconded from his hospital bed, he realized he was a key player in the very same movie.

The vivid orange car's reverse lights flashed white, and Max did not hesitate another second. His foot stomped on the gas pedal.

Max steered the Smart car like a stubby black and silver bullet past the pimped Oldsmobile that brimmed with armed gangbangers. He navigated his way through the parking lot, spinning his wheels as he turned the corner onto the busy avenue that skirted Reed Memorial's parking lot.

The Smart narrowly missed sideswiping a city bus as it drifted out into traffic. Max clutched the wheel tightly with both hands. He turned and looked back through the rear windshield just as the first bullet flew past, striking the street in front of the short car with a bright spark.

"So much for a clean getaway," Max said.

CHAPTER 44

MAX FLIPPED THROUGH THE SMART Fortwo's gears quickly, the gas pedal pinned to the floor. His fingers settled behind the paddle shifters on either side of the steering wheel, and he tapped one to upshift, finding a pronounced lag in between gears. Each slacking shift made his pulse race and his blood boil. Then the next gear engaged, and he sped onward like a madman through the sparse predawn traffic of Brain Coral Avenue.

Barry Manilow's *Copacabana* blared from the speakers; Max still hadn't gotten the stereo's controls to work. Not that he'd had much time to fiddle with it.

Max's heart sank when he checked his rearview mirror. The shiny orange Cutlass Supreme drifted wildly out of the hospital parking lot, losing control and ripping the bumper off a passing Volkswagen Rabbit, about two hundred yards behind.

"Hang on, Josue," Max shouted, his voice sounding maniacal. He noticed that Josue clung on tightly, one hand gripping the Smart's window frame, his other hand pressed firmly against the dashboard.

Max pinned the throttle again, turning onto the street that fronted the river. His route snaked left and right as he and Josue circumnavigated countless city blocks, before he shot the car like a bullet over the Sea Crest Avenue bridge that stretched across the murky green water of the Miami River.

Max honked his horn and swerved into oncoming traffic to

pass an old Cadillac Seville. He swore he saw the surprised face of the man in the little domed bridge tender house off to the side of the lowered drawbridge as the Smart Fortwo whizzed past like a tiny streak of lightning.

The pimped-out Oldsmobile kept pace. Max watched his pursuers in his rearview mirror all the time.

Other than the delayed shifting, Max found the Smart to be a zippy little car. Despite the fact that he tore through the morning like a menace, Max didn't want to attract too much attention; he avoided the busiest streets as much as possible, and he stayed away from the most highly populated areas as he wound his way west through Little Havana.

"Hold on, Josue!" Max shouted as he turned yet another corner.

Josue braced himself, staring through the windshield with wide eyes. He pressed himself in place with his strong arms.

Max had fully expected to be pursued by the police. But now, being chased by the same violent gang members who had planned to kill Josue gave Max an icy chill. With the gangbangers in pursuit, Max knew things would get ugly if they were caught. So his plan *had* to work.

Max rocketed down a quiet street lined mostly with commercial properties: he passed a small power plant; a fenced lot used for boat storage; some scattered houses; and a decades-old Spanish-style mini-mall. The Smart's tiny one liter engine whined as Max milked every ounce of RPM out of it before shifting to the next gear.

Max turned the Smart car at a gas station. He lost traction and the miniature car skidded sideways into oncoming traffic.

"Oh, man, Josue. Thank God no one was in that oncoming lane!" The tires squealed as he raced into the proper lane. Max corrected his trajectory. He sped onward, doing his best to shake the metallic orange Oldsmobile that pursued like a menace.

As chaotic as the pursuit must have appeared, Max followed a carefully preplanned route. He led the other car into a residential street, densely populated with small, tidy houses with red Spanish tile roofs, steel gates around well-kept yards, and mature banyan trees and palms. The unsuspecting residents of the quiet neighborhood would have been shaken awake by the sound of Max's squealing tires, and the roar of the Oldsmobile's engine, as the two cars twisted and turned around the same city blocks again and again, fighting like racing cats and dogs.

Max turned a corner. Then another. Then another still. He felt desperate to confuse or disorient his pursuers.

He checked his rearview again, hoping he had shaken the gang members.

"Damn!" he shouted. He glanced at Josue, still holding on for his life. "These guys are persistent!"

The gang still trailed, though just barely. Max turned the wheel hard, fishtailing the tiny car's rear end. He skidded onto Ponce de Leon Avenue, speeding up over the crest of the bridge to cross the river again, weaving like a desperate man in and out of traffic, dodging early morning commuters on their way to work. He crested the hump in the middle of the bridge, grateful a mega yacht or cargo ship wasn't making its way upriver, forcing the bridge tender to raise the bridge and temporarily cut off access to the other side.

"If they really wanna follow us," Max said, as much to himself as to his frightened passenger, "at least we can make them pay for it."

Max turned the wheel hard left, crossing directly in front of oncoming traffic. His maneuver was met with honking horns and flashing headlights. But Max didn't care. He just drove the Smart car hard toward a side street, jumping the curb of a small median.

He drove a few blocks, snaking his way through more residential streets. The further north he headed, the more neighborhoods diminished into shabby apartment buildings and overcrowded housing projects. Max adjusted his speed, making sure he was ahead of the following Ti Flow members, but not too far ahead.

Gunfire startled Max. He turned his head to see the rear windshield intact, but an arm reached out the Oldsmobile's passenger window firing a pistol after them. It was the same gang member who had shot that detective in the back, killing the helpless man like a dog. The gun appeared tiny in the man's thick fist, but the gunfire was loud, startling. Each shot rattled Max. He shuddered, as he turned the wheel again.

The Smart sped toward an old four-story apartment building, its chipping canary yellow paint having long faded. The steel railings on the apartments' balconies had rusted enough that they looked as if one would only have to lean against them to break them free from the building. But Max was more interested in the heavy wheeled dumpster out front.

He had spotted it the day before, when he had driven around for hours, trying to scout out his and Josue's best possible escape route. Max had noticed, when driving past, that the driver of a garbage truck had struggled to keep the heavy green dumpster from rolling away on the slight, sloping pavement that slanted away from the front of the building.

Max had seized the opportunity. Just a couple hours earlier, under the cover of darkness, Max had crept outside the apartment building. He'd pushed the dumpster up against the building, wedging the beveled two-by-fours from the hardware store under the dumpster's front wheels, lodging it in place.

Max downshifted now, slowing the Smart car, to let the gang members catch up, just enough. He weaved the car left and right, like a slithering snake, as the gunfire erupted again. Satisfied the pursuing vehicle was close enough for his trap, Max maintained his course and speed, driving straight toward the boards that jammed the wheels of the dumpster.

"Put your head down!" Max shrieked at Josue. He knew it would be tough for the wounded man. His brain might still have swelling from his recent concussion. But Josue crouched as low as he could, just as two shots shattered the rear windshield.

Max drove straight through the two wedged two-by-fours. The boards smashed the front windshield, its laminated film holding the pieces together. The plastic front hood of the petite automobile exploded into a thousand plastic shards.

Max checked his rearview. Half the rear windshield was gone. The rest had shattered. The dumpster, no longer chocked in place by the boards, rolled free into the path of the oncoming Cutlass.

The shiny orange car plowed into the heavy trash receptacle. The hulking hunk of steel, and its entire contents of garbage-filled trash bags, broken furniture, and other debris, all went airborne. Then it toppled over, spilling out onto the street.

Max turned the corner, drove another block, and parked the Smart car. He hummed along to the words, "I write the songs that make the whole world sing."

"Out!" Max shouted to Josue. "Get out, get out, get out!"

He unbuckled his own seatbelt and ran around the other side, to help Josue with his. Josue's hospital gown flapped in the breeze, creating an undignified moment as Max grabbed his friend by the arm, helping to right him.

"Get in the red car," Max shouted. He escorted Josue to the waiting Pontiac Firebird, its t-tops removed. He opened the door, and helped his friend get buckled into his seat.

"My pack!" Max said, remembering he'd left the backpack in the Smart Fortwo again. He ran back and grabbed hold of it. But the bag caught on something. Max tugged hard, and he heard one of the straps ripping free from where it had hung up on the emergency brake handle. He pulled hard and the strap snapped. He yanked the backpack through the window.

Max bolted for the Firebird. He dropped into the driver's

seat and turned the key in the ignition. The car turned over, but didn't fire.

"Come on, come on, come on," Max urged, as he repeatedly tried the key. The starter motor churned. Nothing happened. Max tried it again. Then again.

At last the loud engine sputtered. Max pumped the gas pedal, and the four-hundred-cubic-inch V-8 roared to life with a menacing growl. Max revved the car a few times and then shifted into first gear. He peeled out so hard he left two twenty-foot-long streaks of black rubber on the whitish gray street behind him.

The Firebird was faster than the Smart. Much faster. Max shifted through the gears, reaching the end of the street in about three seconds. He was about to turn the corner when he spotted a blur of mangled orange paint in his rearview. The gang members would have seen the burgundy Firebird just before it turned out of sight.

Max punched the dashboard. He had just missed slipping away clean by about a half a second. Now he found the pimped-out Cutlass Supreme keeping pace with him, the pursuing vehicle running about a block behind. Max was sure he had enough horsepower to keep the other car from catching up. But he didn't think he could get away. The Oldsmobile must have been supercharged or something—it had a lot of juice.

Max's plan was no longer to flee the other vehicle. Indeed, as he led the other car upriver, skirting along the north side of the Miami River, Max allowed the other car to slowly gain ground.

He wound through Little Havana, transitioning from impoverished residential neighborhoods toward more industrial streets. He made his way back toward the river. Like with the dumpster, Max intended to draw his pursuers into his next trap.

Max turned a corner onto a street populated with industrial warehouses, the fenced and gated yards on either side piled high with cargo containers: yellow, green, rusty red-colored, the containers had been stacked high like giant interlocked building blocks, shielding Max's view of the river just beyond. He passed scrap yards, little Cuban diners, auto parts import shops.

Max grabbed the emergency brake and looked at Josue. "Hold on, man."

Max tugged the brake handle as he turned the wheel to the right. The muscular Pontiac slipped sideways, and Max compensated by pressing his foot back down into the gas pedal and steering the wheel left. The Firebird drifted around the corner, and sped on through a narrow street lined with parked cars, delivery trucks, and tall stacks of wooden shipping pallets.

Max could not suppress wild laughter. "Did you see that? Ha ha!"

Josue nodded, sheer terror apparent in the injured man's eyes. He clung to the Firebird's door and seat as if they were keeping him from falling from a great height.

"My wife would have thought that was totally badass!" Max squealed with delight. "Don't think I ever pushed it past sixty-five or seventy in our plum-colored minivan."

The scene in the rearview showed the gang members maintaining their pursuit, though the driver pushed the vehicle too hard and slammed sideways into a stack of pallets, sending them flying everywhere, and denting the side of the orange Cutlass pretty well.

Max laughed. Except for the perilous outcome of the life or death struggle, he was actually having a good time. He allowed the pursuing car to gain a bit of ground, and then he reached into the Firebird's backseat. He grabbed a couple of heavy Ziploc bags and handed them to Josue.

"Open those for me, would you?" Max asked.

Josue ripped open the closed bags and handed them, one by one, to the driver, who hurled them out the open t-tops, onto the road behind them. He threw half a dozen bags, spilling their jagged steel contents into the muscle car's wake: sharpened angular joist hangers; pointed sheet metal screws; long framing nails; even some jagged pieces of thick broken glass from the shelving Max had broken up with a hammer now littered the street.

As he drove the length of the narrow vehicle-lined street, which grew more densely residential as they drove further away from the river, Max watched the Oldsmobile carry on behind him, undeterred by Max's booby traps.

He wondered if the thin, low-profile tires that wrapped the tall, chromed wire wheels of the Cutlass were somehow impervious to the normally tire-piercing hardware. Maybe they were run-flat tires, or maybe they were less susceptible to puncture than more substantial tires with taller sidewalls. But the carload of ultra-violent gangbangers pursued, undaunted, as Max reached the end of the street.

He flew through an intersection, nearly wiping out a passing Pinto. The Firebird screamed past a row of auto repair shops and a city bus depot fortified like Fort Knox, with a razor-wire-topped chain link fence. This time the Oldsmobile caught up, and slammed its front bumper into the rear of Max's Pontiac.

"Oh, jeez!" he shouted, as his head whipped back from the impact. "Okay, Josue?"

Josue clutched his neck and nodded gingerly.

Max reached back and grabbed another Ziploc bag, this one filled with bright pink latex house paint. He tossed the bag through the Firebird's open top, watching his rearview. The bag of paint hit the front grille of the Oldsmobile and shattered, instantly painting the front of the pursuing car an embarrassing bright pink color.

Max threw another couple of bags, and these hit their marks—both bags shattered on the windshield, one with pink paint, another with an ugly olive drab green. The paint covered the entire windshield, completely obstructing the view of both driver and passengers.

"Yesss!" Max hissed. He watched the pursuing driver make the mistake of switching on his windshield wipers, smearing the colorful paint into sick-looking streaks across the vehicle's front glass.

The Oldsmobile swerved and plowed into the front of a parked pickup truck. Max seized upon the advantage. He sped up and turned the corner, twisting and turning his way swiftly around a familiar network of streets until he reached a sleepy neighborhood of houses, with their green rolling trash cans placed on the curbs out front, awaiting pickup.

Max pushed the car hard toward the end of the street, screeching the car to a stop in front of a house with tiny palm trees that must have been planted just last year. His front bumper struck one of the trash cans, knocking it over and spilling out its contents.

"Get out, get out, get out!" Max shouted at Josue again, as he yanked the emergency brake to secure the vehicle in place.

The two men climbed out of the car, with Max acutely aware that the pursuing vehicle might scream around the corner at any moment.

"Get in the truck!" Max called to Josue, as he opened the passenger side door to the suspension-lifted GMC Sierra pickup to help his friend inside.

It was a bit of a climb for both men. And it was a strange feeling to get out of first such a small car, then such an open, sporty one, so low to the ground like the Firebird, and then to climb into a much bigger vehicle. But Max fired up the pickup and peeled out.

He sped toward the end of the street, just as the Oldsmobile came into view again. "Aggghhhh!" Max grunted, as the gang members' car quickly closed the distance to rejoin the pursuit with whatever was left of the paint-splattered and wrecked Cutlass Supreme.

"I'd hoped we'd have thrown them off by now," Max lamented. "We were literally just another second or two from slipping away unnoticed."

Despite his irritation, Max led the pursuing vehicle back toward the Miami River.

"What we do now?" Josue asked. He looked genuinely afraid, and not just of Max's driving.

"I have a plan," Max said. He forced a smile at Josue, though the entire strategy now felt tenuous at best.

Gunfire erupted again behind them. It was clear the gang members were not interested in playing Max's game any longer. "Head down! Get your head down!" Max shouted.

Josue leaned down as best he could. Max thought it must have hurt his swollen brain to crouch like that. And the Haitian refugee's cast-wrapped leg jostled around inside the four-by-four's cab with each turn or swerve. Once in a while the cast would bang hard against the door, and Josue could not suppress a painful shriek of agony.

"Sorry," Max said. "Sorry this is so painful, my friend. We'll make it. We'll get away." He wondered if he was just trying to convince himself. Maybe he was deluding himself, intentionally telling himself something he knew not to be true. But Max refused to give up.

He drove the GMC past a massive parking lot, almost entirely empty, in front of a high-rise structure of low-rent apartment buildings. Just beyond, Max spotted the words Miami Jai Alai—it was Casino Miami, where Max had sat in the jai alai fronton wondering what to do about Josue's predicament.

Now, Max saw the sight of the casino as a beacon of hope. He was so close to the next, hopefully last, part of his plan—his Hail Mary. Max steered the jacked-up four-by-four fast past the parking lot, back toward NW North River Drive, pressing his foot to the floor as he hurtled past the large casino building like a locomotive.

A Metrorail train rattled over the concrete overpass overhead on its way south across the Miami River. Max spotted the railroad grade crossing signals and the railroad crossing crossbuck on a truss over the road where the regular train tracks crossed the road. This was Max's marker.

With the busted, pink, green, and bright orange Oldsmobile gaining ground—Max observed that the gang members had apparently kicked out the front windshield completely—Max turned the wheel of the pickup hard left, cutting into the path of an oncoming semi-truck, and speeding off the road, onto the railroad tracks.

"Woah!" Josue said. He struggled to hang on. The pickup bounced along, straddling the train tracks, and speeding over the raised gravel hump toward the old green train bridge, where the Tri-Rail and Amtrak trains crossed the river.

"This is train track!" Josue shouted. "Not car track!"

Max looked back at his friend, unable to suppress his smile. "I know," he said.

The carload of gangbangers pursued, chasing Max across the big, skeletal, green structure. Max was thankful once again that the bridge had not been raised to allow a passing vessel to slip by.

He pressed his foot once again to the floor. He clung to the steering wheel, desperately trying to keep the four-by-four in the center of the track, as its wheels fought to creep off to one side of the tracks or the other.

On the other side of the bridge, Max sped across NW South River Drive, dodging a little blue Geo Metro, its driver staring at Max with wide, freaked-out eyes as Max swerved to avoid a collision with the other vehicle.

Max continued along the tracks, hurtling toward the Miami

International Airport Station, where the tracks for the Tri-Rail, Amtrak, and Metrorail converged. Max took another look at the pursing vehicle through his rearview mirror. The Oldsmobile kept up, veering all over the railroad tracks behind the bulky pickup.

Max spotted arms reaching out of the pursuing car's windows, pistols in hand. He saw the barrel of a shotgun pointing through the gaping hole where the windshield once was.

"Head down!" Max shouted, as a shotgun blast pelted the truck's tailgate.

"Just a few more seconds," Max said. "Hang on, Josue. This is gonna be a hard turn to the left."

Max spotted the little wooden stake he had planted hours earlier with the fluorescent orange tape jostling in a light breeze. He yanked the wheel hard to the left. The GMC bounded off the railroad tracks, tipping for a second onto two wheels in the wide, sandy area between the train tracks and the adjacent avenue.

Max struggled with the steering wheel to right the vehicle. But he drove hard toward a chain link fence that wrapped the property around the train tracks. Max plowed through the fence like one of the four horsemen of the apocalypse, only slowing when he had burst through, and he steered himself toward the nearby pavement.

Max swerved to avoid hitting a thick-trunked palm tree, and he rolled right over a bright yellow fire hydrant in the process. A foamy white spurt of water surged out of the ground in a powerful geyser that drenched the four-by-four.

"Damn," Max said, looking at Josue with a curt half-smile. "I've always wanted to do that."

Max checked his mirror, finding the gangbangers' Cutlass swamped in the middle of the sandy lot. Though the driver attempted to continue his pursuit, the flamboyant vehicle just spun in circles in the sandy lot.

Max's plan had worked; the other car's tires had been ripped free from their rims by the jagged flukes of the anchors that Max had buried and bolted to the ground—a menacing and insidious hidden booby trap.

A volley of gunfire erupted. "Head down," Max shouted again, as he grabbed hold of Josue's neck and tried to help him lower his neck below the bottom of the truck's rear windshield.

Bullets rained all around the GMC, mostly pelting the vehicle's tailgate, which served to protect them more than anything. A couple of the bullets ripped through the rear windshield, zipping through the front glass as well, and another round glanced off the roof with a bright zinging sound.

When the volley stopped, Max lifted his head to take a wary peek behind him. The gang members had climbed out of the vehicle and fanned out, shooting until they were out of ammo. The GMC was stopped on the side of the desolate avenue maybe 150 yards away. It wasn't long before Max knew the gang's efforts would be for naught.

They realized this quickly too. Max was torn between taking off and watching their curious activities, as one of the men opened the trunk. He pulled out a bright red plastic gas can, and he began to saturate the vehicle with gasoline, both inside and out.

"What the hell are they doing?" Max asked, as Josue sat up to watch as well through the pickup's shattered rear window.

One of the gang members struck a match and tossed it inside the car's passenger side window opening. The car burst into bright, flickering orange flames. Then the gang members scattered, apparently pairing up and running off in different directions.

Max heard sirens in the distance and he didn't waste another second. He stomped his foot to the floor and drove the pickup away from the scene, feeling something he hadn't felt in quite a while. Max felt free.

CHAPTER 45

MAX KNEW HE AND JOSUE were living on borrowed time. Somehow, miraculously, no police had taken chase of either Max or the pursuing gang members during the perilous race to get Josue out of the hospital. Max figured that, by the time the police had received a call from a concerned citizen who'd been cut off during the chase, or from a resident who had spotted the speeding vehicles screaming past, Max and Josue would have already been in another part of the city.

But having narrowly escaped the vengeful members of Ti Flow, leaving them pissed off and stranded by the railroad tracks, Max still felt exposed, driving the conspicuous four-by-four, riddled as it was with bullet holes.

Max drove east, away from the scene of the flaming gang car, winding the jacked-up GMC among the ubiquitous palm-tree-lined streets of Little Havana as he proceeded to his next vehicle transfer.

Josue settled in as best he could, trying to get comfortable in his thin hospital gown and obtrusive leg cast. "When we get to our next car, I'll have a change of clothing for you," Max said. "So hold tight."

Josue nodded, forcing himself to smile. The young man had been through a hell of a lot. He seemed a tad delirious, and obviously in some good measure of pain. Max hoped it would all be over soon, and they could finally breathe.

The curved, retractable white roof of Marlin's Park slowly

drew into view in the distance as the pickup inched further east through Little Havana. Max nudged Josue, who had been staring blankly out the window. His eyes grew huge when he saw the enormous sports stadium.

"The Florida Marlins play their baseball games there," Max said, smiling to himself as his mind drifted back to times he had driven to Miami with his father when he'd been a kid. *Jeez, that must have been twenty-five or more years ago now*, Max thought. *Am I that old?*

He took in the sight of the almost geometrically perfect rectangular apartment buildings clustered in the city blocks closer to the stadium, and the little houses with their patchy lawns, their driveways nothing more than two concrete strips in the middle of the grass.

"I came here a few times with my father when I was about nine, ten years old. There used to be a stadium there called the Miami Orange Bowl—before they tore it down to build the new one."

Josue seemed interested, despite his pain.

"One time my dad took me to a particular night game," Max said, drawing the memory out of his mind as if he were pulling a carrot from the ground; the harder he pulled, the bigger it got. "I guess I was too young to really follow the game, you know. But I was so glad to be there. You know, just to be there with my dad. In the big stadium, tens of thousands of other screaming fans."

Josue smiled and looked at Max. He nodded.

"Dad was really immersed in the game between the New York Jets and the Miami Dolphins. This would have been at the height of the deep-seated rivalry that existed between these teams, back in the early 1980s. This game was close—really close—all the way to the end.

"But both teams fought hard, one team leading first, then the other, and then back to the other. Well, I had to take a leak so bad

I thought I might explode if I waited any longer. So I told my dad, 'Dad, I gotta go. I really gotta go.'"

Max laughed himself as he recalled the story. "Dad didn't want to miss a second of the game, as good a game as it was turning out to be. So he said, 'Go ahead. Go quick and come back here.'

"I went to relieve myself, and in the five minutes I was in the men's room, the game ended. It was actually a tie-game. It was unbelievable. Anyway, I tried to return to my seat, but more than sixty thousand football fans were trying to get out of the stadium, all at the same time. It must have taken me ten, fifteen minutes to get past the crowd and back to my seat. By that time my dad was nowhere in sight."

"What happen?" Josue asked. Max noticed his eyes were big, as if he was concerned, even though it was something that happened a long time ago.

"A nice, elderly couple saw that I was lost. They led me down the stairs to a security guard who walked me across the field to a security office. Imagine that. I normally would have loved to have walked on the same field where the Dolphins played football. But at that time, I was so scared, I wanted nothing else in the whole world than to just find my dad.

"I was taken to a room where about twenty other lost, crying kids sat at desks, across from security guards who did their best to gather up enough information to help the kids find their moms and dads, who must have been frantic as well, searching for their lost children."

"What did *you* say?" Josue asked.

"I didn't say anything," Max said. "I had just sat down, blubbering like a little baby, when I saw my dad walk in a doorway at the other end of the room. It was…I suppose…one of the greatest moments of my life. Just the relief that I had been so lost and without much hope a moment earlier, but then someone had come to rescue me."

"Wow," Josue said, looking pensive as he gazed out the window as they passed the enormous stadium. "Good story, Maxwell."

Max drove the lifted pickup until he reached a quiet street just outside of a gated community. The surrounding area was densely packed with remodeled homes, gated front yards, mature trees growing along the street, and Max stopped the pickup behind the last vehicle he had purchased from Stanley Fump, which was parked against the curb.

Max twisted the ignition key to turn off the truck, and he looked at Josue. "One more car change," he said, grabbing his backpack and opening his door. He stepped down to the ground and walked around the pickup, taking in the haggard sight of it: the tailgate was virtually perforated by bullet holes—Max figured the heavy steel tailgate must have saved both of their lives, more than once; the rear windshield was shattered, with bits of glass falling away as Josue slammed his door behind him; and for the first time, Max noticed that the rear bumper was completely gone, and the left rear tire was halfway flat.

He sniggered to himself as he took in the sorry sight. But his heart still fluttered with anxious pangs of worry that they weren't out of the woods yet.

Max grabbed Josue's arm and put it around his neck to support the other man. They hobbled over to the parked car. "Hop in," Max said, as they reached the convertible Mustang. "Let's get going."

Josue's eyes lit up as he recognized the vehicle. He took one look at the cherry-red, five-liter Mustang, and turned to look at Max. The younger man's expression reminded Max of one of his own children's eyes as they had awoken at a ridiculous hour on Christmas morning to find that Santa had come to leave them presents. "Just like Corbin and Teete!"

Max nodded, feeling unexpectedly emotional in the moment. "Yep."

The two men cruised like a couple of renegade, devil-may-care undercover detectives, down palm-tree-lined South Dixie Highway in Coral Gables. As much as he had wanted to give Josue the full experience of putting the convertible top down so they could cruise like their TV heroes, Max thought better of it. With Josue's flapping hospital gown and bandaged head, the two men would quickly attract a lot of unwanted attention. But it was still obvious to Max that, despite the trials and the horrors witnessed over the day, Josue was still thrilled.

When they reached Homestead, Max turned off the Ronald Reagan Turnpike, winding the Mustang into the parking lot of a Publix grocery store. He drove around back, parking by the store's trash compactor. Max got out and popped open the trunk. He pulled out the Buccaneers duffel bag that had a lot of the new clothes they had bought at Kmart.

Max pulled a button-down black rayon shirt out of the bag, along with a pair of khaki cargo shorts. He stripped off his scrubs top and pants right there by the grocery store's loading dock, changing quickly.

"Here," Max said, handing the bag through Josue's passenger side window. "You get changed into something comfortable, and I'll go into the store and get us something to eat. Okay?"

Josue nodded and took the bag of clothing.

Inside the store, Max grabbed roast beef sandwiches on croissants, cartons of potato and macaroni salads, and some cold chicken wings from the deli. He found himself buying a lot more than he had intended, finally placing a good-sized rolling cooler into his cart, along with a couple of bags of ice. Though he had entered the store intent on only purchasing lunch, Max thought it wise to stock up on food, not knowing how long it would be until they might stumble upon another grocery store. So he piled sliced meats, cheeses, condiments, as well as plastic tubs of cut-up watermelon, cantaloupe, and pineapple into his quickly filling cart. He picked up twelve-packs of soda and even a dozen light beers, as well as some hard cider.

Max bought the groceries and returned to the Mustang, finding Josue changed, his seat fully reclined and his eyes closed. Max popped the trunk and stuffed the small space with as much of the groceries as he could, finding he had to put the cooler filled with ice into the back seat.

Josue sat up when Max opened the driver's side door. "Everything okay, boss?"

Max actually laughed, feeling overcome by a strange sense of mirth. "Yeah, man. It's great. But how are you? I mean, I yanked you out of ICU, for crying out loud. How you feeling?"

"I'm…good," Josue said. Max could see the weariness and the pain in the other man's eyes. Max knew the feeling. The month or so he had spent in the hospital after being shot had taken a toll on him as well. He dug into his backpack and found a bottle of Vicodin he'd gotten from Bongo.

"Take two of these," Max said, handing Josue a fresh bottle of water. "I took a lot of these after I was shot. They helped."

Josue took the meds, and Max handed him a sandwich in a clear plastic clamshell package. "Eat up. The more you eat, the faster your body will heal."

Max fired up the car and hit the freeway again. Josue was only able to take a few bites before he felt sick to his stomach. Max figured he had likely had no solid food for a couple days and now needed to take it easy.

The drive down to Islamorada took a little over an hour longer. Max could not stop checking his rearview mirror, each time expecting to see the flashing lights of a half-dozen Florida state troopers in his wake. But no such pursuit occurred. Either Max wasn't quite the wanted criminal he'd thought he was, or he had simply executed his plans well enough.

Max's thoughts turned back to the two dead detectives. What

a terrible turn of events. He knew the Miami cops would likely be looking for him and Josue, at least as witnesses, if not accessories. Max knew going back to give a statement, to try to help them bring the murderers to justice, would undo everything he had just fought for, all of his desperate efforts to free his friend. Ultimately, Max decided the hospital's surveillance cameras, and the accounts of other witnesses at the hospital, would have to suffice. Max just needed to keep moving forward.

Max had a love-hate relationship with the Florida Keys. When he'd been a kid, he had driven down once. His parents had yanked him and his sister out of school for the day, just to go for the drive down to Key Largo in a borrowed van with captain's chairs in the back along with a sofa that folded into a double bed.

Max had powerful, fond memories of riding in the back of that van with his sister, watching the sea go by as they crossed bridge after bridge connecting one small, mangrove-covered island to the next. He had spotted kite shops, kayak rental places, dive shops, bait shops, and unique seafood shacks all along their route. And though it had only been a day trip, looking back, it was one of the most magical days of Max's childhood.

But the Florida Keys were also the place where Max had watched his family die.

In Islamorada, Max turned off the highway into a pharmacy parking lot. He checked the GPS-oriented map on his smartphone to get his bearings. "The marina is only a mile from here," Max told his groggy friend. He had intentionally left out the details of their arrival, maybe wanting to give the resilient Haitian one more surprise. It was the same way his parents had surprised him when they had driven down twenty-five years earlier, not telling him about the snorkeling trip his father had planned until they arrived. It was the same way Max had surprised his own kids with the rented boat when they had come to Islamorada only a few months ago.

Max steered the Mustang into the expansive parking lot of Bruce & Marta's Marina, a weather-beaten bait and boat rental shop and boat marina that looked as if it had existed long enough for Papa Hemingway to have bought gas and bait there back in the '30s, before heading out to sea on his boat, Pilar, in search of half-ton marlin. The marina was situated at the southern end of Plantation Key, just before the Snake Creek Bridge that connected the narrow island with Windley Key to the south.

Max pulled into a parking space and turned off the engine. He stared out across the half dozen or so piers that snaked away from the parking lot, ultimately leading out to the bait and boat rental shop, built on pilings over the crystal clear aquamarine water. Max squinted through his black Ray Ban wayfarers for almost a minute. Then he spotted it.

"There," Max said, stabbing his finger toward the front windshield. "That one there," he said, pointing out the shiny new Bayliner, swathed in white and Patriot Blue paint. "That's ours."

Josue looked surprised. His dark eyes opened wide, and he stared, as if in disbelief. "That boat?"

Max nodded, and Josue flashed his bright white teeth in a charming smile, as if he were unable to keep it from happening.

"Let's go," Max said. He got out and opened the trunk. He threw his arm through the one good strap of his backpack, slinging it onto his back. He grabbed the Buccaneers duffel, and then got the rolling cooler out of the back seat. He pulled a pair of aluminum crutches he'd bought at Walgreens in Little Haiti out of the trunk and handed them to Josue, quickly explaining how to use them.

Max tossed the car keys onto the driver's seat. He wouldn't be needing the Mustang anymore. He just hoped the car would find a good home.

The two men walked the dock toward the awaiting Bayliner, the vessel appearing as the very image of independence and hard-won freedom to Max. It was the chariot to carry both Max and Josue far away from their tumultuous present, and their tormented recent pasts, carrying each man into a new and excitingly uncertain future.

Josue hobbled along, aided by the crutches. It had only taken the strong Haitian a few steps to get used to them, and he made good time over the weathered dock timbers.

Max stopped halfway down the length of the dock. The hair on the back of his neck bristled. Pronounced goose bumps rippled across his arms, including the area around the scarred flesh of his left forearm. His skin tightened in an electrifying moment that gave him pause.

Max peered over the hull of a small boat, a nineteen-foot center console made by Scout. It was a simple little fishing boat with a hundred horsepower outboard. A large decal of a dolphin covered almost one whole side of the boat's hull near the bow.

Max walked the dock, passing six or seven identical boats, each one decorated with hull decals that depicted a different marine animal: the dolphin; a swimming sea horse; a snapping stone crab; an octopus with its tentacles curling over the side of the boat at the gunwale. He reached the last boat in the lineup, finding that one adorned with a decal of a manatee, the strange "sea cow" that inhabited so much of the shallow waters around the Keys.

Max took a step forward, but his body protested. His knees hinged, and he fell to the dock, his hands breaking his fall as he dropped his duffel bag and released the handle of the wheeled cooler, letting it topple over on the dock.

Max gazed across the length of the compact fishing boat. Small deformities appeared in various places across the pristine white hull where holes in the fiberglass had been repaired, all along the port side of the vessel—bullet holes.

Max felt his chest tighten.

"Boss?" Josue said, limping over to Max's side as quickly as he could. He placed a hand on Max's shoulder.

Max struggled just to take a breath. He fought hard against the tears that welled up, but to no avail. Max broke down in sobs that wracked his body in sickening heaves as he reached out, grasping the bow of the manatee-covered boat for support.

"What is it, Maxwell?" Josue asked. He knelt down next to Max.

Bystanders on the docks stared. A few changed direction to avoid passing too closely to the sobbing man.

Max took a series of deep breaths. He looked up at Josue and struggled to speak. "This boat. I can't believe they still have it..."

"What about the boat?"

"This is the boat I rented," Max said, his throat dry and aching. "My family was killed on this boat. My kids, my wife... they died here. They died...on *this* boat."

Max felt his sorrow quickly change to bitter anger. He seethed at the thought of the small fishing boat's existence. "Instead of destroying it, they just hosed out the blood, my wife's blood, my children's blood, my blood, and they fixed it so they could continue renting it out."

Max had never before considered the fate of the boat that had been the scene of such horror, not after he had recovered the submachine gun magazine he'd found at the scene, so he could retrieve the three fateful bullets he now carried with him.

"I am sorry, Maxwell," Josue said. He rubbed Max's shoulder, kneading his muscle with his long slender fingers. "So sorry, my friend."

Max stood up. He lifted the front of his button-down rayon shirt to wipe his eyes. He sniffed sharply, and his head turned toward the Bayliner, which bobbed gently in the light breeze of the late morning. He took a deep breath and stood up, picking up his bags and taking the handle of the cooler, and then striding toward the new boat. Josue kept in step, hobbling on his crutches close behind.

Max stepped onto the rear swim platform of the boat, offering Josue a hand. It was a bit unnerving watching the wounded man hobble across the gap between the dock and the wide, molded fiberglass swim platform, but the young refugee was able to manage.

Max opened the boat's short transom gate to access the rear deck. He put his bags and the cooler on one of the cushioned seats in the rear of the cockpit area, and he stepped forward toward the helm, where he found a sealed manila envelope on the seat in front of the steering wheel. Written in black Sharpie letters was the name Max. He ripped the envelope open, finding boat keys, registration papers, and a handwritten note from the boat dealer Stanley Fump:

Max,

The boat's all set. Got the fuel bladders installed and filled. Instructions on how to transfer fuel are on the next page. I took care of the registration and all the paperwork is in the envelope.

Thank you so much for your business, Maxwell! Even more than that, I am grateful for your friendship. It has truly been an honor to serve you. I trust that any future maritime transportation needs you have will lead you back to my door.

Until then... Yours truly,

Stan

"Let me show you around the boat," Max said to Josue. He tried to shrug off the sickened feeling he felt at seeing the manatee boat like a ghost against the dock. He opened the companionway door, stepping down into the boat's galley area to show Josue the small ceramic stove, microwave, sink, and under-counter refrigerator. He opened a door to the boat's head, revealing the toilet and sink.

"You can shower in this room too," Max said. "Just close the door and use this showerhead. There's a drain in the floor."

Max sat down on the double-sized v-shaped bed in the forward berth, separated off from the galley area by a privacy curtain. It was comfortable and inviting after a bone-wearying several days.

"This is where you'll sleep," Max said. "I figure you'll be comfy here. Easier to move around out here with your cast, close to the kitchen and toilet."

Josue nodded. "It very nice. Thank you, Maxwell."

Max opened another door, to show Josue the small secluded stateroom that was tucked away like a secret in the middle of the brand-new boat. Josue had to crane his neck into the doorway to get a good glimpse of the space, but he smiled and nodded with a slight, "Hmm" that told Max he approved.

"The mid-cabin berth is where I'll sleep," Max said. He knew he would need a door to close from time to time if he were to share a space with another human being.

"I think we're going to be comfortable on here," Max said, taking another look around the somewhat modest, yet well-appointed, new digs of the thirty-three-foot cabin cruiser.

"Let's take her out," Max said, leading Josue back up the companionway steps. "How's your head?"

"Hurts...a lot," Josue said. He smiled, though. "But I'm okay. Going to be okay, my friend."

Max went over the controls to the Bayliner's helm with Josue. At least a dozen round-faced gauges resided in the dash above the steering wheel, along with a Garmin GPS Chartplotter with an eight-inch LED display. Max explained everything as best he could, just as Stanley Fump had explained it all to Max.

He showed Josue how to operate the throttles, how to use the trim tabs, how to operate the GPS unit to navigate preloaded maps, and even how to use sonar to locate schools of fish below the boat. In no time, the two men were firing up the twin 260-horsepower Mercury engines, and were shoving off from Bruce & Marta's dock.

Max let Josue drive the boat, standing beside him, keeping an eye on him, while the other man sat at the helm, trying to make himself comfortable, positioning his heavy leg cast as best he could on the foot rest below his seat. It didn't take long for the young Haitian to become proficient with the controls; he maneuvered the express cruiser with ease, handling the twin throttle levers, and steering the boat with precision, like a seasoned mariner. They spent a good couple of hours driving the boat in the open water of the Atlantic Ocean, but staying close to the cluster of islands that made up the city of Islamorada.

Max spent a little time messing with the Garmin Chartplotter, teaching himself and the other man how to set GPS waypoints, and how to navigate the boat to another position on the map. Josue absorbed all the information like a human sponge.

Max was pleased. It was important to him to know that, left alone, Josue would be well-equipped to handle the vessel on his own, should he find himself needing to.

After taking a leisurely hour or so for a lunch of sandwiches and fruit, Max went down below into the head to dye his hair black with a hair dye kit he'd bought at Walgreens. He figured that a new identity should have a new look. And so he returned on deck an hour later with messy coal black hair.

"Hey, who are you?" Josue joked. "Who let you on boat?"

Max laughed and took a long draw from a cold cider. It tasted sweet, slightly astringent, and extremely refreshing. He lay down on one of the cushioned cockpit seats and instructed Josue to pilot the boat out toward open ocean, through the Whale Harbor Channel. Soon they approached about a dozen other boats, anchored up over a sandbar beside the channel.

Revelers from the boats stood on the shallow sandbar; some danced while loud music pumped through the speakers on one or two of the anchored boats. The smell of sizzling steaks, hot dogs, and hamburgers reached Max's nostrils. He instructed Josue to power down to an idle, and then to cut the engines altogether. They dropped their anchor near the sandbar, about a half mile from the other boats.

Max pushed buttons on the Bayliner's Garmin unit. "I'm setting a waypoint here called Home," Max said, suddenly taking a serious tone. "I've got to go take care of one more bit of business, Josue. I want you to drop me off at the Bruce & Marta's dock, and then I want you to come back here, drop the anchor, and wait for me."

Josue's face wore a sober expression. "Yes, boss," he said. "Anything you want."

"Now this is very important," Max said, locking eyes with the other man. "I want you to wait for me here. But only wait until five o'clock. If I am not back here by five o'clock this evening, I want you to go to Bimini without me. See, I've got it programmed into the GPS. This will lead you all the way there."

Josue nodded, looking a little frightened.

"I'm leaving my backpack here on the boat, Josue. If I'm not back here by five, this boat and everything in my pack belongs to you. I want you to set up a new life for yourself. Find a good place to live, whether it's in the Bahamas or another one of the islands, but don't come back to the US.

"Do you hear me?" Max implored. "You'll be okay. I promise."

"You *will* come back," Josue said, an urgent tone in his voice.

Max paused. "Yes, of course, I'll come back. Don't worry. But if something happens to me, I want you to go on. I want you to look out for yourself. Okay?"

Josue nodded, an obvious reluctance showing in his countenance.

"All right then, my friend," Max said, slapping Josue lightly on the back. "Why don't you take me back to the marina."

CHAPTER 46

"I WANT TO RENT A BOAT," Max said, placing his Florida driver's license and his Platinum Visa card on the glass-topped counter beside the cash register inside Bruce & Marta's bait shop. He noticed his hand trembling as he placed the plastic cards on the countertop. He let his hand settle onto the surface of the countertop to steady it.

"Have you rented from us before?" asked the girl at the counter, a cute teenager with sun-bleached blonde hair who wore a Bruce & Marta's tank top and a bikini bottom. She looked up at Max's face, as if trying to recognize him as a customer.

"I have," Max said hoarsely.

The counter girl punched his name into a computer. Max hoped desperately that she wouldn't recognize him as the man whose family had been murdered on one of their rented boats. "Oh, there you are, Mr. Sutherland. You know the drill: five-hundred-dollar deposit, you pay for the fuel, blah, blah, blah."

Max forced a smile.

"How long do you want it?" the girl asked, and Max noticed that she wore a small, magnetized name tag that said, Brooke.

"Just for today," Max said.

It took a few minutes for Brooke to prepare the rental paperwork, and it seemed like an eternity to Max, standing, waiting for the documents to come off of the printer so he could sign them and take the keys to the rented boat.

"Oh, one more thing," Max said to the teen, who was in the

process of handing him a boat key attached to a floating orange foam keychain with the printed name and address of Bruce and Marta's Marina. "I'd like the manatee boat."

"The manatee boat?" Brooke asked.

"Yeah," Max said. "The one with the manatee decal on the side. I think they're...lucky," he fibbed.

"No problem," the bubbly bait shop keeper said, as she scrutinized the other keys that hung from a peg board behind the counter. "There it is! The manatee boat key." She dropped it into Max's hand.

"Thanks, Brooke," Max said, doing his best to smile politely at the girl. "Do you have a pen and paper I can use?"

"Sure do." Brooke handed Max a branded ballpoint pen and notepad. "Those are yours to keep."

Max nodded and turned to walk out of the shop. Outside the door, he leaned on the wooden railing that served to keep one from walking right off the edge of the dock into the gentle water beneath. He set the notepad on the railing and began to scrawl on the paper in blue ballpoint ink. A nosy pelican walked up to him on the dock, nipping at his ankle, as if expecting Max to give it something. A herring, maybe.

"Get lost," Max said, kicking his foot near the bird's face, being careful not to actually strike it. Last thing he needed now was someone calling the cops on him for animal cruelty.

Max read the note back to himself:

The loss of my family has been the greatest, most unexpected pain of my life. I have not been able to move on from their passing. Each day, I've wanted to do nothing but simply lay down and die. If there's anyone I leave behind who cares about me, and who wonders why I did what I did, just know I have gone on to be with my family. I belong with them.

Maxwell Sutherland.

Max stuffed the suicide note into his wallet that was thick with the bulge of his identification, credit cards, and any other remnant left of the man known as Maxwell Sutherland. He dropped the black leather wallet on the dock, just outside the bait shop door. He wouldn't be needing it anymore, not where he was going.

Max walked to the bow of the manatee boat and paused. He spotted two beat-up red metal Jerry cans in the stern of a tatty fishing boat tied off beside his rented boat. Max made a surreptitious glance around him, before stepping onto the other boat's rear deck. He snatched the two heavy gas cans and passed them over the side, into the stern of the manatee-stickered Scout center console.

Max threw off the ropes that tied the small fishing boat to the dock, turned the key in the ignition, and motored away from the dock.

As he steered the boat through a narrow channel away from Bruce and Marta's, and past the Coast Guard station, Max lifted his shirt to check the 9mm Smith & Wesson pistol, tucked into his front waistband.

He turned west onto Snake Creek, driving the boat toward a bay punctuated by its thick clusters of wildly growing mangroves. Once he was clear of the narrow channel, and he faced the expanse of Cotton Key Basin, Max opened the throttle and headed south. It would only take about ten minutes for him to reach the tangled mangrove maze not far from Windley Harbor. It wouldn't be long before Max had reached the very spot where his wife, his daughter, and his son, had recently been cut down by a cold-blooded and vicious murderer.

Josue tried to make himself comfortable on one of the cushioned waterproof seats in the cockpit area of the new boat. It was tricky work. His heavy cast was cumbersome at best, and each shift in position sent a rift of pain deep into the marrow of his left leg. But he was grateful to have a soft place to sit. The boat reminded Josue of the fast boat that had carried him and so many others from the devastated shore of his home country to his first steps onto unfamiliar American soil, which he guessed had not been too far from where he now sat.

He didn't remember much about the accident. He remembered leaving Shakey Redbone's, stepping out into the street, heavy-laden with bags of crispy chicken and polystyrene cartons full of side dishes. His next memory was of waking up, staring at a fluorescent ceiling light inside the hospital.

Josue had not expected to ever see Maxwell again. And he had never expected Maxwell to come back to rescue him out of the hospital.

Back home, living on his farm, Josue had known family. But he had never before known a friend as close as Maxwell—he had never before known a friend who would risk his own life and freedom for him.

As the afternoon wore on, Josue hobbled down the companionway steps. He did his best to make himself comfortable on the bed in the bow of the new boat. It was difficult to find a comfortable position so that he could sleep.

The pain in Josue's leg grew more pronounced with each passing minute. He wondered if it would be all right for him to partake of another two of the pills that Maxwell had given him.

He zipped open Maxwell's backpack to read the writing on the bottle—perhaps there would be instructions to tell him if it was safe to take more.

Josue could not believe the thick, paper-wrapped bundles of cash money inside the backpack. He picked up one of the bundles. He flipped through the bulky stack of bills, letting each one flutter against his finger. And then Maxwell's words resounded in his head:

"If I am not back here by five, this boat, and everything in my pack belongs to you," he had said.

Did Maxwell mean that all the money belonged to me? Josue found such a sentiment hard for him to believe. He would wait. Maxwell *would* come back. They would go to Bimini together. Josue had only read about the Bahamian island in the book *Islands in the Stream* by American author Ernest Hemingway. Living outside of Port au Prince, Josue had never dreamed he would go to visit such a place. Yet now he stood, staring, at a small computerized map that would lead him all the way there.

Josue had to open a few of the medicine bottles to find the ones he had taken before, the small white tablets stamped with the word Vicodin. He read the bottle, finding that enough time had passed for him to safely consume two more. Relief came within fifteen minutes. Josue soon found himself drifting off into deep, narcotic-induced sleep on his new bed.

The sound of a squawking gull snapped Josue awake. He felt himself drenched with sweat, and he realized he had been closed up inside the boat's cabin. The porthole windows, as well as the companionway door, were all sealed off, creating an overly warm, stuffy area inside the boat's comfortable living area.

Josue hobbled up the steps to the boat's cockpit and checked the clock on the dashboard of the boat's helm. Four forty-three p.m. Josue called out Max's name, just in case he had come on board while Josue had been asleep.

Receiving no reply, Josue descended the steps again, knocking on the door to the small bathroom before opening it. It was unoccupied. Then he checked Max's stateroom, finding it empty as well.

The concerned Haitian limped back up to the deck and took a seat, facing his attention toward the land. From his position,

Josue watched cars pass as they traveled across the bridge from one island to the next.

A stark sight startled him—curls of thick black smoke raised toward the sky from a tangle of green foliage on the opposite side of the island in front of him.

The thick mangroves reminded Josue of the ones he and Foret had waded through after eluding the Coast Guard boat, upon first landing on Florida soil—maybe they were the same ones. He thought about how terrified he had been. And now, hearing the wailing sirens in the distance and seeing the strobe-like flashing of a police boat's lights as it raced toward the origin of the thick smoke, Josue felt no less afraid.

His mind drifted back to the way Maxwell had broken down on the dock. How he had told Josue the manatee boat was the one upon which his family was killed.

Josue wondered if it was possible Max had done something to harm himself. As unlikely as it felt, Josue could not scrub the thought from his mind.

The young refugee sat anxiously, wringing his hands together. He kept his attention rapt across the drawbridge, as another boat sped toward the scene of the smoke. Josue could not see what it was that was on fire. He watched a thick stream of water extruded from a fire hose. Whether the stream came from a boat or from a vehicle on the land, Josue could not tell. The foamy white spray of water showered down over the thick mangroves toward the unseen source of the smoke.

Josue watched the clock tick all the way down to five o'clock. "He's not coming back," a voice inside Josue's head told him. Josue knew it was only his subconscious mind playing with him, motivated by his own fears. But the nagging voice, along with all of his physical pain, and the stress of the past couple weeks, had worn the young refugee down so that he felt thinner than a piece of paper.

Josue anxiously watched the clock. He stared at its face for minutes at a time. He stopped to gaze across the island at the smoke.

Was it Maxwell's body, burning on the boat where his family died?

Josue urged himself not to think such things. He struggled to think other thoughts. For a short time, maybe a minute, he dwelt on the beauty of his surroundings.

Thick white clouds floated in a serene azure sky as far as Josue could see. It was hard for him to believe that people lived in such a beautiful place. Noisy gulls, like the one that had awoken him, buzzed by overhead in clusters of six or eight, the noisy scavengers swooping low and begging for a scrap. A pair of magnificent great white herons swooped close against the clear water of the ocean, hunting for small fish near the surface.

But Josue's mind inevitably drifted back toward the clock.

Five o'clock came and went. It was nearly five twenty when Josue finally broke down. It happened to him so suddenly and powerfully, that he wondered what was happening to him. But Josue started to blubber in a way he could not seem to control, like a small child.

Tears drenched his cheeks as he considered the reality of his situation. Maybe many people would have found it an enviable position to be in: having possession of a brand-new cabin cruiser, a backpack full of cash, the freedom to go anywhere he wished. But Josue knew he did not want to go alone. He had only known Max for a very short period of time, but Max had already proven to be his best friend in the world, having risked so much to save him.

Josue stood up, balancing himself carefully on the deck. With his good foot, he kicked the long seat at the port side of the vessel. He kicked it over and over again with as much force as he could, feeling enraged.

Why did his mother have to die? His sister? His uncle?

Why did their home have to be destroyed? Why did his aunt turn him away as if he were a vagabond, a stranger? Why did he have to meet those terrible members of the Ti Flow gang, to participate in their vicious robbery and murders? Why was he hurt so badly and put into the hospital? Why did so much pain and sorrow have to fill such a short span of man's life? When would he find relief from the hurt he felt? Would he have to die first?

Josue kicked the soft, padded seat until he pivoted wrong on his cast-wrapped foot, and he felt the sharpest, most intense pain he had ever experienced. He dropped to his hands and knees in agony. "Aaaaggghhh!" he screamed. His eyes bulged in their sockets as he vented his rage.

Then Josue let his forehead touch the deck of the boat, and he allowed his bitter tears to flow freely.

———————

Max stopped the boat in the approximate spot where he had stopped the rented Scout, only a few months ago, to drop anchor and begin fishing with Lovelle and the kids. It was hard to know the exact spot; the mangroves grew in thick, tangled webs, making it almost impossible to discern one place from another.

Max knelt to his knees on the deck and prayed. His prayer, as it turned out, mostly involved him asking God why He had to take away his family from him. Why would he never again see their faces?

Max supposed it was sort of therapeutic, as much as it hurt to be there, in that terrible, beautiful place. It helped to know the boat would be destroyed, that it would never again be rented out to pleasure seekers, who could not possibly know that three people were brutally murdered upon the very deck from which they cast their fishing lines.

Max made short work of it. He poured out all ten gallons from the Jerry cans until a shallow pool of amber gasoline covered the entire surface of the boat's deck. And there Max stood, an Orion marine flare in hand, ready to strike.

"Goodbye, Lovelle," Max said, as he looked down at the pool of flammable liquid inside the boat. He placed his hand to his chest, over his heart. "I'll carry you with me always. I promise you I will.

"Goodbye, Lionel. You were such a good boy, such a smart little thing. You would have become such a great man, given time. I know you would have."

Tears rolled down Max's cheeks.

"Goodbye, Lucy, my sweet little mouse. I will miss your laugh every day I draw breath. I *will* see you again, Sweetie. I promise you I will."

Max stepped off the boat into the shallow, waist-deep water. He removed the cap from the flare and rubbed the scratch surface against the igniter. A blinding orange flame seared outward like a welding torch from the end of the small orange tube.

Max tossed the flare into the boat. The entire deck flashed with a powerful eruption of flames, knocking Max backward in the water. He righted himself and waded back away from the boat. He watched the fiberglass boat overcome with the intense fire and heat.

It was beautiful.

Max knew he didn't need the complication of being caught near the smoldering vessel. He trudged away from the mangroves until he reached water too deep for him to stand.

Then Max swam.

He swam away from the fiery boat for a long time, maybe a half-hour, alternating between a freestyle swimming stroke, and occasionally flipping over for a backstroke. As he neared the bridge that connected Windley Key with Upper Matecumbe Key, the distance of Max's swim became more apparent to him. He was maybe only halfway to the boat.

Max had already kicked off his slip-on boat shoes. He stripped off his button-down Tommy Bahama shirt, leaving it adrift in the channel. But he felt that he still had the Smith & Wesson pistol, tucked securely into his waistband.

Max swam under the overpass, watching the cars and trucks passing by overhead. He knew he needed to swim for another three-quarters of a mile or so, despite the cramp he felt developing in his side. So he slogged through it, stopping to rest on one of the nearby sandbars now and then. He avoided passing boats and kayaks, hoping he wouldn't be seen, lest they might assume he'd have anything to do with the torched rental fishing boat.

Max had swum for over an hour by the time he reached the rear swim platform of the Bayliner. Out of breath, exhausted, and most likely dehydrated, Max hoisted himself up and out of the water. He breathed a deep sigh.

Max peered over the transom, seeing no one on deck.

Max turned to look at the island, seeing the pillar of black smoke that billowed into the serene blue sky. The sight of it comforted him. It represented as much closure as he was going to get, at least for now.

"Maxwell?" a voice shouted behind him.

Max turned to see Josue, picking himself up from the deck. His face was slick with tears. He winced as he stood.

"Josue, are you all right?"

"You come back," Josue said, and Max had never seen such a palpable sense of relief on a man's face before. Max wasn't sure of the time, but he realized that Josue must have written him off.

"Yeah," Max said. "I'm back. You ready to go to Bimini?"

"I'm ready," Josue said. The young Haitian wiped his eyes with his shirtsleeve. He sat back down onto the soft, cushioned port side seat.

"There's something else I have to show you before we go," Max said, walking past Josue and stepping down through the companionway. He entered his stateroom and picked up the two garment bags that lay on his double bed, placed there by Stanley Fump, obviously eager to earn another two thousand bucks. Max carried them back up on deck, and zipped them both open.

Out of one, Max removed a turquoise linen suit, along with a bright yellow t-shirt. In the other bag, Max found a pair of white button-fly jeans, a black tank top, and a pair of red suspenders along with a black Greek fisherman's hat, made by Aegean.

"Just like Corbin and Teete!" Josue beamed. "Now I can wear clothing of Charleston Corbin, you can dress to be Palomar Teete."

Max laughed. That hadn't exactly been what he'd had in mind when he'd written the list of clothing articles down and handed it to the slick boat salesman. But if Josue visualized himself as the stylish redhead Charleston Corbin, then Max figured he could humor his friend and don the outfit of the streetwise cop from the rough streets of Kingston, Jamaica. "Sorry I don't have dreadlocks like Pal Teete," Max said.

Josue laughed.

"Get dressed, and we'll get ready to shove off," Max said. "We'll make Bimini in time for dinner."

Josue took his garment bag down below to get dressed. Max found his backpack, along with all of the cash sitting open on the cockpit seat. He dug through it until he found his and Josue's passports. Max opened his own and looked at his name.

Maxwell Sutherland was dead. Max had officially killed him. A flutter of excitement stirred in his gut as he considered the possibilities he now faced. Maxwell Craig had just been born, and his future was a clean slate.

"What you think?" Josue asked, as he appeared on deck, dressed as the charismatic narcotics detective, Charleston Corbin.

"You look great," Max said.

"Why you not dressed?" Josue asked.

Max looked down at the Palomar Teete outfit. He shuddered to think of what folks in Bimini would think when he showed up wearing the white jeans, black tank top, and suspenders. But he humored his friend, stepping down below to change. As he returned on deck, Josue handed Max the Greek sailor hat. Max nestled it on top of his head.

"You look good, Pal," Josue said.

Max handed Josue his passport. "Take a look, Josue. If anyone 'official' asks you who you are, your name is now Josue Dumas."

"Like Monsieur Dumas," Josue said. "One of my favorite writers."

"I know," Max said. "You told me the other day, and I thought you'd like it as your alias. But pretty much no one knows who you really are, so I can just call you Josue Remy if you like."

"Just call me Josue," the energized young man said, flashing his ivory white grin.

"When I needed to come up with a name for you I thought about the Count of Monte Cristo," Max said. "He was a great character. He implemented a years-long revenge plot to get even with his enemies, ultimately finding some peace and redemption at the end."

"Good choice," Josue said.

"You can call me Maxwell Craig," Max said.

"Good to meet you, Maxwell Craig," Josue said.

Max could tell Josue was in a great deal of pain from his wounded leg. "Look, when we get to Bimini, we'll check in with a doctor there, have you looked at. Okay?"

Josue nodded.

"You wanna drive?" Max asked.

"Yes," Josue said eagerly, positioning himself behind the wheel, and firing up the twin Mercury engines. As the motors rumbled to life underfoot, Max remembered just one more thing.

"Almost forgot, Josue. I asked Stanley—the guy I bought the boat from—to get me something else." Max reached into the manila envelope and slipped out a CD. Almost as an afterthought to their transaction, Max had asked Stanley Fump to get him a copy of the soundtrack to *Miami Crime Squad* so that he and Josue could make the most dramatic exit from the Florida Keys as possible.

Max slipped the CD into the weather-resistant player in the dash. He turned the volume knob all the way up in anticipation of the flangey guitar and slick keyboard riffs of the crime drama's eighties era theme song.

The trumpet intro of Barry Manilow's *Looks Like We Made It* started to play through the weatherproof speakers on the spoiler overhead.

Josue looked confused.

Max just shrugged his shoulders and laughed. "To Bimini!"

Josue pushed the throttle levers forward. The bow rose, and as they gained speed, the young Haitian trimmed the boat to level it off. The Bayliner, covered in fuel bladders, and carrying the most bizarre doppelgangers for Charleston Corbin and Palomar Teete imaginable, drove northeastward with the glimmering sunset sparkling at their backs.

Max had no idea what would come next. The last few weeks—indeed, the last several months, flashed through his mind as a mind-numbing blur. With one last glimpse of the smoke from the burning boat behind him, Max considered how he had essentially burned his last bridge in the United States. He was heading now for uncharted waters. But Max was confident that with Josue beside him, whatever they got themselves into, it would be nothing short of an adventure.

THE END

About The Author

Growing up in sunny south Florida, Dannal fished, snorkeled, and dodged jellyfish washed up on the beach. His frequent exploration of Florida's A1A Scenic & Historic Coastal Byway on his bike without permission resulted in numerous groundings. Dannal eventually moved out west, settling in southern Oregon, where he currently resides with his wife and two kids.

In addition to the Maxwell Craig series of thrillers, Dannal is also the author of a quirky series of short reads for younger readers, called *The Trying Tales of Chumbles & Grim.*

Catch up with Dannal at his website Dannal.com, or go to

 www.facebook.com/dannaljnewman

Twitter@thedannal

Instagram@thedannal

www.ingramcontent.com/pod-product-compliance
Lightning Source LLC
Chambersburg PA
CBHW030556180626
46816CB00005B/1570

9780692881019